KNUCKLE BONES

A DCI ROBERT KETT NOVEL

ALEX SMITH

RELENTLESS
MEDIA

KNUCKLE BONES
Published Worldwide by Relentless Media.
This edition published in 2023.

All characters and events in this book are entirely fictional. Any references to historical events, real people, or real locales are used fictitiously. Other names, characters, places, and incidents are the product of the author's imagination, and any resemblance to actual events or locales or persons, living or dead, is entirely coincidental.

Edited by Hanna Elizabeth

ISBN: 978-1-913877-12-5

www.alexsmithbooks.com
relentless.media

ALSO BY ALEX SMITH

The DCI Robert Kett Thrillers

Paper Girls

Bad Dog

Three Little Pigs

Whip Crack

Run Rabbit Run

Stone Cold Dead

Every Mother's Son

Sweet Briar Rose

Jaw Breaker

Knock Knock

King Rat

Knuckle Bones

Lucky Number Seven

Unholy Saints

Cry Baby: A Novella

Other Books

The Harder They Fall

Six Days, Six Hours, Six Minutes

For all the mothers and fathers with empty arms.

A BONUS STORY

I have included this short story as part of Knuckle Bones.

Merry Tossing Christmas takes place in the months between King Rat and Knuckle Bones, and although it's a little bit of fun, it isn't relevant to the main novel so there is no obligation to read it. It was also available for a short while on my website, so you may already have read it.

Feel free to skip to the main event on Page 37.

MERRY TOSSING CHRISTMAS

A DCI KETT CHRISTMAS SPECIAL

"Well, it wouldn't be a proper Kett Christmas without a little bit of chaos, right?"

Billie let loose a little laugh as she spoke, but there was a definite edge of panic in her voice. She held Kett's hand with the strength of somebody who was standing on the edge of a cliff in the middle of a storm, and he was holding her back just as hard. The cliff, in this instance, was the driveway of their brand-new house, and the storm was the fact that Christmas was two days away and every single thing they owned was currently packed away in boxes.

Including their children.

"Get out of there, Evie," said Billie, letting go of Kett's hand in order to lift the flap of the nearest box. It was one of seven that had been left out here by the delivery drivers, simply because they'd run out of space inside.

Evie's head appeared, her grin covered in chocolate. They'd offered her Smarties as a bribe to keep her out of the way, but evidently it hadn't worked.

"Come on, you dope," said Kett. "That's all our bedding, and you're making it wet."

"I'm not," said Evie. "*She* is."

Moira's head emerged from the box, like a game of Whack-a-Mole. Kett frowned at her, but her chuckling laughter was so contagious he found himself smiling. Billie glowered at the girls, then at him, but a heartbeat later there was a smile on her face too. She lifted Evie out of the box, then Moira, watching them run inside. There was a crash, a shout, and more laughter as their footsteps drummed up the stairs.

"What are the odds of this place still standing by the end of the day?" asked Kett.

"There is *so* much work to do," said Billie, closing the flap of the box. She looked up into a grey sky that promised rain, maybe even snow. It was so cold that even though it was nearly lunchtime the plants that edged the driveway were still crisp with frost.

He took Billie's hand again, pulling her into a hug. He could feel her shivering against him, partly the weather, yes, but partly relief, because they were finally here.

"It doesn't matter," he said. "We've got all the time we need to do it. We've got all the time in the world."

He felt her nod, then she leaned up and kissed him. Her lips tasted of salted caramel from the hot chocolates they'd had on the drive over from their old house—house, not home. That place had been where he'd fought to survive when his wife had been taken, where Billie had suffered endless nightmares when she'd returned, and where Kett had been dragged into Hollenbeck's van on his way to hell. He would gladly never think about it again.

This one, though...

They both turned and looked up at the house. At *their* house. The past didn't exist here. The Pig Man didn't exist here. Hollenbeck didn't exist here. There was only him and Billie and the kids and a whole lot of future that seemed to unfold in his imagination like a tapestry. This place was a gift, and he felt the same sense of breathless excitement he'd always felt as a child, waking up on Christmas Day.

Only good things could happen here.

"We're home," he said.

"We're home," echoed Billie.

"Mum," said Alice, appearing in the doorway. "Moira's got her head stuck in the toilet. I thought you should know."

"Right," said Kett. "Of course she has. Wouldn't be Christmas without somebody getting their head stuck in the toilet."

He gave Billie another smile.

"Home," he said.

OF COURSE, it didn't look much like a home. It looked more like a cross between an Amazon warehouse and a flat-pack furniture shop. There were so many boxes that Kett had to squeeze between them as he made his way towards the stairs—tripping twice. He hauled himself up onto the landing, where more containers waited, bracing himself as he entered the family bathroom.

Fortunately, Moira didn't have her head stuck in the actual toilet. But their youngest daughter did appear to have wedged herself firmly behind the pedestal that held up the sink. Evie squatted next to her little sister, scratching her head and looking like an engineer faced with an impossible task.

"I'll squirt soap on you," Evie said. "Then you'll slip right out."

"No!" said Moira.

"Then I'll ask Daddy for a saw and we can cut your legs off, then you'll come free."

Moira's eyes widened in horror.

"Nobody is losing their legs," said Kett, waving Evie out of the way. "How on earth did you get behind there, Moo-moo?"

"She told me to do it," Moira said. She tried to point a finger at Evie, but she was stuck in a way that made it impossible for her to move her arms.

"I didn't!" Evie protested. "You said we should play hide and seek, and I just *suggested* it."

"Right," said Kett. He took hold of Moira's legs and gently tugged until she slipped free. By the time he'd scooped her into his arms, she was laughing hysterically. He went to put her down then changed his mind, lowering her into the bath instead.

"What are you doing?" screeched Evie, giggling.

"Putting you somewhere safe," he said, lifting his other daughter and dropping her into the bath alongside her sister. "Stay in here."

"No!" said Moira.

"No!" echoed Evie, clambering out and running from the room.

"Wait for me!" yelled Moira.

Kett helped her out and watched her bolt, both of them laughing again. It might have been his imagination, but the house seemed to laugh with them in the way the floorboards squeaked. It felt good, it felt like they were being welcomed.

"Just try to stay out of trouble!" he called after them, hearing the futility in his voice.

He walked onto the landing, checking the middle room to see Alice wedged in the corner. She was holding her iPad in her lap, her hair over her face and a miserable expression visible beneath. She looked tiny in the empty room, as if the house had made her younger.

"No Wi-Fi," said Kett, guessing the source of her sadness. "I'm sorry. They're coming next week."

"Next *week*?" said Alice, her jaw dropping.

"You want my phone?"

She nodded and he pulled it out of his pocket, sliding it over the floor. She scuttled out of her corner, snatched it, then retreated, looking like Gollum in his cave.

"If somebody calls, don't hang up on them," he said.

She didn't answer, her nose practically pressed against the screen, YouTube already blaring.

"Right," he said again, rubbing his eyes. Neither he nor Billie had managed to sleep last night, and he was exhausted, running on mince pie and mulled wine fumes. They'd been packing for what seemed like weeks, but they'd still been up past midnight taping the last of the boxes—then awake again before five when Moira had hurled herself elbow-first onto his crotch like a wrestler in her effort to get to Billie.

But he hadn't been lying. They had all the time in the world to make this place their own.

He walked to the stairs, cocking his head as he tried to locate Evie and Moira. The house had fallen eerily quiet, just the tinny rattle of whatever Alice was watching and the sound of Billie lugging boxes. He went to join his wife, finding her in the huge kitchen diner at the back of the house. There were even more boxes in here, a veritable forest of cardboard that blocked most of the light from the bifold doors.

"I don't even remember owning this much stuff," said Kett.

"About ninety percent of it is theirs," Billie said, squinting at the labels on the boxes. "Endless rubbish. Did you get Moira out of the toilet?"

"Yeah," he said. "She was halfway round the u-bend. You looking for anything in particular?"

She frowned up at him like he'd asked the stupidest question in the world, and he answered at the same time she did.

"The kettle."

He walked to the nearest stack of boxes, but she waved him away.

"I'll do it," she said. "We'll just get in each other's way. You go do what you need to do."

"Good luck," he said. "Just call if you need me."

He navigated his way across the front hall into the small, separate dining room. There was no table here but there were plenty of boxes that would do the job. He manoeuvred two big ones over to the window, then made his way back out onto the driveway, shivering as he unlocked the car. His work satchel was lying on the passenger seat and he collected it, running back. He dug a duvet cover out of the box that Evie and Moira had been hiding in, returning to the dining room and throwing it over the makeshift desk as a tablecloth. By the time he'd fumbled his laptop out of his bag, Evie and Moira had materialised.

"What are you doing, Dad?" asked Evie, creeping closer.

"Just got a couple of bits of work to finish," he said, placing the laptop on the covered boxes and opening it up. It whined, as if protesting the fact that it was being asked to work so far into the holidays.

He felt like whining too, if he was honest, but it wasn't like he was back on the job properly. After the horrors of his kidnapping he still hadn't returned to work, but he'd agreed to help Superintendent Clare out by consulting on a handful of cases.

"Can I write something?" Moira asked, slapping her hands on the keys.

"Don't do that, Moira," said Kett. "It's old, and it might break."

"Like Daddy," said Evie matter-of-factly.

"There's some more chocolate somewhere," Kett said. "All the Christmas sweeties. See if you can find them. They're in a box marked *Food*, I think."

They left the room like it was on fire, Billie yelling something in alarm as they flew into the kitchen. Kett felt a little guilty, but because of the move he was ridiculously behind schedule. If he didn't get his report to the Boss before Christmas, he was worried Clare might just show up on the big day itself, nostrils flaring, tossing here, there and everywhere.

He found a smaller box, testing it gingerly before sitting on it. He'd only typed four words, though, before he heard a knock on the open front door.

"Hello?" came a familiar voice. "Robbie? Billie?"

"Kate!" Kett called back, climbing off his box. He poked his head out of the dining room to see Savage framed in the door, mummified in a thick overcoat. "I didn't know you were coming."

"Just tried to call, you hung up on me. This place is amazing. You get in okay?"

Kett nodded, waving her through the door. She didn't close it behind her, looking back. On the driveway, PC Duke was trying to extricate himself from a microscopic pink Fiat 500 that was parked so tightly against the hedge it was proving impossible. He peeled his head and one shoulder free, his face lost in the foliage as he tried to angle himself around.

"What's he doing?" asked Kett.

"I'm not entirely sure, sir," Savage replied with a frown. "But it looks like it might take a while. Shall we go in?"

"I can't stop watching," said Kett. "Is that *his* car?"

"His mum's. Or so he says. He seems weirdly attached to it."

Duke twisted his head round, grimacing at them.

"I'm fine," he said.

"He clearly isn't," Kett said. "Does he need help?"

"That's a question I have asked myself several times in the last few weeks," Savage replied. "Go *through* the car, Aaron. Get out my side."

Duke paused to think about this. He began to work himself back inside the car with all the grace of a grizzly bear. The vehicle wobbled and shook as he moved towards the passenger seat.

"Auntie Kate!" shouted Evie from the hallway. She came running towards the DC and practically leapt into her arms. Savage hefted her up, groaning theatrically.

"What have you been feeding her?" she said. "She weighs more than Duke!"

"I can't find the chocolate," Evie said. "It's not in the kitchen."

"I'll find it," said Kett. "Just give me a second. I want to see how this ends."

The passenger door of the Fiat opened and Duke appeared, sliding out headfirst and literally commando-crawling across the drive until he was completely free. He grunted his way back to his feet, slamming the door shut with such force that Kett half expected the car to disappear through the hedge.

"That was great," Kett said with a smile. "Can you do it again so the kids can watch?"

Duke glowered at him, dusting his hands together as he walked over. He was dressed in black jeans, a black jumper and black shoes, with a black overcoat to match. He looked like a club bouncer, and Kett wasn't sure he'd even get through the door.

"Sir," the PC said with a nod. "Nice place."

"There's not a lot of room," Kett said. "And we haven't found the kettle yet."

He stood to the side to let Duke in, then closed the door. It wasn't much warmer inside than out, the radiators like fridges, and he stumbled over the boxes towards the kitchen, trying to remember where the thermostat was. To his immense relief, he heard the sound of the kettle hissing, and when he stepped through the door he saw Billie standing triumphantly by the counter, her hair all over the place and her cheeks flushed, two mugs in her hand.

He didn't think she'd ever looked more beautiful.

"You are my hero," he said.

"Don't I know it," she replied. "Hi, Kate, good to see you. Aaron. What brings you here?"

"I knew it was moving day," said Savage, trying to lower Evie to the floor. The little girl was resisting, clinging on like a limpet. Moira was trying to climb the DC's leg, in danger of pulling her trousers down. "Figured you might need some help shifting boxes."

"That's really kind of you," said Billie. "We could use some muscle, we're a little low."

"Hey," said Kett. "I'm standing right here."

"Porter's on the way too," Savage added. Moira was still grabbing her trousers, trying to haul herself up. "Aaron will hold you if you like, Moo-moo?"

Duke held out his hands, looking like a fairy tale giant ready to gobble her up. Moira obviously thought the same because she gave the big PC a wary look from behind the safety of Auntie Kate.

"Well, how about we find this chocolate then?" Savage said, and both girls cheered.

"It's in a box marked *Food*," said Kett.

"Then it shouldn't be too hard," Savage said. "Come on, where shall we start?"

"My room!" Evie yelled.

She wiggled herself free and both girls ran through the door, almost pushing each other over. Savage followed, Duke holding back.

"You want me to do anything?" he asked.

"If you can find room somewhere for those boxes outside, I'll love you forever," said Billie, earning another disapproving look from Kett.

"Sure," said Duke, looking happy to have a mission. "No problem."

"Be careful, though," she called after him. "There are breakables."

She turned to Kett.

"He will be careful, won't he?"

"Uh..." said Kett, not wanting to lie. Luckily, the kettle clicked off, distracting her.

"You remember where we put the milk?" he asked.

"Same box as the chocolate, I think," Billie replied.

"I'll go help with the search."

"Don't you have work to do?"

"It'll be fine," he said. "It's not like Clare's going to come looking for it."

The words had barely left his mouth when he heard another knock on the door.

"Oh no," he said.

He walked into the hallway to see that Duke had beaten him to it, the front door open and Porter standing there. The DI was wearing a huge overcoat, but it did little to cover the pounds that he'd packed on in the last six months.

"Thank God," said Kett. "I thought I'd accidentally summoned the Super."

"That you did," came another voice.

Porter stood apologetically to one side to reveal Superintendent Colin Clare on the driveway, glaring at Kett like Kett had just shat in his shoe. He was wearing his Big Tossing Jacket, making him look like a camel's vagina. Standing next to him, her arm looped through his, was Porter's wife, Allie, looking very pregnant.

"That's what happens when you spend your time idly playing with your tosshole, Detective, instead of doing your job."

"I wasn't playing with—" Kett started, but he was bundled out of the way by Porter, the DI shuddering through the door.

"Jesus Christ," he said. "It's so cold my balls have retracted all the way into my stomach."

"Could have done without that mental image," Kett grumbled. "What are you doing here, Pete?"

"Came to help, tried to call but you hung up on me," Porter went on. "Honestly, I think they're still climbing. I'm going to be able to taste them soon."

"For the love of God, Pete," said Allie as Clare let her pass through the door first. She squeezed past Duke. "Nobody wants to think about your balls."

"Thank you," said Kett.

"Especially me," Allie went on, holding her substantial belly. She was six months in and her bump was already enormous. It looked like every step was a struggle. "I wish they'd bloody retracted months ago, or fallen off, then I might be able to go six seconds without needing a pee. Where's your toilet, Robbie?"

"Uh," he said, retreating even further and almost tripping on another box. For a second he couldn't remember, then he pointed down the hall. "Right there, under the stairs. There's no lock on the door, sorry."

"Well, if anyone comes in they'll be scarred for life," she said, pushing past. "There is nothing here anyone wants to see right now."

"You're beautiful," Porter called after her, and she scowled at him as she slammed the toilet door behind her.

"Going well?" Kett asked. Porter grinned.

"Yeah, it's brilliant," he said, his voice low. "I mean, she's amazing, she's doing so well. But she's pretty grumpy."

"I can hear you, Pete," came her voice.

Clare walked in, closing the door just as Duke was about to walk out of it.

"I'm going that way, sir," said Duke.

"Well I'm assuming you know how to open a door, Constable," Clare roared. "I think we cover that in basic training, don't we?"

"Yes, sir," Duke muttered, opening the front door and shuffling outside. He moved towards the nearest box.

"Be careful, Duke," Kett shouted. "There are fragile things in those."

"I'm always careful," said Duke. "It's my middle name."

He lifted the first box and the bottom fell out of it, scattering bed linen all over the damp driveway.

"His middle name's Bellend," said Porter. "I'll give him a hand. Kettle on?"

"Yeah," said Kett. "But we can't find the milk."

"Or the chocolate," came Alice's voice from the top of the stairs. "Can we really eat chocolate if we find it?"

"A little bit," said Kett. "Not all of it."

She ran off, joining the stampede of footsteps overhead as the girls hunted for their treasure.

"Brought you a gift," said Clare, holding out a bottle. It was covered with a thick layer of dust, and Kett winced as he took it from him.

"Eggnog, sir?"

"Best one there is," Clare said. "Got it especially as it's Christmas. Bring a bit of cheer to the new place."

Kett was almost certain he'd seen this exact bottle on a shelf in Clare's larder when they'd visited in the summer for the barbecue, after the Hollenbeck case. He turned it over, looking at the date stamped on the bottom.

"Best before 1998," he said.

"It's like whisky," said Clare. "Gets better as it ages."

"It's got eggs in, hasn't it?"

"Show a little gratitude, Kett," said Clare, surveying the forest of boxes. "I can see you've got a job on here. I'll cut you some slack with the reports. Where do you want these things?"

He shrugged off his jacket, holding it out. Kett took it, half expecting the monstrous coat to fight back as he hung it on the living room door.

"It's honestly fine," said Kett. "We can sort through it later."

But Clare had already picked up the nearest box. It was obviously heavier than he'd expected, his eyes bulging, his jaw clamped. His entire body seemed to rattle.

"That's for upstairs," Kett said with an apologetic shrug.

"That's... tossing... brilliant..." Clare grunted as he

moved away, looking like he'd already given himself a hernia.

"Coming through," said Duke, crossing the hallway with a bundle of blankets scooped into his bear-like arms. "Upstairs?"

"Yes, please," said Kett.

Clare had mounted one step and looked like he was about to keel over. Duke walked up behind him.

"Need some help, sir?"

"Go... toss... your..." Clare barked back as he took each step painfully slowly. He had to stop talking to get his breath back.

"What about this one?" said Porter, appearing with another box. "Says *Bathroom.*"

"That one goes in the bathroom, Pete," said Kett.

Porter joined the queue of people travelling at a snail's pace up the stairs. Evie appeared at the top of them, frowning at Clare.

"Daddy? Why does Uncle Colin look like he's going to pop?"

"He looks like he's going to *poop*," added Moira as she appeared.

Neither of them were wrong.

"Just move please, Evie," said Kett. "Let them through. You found the food box?"

She shook her head, not budging until Savage appeared and guided her out of the way.

"It's not in any of the rooms up here," she said, turning to the Super. "You want a hand with that, sir?"

"I'm... not... an... invalid," Clare snorted back, finally reaching the landing.

Billie walked out of the kitchen, shocked by the crowd who had gathered there.

"Oh wow, it's really good of you all to help," she said. "Uh, Colin, that box is for the kitchen, sorry."

Kett had seen Colin Clare give some withering looks in his time, hard stares that had cut the legs out from even the most experienced criminal, but the glare he threw at Kett beat them all. He manoeuvred himself around, forcing everyone back down the stairs as he struggled to the ground floor. By the time he'd disappeared into the kitchen, he was sweating like he'd spent the last four hours in the sauna.

"Thank you, Colin," said Billie as she walked in after him. "I did tell Robbie not to put all the cookbooks in the same box."

"Sorry," said Kett.

Porter and Duke raced each other up the steps, fighting to be the first one on the landing. The door to the toilet under the stairs opened and Allie appeared, her hands on her head.

"What the hell is going on?" she asked. "I thought the house was collapsing."

"Give it time," said Kett. "I'll find you a chair in a second, Allie, sorry."

She waved him away, her hands on her hips as she arched her back.

"I could do with a walk. Can I look at your garden? It's all a bit crazy in here for me."

"Help yourself," Kett said. "But you'll have to go out the front, no idea where the back door keys are."

"The chocolate!" said Evie from the landing. "It's not up here!"

"We'll find it," he said.

"It's been stolen," said Moira. "A poo head stole our sweeties and I want you to arrest them."

"Maybe we *should* open an investigation," Savage said to them, and they both cheered.

"I'll get some paper!" Evie yelled. "Dad, where's our colouring stuff? I'll make a Wanted poster."

"I have absolutely no idea," he said.

"Open an investigation?" asked Clare as he walked out of the kitchen, his arms so floppy he looked like a sulky orangutang. "Into what?"

"Nothing, sir," said Kett. "We've just misplaced the snacks."

"They're in a box," said Billie.

"It's not urgent," said Kett.

"It is," said Billie. "If you want tea. The milk's in there too."

"Oh, yeah," Kett said. "I forgot. It's *definitely* urgent."

Porter raced down the stairs, Duke right on his tail, the entire house seeming to shake with the weight of them. They almost ran into Clare at the bottom.

"Pack it in, you great buffoons!" he roared at them, and for a second it looked like he was about to clip them around the ear. "There's a new case. We need to find a box, marked..."

"*Food*," said Kett.

"Marked *Food*," Clare said. "Even you two shouldn't struggle with that. Porter, I need you in the kitchen, a comprehensive search. Duke, you take the living room. Savage?"

Savage appeared on the landing, looking over the railing.

"Sir?"

"I need a full sweep upstairs. If that box is here, we'll find it. Is there anything else that can help? Any distinguishing features? Smells?"

"Uh," said Kett, holding his hand to his thigh. "It's about this high, brown, we used a red marker, parcel tape. From memory, it had a faint whiff of cinnamon."

"Very seasonal," said Clare. "Right now, this is priority number one, and time's running out. So *skoosh*."

The team scattered, and Kett couldn't help but laugh.

"Impressive, sir," he said.

"Well, if the cream of the Norfolk Police can't find a box of food marked *Food* then we're well and truly stuffed," he said, looking at the packages that crowded the hallway. "I need you to search this area, Detective, leave no package untossed, no flap unfingered, no crevice unmolested."

"*What*?" said Kett.

Clare stepped over the boxes, disappearing into the dining room, replaced by Billie. She looked flustered, but she was smiling.

"Nice of them to come," she said.

"Yeah," he replied, although he could hear the uncertainty in his voice. "But I suddenly feel like I have twice as many kids as I did this morning. Any luck in there?"

"Pete's going through the boxes now," she said, walking over. "I'll help you out here."

He wrapped her in a hug, pushing his face into her hair and smelling the sweet shampoo scent of her. Then he let go and turned to the army of boxes that surrounded them. Most of the ones that the delivery men had left in the front hall were destined for the garage. Kett had boxed these, and he'd used black duct tape instead of brown parcel tape. There were seven smaller packages, all labelled *Main Bedroom*, and two larger ones. He grabbed the first, tilting it to the side to see *Garden Stuff* written there in Billie's handwriting. The other had no label, and he set about ripping the tape from the top.

"That's definitely not it," said Billie. "I think that's your mum's things from the attic."

When he lifted the flap, he saw that she was right.

"It definitely isn't out here," he said, scratching his head.

"Not in the living room either," said Duke as he reappeared. "Twelve boxes in there plus some furniture, but nothing with *Chocolate* written on it."

"The label doesn't say *Chocolate*," said Kett. "It says *Food*."

Duke frowned.

"Hang on," he said, walking back through the door.

"Dining room is clear," said Clare. "No food. How're we doing out here?"

"No sign of it," said Kett.

"Not in here either," said Duke.

"Upstairs is clear," said Savage, walking carefully down the stairs with Moira in her arms. "No food box."

"That is so weird," said Kett. "It must be in the kitchen."

They filed through the kitchen door, plenty of space for them in the large room. Porter was standing by the counter, far too close to the kettle for Kett's liking.

"How's the search going, Pete?" he asked him.

Porter turned around, a massive grin on his face. There was steam rising from the mugs on the counter, and a weird smell in the air.

"Oh no," said Kett. "What have you done?"

"Fixed the milk problem," said Porter. "Tea's ready."

Kett met Savage's eyes, then Clare's, seeing the same look of horror reflected there.

"What did you use, Pete?" he asked.

"This stuff," said Porter, holding up the bottle that Clare had brought.

"*Eggnog*?" said Kett.

"It's milky, isn't it?" Porter studied the label. "It'll be fine. It'll be Christmassy."

Kett couldn't help himself. Curiosity drove him to the counter and he looked at the mugs, at the unholy travesty that swam inside them. The tea was the colour of a newborn baby's diarrhoea, clusters of oily white lumps floating in it and a weird crust around the edge. The smell was enough to make Kett's eyes water.

"Dear God, man," he said.

"Porter, you're fired," said Clare. "Pack your things. I never want to see you again."

Porter looked genuinely crestfallen.

"It's basically the same as milk," he said, staring at the cups. "I don't know what went wrong."

"You were born," said Clare. "That's what went wrong. I mean it, you're fired."

"It'll be... fine," said Porter, reaching for the nearest cup with a look of grim determination. "I'll test it."

"Don't," said Kett.

"Don't," echoed Savage. "Really."

Porter seemed to think about it for a moment more before deciding it wasn't worth the risk. Billie eased through the crowd and picked up the drinks one by one, tipping them down the sink.

"You'd better chuck the mugs, too," said Kett. "There's no coming back from that."

"Right," said Clare, checking his watch. "Back to work. Savage, Duke, search the kitchen, see if the box is here. Kett, call the removals company, find out if it was left on the truck."

"Yes, sir," they said together.

Kett walked upstairs, wrestling his phone from Alice and bolting back down before the screams of protest could start. He scrolled through his list of previous calls until he found the mobile number for the driver. He opened the front door, stepping into the crisp air, feeling the sting of the cold against his skin.

"Yeah?" came a wet voice after a handful of rings, followed by the sound of chewing.

"Hi," said Kett. "It's Robbie. You just shifted our stuff over to Wroxham Road this morning."

More chewing, then a loud swallow.

"Yeah?"

"Uh, yeah," said Kett. "I think we're missing a box."

"You're not," said the voice. "Both vans are empty, your wife checked them before we left. What have you lost?"

"Nothing much," said Kett, hearing the man take another bite out of whatever he was eating. "Just our food."

The sound of chewing stopped abruptly.

"A big box," Kett said. "Had *Food* written on it. It's got all our snacks, milk, that kind of stuff. Lots of chocolate."

"Okay," said the man. "And what do you want me to do about it?"

Kett cleared his throat, his breath emerging as a cloud.

"You could check again," he said.

"No need," said the man, taking another bite.

"What are you eating?" Kett asked.

"None of your business, mate," came the reply.

"You do know I'm a copper, don't you?" Kett said, the man's rudeness gnawing on his nerves. Again, the chewing stopped, followed by a louder swallow.

"Look, what can I tell you?" said the man. "I haven't stolen your chocolates. This happens every bloody time. It'll be in your house somewhere. If you're a copper, you shouldn't have too much trouble finding it."

"It's—" started Kett, but the man had hung up.

"Any leads?" barked a voice behind him, so close he almost dropped his phone. He turned to see Clare on the doorstep, his face as serious as it was when the team was investigating a murder.

"No," said Kett. "Removals team don't have it."

"Or so they say," said Clare. "I heard you ask him what he was eating."

"Yeah, he was chewing on something," said Kett. "Probably just his lunch."

"Or your snacks," said Clare, eyeballing the street. "Do you remember the registration of the van? I'll have somebody intercept them."

Kett laughed, but the Super's face showed no trace of humour.

"It's really fine," said Kett. "There's a shop down the road, I'll just—"

"Theft is theft," said Clare.

Kett held up a hand.

"I don't think it was them," he said. "I can't see an established removals firm risking their reputation over a box of chocolate and crisps and milk."

Clare grunted, spinning around and heading back inside. Kett picked up one of the boxes from the gravel and followed him, hefting it into the living room. He was surprised to see all three of his girls in there, dragging boxes across the carpeted floor into the corner. Alice seemed to have forgotten all about the phone.

"What are you doing?" he asked.

"Making a cage," said Alice, grinning. "When we find out who stole the sweeties we're going to put them in here so they can't get out."

"And extepute them!" said Moira, doing her best to push a box that was bigger than she was.

"Extepute?" asked Kett.

"She means execute," said Alice. "We'll execute them."

"That's... a little harsh," said Kett. "Please don't talk about that kind of stuff in front of your sisters, Alice."

"We'll just keep them in here forever," said Evie. "But we'll feed them. They'll be like a pet."

She looked up at him imploringly.

"Can we keep them as a pet, Daddy? Please? A pet criminal? Please?"

"Please?" said Moira.

Alice cackled like a madwoman.

"Uh..." said Kett, wondering if the smell of Porter's eggnog tea had made him delirious. "No, sorry."

He left the girls and walked back into the hall, heading for the toilet under the stairs. He'd half opened the door when he heard a scream from inside.

"Oh, shit," he said, catching a glimpse of Porter standing beside the toilet. "Sorry, Pete."

Porter was coughing, like something was stuck in his throat.

"You okay, mate?" Kett asked, peeking around the door again.

Porter turned around, his trousers thankfully done up. He was hiding something behind his back, Kett was sure of it.

And there was a smudge of chocolate on his bottom lip.

"What are you doing, Pete?"

Porter coughed again, his eyes watering.

"Nothing, sir," he croaked. "Was just about to take a leak."

"What have you got there?" Kett asked.

"Nothing, sir," Porter said.

"You're lying."

"Robbie?" came Savage's voice, and a second later, she pushed her head past his shoulder. "Sir? What's going on?"

"Porter's eating something," said Kett.

"I am not!" Porter replied in a falsetto.

"He's got chocolate on his lip," said Savage. "Look."

"What's happening?" asked Duke as he joined the party, peeking over Kett's head. "Why are we all watching Porter taking a whizz?"

"He's not," said Savage. "He's eating."

"In the shitter?" said Duke. "Why?"

"I'm not eating," Porter hissed in a whisper. "Keep your voices down or Allie will hear you."

"Allie will hear what?" said Clare as he joined the back of the queue. "Porter, stop examining your toss porridge in Kett's water closet and get out here."

"Toss porridge?" said Savage, grimacing.

"I'm not..."

Porter sighed, his hand finally appearing. Clasped in his fingers was a Boost bar, half of it eaten.

"I was just hungry. I wasn't expecting the Spanish bloody Inquisition."

"Why are you eating it in there, though?" asked Savage.

"Because he stole it, that's why," boomed Clare. "Where did the chocolate come from, Porter? Where did you find it? From a box marked *Food*, I'd wager."

"I brought it with me," Porter protested. "I swear, I wouldn't steal from a bunch of kids. I wouldn't bloody dare, not from your girls. They'd string me up.

"He's telling the truth," said Kett. "We don't buy Boosts."

"See," said Porter with a breath of relief.

"It doesn't explain what you're doing in there, sir," said Duke.

Porter shot him a look, then seemed to resign himself to the fact that he wasn't getting out of the toilet until he'd told the truth.

"Fine," he said quietly. "If you must know, I've been... I've put on a bit of weight in the last few months."

"No shit," said Duke.

"Because I'm trying to feed Allie up. She's too thin and I want her to be okay with the baby and everything. So I offer her food all the time and I'm eating too, to encourage her. But she's worried I'm eating too much so she doesn't like me snacking, but... But now I've got to the point where I'm hungry all the time, so I..."

He shrugged.

"You sneak off for a treat," said Kett, feeling a rush of sympathy for him. "Don't stress about it, Pete, we've all been there."

Porter looked like he was about to cry.

"Hey," said Kett. "Having kids is *so* hard, every single part of it, even before they get here. You wanna eat, you eat. As much as you want."

Porter lifted the Boost to his mouth and nibbled it.

"You're a good man, Pete," said Savage. "Sorry, we thought, you know..."

"You should probably stop, though," said Duke, glancing at Porter's stomach. Savage elbowed him in the ribs hard enough to make him grunt.

"Pack it in, Aaron," she said. "Move back, let the poor guy out."

They all stood to one side as Porter ducked out of the low door. He folded the wrapper carefully around the Boost and dropped it into his pocket. Then, as one, Kett and Savage enveloped the big DI in a hug. A second or two later Duke joined in, Porter's body trembling.

"Well, that's twenty seconds of my life I'm never getting back," said Clare as they all let go. Porter wiped his eyes. "Stop crying, Porter, we're working a case. The chocolate's not here, it hasn't been taken by the removals company, Porter hasn't snuck into the toilet to gobble it all up. Where does that leave us?"

"Aliens?" said Duke with a shrug. Kett glanced at him, not quite sure whether it was a serious suggestion or not.

"It's really no problem," Billie said as she walked into the hall. "The shop's a five-minute walk. We could have been there and back half a dozen times by now."

"I kind of want to know what happened," said Savage. "It's like one of those true crime podcasts."

"It really isn't," said Kett.

"We need a spreadsheet," Clare barked. "We need to get some suspects up on the wall. Where's your laptop, Kett?"

Kett sighed, rubbing his eyes again until fireworks exploded across the dark.

"Through here," he said after a moment, heading for the dining room.

"Honestly, we really don't have to do this," said Billie. "Kett's mum is coming over in a little while with the chinchilla, she can bring some milk and treats."

"It would be good to know where it went," said Kett. "It doesn't make sense."

"And if we let the small crimes go, then the big crimes just get bigger," said Clare. "Criminals will start tossing all over us, everywhere we go. We won't be able to move for tossing. We'll be swimming upstream in toss, all day every day."

"So wrong," said Savage.

"So whoever is responsible for this, they have to pay,"

Clare went on. "I want a list of everyone who's had contact with your belongings for the last few days. Every single person, Kett. We're going to find the criminal responsible. We're going to find the truth."

"But—" Billie said, only for the Super to cut her off again.

"Billie, when your husband was taken by Hollenbeck, did we just pop to the shop and buy another one?" he asked. "No, we didn't. We used all the resources at our disposal to track him down. We do that with every single case. We do, because we must."

"It's some milk and like half a packet of bourbons, sir," said Kett, but the look Clare threw him made him crash down on his improvised chair, the little box almost buckling beneath him. He prodded the laptop's trackpad until it woke up, typing his password.

"Nice desk," said Duke from the dining room door.

Kett ignored him, opening a new Excel document.

Then immediately closing it.

"Oh," he said.

His knees were pressing against the first of the two boxes that he'd used as a table, the sides soft and squashy.

He thought he might have caught a whiff of cinnamon.

"What is it, sir?" asked Savage.

"Nothing," he said. "Why don't you lot head back to the kitchen, let me focus on this?"

Nobody moved.

"It's right there, isn't it, sir?" said Savage. "The box."

"Uh..." said Kett.

"Where?" asked Duke.

"It is," said Porter. "I bet it's literally right in front of you."

"*Where?*" Duke said.

"For the love of..." groaned Clare. He stomped over, and Kett had to snatch up his laptop as the Super ripped the duvet cover away.

Sure enough, the box that was making up half of his desk boasted the word *Food* in big, red letters.

"Yeah," said Kett, feeling his cheeks burn. "My bad."

"Porter," said Clare. "You're hired again. And promoted to DCI. Kett, clean out your locker."

"That's fair enough," said Savage with a smile.

Kett nodded, putting the laptop on the floor and holding up his hands.

"I confess," he said. "You'd better arrest me."

"Girls," said Savage. "We've solved the case."

There was a chorus of whoops and a thunder of feet as the girls crossed the hall. Alice appeared first, looking at the scene with wide eyes. Evie pushed past her, running over and pointing a finger at Kett.

"It was you, Daddy!" she said, aghast.

"Not intentionally," said Kett.

"That's for the courts to decide," said Clare.

"You just wanted all the chocolate for yourself!" said Alice.

Moira was more interested in the box, wrestling with the tape.

"I'll do it," said Kett. "Stand back."

"Oh no, you won't," said Clare with a glint in his eye. "That's evidence. You, Robert Kett, are now under arrest. Girls, take him to prison."

Kett laughed but Clare was deadly serious, and so were the girls. Alice grabbed his arm and yanked so hard he almost fell off his improvised chair. Evie took his other hand and together they marched him into the living room, to the fortress of boxes in the corner.

"Get in," said Evie, and she was smiling so hard he didn't have the heart to disobey her. He clambered over the lowest section, his bottom lip pouting. Evie laughed. "And don't come out, not ever."

"Never?" he asked.

"Never," said Alice and Evie together. "Now let's get our reward."

They scarpered from the room and Kett breathed a laugh through his nose, enjoying the relative quiet. The girls had thrown some cushions in, and one of the boxes held his books. If this was to be his prison until the end of time, it wouldn't be so bad.

He sat on the cushion and stretched his legs, feeling once again like he was dreaming. The house smelled so different, it sounded so different, it felt so different—and yet it still felt welcome, it was still undeniably *home*.

"You okay in there?" came a voice, and a second later Billie peeked over the wall of boxes.

"I'm fine," he said. "Quite cosy, to be honest. You could join me if you like."

He wiggled his eyebrows, and she laughed.

"I don't think conjugal visits are allowed, sorry," she said. "I'll see what I can do about commuting your sentence."

"No chance," came Clare's voice from the door. "He'll sit in there until he's learned his lesson. We, in the meantime, will take care of the mess."

"Oh, really, it's no bother," said Billie. "You don't have to—"

"I insist," said Clare. "We'll start in the living room. It's what families do, Billie. And we're family."

"Thank you," she said. "I'll put the kettle on."

She blew Kett a kiss and walked out of the room.

Kett leaned back against the wall, closing his eyes and listening to the laughter, to the happy calls of his children, to the kettle coming to a boil. The exhaustion was like a weighted blanket, sleep right there, and he wondered if he had drifted off for a moment because suddenly Duke and Porter were above him, dismantling the walls of his prison. Past them, he could see the sofa against the far wall, a shelf full of books.

"Oh," he said.

"Oh is right," said Porter with a grin. "They obviously make prisons far too comfortable these days."

Kett struggled up, his body stiff.

"How long was I out?"

"Only half an hour, sir," said Porter. "We work fast."

"I can see that."

"Daddy!" Evie yelled as she ran into the room, more chocolate smeared over her face. "I'm glad you're free. I wouldn't want you to be in prison forever."

He lifted her up, giving her a hug that she returned with all her strength.

"Auntie Katie put my bed up, and Moo-moo's, my room looks pretty."

"That's great," said Kett. "I'm really pleased."

"I love our new house," she said, wiggling until he dropped her. "I want to live here forever."

"Me too," he told her as she ran from the room. "Me too."

He followed her into the hall to see Superintendent Clare by the door, drowning in his Big Tossing Jacket.

"I'm off," he said. "Some of us have proper work to do."

"Thank you, sir," said Kett, noticing that all the boxes in the hall were now gone. "I really appreciate it. We both do."

"It wasn't done out of kindness," Clare replied. "It was

done so you could get on that computer and start your tossing work."

"Won't be doing *that*," Kett muttered.

"I want them before the New Year, Kett," said Clare as he opened the front door. "Merry Christmas."

"And to you, sir," Kett said.

He started to close the door but stopped when he heard a shout behind him. Savage was walking out of the kitchen, pulling on her coat.

"We've got to split too," she said. "Sorry, sir. Duke's mum needs her car back for the bingo."

"It's a 'we' now, is it?" said Kett with a smile.

"Well, you know," Savage blustered. "Not a... I mean only because he's driving and... It's not like we're, you know..."

"You ready, hon?" said Duke as he appeared from the dining room. Savage put a hand to her face.

"Hon, eh?" Kett said quietly, his grin growing. He offered his arms and Savage moved in for a hug. "I'm happy you're happy," Kett said when they'd parted.

"I am," she replied. "Really."

"Come here," said Duke, and before Kett could tell him not to dare, he'd wrapped his giant arms around him, his beard tickling Kett's face. The hug seemed to go on forever, but it was so tight that Kett couldn't find the air to protest with. Duke gave him a couple of slaps on the back that could have knocked him through the wall.

"Happy homecoming," he said.

"Wrong word, Aaron," said Savage as she stepped outside. "Come on, let's see if we can figure out how to get you back in the car."

"Merry Christmas," Kett called after them.

"You're all sorted," said Porter as he appeared from the

kitchen, Allie's arm looped through his. Billie was right behind him. "You'll still have to unpack some of your own stuff. I'm not going through your underwear."

"Small mercies," said Kett. "Thank you, Pete."

"It's a pleasure," he said.

He offered a hand but Kett hugged him instead. The big DI gripped him back.

"Merry Christmas, Robbie," he said. "And to you, Billie."

"Merry Christmas," said Billie. "Look after yourselves, all three of you."

"And no more stealing the kids' food," Porter said, pointing a finger at Kett. "They've already told me they won't go so easy on you next time."

"I've learned my lesson," said Kett. "I'm well and truly reformed."

Porter let Allie through the door first.

"You need anything at all, mate," Kett told him before he could follow her. "I mean anything, then you just ask. Okay? It's an emotional rollercoaster, for both of you, and we're here if you need us."

Porter nodded his thanks, looking for a second like he might burst into tears again. He set off after his wife.

Kett closed the door, letting out a long, slow breath. Billie walked up behind him and slid her arms around his waist, resting her head against his back.

"I was not expecting *that*," Kett said. "I can't believe they did that for us."

"I can," she said, her words hot against his skin. "They're good people. They're the best people."

"They are," said Kett.

He swivelled around and held her.

"Looks a little less like a stable now, anyway," he said. "Where are the girls? It's suspiciously quiet."

"Upstairs, with chocolate and my phone. They're watching *Elf*."

Kett laughed, feeling a sudden rush of relief, like sinking into a hot bath after a cold day. He shuddered and Billie held him tighter.

"You missed your cuppa," she said. "You were asleep."

"I wasn't asleep," he protested, finally letting her go. "I was in prison, contemplating the error of my ways."

"Well, whatever it was, I'll make another one."

She took a couple of steps back, studying him—and there in the quiet light of the hallway she seemed to have shed the last two years of her life. She seemed almost as young, almost as carefree, as the woman he'd first fallen in love with all those years ago.

"I love you," he said, the words out of his mouth before he even knew they were coming.

"I know," she said. "I love you too, Robbie."

She walked into the kitchen and he heard the sound of the kettle leaving the cradle, the tap running, the click of the switch.

The best sounds in the world, surely.

Then he heard a scream of anger from upstairs.

"It's my turn, Moira! It's not fair!"

"No!"

"Give it!"

Another scream, then footsteps pounding across the landing.

Kett took a breath, feeding off those last few moments of peace. Then he set off towards the stairs.

"Come on," he called to his girls. "No arguing, unless you want me to put you guys in prison."

More screams, these full of laughter. He didn't mind. He didn't mind one bit, because they were home, they were safe, they were together.

And it wouldn't be a Kett Christmas without a little chaos, after all.

KNUCKLE BONES

PROLOGUE

Wednesday

There was nothing on Earth more dangerous, thought Geoffrey Wilcman, than a group of riled-up grannies high on tea and digestives.

There were fourteen of them now, clustered around the edge of the building site, their hair the same colour as the miserable winter sky. Half were wrapped up in thick coats of tweed and tartan, the rest wore velour tracksuits in various shades of pink and green, but all were united by three things: the homemade signs they held, their expressions of outright indignation, and the words that were spewing out of their wrinkled mouths.

"Stick your digger up your arsehole!" yelled one, loud enough to be heard over the fourteen-tonne JCB excavator that was carving trenches in the dirt. The woman was easily the most formidable of the lot, probably not far off fourteen tonnes herself. She held a sign that read, "Say NO to the expansion of County Hall!" It was gripped in both of her hands like a battle axe, her knuckles white. Geoffrey guessed she was in her late fifties, a good decade older than him, but he wouldn't have fancied his chances against her in a fight.

"And the rest of them!" shouted another woman, far smaller but no less terrifying. She was pouring tea from a thermos into a plastic cup with the mad-eyed determination of somebody about to launch a Molotov cocktail. "All the bloody diggers, right up your bumhole!"

He pretended not to hear them, adjusting his hard hat and holding his clipboard like a shield. It had started to rain an hour ago—not proper rain, just that infuriating February drizzle that stuck to you like wet gauze. It had churned the construction site into a moonscape of mud, the ground sucking at his boots as he tried to walk. To his right, past the excavator and the huddle of terrifying old ladies, towered the enormous bulk of Norfolk's County Hall—ten stories of brutalist bureaucratic ugliness that dominated the skyline. To his left, past the remainder of the football-pitch-sized zone of destruction, was what was left of the woodland that had once surrounded this place, another JCB currently ripping up the roots of a once-mighty beech tree.

"You should be ashamed of yourselves!" screamed one of the protesters. "Your mother would stick you back up her fanny if she could!"

He wasn't sure his mother would do anything of the sort, but the woman was right, they *should* be ashamed. There was no excuse to flatten a woodland like this, not when these trees had been growing here for a hundred years or more, and certainly not because the sad old farts on the council wanted a bigger building to be sad old farts in. He didn't even understand why they needed any more space. County Hall was already far bigger than any building in this little city had any right to be. He'd heard countless justifications for it over the last three years, but the simple truth was that the council had too much money and they didn't like blowing their wad on anyone who actually needed it.

Still, a job was a job, and this was his.

And God only knew he needed the money, because the betting shops had rinsed him these last few weeks.

Months, he thought, then, *well, years*.

He heard more shouting from the direction of the women and did his best to ignore it, watching as the beech finally gave up and tore its way free from the wet earth. The sound it made was almost human, a gravelly cry of grief.

"Geoff!" the shout came again, and this time he turned to see Mike 'Peewee' Persons slipping and sliding through the mud towards him. The short guy doffed his hard hat like he was talking to a lord, not the foreman.

"What's up, Mikey?" said Geoff, knowing full well how much the guy hated his nickname.

"We've hit masonry," he said. "Up the hill."

Geoff followed the man's finger over the sea of mud to where a third digger, this one smaller, was working on the perimeter of the build. It had come to a standstill, four men in hi-vis vests idling beside it, two of them smoking even though they knew perfectly well they weren't allowed to do that near the machinery. Geoff opened his mouth to reply but was cut off by the roar of the nearest excavator's belching exhaust as it reversed. He leaned closer, shouting.

"You've hit masonry? What kind?"

"Not sure," said Mikey, shrugging his shoulders. "Flint and brick, an old basement or something."

Geoff swore, looking at his clipboard like it might

provide him with an answer and seeing only budget notes. In the three years that this project had been in the works, he'd studied dozens of historical documents, ancient deeds and crumbling maps that told the story of this little pocket of Norwich. He'd consulted with every single heritage group in the city with the express purpose of making sure they didn't disturb anything that might be considered archaeologically relevant.

There was no way they could have missed something.

"You're sure it's not just a rock?" Geoff asked. Mikey's greying eyebrow climbed upwards.

"It's not a rock," he said. "I know what a rock looks like, Geoff."

"Hey!" came a cry from the posse of angry grandmothers.

"Don't pay them any attention," said Geoff.

"Yeah, you," said the biggest woman, extending a finger that was the same size, shape and colour as a raw sausage. "I hope your willy falls off."

Mikey almost choked.

"Did she say she hoped my *willy* fell off?" he said.

"I think that was the gist of it."

"Bit harsh," said Mikey.

"And gets eaten by cats!" the woman persisted, her voice unfathomably loud.

Mikey pulled a face.

"Sounds just like my wife," he said.

Despite everything, Geoff managed a smile. He set off into the mud and the noise, feeling like a soldier during the Great War stumbling towards the sound of artillery fire. After a dozen steps his boot slipped off to the side and he almost did the splits, his clipboard hitting the dirt. A cheer rose up from the bunch of old biddies, and he shot them a murderous glance that only brought about an even louder round of applause.

He swore again, waving his arms at the excavator until the driver spotted him. The engine grumbled into silence, the shouts from the protestors suddenly much louder.

"I hope you get diphtheria from all that mud!" yelled one. "And dysentery! And syphilis! I hope you shit yourself to death!"

"Syphilis?" said Mikey as he followed. "You're not putting your knob in it, are you?"

"I said ignore them," said Geoff, his patience razor-thin as he stumbled past the enormous digger. "They've got nothing better to do with themselves."

That was apparent in the way the women were shuffling along the length of the dig, keeping pace with him as he moved towards the far side. Their signs pointed to the sky, their breath collecting around them like a fog. One, a woman in her seventies wearing a smart beige skirt suit and matching hat—Kitty Lewington, he knew, because he'd argued with her in endless council meetings—had ducked beneath the flimsy line of red and white tape that marked the edge of the excavated pit.

"Hey!" Geoff yelled, shooing her away like she was a pigeon. "Get back. You're not allowed to cross the line."

"And you're not allowed to destroy our city," she shot back, marching into the mud. "We've all warned you, this isn't your place."

"Get back, or I'll call the police," Geoff said, but the woman showed no sign of stopping. Like him, she was heading for the third digger, and she was dragging the collective of grannies behind her.

"We'll make sure you lose your job for this!" she said.

"For heaven's sake," said Geoff. "Do me a favour, Mikey, would you? Call the coppers, get somebody down here. As much as I'd like to see the lot of them disappear beneath that JCB I'll never hear the end of it if they do."

"Sure thing," said Mikey, using his teeth to pull off his glove.

Geoff left him to it, passing a group of workers who had paused to watch the women.

"Ignore them," he ordered. "Everyone just ignore them."

"Hard to," said one of the men. "That big one told me to eat my own sphincter yesterday."

"He didn't even know what *sphincter* meant," said another guy with a wheezing laugh. "Thought it was an Egyptian monument."

Geoff marched on with steely determination, giving the twelve-foot-deep excavation a wide berth. The huddle of women matched him step for step, converging on the far side of the site at the same time. The workmen stood in the shadow of their digger, dousing their cigarettes in the mud and watching the advancing army warily.

"This is your last warning," Geoff told them when they were within earshot. "This place is dangerous. I've called the police."

"Good," said Kitty Lewington. She was still at the head of the pack, but the giant Miss Trunchbull lookalike was close behind, huffing and puffing like a bull. Their signs clacked together like the percussion section of an orchestra. "Then we'll point out that despite your claims to the contrary, you have indeed disturbed an archaeological site."

"It's nothing of the sort," said Geoff, moving towards the digger. "It's a rock or something. We took every precaution, as you well know. We've..."

And his words died on his lips as he passed the digger and saw what lay in front of it. Down a shallow slope of earth was the excavated pit that would eventually house the plant room for the gym and swimming pool. A monumental slab of stone had been shunted to the side to reveal a ruin of brick and flint beneath it, the circular pattern far too neat to be anything but deliberate.

Geoff ran through pretty much every swear word he knew beneath his breath, wondering if there was any way he could hide the revelation before Mrs Lewington made her way around the digger.

It was already too late.

"I knew it," she said. "What did I tell you? You and your idiot masters. That's a heritage site. You almost destroyed it!"

"I very much doubt it," said Geoff. "It's an old soakaway or something. Now back off, or I swear to God..."

"Police are on the way," said Mikey, reappearing behind the growing crowd of angry women and smirking workmen. "Five minutes."

It wasn't the deterrent he'd hoped for, because Mrs Lewington was marching past him and struggling down the slope, her enormous companion by her side. They were both using their signs as walking sticks to stop themselves from falling over.

"Don't," said Geoff. "I'm not joking. Can one of you grab them?"

"Touch me and I'll fuck you up!" roared the bigger woman, with no trace of a lie in her features.

"Anyone?" said Geoff, almost whining.

Nobody volunteered. He walked after them, almost losing his balance on the slope. The pit was deeper than it looked, the world fast disappearing behind its steep banks.

Only the tops of the trees crowded overhead, and he had the uncanny notion that they were waiting for the right moment to bury him alive in the sea of mud as punishment for what he'd done to their friends.

Mrs Lewington had reached the circle of bricks and she had a camera in her hands—an *actual* camera, not a phone. He heard the snap of the shutter as she took a photo.

"Look," said Geoff, out of breath as he caught up to them. "I know we haven't always seen eye to eye, Mrs Lewington, but you really can't be down here. It's not safe."

She took another photograph, her bullish friend standing between them like a bodyguard. He stopped walking, not wanting to get within swinging-handbag distance, trying to fathom how on Earth he'd ended up in a pit trying not to get beaten up by two women.

"We'll down tools, I promise," he said. "We won't do anything else until we figure out what this is."

"I know what it is," said Mrs Lewington, taking a third photo. "Don't you? It would be fairly apparent, one would think. What did I tell you would happen if you kept going? Nothing good, nothing good."

Geoff had to step to the side to see past the second woman, and he took his first proper look at what the excavator had revealed. The circle of bricks in the mud was bigger than he'd first thought, six feet or so from side to side. There were slabs of stone set into it, each one lower than the last. Steps, he realised, spiralling into a shaft of darkness. The immense stone slab lay next to it like the top of a giant's sarcophagus.

"It's a staircase," he said, wondering again how the surveyors could have missed it.

"Digger was trying to shift the slab," said Mikey as he slid down the slope. "We saw that underneath."

"I told you, didn't I?" said Mrs Lewington, finally looking at him. She wore an expression of profound anger and disappointment, one that made him feel like he was five years old. "You didn't listen."

"*I* had nothing to do with it," said Geoff. "I'm just the bloody foreman. What are you doing?"

Mrs Lewington was approaching the staircase, testing the topmost step with her mud-caked shoes.

"What do you think?" she asked. "I want to see what you've almost destroyed."

"You're not going down there."

It was meant as a statement, not a question, but either way, it was ignored. Mrs Lewington dropped onto the second step, then the third, and it was only when her bottom half had disappeared into the gloom entirely that she looked back—the first hint of uncertainty on her face.

"Do you happen to have a torch, Mr Wileman?"

"I've got one, miss," said Mikey, pulling out his keys and releasing the torch on the ring. Geoff shot him a look that might have blasted him right out of the pit, and Mikey shrugged apologetically. "Sorry," he said. "Don't want her having an accident."

Right now, Geoff wanted nothing more than for the old woman to tumble down the stairs and for the stone slab to magically seal her down there, but he didn't think it would do his career any good. He snatched the tiny torch from Mikey and set off towards the stairs, passing the second woman. She, at least, seemed to want nothing to do with the subterranean chamber they'd uncovered—he wasn't even sure she'd fit down the steps.

"May I?" said Mrs Lewington as he joined her in the claustrophobic stairwell.

"No," he replied. "If you're going to make me do this, then I'm going first. Move over."

She did as she was told, her mouth a tight line and her watery eyes watching him intently as he squeezed past, as if she feared he might try to give her a shove. The thought had crossed his mind, of course, but by now the edge of the pit and the shallow slope were crowded with people. It seemed the entire workforce had come to watch, as well as a growing number of staff from inside County Hall. He felt almost like a gladiator in front of a crowd of jeering Romans, and his stomach clenched like a fist.

The yawning darkness beneath him didn't help, either. He angled the torch down the steps but it did nothing to peel away the shadows which had been buried there for God only knew how long. Fingers of freezing air reached up and caressed his face as if thanking him for freeing them, stinking of dirt and age and rot and something else, something *worse*.

"We really should wait until we know it's safe," he said, his voice a whisper.

"It's safe," said Mrs Lewington, a finger prodding Geoff between his shoulder blades. "These things were built to last a thousand years. On you go, or step aside."

The crowd watched, the builders in their bright coats nudging each other and laughing. He was well aware that if he backed away now, his reputation would be forever in tatters. *Geoff Wileman the chicken, Geoff Wileman, bullied by grannies*. He'd never live it down.

And it was that thought that made him take another step, then another, one hand holding the useless torch while the other snatched at the slick brick walls to stop the vertigo from taking him. The stone slab had done its job well, stopping the soil from compacting inside the stairwell. There was only dust here, kicked up into a whirling cloud that danced in the light from the torch.

He dropped down another three steps, fully underground now. Mrs Lewington followed, her breaths fast and hoarse, her hand still resting on his back. Geoff glanced up at the sky, which seemed too far away. It was utterly silent down here, terrifyingly silent, and he imagined himself sliding down the gullet of some patient predator, the stairwell suddenly snapping shut and plunging them into darkness, the stone jaw grinding him to a paste.

He stopped, overwhelmed by claustrophobic panic.

"Let's go back," he said, his throat too tight for the words to form properly. He started to turn only to feel the old woman's finger in his back again, prodding insistently. He would have screamed at her if she hadn't spoken first.

"That's the bottom, Mr Wileman," she said. "Right there."

He aimed the torch at his feet and saw the last two steps.

"I know," he snapped, dropping down them onto a brick floor that felt wonderfully firm. Mrs Lewington walked to his side, and they both looked up to where daylight trickled down behind them, as if emboldened by their success. They were maybe ten feet underground, Geoff thought, the pressure in his chest relaxing. Even if the stairwell collapsed—which it would never do, he knew, because he could see how well it had been constructed—the boys would be able to dig them out in minutes with the excavator.

"I know," he said again, even though Mrs Lewington hadn't spoken. "I was just saying that the police are probably here. We should let them check it out first."

"Why?" the woman replied, pushing past him.

He didn't have an answer for her. He lifted the torch

and swung the paltry light in a circle, revealing a cellar that was maybe ten feet wide and twice as long. The walls were made of brick, vaulted overhead, with a large circular column—like a tree trunk—in the middle, holding everything up. Four or five tall, wide alcoves split both sides of the room into pockets of shadow, and he had to swing the torch towards them to check that nothing was hiding there. The air was cold and entirely motionless, still fast asleep. He wondered how long this place had gone undisturbed, and what it would do to them when it realised they had woken it.

"This is definitely part of the old hall," said Mrs Lewington, her fingers resting lightly on the wall. "This brickwork is Tudor. It must have been left behind by the heathens who tore the place down. They can't have known about it or they would have filled it in."

"Someone knew about it," said Geoff. "Or why would they have covered it up?"

She didn't answer, taking hold of his sleeve like he was a child and pulling him towards the central column.

"You okay, Geoff?" shouted Mikey from overhead.

"Yeah," he croaked, his voice swallowed whole by the room.

"There would have been several cellars in the old hall," Mrs Lewington was saying, as if he might hold a shred of interest. "They used them for meat, cheese, wine, even ice."

They rounded the central column and Geoff aimed the torch at the far end of the room. There was another alcove there, this one bigger, darker.

"They used them as hiding places, too," the woman went on. "During the Civil War. Not that we saw much action around these parts. But this is history, Mr Wileman.

History is a vulnerable creature, and it is up to us to keep it alive."

She marched towards the alcove at the end and he followed, if only because he didn't want to be left on his own. It was only when he was standing right next to it that he realised it wasn't an alcove at all but an opening, leading into a smaller space.

Don't go in there, he said, or at least he *thought* he'd said it. Either way, Mrs Lewington ducked through the gap.

"Oh," he heard her say. "Oh my. Hurry up, man, bring the torch."

He followed her into the smaller room, barely enough space for both of them. There was something mounted on the wall, a collection of bits and pieces that looked like old rope, or maybe even riding tack. Even with the torch, it was too dark to tell. They seemed to have been arranged in the shape of a cobweb, with a disc in the centre.

"What *is* that?" he asked, trying to peer over the little woman's head.

"History," the woman answered as she stepped forward. Her hand held the sleeve of his coat again, but it felt less like an act of aggression now and more one of apprehension. "It's a part of a world that..."

Her voice tailed off into a dry croak as they stepped up to the wall and the little torch finally penetrated the inky dark. The light was trembling, and it took Geoff a moment to understand that it was because his hand was shaking. His entire body was shaking, his teeth doing a macabre chattering dance that he couldn't seem to stop.

The objects on the walls were bones, dozens of them —*hundreds*, maybe. He recognised some of them, the long, ball-jointed length of a thigh bone, the spidery curves of half a dozen ribs, the wing-like plates of the pelvis, all arranged in a series of concentric circles that was almost perfectly symmetrical.

And in the centre of it all was a skull, looking right at him, its eyes blazing darkness.

"Nope," Geoff whispered, backing away. This time he grabbed hold of Mrs Lewington's sleeve, feeling like a kid reaching for his mother. She shook him off like he might have been responsible for whatever this was, and he staggered away without her, retreating into the bigger part of the cellar. There was a high-pitched ringing in his ears, as if somebody had hammered a tuning fork inside his skull.

He kept moving, not turning away from the room with the bones even when he hit the central column hard enough to jar the wind from his lungs. The bottom step caught him by surprise, as if it had crept closer while his back was turned, and he tumbled onto his backside. The torchlight hit the ceiling, liquid night flooding the cellar instantly. And in that gloom he imagined the bones jumping off the wall and scuttling towards him, the skull's jawbone snapping.

He had to shove a fist to his mouth to stop the scream, pushing himself up the steps on his arse. The torch was forgotten, Mrs Lewington was forgotten, there was only the stairwell which seemed to shrink around him, choking him; only that stinking, ancient darkness which tried to wrench him back. He spun around, crawling up the steps on his hands and knees until he pushed into the day like a man who had almost drowned, gasping for air.

"Jesus, Geoff," said Mikey, grabbing his hand and hauling him the rest of the way. "What did she do to you?"

Nothing, he tried to say, his lungs empty. He took a couple of giant strides away from the stairwell, scrubbing his hands down his trousers again and again and again to try to remove every last trace of the place.

Mikey and the second woman were helping Mrs Lewington up the last few steps. She, at least, had managed to keep her composure—although only just. The audience had noticed it as well, at least twice as many people watching now as there had been when he'd started down those infernal stairs. They pointed, they smiled, they laughed at him as they snapped photographs on their phones, and he didn't know how to tell them that he looked the way he did because he'd seen a dead person arranged on the wall like a piece of art.

He tugged at his jacket with numb fingers, felt for his hard hat before realising he'd lost it somewhere underground. He'd dropped Mikey's torch, too, like some frightened child. The palm of his right hand was bleeding, his trousers ripped over both knees.

"Dear me," said Mrs Lewington, staring back down the hole she'd just emerged from. Her face was the same colour as her hair, just two smudges of bright red where she'd used blusher.

She looked at Geoff, caught his eye and held it in a way he didn't fully understand—as if there was a secret that the two of them now shared. Then she looked over his shoulder and sighed with relief.

Geoff turned and saw two uniformed policemen walking down the slope, both of them struggling not to bugger over in the mud.

"You okay?" said one when he caught sight of Geoff's face. "There been an accident?"

Geoff shook his head, finally remembering how to speak.

"No accident," he said. "But yeah, we're okay. I'm glad you're here."

"What is this place?" asked the same policeman. "What's going on?"

Geoff looked back past Mikey, past Mrs Lewington and her hulking friend, to the gaping maw that seemed to lead towards all the horror and hopelessness of hell. And there was only one answer he could give to the question.

"It's a tomb," he said. "It's a fucking tomb."

CHAPTER ONE

Wednesday

DI Peter Porter eased the Mondeo up the slope that led towards County Hall, stopping when he reached the IRV that blocked the access road. He wound down his window, a shudder ripping through him as a blast of cold, damp air took shelter inside the car. A young PC walked up, squinting until she recognised him.

"Afternoon, sir," she said, running back to the IRV. "I'll just move it."

Porter raised the window again, drumming out a beat on the wheel to the soft, smooth rhythms of Kenny G until the police car had shifted. He waved a thanks to the officer as he drove by, crawling past the immense bulk of County Hall towards a storm of blue lights that sat at the far corner of the building. There were four IRVs, two ambulances and a fire engine too, although he couldn't for the life of him work out why half of Norfolk's emergency services were here. All he'd heard from Savage's report was that they'd found a handful of bones in the mud.

He parked the Mondeo behind the last ambulance, bracing himself before clambering out into the cold. Even with the extra few inches he'd packed on around the waist these last few months, he felt it. It was February, his least favourite time of year. There was a reason February was the shortest month, he always thought. Because it was unbearably shit.

Still, it was one month closer to meeting his kid. Allie was eight months in now, and the size of a small house. She kept needling him about the fact she should have had a baby with somebody smaller—"*Your sprog's a bloody lump, Pete*!"—but he honestly couldn't remember the last time he'd seen her this happy and this content. Still worried, sure, because who wouldn't be worried? Porter had never really given any thought to how much pressure there was on a mother-to-be. How strong you had to be to carry a child inside you, to carry all those hopes and dreams in your own body, that immense future. He couldn't have done it, not in a million years, and he was infinitely grateful to Allie that she could.

They still hadn't decided on a name, even though he'd suggested just about everything he'd found on the internet. What kind of woman didn't want her kid to be called Warrior?

"Have you broken, sir?"

Porter turned to see DC Kate Savage walking towards him, wrapped in a black overcoat and wearing a red woolly hat over her dark hair. The wind tugged at her clothes, the gusts hard enough to make her wince. She clung onto her hat as she broke free of the shelter of County Hall, her voice broken up and carried off.

"What, Kate?" Porter yelled. He felt a sneeze building, and pinched his nose until it went away.

"I said have you broken?" she tried again when she was closer. "You were just standing there, staring into space. I think you were dribbling a bit."

"Oh, right," he said. "I was just thinking."

"That explains it, sir," Savage said with a gentle smile. "You just arrived?"

"Yeah," he said. "I was working the Hopper case down in Poringland. Clare told me to come here instead. You've found a body?"

Savage nodded, looking past the huddle of frozen emergency vehicles to an ocean of mud that flanked County Hall. Porter could make out a couple of enormous excavators, as still as statues. It looked like quite a crowd of people had gathered there, builders in their fluorescent jackets, more uniformed coppers, and what might have been a group of protesters holding signs. In the moments where the wind dropped, he thought he could hear chanting.

"Kind of," said Savage. "You have to see it to believe it, sir."

"Then lead the way."

Savage walked into the wind, one hand still clamped on her hat and the other around her waist as if she was worried she was going to lose her coat. Porter did his best to hunker behind her as they moved past the police cars, a constable lifting a line of police tape as they approached the building site. It was vast, half the hillside churned into mud and a pit in the middle of it that had to have been twenty-foot deep.

"What the hell are they building here?" he asked. "A goldmine?"

"Foundations for the new wing," said Savage. "It's controversial. They uprooted a lot of trees. Hence that lot."

They were closer to the chanting protesters now, and Porter saw that they were almost exclusively older women. Most were elegantly dressed, although the rain and wind had battered them so much they looked like they'd just been rescued from the Titanic. They were as miserable as it was possible to be, but their voices were loud and clear.

Maybe a little bit *too* clear.

"Are they singing 'I hope you choke on a squirrel's nuts'?" asked Porter.

"That's not the worst I've heard since I've been here," Savage replied. "They're pretty creative. Duke's up there with the two people who found the body."

"Duke, eh," said Porter with a wry smile of his own. He gave her a soft elbow in the arm, wiggling his eyebrows. "You two are inseparable these days."

"I would hardly call us that, sir," mumbled Savage. "I mean, we work together, it's not my fault we get posted to the same jobs sometimes, and we've only had a couple of dates and it's—"

"I was joking, Kate," said Porter, lifting a hand in apology. "It's cool. I'm glad things are going well."

She gave him a tight-lipped frown, then focussed on where she was going, leading the way past the shorter end of the building towards a second pit a hundred feet away. There was another digger inside it, and a smaller crowd of people around the edge. Porter could make out Duke even from here, the enormous, bearded PC towering over everyone else. Weirdly, he looked like he was taking photographs on his phone.

"You seen the actual body?" Porter asked as they closed in. He felt the tickle of another sneeze and pinched his nose until it had gone.

"Not yet, sir," said Savage. "It's underground, an old

cellar. Fire service needed to make sure it was safe. They looked pretty shaken up when they came out."

Porter could see that for himself, now that they were closer. Two firemen stood on the edge of the dig, wearing grim expressions. In between them and Duke were two other people, a weary-looking man in his late forties or early fifties dressed in a suit and a yellow fluorescent jacket, and a woman who had to be pushing 80, wrapped in tartan. Both were leaning into the wind as it did its best to bully them off the lip of the excavation.

"I asked Duke to get her a chair," said Savage.

"Does he know what a chair..." Porter started to reply, but the sentence was truncated by a violent sneeze. He loosed three more in quick succession, groaning.

"Bless you, sir," said Savage. "You okay?"

"Fucking February," he said.

"Are you going to keep us here much longer?" asked the man in the jacket as they joined the group. He was doing his best to hold on to a clipboard that snapped and shook in the wind. "I don't know what to tell the workers. I don't know if I need to cut them loose for the day."

"I'd say that's a safe bet," said Porter. "Mr..."

"Geoffrey Wileman," he replied, offering a gloved hand that Porter ignored, mainly because he didn't want to pull his hands out of his warm pockets. He tried the name out in his head the way he did with everybody he met these days, wondering if it would be suitable for the baby. *Geoffrey Porter*. He pulled a face without realising it, but the man didn't notice. "Geoff. I'm the foreman here. We were—"

"Destroying this parcel of historic England," the older woman cut in, her voice far more theatrical than it needed to be, and far louder than Porter would have expected.

"That's what they were doing. We warned them not to do it and yet here we are, somebody has died."

"*We* didn't bloody kill them," Wileman spat back. "He must have died years ago. Got nothing to do with the dig."

"It does, and you know it," the woman argued. "You and your—"

"Enough," said Porter, looking at the woman. There was another sneeze tickling his nose but he tried to ignore it. "Who are you?"

"Kitty Lewington," she said in a tone of voice that made it sound as if she was surprised he didn't know her. "Chair of the Norwich and Outer Norwich Heritage Society, co-founder of the County Hall Crisis Team, co-director of the Fine City Conservation Trust and—"

"The Queen of England, Ruler of the Commonwealth and Defender of the Faith," Porter interrupted, thinking *Kitty Porter* had a nice ring to it. "Got it. You're here protesting the build?"

"I am," she said. "It's absolutely scandalous that—"

"And what brought you over here?" Porter said, shivering in the brutal cold. "Why were you in the pit?"

"Because of what they found there," she said. "I always told them this was going to happen. There have been countless historical buildings on this site over the centuries, not least a Jacobean manor house of huge importance. We knew there would be foundations, maybe even basements, and we pressed for an archaeological intervention. The arseholes on the council denied it, but I knew they'd find something eventually. They almost bulldozed it into dust, they almost buried it."

"It was already buried," Wileman cut in. "You never would have known about it if we hadn't been digging here, you old bat."

"Enough," Porter said again with more force. "So you found the stairs, and for some reason I can't quite get my head around you decided to walk down them. Both of you?"

"She did," said Wileman. "I had no choice but to follow, to stop her falling over on her arse."

"I believe the only person to fall over on his arse was you, Mr Wileman," she replied. "As a number of witnesses will testify."

Wileman shot daggers at her, but only for a second, his head dropping.

"When was this, exactly?" Porter pressed.

"Just after three," said Wileman. "Had the dozer working this section of the dig and they uncovered..."

The man stared into the pit and Porter looked with him, seeing a throat of darkness in the mud, lined with stone steps that looked like teeth. He actually felt a shudder pass through him at the thought of going down those stairs. There was nothing good down there, he was certain of it.

"Just after three," Porter said, checking his watch to see that it wasn't even four yet. "How'd we all get here so fast?"

"Control sent a couple of Uniforms up because of the protests," Savage said. "They were here when the discovery was made, threw it up the chain in a heartbeat. I got here twenty minutes ago, just been trying to secure the scene."

Duke was on his way over, his boots so caked in mud he might have been wearing a couple of coconuts. The wind had blown so many leaves and twigs into his beard that he looked like Stig of the Dump. The sneeze was back with a vengeance and Porter let it out, noticing as he did so that Duke was taking a photograph of him on his phone.

"What are you doing, Duke?" Porter asked, wiping his dripping nose.

"It's for the Force's social media, sir," the PC answered, checking his phone. "The Boss put me in charge."

"Superintendent Clare put *you* in charge of social media?" Porter said. "For the *police*?"

Duke lifted the phone again, but this time he must have been taking a selfie because he pouted his lips like a hairy fish. Porter glanced incredulously at Savage, and she shrugged.

"He's quite good at it, apparently," she said.

"You do realise this is a crime scene, Duke?" Porter said. "As in, put the bloody phone away."

Duke took one more photograph, then slid the phone into his pocket.

"Sorry, sir," he said.

"Unbelievable," muttered Porter, turning to Geoff Wileman and Kitty Lewington. "Right, so it's just you two and the fire service who've seen the body?"

They both nodded.

"It's not a body," said Wileman. "It's... it's something else."

"What?" Porter asked, but the man couldn't seem to find an answer.

"You'll see," said Lewington.

"You found the stairs, you went down them together," Porter said, feeling the frustration gnaw at him. "Then what?"

"You really do have to see it for yourself, Detective."

But I really don't want to, thought Porter.

"Mr Wileman, shut everything down until we know what's going on," he said. "Duke, can you take them inside, get them warm, maybe fix up a cup of tea for them?"

"Sir," said Duke with a nod.

"I need a full statement from both of you. You going to

be able to stop yourselves killing each other before that happens?"

They both nodded, although the looks they aimed at each other as they followed Duke made it clear there was no guarantee.

Porter stared into the pit once again, his skin crawling as though he'd already descended those steps, as though all the creatures of the earth were scuttling and squirming beneath his clothes.

"Kate," he said after a moment. "You're with me."

CHAPTER TWO

Savage followed Porter to the edge of the pit, more than happy for him to go first. The steps looked far too much like a tomb, like she was about to walk into her own grave, and the last thing she wanted to do was lead the way.

She felt considerable dismay, then, when Porter gestured towards the stairs with both hands.

"After you," he said, sniffing.

"Really, sir?" she replied, pulling the hat down over her ears. It had been a Christmas present from Duke when she'd told him she didn't own a hat, one of several thoughtful gestures he'd surprised her with over the last few months. "What happened to the golden age of chivalry?"

"I am being chivalrous," he said. "Ladies first, right?"

"As a superior officer, sir, I think it's your duty to take the lead on this."

"But as my subordinate, Kate, you kind of have to do what you're told."

They both studied the opening of the cellar, which sat a dozen yards away from where they stood. A couple of constables had hammered four wooden posts into the ground and tied a square of wind-maddened police tape around it, but it didn't look like much of a cage.

Cage? she thought, wondering why that word had popped into her head. And suddenly she was picturing something crawling up from the dark, a sculpture of yellow bones click-clacking towards them over the mud.

It was ridiculous, and it was as much to prove her imagination wrong as follow orders that she set off again. It was tough going in the sludge, and at one point she slipped, but Porter was close enough behind to catch her—the effort of it almost causing both of them to fall over.

"Bastard bloody mud," Porter muttered. "Tell me again why I live in this bloody country?"

"Because of all the lovely trees, isn't it, sir?"

"*You're* a bloody tree, Kate," he spat back.

They'd reached the entrance to the cellar, an obscene mouth of stone and brick which seemed to have tightened in the time that Savage had last stood here. It reminded her of the worms you saw on the beach sometimes, the ones that sat with their mouths open, waiting for something stupid enough to crawl in.

And here they were.

"You got your torch, sir?" she asked, pulling a pencil torch out of her trouser pocket. Porter grunted a reply, his own torch clicking on.

She walked onto the first step, wobbling in the absence of a handrail. Porter took her arm until she'd steadied herself.

"Thank you, sir," she said. "Very *chivalrous* of you."

"It is," he said as she took another step. "It's not my fault you're more expendable than me. I didn't make the rules."

His words fell flat this time, sucked into the void of shadow at her feet. Savage breathed in a lungful of damp air then went down the stairs as fast as she dared. The light from her torch barely touched the sides, lost long before it struck the floor below. The air stank of mildew and rot, the chill of it settling right in the core of her bones and making her shake so hard her torch rattled. She put her free hand to her chest, feeling her granddad's silver police whistle beneath her shirt and drawing strength from it the way she always did.

"So why is this thing out here in the middle of nowhere?" Porter asked, his voice welcome as they continued to descend. "Weird place to build a cellar."

"I'm guessing it was part of the old hall," said Savage. "Whole place went to ruin decades ago and they bulldozed the rest to make way for County Hall. Spalding's looking for any old plans so we can be sure, but she's not having much luck."

"So they flattened the house but didn't fill in the cellars?" Porter said. "Weird."

"They would have filled them if it had been part of the new building. They'd have had to, for the foundations. Out here there's nothing but grass and trees, though. They covered the entrance with that stone slab, buried it in earth and just left it."

Her foot hit the bottom before she was ready for it, jarring her spine. She turned back, seeing Porter right behind her, wide enough that he blocked the weak trickle of daylight, seeming to plug the opening like the slab had done. She had to bite down on a wave of claustrophobia that made her skull ring like a bell.

"What a shithole," said Porter.

He dropped off the last step and aimed his torch past Savage, sweeping it around the small chamber. Shadows danced and spun around a squat column that sat in the middle of the space, crawling out of the vaulted brickwork in the ceiling and swarming like bats. The alcoves in the wall were drenched in a darkness so thick that Savage had to fill them with light again just to chase away any thoughts of monsters.

"Where's the body?" he asked.

"I think it's in a smaller room at the back," she told him. "Must be this way."

She set off, holding her torch like a weapon as she stepped around the column. The far side of the cellar came into view, a slim opening in the wall that bled liquid night.

"Right," she said.

She pushed through the gap, lighting up a choked pocket of space that she could have bridged with her arms—if she'd wanted to put them anywhere near the far wall. Even though she knew what had been found down here, she couldn't believe what she was seeing.

"Holy shit," said Porter as he squeezed in beside her. "That is not what I was expecting to find."

It *was* a body, there was no doubt about that. Every single bone had been cleaned and polished and hammered into the brick with a forest of long, black nails. Savage ran her eyes over them, seeing everything from tiny finger bones which had shattered into fragments—some of which littered the floor like snow, along with a handful of teeth—to thigh bones that looked more like medieval clubs. They had been arranged in a series of concentric circles, three of them, like a horror-show spiderweb. And right in the middle of it all was a single skull, its jaw open in a silent scream.

"They're real?" Porter asked, taking a step closer, his torchlight rolling over the bones.

"I don't know," Savage said.

The display looked more like a Halloween prank than a

crime scene, a joke left behind by whoever the last people to leave this place had been. Porter must have had the same thought.

"Nah," he said. "It's a prank. Some kids must have found their way down here one day, set this up to scare the bollocks off people."

"My granddad did the same thing," said Savage. "Years ago, before he died. He was getting new carpets, and he used red paint to leave handprints and messages all over his floor. 'Save me!' That kind of thing. Whoever got the bungalow next would have been scared witless. He thought it was hilarious. Gran, not so much."

Porter hissed a laugh.

"But no," she went on. "These look real. We've seen enough bones, sir. It's not hard to tell the difference, not really."

"Shit," he said. He swung his torch left and right, the motion of it making Savage feel seasick. Then he aimed it up. "What's that?"

At first, Savage couldn't see what he meant, because there was nothing there. Then she realised that's exactly what he was looking at. Somebody had chipped out a circular hollow in the bricks, roughly the size of a dinner plate. She aimed her torch down and saw scraps of masonry on the floor, mixed with the bones.

"Weird," she said. "Looks like somebody didn't like what was there, cut it out."

"Huh," said Porter. "What are you thinking?"

"I'm thinking it's a hidden cellar, sir. There could be secret rooms, compartments behind the bricks, loose flagstones. We'll need a proper forensic team down here; they've been informed."

"We'll need Emily, too," said Porter.

"Then you're in luck," came a voice.

Savage peeked through the opening of the smaller room, seeing Emily Franklin step around the central column. The young pathologist was wearing pink jeans and the biggest, yellowest puffer jacket Savage had ever seen, almost reaching her ankles. It looked like she'd come to work in a sleeping bag.

"Were you just waiting up there until you heard your name?" asked Porter.

"No need. I know you're always thinking of me, Pete. You had that baby yet?"

"Nope," he said, thinking *Emily Porter* and shaking his head. "Soon."

"How're things, Kate?"

"Ask me when we're back above ground," Savage replied. "Thanks for coming so quickly."

"Well, you know how to appeal to a girl's heart. An artwork made from bones, how could I stay away? Where is it?"

Savage gestured over her shoulder, moving out of the way to let Franklin step past.

"Little light?" Franklin asked, and when Porter shone his torch at her, she gave him a withering look. "On the bones, Pete, not me."

"Oh, right," he said, angling his torch at the far wall. Savage did the same.

"Oh, my!" said Franklin with a shudder of genuine excitement. "I've never seen anything like it."

She walked up to the bones and Savage walked with her so that the macabre display wouldn't be lost behind the pathologist's shadow. Franklin snapped on a glove, but when she reached for the skull she held back, her fingers hovering a few inches away.

"Cara's not been yet, has she?" she asked.

"No," said Porter.

"I'm actually not sure there's much point."

"What?" said Savage. "Why? They're not real?"

"Oh, they're real," said Franklin. "It's quite a display. I'd guess the skull belonged to a young man, a teenager maybe, or a child. Probably a boy. The shape of it—see how narrow it is, less pronounced cheek bones, elongated chin—suggests a Caucasian. Triangular nasal cavity, rectangular eye orbits. Yes, for sure."

She paused for a moment, her eyes sharp and serious as they navigated the wall.

"Now, this is interesting," she said, pointing her gloved finger at a long, jointed bone in the outer ring. "See that, that's a thigh bone, a fully grown femur."

"Fully grown?" asked Savage.

"Yes. Your bones don't fully mature until you're between seventeen and twenty-five, which is older than I'd guess for the skull. And this..."

She shifted her finger to a pair of bones in the inner concentric circle, these ones much smaller.

"It's a tib and fib," she said.

"Leg bones?" said Savage. "But they're tiny."

"And still fused together," said Franklin. "They belong to a much younger child."

"Jesus," said Porter. "So this isn't one victim?"

"Not even close," said Franklin. "At a glance I can't see even two bones that look like they've come from the same body. The ends of those ribs suggest somebody much older, as does the wear and tear on those pelvic wings. But there are fingers here that could have come from a baby. You've counted them?"

"Not yet," said Savage.

Franklin moved her finger, following the lines of bones and muttering beneath her breath.

"Sixty-four," she said. "If we're lucky, we're looking at sixty-four dead people arranged here."

"If we're lucky?" said Savage, turning to Franklin. There was a definite gleam in the pathologist's eye, picked out by torchlight.

"I'm not saying *they're* lucky," she said. "Far from it. But this is uniquely fascinating for me. It will be quite a project."

She must have seen the look on Savage's face, because she suddenly shook her head.

"Sorry, Kate. That probably sounded a little insensitive."

"A little?" muttered Porter.

"But I left out the most important thing," Franklin went on. "These bones are old. You can see that in the residue that's formed on them, on all of them. We're talking decades, maybe even centuries. Whoever these people were, and I pity them, of course, they died long before any of us were born."

"Shit," said Porter. "You're sure?"

"I will be when I get them back to the lab," said Franklin. "But I'm almost positive. Nobody here died recently. You said this place was sealed?"

"Yeah," said Savage. "Buried in the dirt."

"Then I sincerely doubt we'll ever know what happened to these poor sods," said Franklin. "I'll wait for Cara to do her thing, and I'll give these bones the due care they deserve, but this is a cold case. As cold as you're ever going to get."

She looked at Porter, then at Savage.

"Sorry," she said.

She squeezed between them and made her way out of the smaller room, heading back towards the stairs.

"Just going to grab my stuff," she shouted back. "Quite nice down here, isn't it?"

"Well, that was a bloody waste of time," Porter said, following the pathologist. "Come on, let's get out of here."

Savage didn't move, keeping her torch on the bones. The remains of sixty-four dead people arranged like a mosaic on the wall of a buried cellar. Kids, adults, old people—maybe even babies. They may have lived a long time ago, but it didn't mean that they had to be forgotten. It didn't mean the world would give up on them.

It didn't mean they didn't deserve justice.

"I'm sorry this happened to you," she told them, and her voice was a whisper that echoed from the wall as if the dead were talking back to her.

CHAPTER THREE

Thursday

"The whole point of asking for jam on toast, Moira, is that you actually have some toast with your jam."

DCI Robbie Kett sat at their brand-new dining table in their brand-new kitchen in their brand-new house, wondering whether it was time to get some brand-new children. For much of the day this was a place of calm, but right now he was caught in the middle of a feeding frenzy of epic proportions. It was like being at a zoo, he thought, except he was pretty sure most animals had better manners than this.

To his right, Moira was ignoring the slice of toast on her plate and was spooning raspberry jam directly out of the jar into her mouth—ignoring the sacred rule of no double dipping. She had so much of it smeared on her chin, her cheeks and her forehead that a passerby would have assumed she'd been in some kind of horrific accident.

On his left, Alice had a bowl of pasta and cheese held

up to her face and was actually shovelling it into her gullet. He wasn't sure how she was managing to breathe. She insisted on cooking pasta every single morning now, even though it always made them late for school and left the kitchen looking like a demolition site. She eyeballed him over the top of the bowl like a starving dog prepared to fight for its food.

Only Evie wasn't eating, because they'd run out of the branded cereal she liked and he'd had the audacity to replace it with Asda's own. It was identical, probably made in the same factory, and Kett had shoved the bag into the old box so that she wouldn't notice. But Evie seemed to have ten times as many taste buds as a normal human being—either that or she was psychic—and the first spoonful had touched her tongue for about a tenth of a second before she'd cottoned on. Now she was doing her best to obliterate her breakfast by staring at it, her teeth bared.

"Moira," said Kett, taking the girl's spoon before it could reach her mouth again. "You can't just eat jam."

He spread it onto her toast, then sealed the jar and moved it out of reach. The four-year-old picked up the toast and began to lick the jam off the top.

"Right," said Kett, rubbing his eyes.

Alice made a noise like she was choking, and he was halfway out of his seat and ready to attempt the Heimlich manoeuvre before he realised she was just trying to talk with a throatful of pasta.

"What?" he said, crashing back down again.

She swallowed like a python working down a whole rabbit, then tried again.

"How long have I got?"

Kett checked his watch.

"Fifteen minutes. You're fine."

Alice leapt up with enough force to set her bowl spinning. She bolted from the room, heading past the toilet that was hidden beneath the stairs before spinning around and doubling back.

"Why is everything in the wrong place in this stupid house?" she screamed as she slammed the toilet door behind her.

Kett let it go. The move had been tough on her. *Any* change was tough on her, and one this big had left her reeling, especially considering she'd only just got used to the other house. When she wasn't running late for school, when the pressure was off, she loved it. Alice had the room at the front next to his and Billie's. She cocooned herself inside it and she'd told Kett a number of times how safe she felt here. How happy. It was a word she'd never used to describe herself, and it made his heart sing to hear it.

It wasn't just their oldest daughter who had found peace here, either. Billie had been a different woman since they'd moved. No, not different, but *healed*. She'd found her way back to the person she'd been when he'd first met her, as if she'd finally managed to shed the armour of fear and anger that she'd grown in the last three years.

It had happened almost immediately, as soon as she'd closed the front door behind her on their first day, with the moving vans still pulling out of the driveway. Porter, Savage, Duke and even Colin Clare had arrived to help them unpack, and after they'd left, Billie had taken a breath that might have been her first. She'd looked up at him and smiled, and he'd had the uncanny notion that he was looking at a ghost from another world, another life.

It helped immensely, of course, that Hollenbeck—the group of people who'd put her through hell, put them *all* through hell—were now dead and buried.

"Don't let her eat jam out of the jar, Robbie!"

Billie walked into the room, scrubbing her hair with a towel. She gave him the same smile now that she had on that first day, and every day since, and he found himself grinning at her like he was twelve years old and she was his first crush. The light outside was dreary but she still seemed to glow, and not for the first time since they'd moved here he saw that the scars on her neck and face had faded just that little bit more. Some kind of magic.

"Jam," she said, and Kett saw that Moira had managed to get hold of the jam jar again, her spoon a blur.

"Moo-moo, no!" he said, taking it from her. "How did you even..."

He scowled at Evie and she met his eye defiantly.

"Did you give it to her?" he started, then realised it really wasn't worth the hassle. "Just eat your cereal, okay? We've got to go."

"It's not cereal," she said. "It's dried worms."

"Eat your dried worms then," he said, getting up and joining Billie by the sink. "Honestly," he said, "do you ever feel these aren't actually our kids?"

"All the time," she replied. "I think we must have found them somewhere."

"Yeah, we found them in a bin. And we just forgot about it, because there's no way they can be ours."

He gave Billie a hug that she returned with all her strength, and they held each other tight until Evie and Moira started making smoochie noises.

"Time's up," Billie said. "Evie, go and put your shoes on. Moira, I can't even see your face past all that jam. Come here."

She set to work the way only a mother could, using one hand to clean the jam from Moira's face with a towel and the other to pull a slice of plain bread from the packet on the counter, lobbing it onto Evie's plate without even looking. Evie snatched it up and began devouring it like it was a gourmet dinner.

"Shoes," said Billie, lifting Moira from her chair and clipping her hair back.

"You want me to take them?" asked Kett. "It's no trouble."

"Nah," she replied, carrying their youngest out of the kitchen. "I'm going to the food bank for a couple of hours, Danielle's off sick again. You want a ride in?"

"No thanks," he said, following them into the wide hall. "I'll grab a taxi."

Alice came barging out of the downstairs toilet, her hair tangled into wild, uneven plaits that hung over her face. Kett raised his eyebrows.

"What?" she said, looking like she might punch him if he gave an answer. He lifted his hands in surrender and she stormed off, grunting. "Where are my shoes? Why is everything so stupid?"

"Definitely not ours," Kett muttered.

Billie slung her towel into the utility room, grabbed the kids' bags and opened the front door, all in one fluid motion.

"Car," she said, ushering the girls out. "Moira, you've got your shoes on the wrong feet."

"No, I haven't," said Moira as she tripped over the stoop onto the gravel drive. "I swapped my feet around last night."

"Bye, girls," Kett called after them. "Be good."

"Never!" shouted Evie.

Billie looked back.

"Remember, take it easy," she said.

"I will. Love you."

"Always," she replied, closing the door behind her.

For a few seconds he listened to the muffled shouts from the driveway, the sound of the Volvo's engine starting, the rumble of tyres on gravel.

Then there was silence—utterly peaceful, completely unbroken.

And the truth was, he hated it.

Because this house was a blessing, it really was; a fresh start away from the horrors of his move to Norwich, away from those awful months when Billie had been missing, away from the memories of what had happened to her and the subsequent nightmare of Hollenbeck's attack. It was a clean slate where—for so much of the time—he and Billie and the kids could almost believe that none of it had happened, that it had all been some kind of fever dream. When the house was busy, when the kids were here, this place was the best thing he ever could have asked for.

But when it was empty...

Here, in the quiet, it all came creeping back. Here, in this unbearable stillness, it wasn't his house anymore. It was a warehouse with bricked-up windows and mannequins dressed like his family and cameras that watched his every move and masked killers who waited with bated breath behind every closed door.

Hollenbeck was gone, but when he was alone in this house they were as real as they ever were, and they lived right here beneath his roof.

Kett switched on the digital radio before collecting the plates and bowls from the table, loading them into the dishwasher. He cleaned up the hurricane of mess that the kids had left then made his way upstairs. His phone was where he'd left it on his pillow and he was surprised to see a call there from Savage.

He sat on the bed and called her back. From here he

could see the main bathroom, the door almost closed and the light off inside. He couldn't shake the notion that somebody was watching him from the darkness—somebody with a fox's grin.

"Hi, sir," said Savage, making him flinch. "How's it all going? Still enjoying the new house?"

"Yeah," he said. "Mostly. How're you?"

"Living the dream," she said.

"Yeah?"

"That was sarcasm, sir," she said. "But things aren't too bad. Still quiet. At least, it was until yesterday."

Her words were like a kick to Kett's heart, his pulse drumming.

"Something happened?" he asked, and he had to fight to stop the rest of the words from tumbling out of his lips. *Something about Hollenbeck?*

"Nothing to do with you-know-who, sir," she said, reading his mind. "We found bones, up at County Hall."

"I'm guessing they're human," he said, the relief short-lived.

"Mostly. But they're old."

Kett stood up, the bed springs groaning. He walked to the window, looking past the drive, past the two bare magnolias and the road, to the satellite police station beyond. A couple of constables were milling by the front door, one of them tossing his car keys up and catching them, over and over, as they chatted.

"How old?" he asked.

"Like, decades, sir," she said. "We think it was part of an old house that sat on the hill. Knucklebone Hall, some people call it. It was demolished to make way for the council buildings. Would have stayed buried except they're doing construction work."

"Old bones," said Kett. "That's why you called?"

"Charming, sir," said Savage. "I called to say hi. The bones were an extra. Superintendent Clare was hoping it might be enough of a mystery to lure you back in."

Although Kett had kept himself busy these last few months consulting on open cases, he hadn't been back to work since the Hollenbeck incident.

"It's hardly an extreme crime if they're a few decades old," he said, watching the copper with the keys climb into an IRV and pull onto the road.

"Yeah, but Clare thought a cold case might be what you need to get you back into the swing of things."

The car had vanished, but he heard the siren as it gunned towards town. His pulse quickened even more, powered by an unmistakable jolt of nostalgia.

"Would it change things if I told you that some of the bones belonged to children?" Savage asked.

It wouldn't change anything, because he'd already made his mind up. The house sat quiet around him, brand new and yet somehow still full of memories. He could spend the day here with the ghosts of Hollenbeck, or he could do something better.

He could do something good.

"You at HQ?" he asked.

"Heading over now, sir."

"I'll meet you there," he said. "I'm coming in."

CHAPTER FOUR

Kett wasn't sure what kind of welcome he'd receive after so long away from HQ, but when he walked into the Major Investigation Team's open plan offices an hour later, it was a rousing cheer that greeted him.

Admittedly, it was only one person doing the cheering, but it still brought a smile to his face.

"Thanks, Kate," he said as he walked over to Savage's desk. She was the only person in the expansive space and she was practically mummified in an overcoat and a red beanie hat. Kett started to take off his coat, then realised it was almost as cold inside the room as it was outside. "What's happened to the heat?"

"According to the boss, the boiler is broken," she said, her words almost visible in the cold. "But I think they're just trying to save money. Good to see you back, sir. How does it feel?"

"Honestly?" he said, looking around at the empty desks. "Weird."

"Good weird?"

He didn't answer immediately, because he wasn't sure

what to say. It had been almost eight months since he'd last been here, working on the Monk case. Eight months since he'd driven home from work only for DI Dunst to knock on his door and blow his world apart.

Knock. Knock.

He closed his eyes for a moment, but the quiet was too loud and the surge of panic kicked his heart into overdrive.

"Sir?" asked Savage.

Kett looked at her and nodded, and she must have seen the emotion on his face because she mirrored it, an expression of sympathy and grief and compassion that genuinely moved him. He dredged up a smile.

"Yeah," he said. "Good weird. I'm okay. Where is everyone?"

"A photoshoot," said Savage.

"A *what*?"

She laughed.

"Duke's got a new side job. He's moonlighting as the Force's official photographer, for Twitter and Facebook and stuff. He's corralled them all in the Incident Room."

Kett shook his head in disbelief.

"Duke as an influencer," he said. "Next you'll be telling me Pete's made a decent cup of tea."

"You haven't been away that long, sir," she said. "Go and join them. It's almost certainly guaranteed to be hilarious."

"You not coming?"

"Some of us have work to do," she said, turning back to her desk.

Kett left her to it, heading across the bullpen to the corridor beyond. He could hear arguing even before he'd opened the Incident Room door, and when he poked his head inside he half-expected to witness a full-on brawl.

Instead, he saw Duke sitting at one of the desks with a laptop in front of him, DI Porter leaning over one of his broad shoulders and Superintendent Clare the other. He hadn't seen Porter since Christmas and he was surprised how portly the DI looked.

"I'm not letting you post that," said Porter. "No bloody way, Constable. Take it down, right now."

"I think it's quite flattering, sir," said Duke. "And to be honest, it's the best one we've got. You're not what I'd call photogenic."

"What?" spluttered Porter. "*Me*? Not photogenic? You're kidding, aren't you?"

Kett walked over quietly enough that nobody heard him. He peeked past Clare to see a Facebook page on the laptop, a photograph of Pete Porter filling most of the screen. The DI was standing in the middle of a muddy field and he looked like a man who was in the process of shitting his pants: hunched over, face gurning, his watery eyes almost crossed.

"That's not the best photo you've got," Porter said. "It can't be. Check again."

"I did," Duke said. "I would have taken another one but you told me to put my camera away, remember?"

"Your tossing photo's fine," barked Clare. "Just click the damned thing already."

"It's not a *tossing* photo, sir," said Porter.

"To be fair," said Duke, "you look like you *could* be tossing. You do have your hands in your pockets, and that expression's—"

"Duke, I swear to God, if you—"

"Just click the thing," roared Clare.

"Don't," said Porter.

"Click it or you're both fired."

"Don't do it," Porter growled.

Duke grinned at the DI as he clicked the button. The laptop dinged as the photograph was posted, Porter somehow looking *worse* now that it was official.

"I look like the Hunchback of Notre Dame," he said.

"The *tossing* Hunchback of Notre Dame," said Duke.

"That's my word, Constable," said Clare. "Find your own."

"I don't even know how you managed to make me look so bad. You must have used Photoshop or something."

"I just capture people as they really are," said Duke, still grinning. "The camera never lies, and I'm an *artiste*."

"*Arse*-tiste," Porter muttered.

"I think it's quite fetching," said Kett, and all three men whirled around in shock.

"Robbie!" Porter yelled, and he wrapped Kett in a hug, slapping him on the back hard enough to knock the wind out of him. "Holy shit, the legend returns. It's good to see you, sir."

"And you," said Kett when he'd let go. He nodded to Clare, who was offering him something that might have passed as a smile. "Sir."

"I knew you couldn't resist it," said the Super. "A good old-fashioned whodunit. It's nice to have you back, Detective."

"It's nice to be here," Kett said, looking at the laptop. "I see the Force has finally entered the 21st century."

"Yes," said Clare. "A new-fangled thing called Face-book. Apparently all the kids are using it."

"They were," said Duke. "About fifteen years ago."

"I thought it would be nice for people to know who we are," the Super went on. "The real people at the heart of Norfolk Constabulary. There's been a huge surge of interest from the general population after your kidnapping and rescue, Kett, and I want the population to know the truth behind the media storm. I want them to know that we are real people with real lives."

"And you're posting *that* photo?" Kett said, lifting an eyebrow. "He doesn't look real, he looks like some kind of horrible sock puppet."

"Thank you," said Porter. "Which is why we should take it down."

"Why *do* you look like that, Pete?" Kett asked.

"It was cold!" the DI protested. "And windy, and I was bloody sneezing. Everybody looks like that when they sneeze."

"They really don't," said Kett.

"Enough," snapped Clare. "It's up, it's out there, there's nothing we can do about it now."

"We can delete—"

"Shut your tosshole, Porter," Clare interrupted. "I just said there's nothing we can do. Get back to work, both of you."

Porter's bottom lip slid out like a pouting child, his eyes pleading. There was the sound of a camera shutter as Duke took a photograph on his phone.

"Don't you bloody dare," Porter said, diving for it. Duke skittered out of the way, making a break for the door, Porter hot on his heels. They left the room like a couple of charging elephants, their shouts fading.

"That really is a terrible photo," said Kett.

Clare actually laughed.

"I know. It'll serve him right for all those photographs he took of poor old Duke."

The Super put a hand on Kett's shoulder, guiding him towards the door.

"It genuinely is good to see you, Robbie. You're looking well, I must say. The new house must agree with you."

"Yeah," he said as they walked into the corridor. "It's partly the house, partly the fact that I'm not looking over my shoulder every five minutes. Any word?"

"Nothing you don't already know," said Clare. "Three down for life, six awaiting trial, one dead from a heart attack, and two on the loose. But we're not picking up anything that suggests they're coming back, or that they have any kind of vendetta against you. It was a fair fight and we won, that's the end of it. Old cases need to be forgotten."

He sighed, then led the way down the corridor away from the bullpen.

"Apart from this one," he went on. "Bones, discovered at County Hall yesterday inside a cellar that had been sealed beneath some kind of sarcophagi-like stone. Franklin claims they've been there for decades, so I don't think there's much we can do for them."

"Them?" asked Kett.

They rounded the corner into a dark, quiet stretch of corridor that ended in a door. Clare opened it to reveal a set of stairs dropping into the basement. Kett wasn't sure he'd ever been this deep into the heart of HQ before.

"Franklin suspects there are over sixty victims," said Clare as they descended.

"Sixty?"

"All arranged in some kind of display. Fire department told us the cellar where we found them isn't as sound as they'd like it to be, the weight of the diggers damaged the ceiling. So we've moved them down here."

"Into the basement?"

"Franklin's choice," said Clare. "She likes the quiet, apparently."

They made their way past three closed doors before finding one that was open, and here Clare stopped and knocked.

"Franklin, you decent?" he boomed.

"Well I'm not stark bloody naked and cavorting with the dead, if that's what you're worried about," came the reply. "Yes, come in."

Clare stood to the side and Kett walked through the door, seeing a classroom-sized space dotted with desks. The overhead lights were off but an enormous halogen field lamp was burning a hole in the middle of the room, too bright for Kett to even look at. Emily Franklin was a silhouette against it, one hand waving. Kett waved back, using his other hand to shield his eyes.

Only then did he see what lay on the large central table.

Old bones. Dozens of them, arranged in a series of concentric circles with a slack-jawed skull right in the middle of them.

"Bloody hell," he said.

"Indeed," Franklin replied.

"I'm going to leave you to it," said Clare from the other side of the door.

"Sure, sir. You must have plenty to do."

"No, I just don't like it down here," the Super replied. "Makes my tossbone all shivery."

He darted out of sight, the sound of his footsteps echoing as he retreated.

"That's an image I could happily have done without," said Franklin.

"I find myself saying that more and more with the Super," Kett replied, turning back to her. The halogen almost blew the back of his head off.

"Oh, sorry," Franklin said, adjusting the light so that it hit the top of the table. "Better?"

"Better," he said, blinking the spots from his vision.

He walked to the young woman's side, noticing that Franklin was dressed like she was going on holiday: bare feet, knee-length striped shorts and a T-shirt that displayed a walking, grinning ice cream. Rather disturbingly, the ice cream was holding—and eating—a smaller ice cream that appeared to be crying.

"Nice, isn't it?" she said, following his gaze. "Made it myself."

"Impressive. You not cold?"

"Not with the light on," she said. "Like a furnace down here. Probably the hottest place in HQ right now. They've turned the heat off."

"I heard," said Kett. He looked at the bones, unable to stop the shudder running through him. "Where do you want to start?"

"I'll start by welcoming you back, Robbie," she said. "I'm glad you're here."

"Thanks," he said.

"Because we had a pool going, about whether you'd come back to work or not. I'm about to cash in."

"Right."

"Never doubted it," she said. "You ever been to the Catacombs?"

"Huh?" Kett said, the change of topic throwing him.

"In Paris, the underground graves. Ossuaries, they're called. Hundreds of thousands of corpses just sitting there beneath the ground. The whole city is built on the bones of the dead."

"Uh, no," said Kett. Franklin shrugged.

"Just the first thing that came to mind when I saw these.

Ossuaries are surprisingly common. We have a few in this country and you can't throw a stick without hitting one in Europe. Anyway, what you see here is the exact arrangement of bones that was found yesterday. Cara and I carefully documented the display and then removed them last night, and I repositioned them on the table. That masking tape arrow points directly to where the ceiling was, just so you can get your bearings. Check the photographs if you're confused."

She gestured without looking and Kett saw a series of photos mounted on the wall. The skull stared back at him from more than half, its dark eyes full of secrets.

"How much do you already know?" she asked.

"Assume nothing."

"Okay. Then I guess the most important thing is that these bones don't belong to one victim. As far as I can figure out—and much of this is guesswork—we have sixty-four bones, belonging to sixty-four separate victims."

"How can you tell?"

"Like I said, mostly guesswork," she replied. "The best clue is that we have more types of certain bones than you find inside a human body. Nobody has four legs, for example, or six scapulas."

"Fair point," said Kett, trying to remember what a scapula was.

"Shoulder blade," said Franklin, seeing him struggle. "Then we go by size. Assuming the victims were all of average size and weight for their age, we see an enormous variety of ages on display. From old folks..."

She gestured at a pelvis that looked like it was seconds away from crumbling into dust. Then she moved her finger to a sliver of white bone.

"To babies."

"Babies?" he said, almost choking on the sudden horror.

"Yes. That's an infant's finger. Less than a year old, but of course that's just an educated guess. There's also this."

She pointed to another bone, this one just a fragment.

"Found this on the ground beneath the display. It's not human, I'm fairly sure about that. I can't figure out where it came from."

It looked exactly the same as the others, but Kett didn't comment.

"There are countless factors to consider, but using that criteria we can split the bones into at least twenty-four different victims. We separate them further by the age of the bones themselves. Ideally, I'd like to use radiocarbon dating to determine a precise year of birth, and isotope analysis to work out where they were born, but for now I can safely say some of these bones are going on 200 years old. Others are much newer. Possibly within the last fifty years. But without the right equipment, that's entirely—"

"Guesswork," guessed Kett, and she nodded.

"Exactly. I've ascertained that we have at least forty-three unique individuals here. It stands to reason, then, that whoever made this macabre wall art picked a single bone from each victim."

"Like a trophy," said Kett.

"If you like," she replied. "But of course you're making a rather large assumption, DCI Kett."

Kett chewed on it for a moment, studying the bones. Franklin gave him all the time he needed.

"They're old bones," he said. "They're not necessarily victims of a crime."

"Quite," said Franklin. "You can find bones like these in literally every village, town and city in the country, if you're willing to dig for them. And an estate like the one where we found these would almost certainly have had its own cemetery. Our artist could have simply removed the bones from their resting place and arranged them to their fancy."

"Still a little sinister, though, isn't it?" Kett asked.

"To us, maybe. But remember, some of these bones are centuries old, and the Victorians were obsessed with death. I've seen dioramas far weirder than this on my travels. For all we know, this might have been the workshop of an anatomist, or a medical student."

"Or a serial killer," said Kett.

"Perhaps," she replied with a shrug. "I'm honestly not sure we'll ever know the truth. Maybe it's enough that whoever these bones once belonged to, they'll get a burial now. They'll find peace."

Kett nodded. He could feel the heat of the lamp now, his skin prickling with sweat under his shirt, jacket and coat.

"You said some of the bones are newer?" he asked. "Which ones?"

"That ischium," she said, nodding to the top of the display. "Part of the pelvic girdle. Not much wear and tear, hardly any ageing. A teenager, perhaps, or a young adult. Almost certainly male. I'm guessing it's between thirty and fifty years old—the bone, that is, not the owner."

She sighed, then nodded at the skull.

"And there's this," she said. "At a guess, it's even newer."

"That doesn't make any sense," said Kett. "Some of these bones are a hundred years old or more, and some are from the last few decades. And all of them found in a sealed chamber that hasn't been opened for, what, sixty years?"

"At least," said Franklin. "But that's not the weirdest part of all this."

"It's not?"

She shook her head.

"You're right about the chamber not being opened for decades. Has Kate shown you the photos?"

"No," said Kett.

"Well, we've got photographic evidence that the cellar was covered as far back as 1968, which is when County Hall was opened. It's never been unsealed, as far as we can see."

Franklin smiled, almost mischievously. She backed across the room to another table, which was completely clear apart from a scrap of orange and purple paper that was maybe two centimetres square. She pointed both her index fingers at it, then mimicked shooting a pair of pistols.

"What?" asked Kett.

"Recognise it?"

"That?"

He shook his head, although something about the colours was familiar. He almost had it before Franklin started talking again.

"That is a Double Decker," she said. "Or at least part of the wrapper for one, still has a scrap of chocolate on it. As I'm sure you know, Double Deckers were invented in 1975, but whoever opened this one did us a favour by doing so at the end where the Best Before date was located, so we know that this particular piece of confectionary was made in late 2018 or early 2019."

"And you found that in the chamber?" asked Kett.

"We did," she replied. "Which makes the most interesting question of the day, how the hell did somebody from 2018 manage to drop their chocolate wrapper inside a room that was sealed up sometime in the last century?"

CHAPTER FIVE

After the revelation of the Double Decker, Franklin didn't have much else to offer, and it was painfully obvious that she was champing at the bit to return to work. Kett trod back up the basement steps, weaving his way through the labyrinth of corridors until he found the Major Investigation Team's bullpen.

Savage hadn't moved, sitting in her chair toying with the lucky silver police whistle she always wore around her neck. Duke was perched on the edge of her desk with a big, goofy grin on his face. Savage said something and he laughed, sounding like a braying donkey.

Kett cleared his throat and Duke almost fell off the desk as he stood to attention.

"Hello, sir," he said. "Sorry, we weren't, ah..."

"You weren't *ah*?" said Kett as he walked over.

"I'd better, ah," Duke said, shrugging as if he'd forgotten every word in the dictionary. He made an odd motion with his arms like he was directing a plane to the runway, then turned and marched out of the room.

"Right," said Kett, turning to Savage.

She scratched her cheek, picked up a pen, dropped it again, then finally met his eye.

"You saw the bones?"

"I did," he said, pulling a chair from the next desk over and sitting down. "And the chocolate wrapper. Seriously weird."

"Seriously weird that somebody would be eating a Double Decker at all, sir," said Savage. "They're grim."

"That's a joke, right?" said Kett. "The Double Decker is the king of chocolate bars. It's chocolate, biscuit, nougat. All the amazing things. You literally can't beat it."

There was a clattering sound from Clare's office, and a second later the Super appeared. He was wearing his atrocious Big Tossing Jacket, which looked like the entire hide of a long-dead camel, but even so he was shivering like he'd just stepped out of a fridge.

"There's only one king of chocolate bars, Detective," he said, genuinely furious. "And that's a Bounty. No discussion, no argument. It's royalty."

"Sure," said Kett, pulling a face. "If you mean it's like some kind of inbred prince. Looks okay from a distance, but up close everything about it is wrong."

"I quite like a Bounty," said Savage. "More than I like a Double Decker. Bounty wins."

"The Double Decker would literally deck a Bounty," Kett went on. "Twice. What the hell is wrong with you both?"

"I think I've made myself very clear," said Clare. "Any more talk like that will be considered subordination."

He slunk back into his office, slamming his door behind him.

"Who found the wrapper?" Kett asked.

"I did, sir," she said. "On my third trip."

"So the stairway had been open for a while?"

"A couple of hours, yeah. And I know what you're going to ask next. Could it have blown in? Or could somebody have dropped it?"

Kett nodded. Savage leaned back in her chair, lacing her fingers behind her head.

"I mean, it's not impossible," she said. "Seven people walked down those stairs before I found the Double Decker. The foreman, Geoff Wileman, and Kitty Lewington. You heard about those two yet?"

"No," said Kett.

"They're quite a double act. Then a couple of firefighters, me and Porter, and lastly Franklin. No chance of me bringing a Double Decker wrapper with me, but Porter's..."

She glanced over her shoulder, then leaned forward again and spoke in a whisper.

"I mean, he's packing on the pounds, isn't he?"

Kett nodded.

"He's stressed about the baby," he said.

"Yeah, poor guy. Anyway, I asked him and it's not his. Neither of the smokies claimed it. There was quite a crowd watching and it could have belonged to somebody there, the wind could have carried it down. But here's the thing. The wrapper wasn't just lying there, it was caught under some cement."

"What kind of cement?"

"Mortar," said Savage. "From the walls, maybe. It was trapped."

"You're sure?"

"I am," she said. "And it was dusty, too. Date on the wrapper was April 2019, and judging by the amount of dust and grime on it, it could easily have been sitting there since then."

"So unless we're looking at a time traveller, somebody has been down in that basement in the last three years," said Kett. "Somebody found their way inside, discovered the bones, ate some chocolate, escaped, buried the chamber again and forgot to tell the police."

Savage shrugged.

"Something like that," she said. "Which is, as far as I can tell, completely impossible. Look."

She woke up her computer and opened the browser, clicking on a few tabs before finding the one she wanted. Kett pulled his glasses from his pocket and slid them on, turning the blur into a photograph of a building site. He recognised the ground floor of County Hall, and there was nothing above it except for the big Norfolk sky.

"1967," said Savage. "They'd just started work. You can see up the hill there, towards those trees. It's grassland. Chamber would be right about here."

She tapped the screen, making it wobble.

"Completely covered up. Same on this one, from five years later."

She clicked the next tab to reveal an aerial shot of the building and its grounds. Kett leaned in, seeing the woodland to the north and the main road to the south. Savage tapped the screen again.

"I measured it out, the stairs we found are right there. It's completely hidden, you can't even get a sense of the chamber from overhead."

She clicked through four more photos, ending with one taken in 2020. There was no hint in any of them that there was a room buried beneath the ground.

"I'm still looking," she said. "But as far as I can see, the chamber's been sealed for sixty-odd years, and quite possibly a lot longer."

"Except it hasn't," said Kett.

"Except it hasn't," she echoed.

"You know what it was originally?" he asked. "There must have been a building there."

"There was," said Savage. "It's on a few old maps. Knucklebone Hall."

"Seriously?"

"Yeah, good name, right? Honestly, I haven't found out much, but we're going back a couple of centuries at least. It was a manor house that went to ruin. People have been finding pieces of it for decades. I knew about it because there's a stone archway in the woods. The legends say the floor was a mosaic made from sheep knuckle bones."

"I don't even know what that means," said Kett. "Sheep have knuckles?"

"Apparently so. In the legs. Anyway, that's not important. What matters is that the house was demolished but the basements weren't filled in. At least this one wasn't. My guess is that it wasn't part of the main house. That's further up the hill. I bet this was an outbuilding of some kind, maybe even an icehouse, a stable, something like that. They tore the top of it down, but they didn't touch the basement."

"Because they didn't know about it," said Kett.

"That's my guess, sir. All those bones, somebody would have wanted to keep that secret. It was hidden, then it was covered, then it was forgotten. Along with what was left of all those poor people."

She shuddered.

"I've asked Kitty Lewington if she'll tell me more about the place."

"The woman who went down there?" Kett asked.

"Yeah. Her and some others were up at County Hall protesting the dig. She's a keen heritage enthusiast, wanted to preserve the site and the woods. They've been campaigning against the build for months. If anyone knows what that chamber's all about, she will."

"Nobody's interviewed her?" asked Kett.

"Duke asked her a couple of questions," Savage said, rolling her eyes. "But they weren't good ones. I said somebody would drop by."

She wiggled her eyebrows at him beneath the brow of her hat.

"Sure, I'll do it," he said. "Not exactly extreme crime, though, is it?"

"We're a bit short on that these days, sir," said Savage. "I'm not complaining."

"Me neither," he said, heading for the door. "You got an address?"

"I'll text you."

"Thanks, Kate," he said.

"No worries," she called after him. "It really is great to see you back, sir."

It felt great too, Kett thought. He'd slipped back in here as easily as a jigsaw puzzle piece, and he was smiling as he walked into reception. His good mood didn't last, though, because two men stood by the main desk, the bigger of them shouting at Shelley, who sat on the other side looking deeply unimpressed. His finger jabbed the air like a blade, specks of his spit caught in the overhead lights. He held a walking stick in his other hand, which bent beneath the sheer bulk of him. He had to have been approaching six-foot-six and pushing twenty-stone.

"... then what's the point of me even being here?" he yelled, his deep voice rolling effortlessly across the room. His accent was pure Norfolk, as strong as Kett had ever heard. "Do you have any idea how busy I am?"

"I've told you, sir," said Shelley, lifting her hands like she was trying to defend herself from an angry boar. "I can't just—"

"Get your shit sorted," the man said. "I do not—"

"Hey," Kett barked, loud enough for silence to drop like a guillotine blade.

The big man flinched, spinning around as quickly as his immense body would let him. He was well into his sixties with a round, red-cheeked face and two eyes that boiled like blisters. Most of his hair had fled, the wisps that were left mostly grey and planted into a scalp that was raw with psoriasis. He was wearing an expensive suit, a cheap shirt—the middle button undone, exposing an unwelcome glimpse of his substantial belly—and an awful tie emblazoned with the yellow and black Norfolk flag. When he opened his mouth his teeth were like yellow tombstones, and the look he gave Kett was that of somebody who was used to getting his own way.

"Don't 'hey' me," he said, more spittle than speech. He lifted the stick in order to point the end at Kett. "I'm—"

"Hey," Kett said again. It wasn't a shout this time, but it had the effect of one. "Calm down or get out. Those are your choices."

The man's jaw dropped, his substantial chin vibrating as he planted his walking stick back on the ground. He glanced at the guy next to him, who was a couple of decades younger and much skinnier. He was dressed in jeans and a black polo, and the embarrassment on his face spoke volumes. He looked at Kett helplessly, managing the smallest of apologetic shrugs.

"Do you know who I am?" the bigger man wheezed.

"No," said Kett. "I find that people who have to ask that question are seldom memorable."

Behind the desk, Shelley smiled, hiding it behind her hand. The man took a step towards Kett, making the most of his height. This time, when he jabbed his finger, the blunt yellow nail made contact with Kett's shoulder, hard enough to hurt.

"It might serve you well to figure it out, Detective," he said, leaning in. "Because I pay your fucking wages. Derek Foulger. Ring any bells?"

"No," said Kett, his shoulder throbbing. "But touch me again and you're under arrest, whoever you are."

He met Foulger's furious gaze until the other man swallowed and stepped back, tapping his stick on the floor like he was sending a secret message in Morse code. He sneered at Kett with such arrogance that it took every ounce of restraint he had not to slap the look off his face.

"I'm the Governor of Norfolk County Council," he said. "And I'll be speaking with your senior officer as soon as I'm finished here. What's your name?"

"You mean you don't know who *I* am?" said Kett.

The man aimed his finger again, but he was cut off by a roar from the other side of the room.

"Kett!"

It was Superintendent Clare, and he crossed the lobby like a possessed marionette. He eyeballed Kett before grabbing the other man's mutton chop of a hand and shaking it.

"Derek, good of you to come. Sorry, they should have told me you were here. This way."

Kett stepped out of the way to let the two men pass, Foulger wearing a look of pure smugness as he limped into the corridor. The other man waited by the desk, scratching his head like Stan Laurel. He clearly had no idea what to do with himself.

"You okay?" Kett asked Shelley, and she nodded.

"Not bothered," she said. "My dad was a butcher. I've seen scarier lumps of gammon than that."

Kett laughed.

"You two are together?" he asked the man who had been left behind.

"God, don't say it like that," he replied. "I'm having enough nightmares as it is. My name's Geoff Wileman, I'm the foreman up at the County Hall dig."

He offered his hand and Kett shook it, surprised at the strength of the man's grip. He almost yelped.

"Mr Wileman," he said, flexing his fingers. "Good to see you. You're here for an interview?"

The man shrugged.

"I don't know what's going on, to be honest," he said, scratching his head again. "I've lost the plot. Derek was asked to come down, he wanted me here too."

"He's quite something," said Kett.

"If by 'something' you mean a horrendous arsehole, then yeah," said Wileman, keeping his voice low. "Absolute prick. He's the man who pushed for the whole County Hall extension thing, even though every single person I've spoken to thinks it's a bad idea. He believes he's God."

"I can tell," said Kett. "I'm happy to inform him he's not."

"He won't appreciate that," said Wileman. "He knows a lot of people, a lot of powerful people. That whole Governor thing isn't even a real job title, you know that?"

Kett shook his head.

"He made it up when he retired, now he won't bloody leave. Got that stick of his in a whole lot of pies and none of them are good."

"Noted. You want to come with me, Mr Wileman? I can take your statement."

He started to move away, but Wileman grabbed his arm, rooting him in place. He leaned in, his voice once again so low it was almost a whisper.

"I mean it," he said. "Men like Foulger, they're dangerous. They always have been. Tread carefully."

CHAPTER SIX

"Go fuck yourself, tree."

Porter pushed the branches of a scraggly hawthorn out of his way, wincing as they scraped across the frozen skin of his face. He let go and they bounced back in a full slap, almost knocking him off his feet.

"I said fuck off!" he growled, tempted to march back down the hill to the building site, jump in a digger and uproot the woody bastard here and now.

He changed direction instead, giving the tree a wide berth as he pushed into the dense woodland that sat to the west of County Hall. The hawthorn whispered in the wind, like it was laughing at him.

"I'm not done with you," he told it, the anger boiling inside him. "Any of you. Bloody arsehole bloody bastard trees."

The woodland shivered and Porter shook his head, a laugh escaping his lips.

"Talking to trees, Pete," he said. "You're losing it, mate."

He did feel a bit like he was going mad, and it wasn't

just this case that was doing it. It was stressful as hell at home because Allie wasn't sleeping—Porter didn't know how anyone could sleep when you had a squirming lump the size of a space hopper bulging out of your stomach, compressing your organs, weird hands and feet pressing against the skin every now and again like something from a horror film. It felt like every thirty seconds he had to help her out of the bed and hobble to the toilet due to the fact that, in her words, her bladder was now smaller than her belly button. He couldn't remember the last time he'd slept for longer than an hour straight, and he knew it was only going to get harder when the little fella arrived.

"It's going to be worth it, though," he said. "It's going to be awesome."

The trees sucked up his voice, almost hissing with delight in another gust of wind.

"Wasn't talking to you," he told them. "Was talking to myself."

Which is far better, he thought with another laugh.

He broke free from the arms of a tall bush and staggered onto something that might have been a path. It was almost too dark to tell, because even though it was mid-morning the clouds were as solid as stone and the skeletal canopy blocked out most of that. He didn't even know what he was looking for up here, and more important than that, he didn't know *why* he was looking for anything at all. The bones they'd found were old, maybe centuries old. When a body was as old as that, surely there was no hope for any kind of explanation, or any kind of justice.

So surely there was no point schlepping up a muddy hill in the arse end of February being assaulted by trees.

At least there was one consolation, he thought. He looked behind him, down the hill and through the clustered branches to the bulk of County Hall. He was alone up here, there was nobody to witness him. Reaching into his pocket, he pulled out a Boost bar and unwrapped it with the urgency of an addict. He bit half of it off in one go, chewing relentlessly as he continued up the hill. He swallowed so hard he almost choked, banging a fist on his chest. Then he devoured the second half with equal enthusiasm.

The sugar rush hit him almost immediately and he marched onwards with renewed vigour—mental vigour, that was, because he was seriously out of breath. That was the other thing about Allie needing him so much at home, he hadn't had any time to go to the gym.

"Come on, you old fart," he wheezed. "It's just a hill."

He set off to the side instead to avoid having to climb, the trees around him like a crowd of frozen people. The ground was treacherous, his shoes slipping with every other step, and more than once he thought about just heading back to HQ, telling everyone he couldn't find anything.

Old bones. It didn't even matter.

But he kept going, because he was Detective Inspector Pete Porter. He didn't know how to turn his back on a case, even this one.

"Yeah," he said. "So fuck you, trees."

He rounded a corner, staring so intently at the slippery path that it took him a moment to notice there was something other than vegetation up ahead. Sitting in the middle of a patch of dense bushes, so smothered in ivy that it was almost invisible, was a stone archway. It was maybe ten foot high and half that in width, with a pointed top and a small, circular window over the archway. It looked so out of place that Porter almost felt sorry for it, as if it was a child lost in the woods.

"What on earth are you doing out here?" he asked it.

He pulled his phone from his pocket, opening the camera app and taking a couple of shots. According to Savage—or Encyclopaedia Jones, because she knew just about everything when it came to the weirder parts of Norfolk—this was all that was left of Knucklebone Hall. Why this bit had survived and nothing else was one of the many mysteries he gave absolutely no shits about.

He kept his phone out, firing up the torch as he closed in. It was so dark in this part of the woods that even with the light on he couldn't see the archway in much detail. Not that there was much to see. The stones were old and covered in graffiti—some of it drawn, some of it etched into it over the centuries.

"'Rudy has a bent todger'," he said, reading one. "Sorry to hear it, Rudy."

Rudy Porter?

He frowned.

"Rudy? Is that even a name?"

He started to walk through the arch, then decided against it. Something about passing under this weird monument seemed to be asking for trouble. He skirted around it instead, tripping on a root and almost braining himself on the stone. A smell hit him as he staggered to the other side, the stench of rot. It was easy to see where it was coming from. There was a pile of flowers here that almost reached his knees. They weren't wildflowers, they were the kind you got from the florist or—in his case, usually—the garage, most still wrapped in cellophane and paper even though their contents had turned to mush. Some of the bunches on the top looked newer, a couple so fresh they could have been bought that morning. He didn't recognise all the flowers but he was fairly sure the white ones were lilies, and the blood-red ones tulips.

Porter took a couple of photos, his breath locked in his lungs and his eyes watering. He used the toe of his shoe to flip one of the newer bunches—tulips, so bright they could have been artificial—seeing that they'd come from Sainsbury's. He wondered if flowers had a Best Before date but he couldn't see one.

"Because you don't eat them, Pete," he told himself.

There were some labels buried in the slush but it was so rancid in there he left them well alone. His phone was dinging anyway, a text from Allie.

Is this you???

There was an image attached and he clicked on it to see the photograph that Duke had taken of him yesterday morning. He seemed to have deteriorated even further, as if by magic, his face puffy and his chin drooping, his eyes almost crossed. He gurned at the camera like an angry orangutang at the zoo.

You look like the Swamp Thing!!! came another text from Allie.

"Thanks," he said, firing a reply.

Not me. It's a mistake. Photoshop.

He saw the three dots as she typed, then her text arrived.

It's on the Force's FB page, it says "DI Peter Porter tries his best."

"Tries his best?" said Porter. "I'm going to kill Duke, that cheeky mother—"

A branch cracked in the woods, loud enough to be a gunshot. At once, two dozen birds scattered from the trees in a rush of movement and sound and a bullet of adrenaline ripped through Porter hard enough to make him drop his phone.

"Bloody hell," he said, scooping it up and blowing off the dirt. "Hello?"

The woods had pulled a blanket of silence over themselves again. Porter clamped the air in his lungs, his pulse hammering at his eardrums. He heard the crack of another stick breaking, further away this time.

"Hello?" he called out, pushing away from the stone arch and deeper into the woods. "This is the police. If you can hear my voice, then stay where you are."

There were too many trees to see what lay ahead, as if they were deliberately concealing something. He struggled through knots of undergrowth and low-hanging branches until he found himself on another path, this one paved. Up ahead, to his right, a man was walking away at some speed, dressed in jeans, trainers and a red and blue windbreaker.

"Hey," Porter yelled. "Stop."

He broke into a run, not liking the way his body jiggled beneath his suit. The Boost bar wasn't sitting well in his stomach—along with the two he'd already scarfed that morning—and he belched chocolate-flavoured acid as he closed in.

"Stop!" he called again, too close for the man not to be able to hear him. The guy didn't show any sign of wanting to stop, speed-walking down the path with some urgency.

It only took twenty seconds for Porter to reach him, and he grabbed the man's shoulder. It was like somebody had set off a firework in the guy's underwear, his entire body jolting up off the ground. He loosed a high-pitched scream that a seven-year-old girl would have been proud of, ducking and dropping onto his haunches with his hands in front of his face. From this angle, Porter could see that he wasn't a man at all, he was a teenage boy. He was almost completely bald, his face so thin that his cheekbones jutted through the dark skin, sharp enough to be dangerous. His wide eyes were sunk deep into their sockets, and they were full of panic.

He was wearing EarPods, Porter saw, and he could hear tinny music spilling out of them.

"Please don't," the kid said. "Please. You can have my phone, just don't hurt me."

Porter stood back, his own hands up.

"Sorry," he said. "I thought you were running away from me."

He reached into his pocket and pulled out his warrant card.

"Police," he said, holding it up. "DI Peter Porter. You okay?"

He pocketed the warrant card and offered his hand, but the kid didn't take it. He struggled up by himself, the act looking like it took a monumental effort. Beneath his windbreaker he looked like a scarecrow, like the slightest of breezes would carry him off into the cloudy sky. He was sick, Porter realised. The hair, the deep pockets around his eyes, the way he rocked unsteadily. The kid looked *really* sick.

"You okay?" Porter asked again. "I'm sorry I startled you."

"I almost shit myself," the kid said. He looked down the path, then into the woods. He took a breath and called out in a weak shout, "Chainsaw?"

"Chainsaw?" asked Porter, expecting to see somebody appear from the trees.

"Lost him," said the kid. "He ran off."

"He's your dog?"

The kid nodded, searching the woods for a second more before finally meeting Porter's eyes.

"Lucky he wasn't here, mate," he said. "He'd have had

you for that."

"Fair enough," said Porter. "What's your name?"

"Why do you want to know?" he replied. His eyes were watering, but there was a fierceness in them that took Porter by surprise.

"Because I'm a copper," he said. "And I want to know what you're doing in the woods."

"Gee, let me think," said the kid, putting his hand beneath his chin like a Rodin statue. "I'm walking along a path used by dog walkers. And my dog is here somewhere. I must be..." He opened his mouth and gasped. "I must be walking my dog!"

"Ha bloody ha," said Porter. "You get a lot of dog walkers along here?"

As if the universe was answering him, a dog scampered into sight at the far end of the track. It was a terrier of some sort, more mud than fur, and it threw them a cautious look before advancing. A young woman followed, talking on her phone.

"Nah," said the kid, his voice heavy with sarcasm. "Never see people walking their dogs here."

The terrier blasted past, panting hard, and the woman followed. She looked at Porter, then at the kid, and lowered the phone.

"You okay?" she asked the boy.

"No," he said. "This weirdo attacked me. Call the police."

"I am the bloody police," said Porter, pulling the warrant card out again. "I didn't attack him, I wanted to ask him some questions."

"About what?" she said, and Porter lifted his arms in frustration.

"Flowers, I guess," he said. "Either of you know

anything about flowers in the woods, over there by a stone arch?"

The kid's eyebrow lifted, and he looked at Porter like he'd gone mad.

"Flowers," Porter said again. "Never mind. It doesn't matter."

The woman moved on, lifting her phone again.

"Hey," Porter called to her. "You seen another dog back there? A..."

He looked to the kid.

"Big one," the boy replied. "Like a wolf. Bit wild, kind of crazy. Answers to Chainsaw."

The young woman shook her head, hurrying off after her terrier.

"Big, wolf-like and kind of crazy?" said Porter when she'd gone. "Are you sure he should be off the lead?"

"He hardly ever bites anyone," said the kid.

"Reassuring," said Porter. "Look, you want me to help you find him? Least I can do after, you know..."

The kid shook his head, but he was exhausted. His shoulders were slumped, his hands trembling, and his breathing was so shallow it was like he wasn't taking in any air at all.

"Where did you see him last?" Porter asked.

The kid nodded to the woods.

"Chainsaw?" Porter yelled, slapping his cold thighs. "Chainsaw, here boy."

He walked to the edge of the trees, leaning on a wide trunk.

"Hey, Chainsaw, come on."

"It's no good," said the kid from the path. "He's the devil's bloody dog. He won't come until he's ready."

Porter whistled a couple of times, and after the second

attempt he heard the crack of branches as something came charging through the undergrowth. He staggered back to the path, trying to put the boy between him and whatever monster was about to explode from the trees.

"You sure he doesn't bite?" he asked.

"I said he *hardly* ever bites," the kid corrected. "Just don't look him in the eye."

The crashing sounds grew closer, then the smallest dog Porter had ever seen shot from the bushes. It was going so fast that its legs tangled beneath it and it did an almost perfect somersault, landing on its backside and staring up into the sky with eyes like Gobstoppers. It loosed a bark that was almost too high on the spectrum for Porter to hear, then it angled its head and spotted the kid.

"*That's* Chainsaw?" said Porter, who couldn't work out if he was relieved or disappointed.

"Yeah."

"Mate, I hate to break it to you, but I'm not even sure that's a dog."

Chainsaw scampered over, looking every bit like a drowned rat. He yelped repeatedly at Porter, sounding like a squeaky toy.

"I said don't look him in the eye," said the kid.

"I'm not even sure which end is his head," Porter replied.

At this, the kid almost smiled. He ducked down with some effort, bracing his elbow on his leg to steady himself. The dog ran over to him and began to furiously lick his fingers, something that might have been a tail flapping back and forth faster than a hummingbird's wings.

"Don't you go running off again," the kid said, using his free hand to scratch the dog's back. Chainsaw began to turn in tight, ecstatic circles, his tongue out. "I told you, you'll get eaten out there, you terror."

The kid was trying to pull something out of the pocket of his coat, and after watching him struggle for a few seconds, Porter leaned down to help. It was a lead, and he secured the clip to Chainsaw's collar before passing the loop to the boy. He offered him a hand, and this time he took it. Porter could feel the tremor that ran through him. Every single bone must have been rattling as he struggled up.

"Thanks," said the kid. "He likes you."

"Everyone likes me," said Porter. "You sure you're okay? You need some help getting home?"

"No thanks, weirdo," he said, but there was no malice there. He looked down the path as if he was trying to gather the strength to press on. "I only live round the corner there. Lakenfields. I'll survive."

He glanced back at Porter.

"What're you doing here, anyway? Something happened? When I was at school, we used to call this path the *Rape*bow Highway. Like Rainbow Highway from Mario Kart, but, you know, not. Nice, right? Wasn't a good place back then but everyone uses it now."

"Nothing's happened," said Porter. "Nothing recently, anyway. We just found something, you'll probably hear about it on the news tonight. Old bones."

The kid turned his dark, serious eyes to Porter.

"Old bones?"

"Yeah. Like, *really* old. Hundreds of years. I don't think they matter."

The kid shook his head.

"We'll all be old bones one day," he said. "They don't stay inside us forever."

Porter pulled a face.

"I guess, when you put it like that..." he said.

"These woods don't look like much," the kid went on. "But they're older than you think. There's a lot of history here. Some say magic, too."

"Magic?"

The boy shrugged his bony shoulders.

"Bones aren't the only things planted here, mate," he said. "Dig deep enough, you'll find all kinds of secrets."

"Like?" asked Porter when the boy didn't continue.

He grinned.

"I'm fucking with you," he said. "I'm seventeen, how the fuck would I know?"

Porter laughed too.

"You'd better get off then," he said. "Before I arrest you."

"For what?"

"For being a dick," said Porter, flapping his arms. "Go home."

The boy hesitated for a moment.

"Name's Daniel," he said.

"Good to meet you, Daniel," said Porter. "You look after yourself."

Daniel nodded, sighing, but he still didn't move. The little dog busied itself around Porter's shoes.

"Chainsaw *really* likes you," Daniel said after a moment.

"Yeah, like I said, I'm a likeable guy," Porter said. "I—"

"No, I mean he's pissing on your shoes."

Porter looked down and saw the kid was right. The dog was unleashing a veritable torrent of yellow piss all over his mud-caked Cleverleys, its enormous bug-eyes staring at Porter with unmistakable glee.

"Hey!" he yelled, staggering back.

The boy laughed, giving the lead a gentle tug as he set off up the path.

"Nice to meet you, weirdo," he shouted back. "Good luck with your bones!"

CHAPTER SEVEN

Kett led Geoff Wileman back through Norfolk Constabulary HQ's winding corridors and into the Major Investigation Team's offices, offering him a seat at his desk—or at least the desk that had once belonged to him but which was now completely empty. Savage nodded a welcome, but Wileman was too agitated to return it. He sat almost doubled over in his chair, his hands locked between his knees and his head down. He looked stressed, there was no doubt about that. But there was something else, too.

He looked *guilty*.

"You want a tea or something?" asked Kett.

"No, thanks," he replied. "Bit nippy in here, innit?"

"Heating's broken," said Kett. "Sure you don't want a cuppa?"

"I'll wet myself if I have any more tea," he said.

"We've got a toilet, if that helps?" said Kett, but Wileman was having none of it. He lowered his head even further, sniffing loudly. Kett rolled a chair over from an empty desk and sat opposite him, patting his empty pockets for a pen.

"Catch, sir," said Savage, way ahead of him. She lobbed a pen from her desk and Kett missed it completely, watching it spin under a desk halfway across the room. He looked at Savage and she dashed out of her chair to retrieve it. "Sorry, sir. Don't know my own strength."

"So, Mr Wileman," Kett said when she'd passed it to him. He jotted the name in his notebook. "You're the supervisor?"

"Foreman," Wileman replied. "Same thing, I guess. I'm in charge of the site."

"And you found the underground room?" asked Kett. "The cellar with the bones?"

"No," said Wileman, rocking gently back and forth, his hands still clamped between his knees. "That was Budgie. Oliver Budge. He's an operator, part of the team that's digging out the basement for the plant room. His excavator hit stone yesterday morning. He thought it was foundations but it was a single slab. When he shifted it, he found the stairs."

"But you were the first person down them?" asked Kett.

"I was," he replied, speaking to the floor. "Me and that woman, Kitty Lewington."

"You're absolutely sure nobody else entered the basement before you? Not Budgie, not any of the other workers?"

"I'm sure," he said. "They would have told me, and we've got CCTV on the dig, for insurance purposes. You can check it if you like."

Kett looked at Savage and she nodded.

"And you have absolutely no idea what this basement room is or what it used to belong to?" Kett asked.

Wileman took a deep breath, his eyes screwed shut.

"Mr Wileman?" said Kett. "What aren't you telling me?"

It took the man another half a minute to look up.

"Where's Derek?" he asked.

"I have no idea," said Kett. "Kate?"

"The big guy with Clare?" Savage said. "They went that way."

She nodded to the doors that led to the kitchen, and Wileman seemed to relax.

"This whole thing is my fault," he said. "Somebody could have died. I'm such an idiot."

"What's your fault?" asked Kett. "The bones?"

Wileman frowned, as if he couldn't work out what Kett was talking about.

"No, the *cellar*," he said. "We're lucky it had a vaulted ceiling or that JCB would've gone right through it. Budgie would've been buried alive down there. He's got two little'uns, six and four. Can you imagine? I'd have had to tell them about their dad, all because..."

He stopped, and Kett waited patiently for him to continue.

"Because those wankers in their ivory tower wouldn't pay for a proper survey," he said quietly. "They're happy to spunk twenty-odd million on a new building with a gym and a pool, but they won't fork out a few thousand for archaeological ultrasounds. Wankers."

"Hang on," said Kett. "You're telling me you started digging without knowing what you were going to find there?"

"Exactly," said Wileman. He sat back, taking a deep breath as if a heavy weight had been removed from his shoulders. "That's exactly what I'm saying. I pushed for a full survey three years ago, but Foulger and his cronies argued they didn't need one, because they'd had one done back in the 60s when they threw up the main building. I never argued with him, but I should have, you know? They didn't have the same equipment back then. At the end of the day, it's all on me."

He glanced at Kett.

"Am I going to get in trouble for that?"

"I have no idea," said Kett. "But thanks for telling us. So you had no idea the cellar room was down there?"

"I bloody should have," he said. "Because of *her*, Kitty Bloody Lewington. She's a pain in my arse, but she kept saying it, over and over, that if we dig the fields and the woods then we'll hit something from the old house. I should have listened to her."

"There are no architectural plans available for Knucklebone Hall," said Savage. "I looked, couldn't find any."

"Yeah, I looked too," Wileman said. "Looked for months, but any record of it's just gone, *poof*, vanished. So we had no idea what we'd find there, and it's why I was pushing Derek to get the sonars out so we could at least be sure, but you can't—"

He cocked his head, looking like a bird that's just sensed a stalking cat. He glanced at the door and a second later it opened, Derek Foulger's meaty voice rising from the corridor beyond.

"All good, Colin, all good. Nothing we can do about it now, eh?"

The so-called Governor marched into the bullpen, looking a little less like a boiled ham than he had in reception, but not by much. He spotted Wileman and his piggy eyes narrowed into a glare.

"Geoff, what the hell are you doing?" he boomed, his

voice reverberating from wall to wall like a trapped bull. "I told you to wait for me in the lobby."

Superintendent Clare walked out after Foulger, closing the door behind him. He looked more irritated than ever. Wileman, meanwhile, was squirming in his chair like a child about to be reprimanded by a furious parent.

"I brought him through," said Kett. "I just wanted to check a couple of things."

"What's the point?" said Foulger, crossing the room like an oil tanker. "You found a cellar, a few bones, and from what Colin's just told me you've cleared them out already. Geoff's going to fill the cellar in tomorrow and we're going to crack on, isn't that right, Colin?"

He lifted a giant hand and brought it down on Clare's shoulder, hard enough to make the Super grunt in pain.

"I don't think that's such a good idea," said Kett. "I—"

"Don't think," said Foulger. "That's good advice, Kett. Do not think. Listen to yourself."

"There's not much left for us to investigate," Clare said, giving Kett another warning look. Foulger was still squeezing Clare's shoulder like he was giving him a massage. "If forensics come up empty-handed then you're welcome to do whatever you want with it. There's no argument here."

"Good man," said Foulger, finally letting go. "Good man. Wileman, get out of that chair, you've got work to do."

Wileman shot up like Foulger had hold of his strings, and together the two men left the room, looking more like Laurel and Hardy than ever. Clare waited for the door to close behind them before rubbing his shoulder.

"Do either of you know how many words there are in the English language?" he asked.

Kett shook his head, but Savage put up her hand.

"170,000, sir, give or take," she said.

"And none of them adequately describes what an absolute tosser that man is. He thinks he can come in here and tell me my job?" Clare spluttered. "Bastard's not wrong, either. Unfortunately."

"Sir?" asked Savage.

"He knows a lot of people," Clare said. "And a lot of people owe him favours. You don't get to his position without serious clout and bollocks the size of beach balls. I should probably mention that he and the Chief Constable are golfing partners. One of them's godfather to the other's kid, I can't remember which way round it is."

"What did he say to you?" asked Kett.

"Told me to leave this well alone. Told me he'd heard from the CC himself that this would not impact the project. Told me to get you out from under his feet or he'd happily stomp you."

"He said that?"

"Yes, and he wasn't beating about the bush, either. He used those exact words."

Clare lifted his head and groaned at the ceiling.

"Wileman told us Foulger vetoed the surveys that would have located the basement," said Kett. "Didn't want to have to pay for them."

"Good to know," Clare said. "He say anything else?"

"He said that Foulger wasn't a man to be trusted. That he can be dangerous."

"Truer words have never been spoken," said Clare. "But I think my hands are tied on this. Old bones, I don't think they're enough to keep the case going, not unless we find something else."

"So they're going to fill in the basement?" said Savage. "Tomorrow?"

"Almost certainly," said Clare, a definite twinkle in his eye. "So you'd better get down there today and find me something good."

IT WAS NEARLY one by the time Savage pulled up to the barrier at County Hall, the brakes of the Audi squealing as she came to a halt. Kett stuffed the last of his petrol station Chicken Mayonnaise sandwich in his mouth as she opened the window and flashed her warrant card to the security guard in the booth.

"I thought you lot were finished up here?" he asked, looking at Savage, then Kett, then at the hulking shape of PC Duke who was crammed into the back.

"Not by a long shot," said Savage.

The man frowned and picked up his phone.

"Just got to check it," he said. "Hang on."

Kett leaned over Savage, furiously chewing his sandwich.

"Open the barrier, now," he ordered. Or *tried* to order. His mouth was too full.

"Say it, sir, don't spray it," muttered Savage.

"What was that?" asked the security guard.

Kett swallowed a lump of bread and chicken, feeling it grind to a halt halfway down his oesophagus. He thumped himself in the chest to get it moving, then tried again.

"I said open the barrier. Now."

Sandwich or no sandwich, the man heard the authority in Kett's voice. He put the phone down and then opened the barrier.

"I'm still going to have to check it with—" he shouted

after them as Savage drove on. His voice faded behind the growl of the Audi's engine.

"If I didn't know any better, I'd say somebody here was trying to hide something," Kett said as they drove alongside the flank of the enormous building.

"Derek Foulger?" asked Savage. "Maybe they're just worried they'll get penalised for not doing the right checks? They might think we're going to shut them down."

"Maybe," said Kett. "Porter still here, you reckon?"

"One way of finding out, sir," said Duke from the back. "Follow the trail of chocolate bar wrappers."

Kett angled himself in his seat so that he could give the young PC a hard stare.

"Porter's going through some stuff, Duke," he said. "Leave him alone."

"Heard and understood, sir," said Duke, but the smile on his face said otherwise.

Savage pulled the car into an empty visitor's space and cut the engine, cricking her neck. Kett opened his door, the cold wind slapping him hard in the face as he shivered his way out. The day was getting darker by the minute, the clouds already scattering sleet and threatening snow. A handful of people milled in and out of County Hall's lobby, but most had the good sense to remain indoors.

Savage pulled her red beanie over her hair and set off, Duke walking by her side—so close that Kett half expected them to start holding hands. Savage must have been conscious of the fact too, because she shifted herself away from the big PC, almost trotting as she rounded the corner.

Kett knew there was a building site here, but the sheer size of it took him by surprise. Ahead of him was a graveyard of mud that stretched a hundred yards to the distant woods, pocked with several immense holes that could have been giants' graves. A mound of uprooted trees sat to the left like a headstone, and Kett felt a sudden and surprising rush of anger that they'd been pulled from the earth so violently.

"How the hell did they get permission to do this?" he said.

Savage shrugged.

"It's been controversial. There have been protests up here every day."

Not now, though. The site stood almost completely empty, other than a handful of men and a single woman on the far side of the field, all decked in hard hats and fluorescent yellow jackets. A lonely copper stood on the lip of the smaller of the two pits, and even from here Kett could see that she was shivering.

"There's Porter," said Savage.

Her hands were in her pockets, but Kett followed her nod to the treeline up the hill. Porter was stomping out of it like some kind of mythological ape, his body hunched and his face creased into a glower that Clare would have been impressed by. He sneezed loudly, the sound of it echoing off the side of the building. He caught sight of them and waved.

"Who's he with?" asked Duke.

"*With*?" said Kett. "He's on his own."

"Oh, right, sir," Duke said, squinting. "Just looks like two of him, he's so big now."

"Last chance, Aaron," said Kett.

He pointed to the lonely copper.

"The cellar's over there?"

Savage nodded, and together they struggled through the ankle-deep mud, past three enormous JCBs that looked like abandoned tanks.

"Thank the heavens," said the young constable, PC Felicity Niven, as they closed in. She smudged the hair out of her eyes and the wind blew it right back again. "Please tell me you're taking over, I can't feel my feet."

"Not for long," said Kett. "But go grab a cuppa, we'll be here for a while."

Niven grinned with relief, almost running as she made her way towards the main building. She looked back as she went.

"Forensics are inside the cellar, just so you know."

Porter had caught up to them and Kett lifted an eyebrow when he saw the state of the man. His shoes were caked in mud, and one leg of his trousers was absolutely slathered in dirt. His jacket, too, was green with moss. He opened his mouth to speak, then held it open, and Kett thought he was having some kind of seizure until he unleashed a deafening sneeze.

Not quite loud enough, though, to cover the sound of Duke's phone as he took a photo.

"Oh God, that's perfect," said the PC, studying his screen.

Porter pointed a finger at him.

"Don't you bloody dare," he said. "I'm already getting calls about the last picture you posted. 'Porter tries his best'? What the hell kind of caption is that?"

"You *are* trying your best, sir," said Duke with a look of pure innocence. "We all are."

"I'm going to make you eat that bloody phone," Porter growled, advancing with such a look of fury that Kett had to step between the two men.

"Enough," he said. "Porter, calm down. Duke, delete that photo. That's an order."

"Can I keep it for personal use, sir?" Duke asked.

"No," said Kett with a glare. "And what is that smell?"

Whatever it was, it was acrid enough to make his eyes water. He looked at Porter, who was staring at his feet.

"Is that *you*, Pete?"

"No, sir," Porter replied. "I mean, maybe. A dog pissed on my shoes."

"Right," said Kett, pinching the bridge of his nose. "Not even going to ask how that happened."

"I was in the woods," Porter said. "Found the remains of the old house."

"The archway from Knucklebone Hall?" said Savage. He nodded.

"Nothing there apart from some flowers. Not the growing kind, the cut kind. From the supermarket. Most are old, but there's a few new bunches there too."

"Mean anything to anyone?" Kett asked, and nobody replied.

"Couldn't see much else, but I bumped into a kid who'd lost his dog," Porter went on.

"You found it?" asked Kett, and the DI gestured towards his shoes.

Kett turned to the pit, noticing for the first time the fluttering square of police tape and the void of darkness that sat in the middle of it. A portable generator rumbled nearby, wires snaking into the spiral stairwell. The hole seemed so alien, so wrong out here in the middle of nowhere, that he felt a shudder rip through him. The idea of somebody filling it in, of obliterating it with stone and cement, suddenly didn't seem so bad.

"Is it as awful as it looks down there?" he asked.

"Oh yes," Savage replied, pulling her hat down over her ears like a gladiator's helmet.

"Great," said Kett. "Then let's get this over with."

CHAPTER EIGHT

IT WASN'T AS BAD AS IT LOOKED, KETT REALISED, AS HE made his way carefully down the stone steps into the cellar.

It was *worse*.

When he'd been a kid, four or five years old, he'd seen a documentary on the TV about eels. The lampreys had absolutely terrified him, their circular jaws with row upon row of barbed teeth. He'd had nightmares for weeks, and still dreamed of them sometimes, if he was particularly stressed.

He'd be dreaming of them tonight, he was sure of it, because that's exactly what this circular hole in the ground reminded him of—a sucking pit with stone teeth and no desire at all other than to feed. He couldn't help but imagine it as the head of some vast subterranean creature, and the idea of being trapped inside the dark and the cold almost stopped him in his tracks.

Fortunately, after a couple of steps, he realised it wasn't dark or cold down here at all. A handful of dull yellow lamps lay on the stairs, powered by the generator overhead, and currents of warm air seemed to wrap him in a hug as he traipsed downwards. He could hear somebody humming softly.

"Hello?" he called out. "Cara?"

The humming stopped.

"Kett?" said the lead forensic technician, her accented voice as warm as the air. "Talking of ghosts. Watch your step."

He did as she advised, lurching over a bundle of electrical cables at the bottom of the spiral staircase. The room was bigger than he'd anticipated, maybe twelve feet wide and twenty in length, although he couldn't see much past the squat column that held up the low, vaulted ceiling. Other than the stairs, everything was made from bricks, all of them angled against each other like parquet flooring. There were alcoves in the walls, three on each side and each big enough to stand in, but other than them there really wasn't a lot to work with.

"I heard you were back," Hay said from wherever she was hiding. "It is good to see you."

"It would be good to see you too," he said "Where are you?"

"At the back."

Savage appeared behind Kett, one hand on his shoulder to steady herself. He could hear Porter and Duke stomping after her, and he wasn't sure which one was making more noise. A moment later, Cara Hay leaned around the side of the column, a big smile on her face. She was holding a lamp in one hand and she used it to beckon Kett forward, her white overalls rustling.

"Watch your head, too," she said, brushing her free hand over her shaved scalp. "I almost gave myself a concussion on those ridges."

Kett ducked beneath the ornate branches of the pillar,

seeing the rest of the cellar. There were two more technicians here, both in matching overalls with gloves and booties, and between them and Hay there was barely any room to move. Past them was an opening into a smaller room, but there were no lights in there, just a darkness that was inkwell deep. A portable heater pumped out hot air, and between that and the claustrophobia that gnawed at his nerves, Kett instantly broke into a sweat.

"Budge up, sir," said Savage, giving him a nudge.

"Budge up where?" he asked, biting down on the panic as he shuffled forwards a few feet to let her in. Porter loomed over her shoulder, looking like he was sucking all of the air out of the space.

"Room for a little one?" came Duke's voice.

"No," said Kett.

He squeezed through the crowd to the opening at the far end of the cellar, firing up the torch on his phone and peering through.

"This is where they were?"

"Yes, sir," said Savage. "Fixed to the back wall."

There were no bones there now, of course, but he could see the pattern of scars where the nails had been hammered into the brick. Something about that cluster of holes was almost worse than what had been displayed in Franklin's photographs, as if any minute now something would hatch inside them and start swarming. He scratched a phantom itch on his stomach, looking at the wall above the bones where some of the brickwork had been cut away, then he retreated.

"How's it going?" he asked Hay, switching off his torch.

"I am having a lovely time," said Hay, and Kett couldn't work out if she was being sarcastic or not. "We started by looking for prints, but we weren't expecting much."

"Hard to get prints from bricks," said Savage.

"It's almost impossible. They're too rough, too porous, and bricks are about all we have down here. I can try to get something from the nails, but I fear it will be a losing battle. They're rosehead nails, antique iron, so it will be difficult to find prints and even then they'll be partials. We could try to make a composite, I'm not saying it's impossible, but that would require a significant organisation of resources and it would take weeks. Hardly worth it, given that whoever did this is almost certainly long dead and therefore unlikely to give us a print to match."

"Anything else?" asked Kett, desperate to head towards the surface again.

"We looked for shoe prints, but everything was kicked up by yesterday's visitors. We have samples from the floor, a few hairs, mostly human but maybe some dog, cat and rat in there too. A lot of dust, which, of course, we can sieve through for anything of interest. Lots of bone fragments which I have bagged up and sent to Emily. You heard about the chocolate bar wrapper?"

"I did," said Kett. "Double Decker from 2018, or thereabouts. Where was it?"

Hay put her hands on the shoulders of the nearest technician and gently steered her out of the way. Behind her was one of the shallow alcoves, maybe six-foot high, half as wide, and half again as deep. The floor here had been pocked with puddles of what looked like mortar, the smallest the size of a pea and the largest no bigger than a fifty-pence piece. They would have been almost invisible against the dusty brick if he hadn't been looking for them.

"It was caught under one of those," said Savage.

"Cement?" he asked.

"Yes," said Hay. "At first I thought it was the same kind

used to make the walls. I wondered if the builders had simply done a sloppy job. It's a basement, after all, not a grand entrance hall."

"It's more than a basement," said Kett, looking at the circular column, at the ornate brick branches that stretched overhead, then at the little room where the bones had been hidden. "Whoever designed this didn't want it to look like your bog-standard storage space."

"Right," said Hay. "I agree. I sent the cement off this morning for testing, but it's obvious this is different to the mortar in the walls. It's far more powdery and not as strong. Whoever mixed this didn't seem to know what they were doing. They added too much water, you can see the air bubbles."

"What's it doing here, then?" asked Kett. "None of the bones were cemented in place, were they?"

"No," said Savage.

Hay smiled, making it very clear she knew the answer to the question.

"Take a look at the floor, Detectives, and tell me what you see."

Kett studied the bricks that made up the ground, spattered with dots of cement. They were old, worn down by time, and there was a long, perfectly curved groove carved across the face of three of them.

"Can I see?" asked Duke from the other side of the pillar.

"No," said Kett, pointing to the groove. "That mark, what made it?"

"It looks like a door, sir," said Savage, peering past his shoulder. "The angle of it, the way it curves away from the wall. It looks like something's opened here."

"And not just once," said Hay, giving Savage a nod of

approval. "It would take a lot of effort to make a mark like that in these bricks. Something has ground its way back and forth in exactly the same way, again and again. Hundreds of times."

"A door," echoed Kett. He stared into the alcove, imagining the back wall on a hinge, moving inwards. Savage was right, if it opened into the room then it could easily account for the scarred bricks. "You've had a look?"

"Of course," said Hay, lifting her lamp to chase the shadows away from the walls. "As you can see, there are no handles, no hinges of any kind. We've pressed every brick looking for a secret mechanism and found nothing. But can you see how the bricks are cut?"

Kett nodded, then shook his head when he realised he had no idea what she was talking about.

"A solid line along the back of the alcove, both sides and the top. In every other alcove the bricks overlap, for strength, but here there is a clear break. I have no doubt that this can be opened."

She sighed.

"At least, that it could *once* be opened."

"Somebody's sealed it," Kett said. "Right? That's what you think the cement was used for."

"It's a theory," said Hay with a shrug. "Somebody came down here, mixed up some cement, and used it to block up the door. From the other side, I think, because there are only smatterings on the floor in here, like droppings from a bucket or a trowel."

"Which means there's not a room in there," said Kett. "There's a tunnel."

"Unless somebody buried themselves alive," added Porter. "Like something out of a Poe story, isn't it?"

Another shudder ripped through Kett as he imagined a

grinning skeleton on the other side of the wall, a Double Decker clenched in its bony hand. He thought about the world above him, about the air up there, and he had to root his feet in place to stop himself from making a break for it.

"This explains the chocolate wrapper, though," he said. "The chamber's been buried for sixty-odd years, but there was a tunnel. Somebody knew about it, and in 2018 or early 2019 they mixed up some cement, ate a Double Decker, and sealed it off from the other side of the wall. Why?"

"Maybe they wanted to eat chocolate bars in secret," said Duke from the other side of the room. "It happens."

Kett thought he heard Porter growl.

"Because they knew what was down here," said Savage. "They knew about the bones and they didn't want anyone to find them."

She cocked her head.

"Hang on, I was doing some reading last night. Plans for the extension to County Hall went public in 2018. Just before Christmas."

"So it fits," said Kett. "The person saw the plans, they knew the groundworks might reveal the cellar and they wanted to hide the tunnel. But why leave the bones? If they were worried about somebody finding this place, why not clear it out?"

Nobody answered, the room silent apart from the rumble of the generator.

"Because they were still using it," said Kett after a moment, answering his own question. "They didn't want to clear it out because they were still using it. Franklin told me some of the bones were newer. What if whoever was using this place was still collecting the bones? Still mounting them here?"

"Christ," muttered Porter.

"That is very possible," said Hay.

Kett looked at the alcove again, picturing the tunnel that they might find on the other side, snaking into darkness.

"You sure you can't get the door open?" he asked.

Cara shook her head.

"Then somebody get up those stairs," he said. "We're on a building site, it shouldn't be too hard to find a sledgehammer."

CHAPTER NINE

Savage made her way carefully up the spiral steps, the rain so heavy now that when she emerged from the cellar it took her a moment to notice the rumble of an engine—far bigger than the generator that purred at her feet.

The JCB digger that had been parked at the bottom of the slope was running, a man sitting in the cab. Two more men stood shivering by the mud-clogged tracks, both of them with cigarettes in their gloved hands. Smoke mixed with the exhaust from the digger, forming a cloud overhead. They were all wearing fluorescent jackets over black overalls, the rain drumming off their hard hats. None of them was older than thirty, and they all sported almost identical neatly cropped beards.

"Hey," Savage said, trudging over, the mud so thick it was like somebody was grabbing her feet. "Anyone here have a sledgehammer?"

One of the men standing beside the digger grinned through his beard.

"I do, love," he said.

The guy next to him laughed, elbowing him in the ribs, none of them taking their eyes off her. Savage threw them a look that told them just how unimpressed she was, but it did little to strip the smirks from their faces.

"A sledgehammer," she said again.

The man who'd told the joke shrugged, taking a drag on his cigarette before making his way up the slope. Savage turned her attention to the guy who was operating the JCB. He was the youngest of the lot, probably not much older than her, and fit, too, his neck thick with muscle. He sat with one boot propped on the dashboard, studying her with undisguised insolence.

"What are you doing?" she asked him, and he cupped a hand to his ear as if he couldn't hear her. She took a couple of steps towards him and shouted the question again.

"Just getting ready to work," he called back.

"Site's shut down," Savage told him. "Police orders."

"Not what I've been told," he said. He lowered his foot, taking hold of one of the digger's levers and gently wiggling it from side to side.

"Well I'm telling you now," Savage said. "Turn it off."

He didn't respond, and she walked closer. She refused to break eye contact and so did he, the smugness never leaving his face.

"Last chance," she said.

It seemed like a small eternity passed before he turned the key and the JCB's engine clattered into silence.

"What's your name?" Savage said.

No answer.

"Budgie, right?" she said, and this wiped the smile clean off his face. "Oliver Budge. We have you to thank for finding this place, don't we?"

Budgie swapped a look with the other man, something in his expression that Savage couldn't make sense of.

"You know anything about it?" she said. "The cellar?"

"No," said Budgie, looking back at her. "Why would I?"

She didn't answer, she just held his gaze until he broke away.

"No idea what you're on about," he said.

"Not on about anything," said Savage. "Has somebody told you to start filling it in?"

He didn't answer, and Savage was on the verge of telling him to get out of the digger when the first man returned. He was holding a bright yellow DeWalt mechanised chisel, struggling with the weight of it as he tripped and slid back down the muddy slope.

"Shit," he said when he almost fell, using the chisel as a crutch to keep himself standing. "No sledge, will this do?"

"It'll do," said Savage.

The man was standing his ground so Savage made her way to him, grabbing the chisel's handle. He let go of it too quickly and the weight almost pulled her over. Only sheer stubbornness kept her standing, because there was no way in hell she was falling over in front of these three muppets. She hefted it up with a smug grin of her own, taking her time as she walked back to the stairs. Only there did she turn back.

"If I hear that engine before we're all above ground again, then I'm taking you in," she told Budgie. "I mean it."

None of the men replied, all three of them watching her like lizards as she dropped down the steps again. Duke was waiting at the bottom and he held out his hands for the chisel, only for Savage to shake her head.

"Three idiots up there," she told him, struggling for

breath. "With a digger. Don't like it. Can you keep an eye on them?"

"Sure," said Duke, cracking his knuckles. "It'll be my pleasure."

Savage carted the chisel around the column, her muscles burning.

"Got this," she said. "Electric. Anywhere to plug it in?"

"Just there," said Hay, pointing to the extension cord that was connected to the heater and the lights. Porter offered to take the chisel, and she gladly handed it to him, flapping her aching arms to get some blood back into them. She plugged the cord into the socket, standing back.

"Not going to bring the walls down, is it?" Porter asked, looking nervously at the ceiling.

"One way to find out," said Kett, standing to one side to allow Porter access to the alcove.

"Does it come with any safety equipment?" the DI asked. "Goggles? Helmet? I mean, it's a powerful bit of kit and—"

"Give it here," said Kett, taking the chisel from Porter's hands. "Stand back, and cover your ears."

Kett braced the point of the chisel against a section of crumbling mortar between two bricks, then fired it up. Down here, in such a confined space, the noise of it was deafening. Savage had her fingers in her ears, but they might as well have been needles pushing towards the tender flesh of her brain. She retreated around the column and onto the first step, followed by Porter, who had his gloved hands pressed against the sides of his head.

The noise stopped, then started again, a pattern of sound and silence that went on for almost ten minutes. When it finally ended, Savage's ears were ringing.

"Probably should have waited outside, sir," she said.

"What?" asked Porter.

"Exactly."

She followed the DI into the other half of the basement to see the chisel on the floor. Kett and Hay were both pulling out loose bricks and stacking them against the wall. There was an opening in the back of the alcove that was maybe eighteen inches high and just as wide, a mouth of toothy masonry leading into a maw of absolute darkness. The current of air which blew out of it was strong and cold, almost Arctic.

"Definitely a tunnel, then," said Savage, wrapping her arms around herself. "Can you see anything?"

"Nope," said Kett. "Has anyone got a—"

Hay was already holding out her lamp and Kett took it, offering it up to the hole in the back of the alcove. His hands were shaking from the effort of operating the chisel, Savage saw, the light almost vibrating. She pushed gently past Porter, peering through the gap to see walls the colour of bone. There was a moaning sound from deep inside, a haunting cry that made her skin crinkle painfully into goosebumps.

"What the fuck is that?" said Porter. "Can anyone else hear it?"

It would be hard not to, because the howling came again, a strangled cry of grief.

"It's the wind," said Savage. "It has to be, right?"

They all fell silent, waiting. And when the noise rose once more it brought with it a gust of dusty air, a dead man's breath.

"The wind," said Kett. "That's probably all it is."

"We should check, though," said Savage. "Can you make the hole any bigger?"

Kett shook his head.

"There's a metal frame," he said. "To support the weight of the bricks, I guess. Chisel won't cut through it, we'll need an angle grinder."

"On it," said Porter, heading for the stairs. The tunnel moaned softly, as if pleading for him to come back.

Kett pushed his head into the hole, looking like he was being eaten alive.

"Can't see far," he said. "There's a corner about fifty feet ahead. Somebody's definitely cemented the door, though, I can see the bucket and the trowel."

He tried to force himself deeper into the gap, but he was too wide, and after a second or two he emerged. There was so much white dust in his hair he looked like he'd aged twenty years or more in the time he'd been in there.

"I'm never getting through that," he said, and he looked expectantly at Savage.

"Uh," she said, glancing at the hole, at the tunnel beyond which had once again flooded with darkness. "You want me to..."

Please say no, she thought, but Kett was smiling.

"Only if you want to, Kate," he said.

"I can't say I want to, sir. But..."

She couldn't think of an excuse, so she shrugged instead.

"Good job," said Kett, giving her the lamp. "Just a peek, okay? Don't go far."

Savage blew out a sigh. Gripping the lamp like it was a weapon, she walked to the opening. Fingers of frozen air caressed her face, and her body locked up, doing everything it could to prevent her from sticking her head through that hole.

Come on, Kate, she told herself. *It's just a tunnel.*

A tunnel that led to this hidden room filled with bones,

she thought, and the high-pitched moan of the wind seemed to laugh at her.

"Any time you like," said Kett, and she clamped her chattering teeth together in case she said something she regretted. "You want a hand?"

She didn't see how she'd be able to do it otherwise, so she nodded. Kett came up behind her and wrapped his arms around her stomach, letting her lift both her feet off the ground.

"Crikey, Kate," he wheezed. "You're heavier than you look."

He shuffled forwards so that she could slide her legs through the hole, then her backside, and she stretched like a cat until she found the ground. Kett supported her weight until she'd slid her body through like she was playing limbo, her back cricking as she stood straight. The wind snatched at her hair with such force she was convinced somebody was standing next to her, the fright of it like a physical punch to the gut. She lifted the lamp with a grunt of breath, seeing nothing but those pale walls. Flecks of dust hung in the bright light, glittering like stars.

"It's bloody freezing in here," she said, the shakes uncontrollable.

"What do you see?" asked Kett.

"It's definitely a door," she said, holding the light to the back of the alcove. There was a sturdy iron frame, bricks mortared to the inside of it. There was no handle, but a crude bolt sat at waist-height, most of it concealed by an enormous lump of rock-hard cement. More cement had been plastered over the three immense hinges. "And somebody definitely sealed it. No way in hell this is going to open, sorry."

She swung the lamp around, finding the bucket. It was

made of bright orange plastic, the handle metal, and inside was an empty bag of cement.

"You got any gloves, Cara?" Savage called back, and a second later Hay handed a set to her. She pulled them on, ducking down beside the bucket and removing the bag. "Lefarge Mastercrete," she said, reading the label. She turned the bag over. "It's got a manufacturing date, September 2018."

She handed it to Cara, searching the bucket to find only the calcified remains of the cement. She hefted it up and passed it through the gap. There was nothing else here, so reluctantly she turned her attention to the tunnel. It seemed smaller than it had a second ago, as if it was contracting, and once again she felt a sudden cold wash of panic. She ran her gloved hand along the wall, looking at the residue it left on her fingertips.

"Chalk," she said. "Must be an old mine. There are miles and miles of these under the city."

"Can you see where it leads?" said Kett.

The tunnel answered before she could, that same spectral groan which made her legs feel too weak to hold her. She rested her hand on the wall again, this time so she wouldn't buckle over.

"Don't go far," said Kett. "Just see what's around the corner."

She nodded, more to herself than to him, and set off, her footsteps echoing back at her like there was an army on her tail. The floor was uneven, filled with ridges and potholes that did their best to trip her up. Scraps of chalk exploded beneath her shoes like rodent bones, filling the air with their earthy scent.

She reached into her shirt and felt the reassuring weight of her granddad's silver police whistle, the way she always did when she was afraid. Slowly, step by step, she closed in on the corner. Only when she reached it did she look back, the yellow light from the underground room surely too far away, Kett's face impossibly small. She had the uncanny feeling that she was an astronaut floating away from her shuttle, and she wondered whether she should ask for a tether so that they could reel her back in.

Focus, she ordered herself. *You're fine.*

She held the lamp in front of her and turned the corner, seeing another section of tunnel that stretched much further. The end of it was pitch black, and anything could have been staring back at her from its fathomless depths.

"Just carries on," she called back, the volume of her voice in the quiet tunnel making her jump. "You want me to..."

She looked back hopefully, but Kett was nodding.

"Only if it looks safe, Kate," he said. "Don't put yourself in any danger."

"I'll put *you* in bloody danger, sir," she muttered beneath her breath. "Too big to fit through the hole, my arse."

She stepped around the corner, losing sight of the secret door. The wind wrapped itself around her like a fist, it pressed its cold lips against her eyes, her ears, thrust its fingers down the collar of her shirt. She put her head down and kept walking, counting her steps as she went, just for something to do to take her mind off where she was.

One, two, three.

The ceiling was so low she had to duck to stop her head from scraping along it, and as she went it seemed to drop further.

Nine, ten, eleven.

The sound of the distant wind picked up again, calling

her forward. It was *so* human, that moan. It was unbearably human, and she couldn't help but imagine a phantom sliding out of the shadows up ahead, its mouth distended, its eyes black.

Twenty-seven, twenty-eight, twenty-nine.

She looked back, the corner of the tunnel no longer visible, like something had erased it. What would happen if she turned back now and she couldn't find it? What if she retraced her steps and the tunnel just kept going in a straight line, forever?

Hold it together, Kate, she thought.

"Kett?" she called out. "Can you hear me?"

She heard his voice but she couldn't make out his reply. It could have come from miles away.

Fifty-nine, sixty, sixty-one.

The ceiling was starting to lift and Savage straightened her back, flexing her neck. The breeze was stronger and colder than ever, and the pitch of it had changed. She counted twenty-one more steps before the tunnel widened out and she found herself in a circular chamber about the size of the Incident Room back at HQ. More tunnels led out from it, seven in total, including the one she'd just left. Random pieces of rusted machinery and old tools littered the floor, including what looked like a section of railway track that led into a tunnel to her left.

She swore under her breath, walking around the circumference of the chamber. It was so cold that her hands had gone numb, the lamp impossibly heavy. Each of the seven tunnels looked identical, and they all led into the same awful dark.

"Kett, can you hear me?" she shouted. "I've found a junction. Six exits. No idea where any of them go."

She held her breath while she waited for a reply, but if

one came it was lost in the mad chatter of the wind as it threw itself around the room.

What now? she thought.

She pulled her phone out and it slid from her gloved fingers, hitting the chalk floor. Swearing again, she used her teeth to pull off the glove, then collected the phone, taking a dozen photographs of the space. There was no signal down here, of course, so she slipped it back into her pocket and turned to head back. There was no way in hell she was going any deeper, not on her own.

She'd only taken a couple of steps, though, when she heard a noise behind her. She stopped, every muscle locked, the pulse of adrenaline so powerful that it was like somebody had crushed her skull in their fist.

It came again, the crumble of something falling from the ceiling, maybe.

Or the scuff of a foot.

Turning her head was almost more than she was capable of. It was like her body wasn't hers to control anymore. But she did, seeing the empty chamber, seeing the dark, coffin-shaped tunnels. The wind tugged at her hair, at her clothes, but past its urgent whimpering she heard the noise again, coming from one of the openings to her right.

Definitely a footstep. She heard the same explosion of chalk beneath the weight of a boot.

Police, she wanted to call out, but there was absolutely no air in her lungs. She breathed in as slowly and as quietly as she dared, listening to another crunch, then another. Whoever it was, they were moving slowly.

And they were moving this way.

Savage studied each of the tunnels in turn, but there was no telling which one the noise was coming from.

Or was there?

She took a deep, unsteady breath.

Then she clicked off the lamp.

Darkness fell instantly and violently, like a hood over her head. The chamber became a void, filled only with phantom sparks as her eyes struggled to process the unfathomable, unbroken dark.

No. Not unbroken.

A soft light pulsed from one of the tunnels, just the faintest of glows that froze like a startled mouse.

And which clicked off almost immediately.

Savage turned her lamp on, and this time when she called out, her voice carried.

"Police! Stay where you are!"

She ran for the tunnel, scuffing her shoe and tripping onto her knee. The lamp struck the stone and for a second the light cut out, plunging her once again into that remorseless dark. Then it flickered back on and she pushed herself up, reaching the tunnel in a handful of seconds.

"Hey!" she cried out, her voice bouncing off the walls before being swallowed whole. "Stop!"

She paused for long enough to hear footsteps, fast and hard, and she was about to start running again when she remembered she was defenceless. She scanned the floor, seeing a lump of dull metal. A hammer. It would have to do. Picking it up, she gave chase. The torch bounced in her grip, its movement bringing the walls to life, making the tunnel feel like a living thing that flexed and twisted around her. The light peeled away the darkness ahead, one foot at a time, no sign of anyone up there, no sign of anything at all.

"Police!" Savage shouted again, breathless.

The tunnel peeled apart, a fork in the path. It was the last thing she wanted to do, but she clicked off her lamp again, seeing the faintest of glows in the passage to her left.

She turned it back on, running another dozen yards before the tunnel split for a second time. The footsteps were echoing so much that they seemed like they were all around her, like they might even be coming up from behind.

"Shit," she said. "Shit, shit, shit."

She glanced back to make sure she was still alone, then shut the lamp off.

Nothing. No sign of light from anywhere, and the footsteps had fallen silent too.

Savage turned on the lamp, swallowing down a throat that was as dry as bone. She took a couple of steps into the tunnel on the left, then stopped, well aware of how stupid it would be to get lost down here.

How dangerous it would be.

And that thought made her spin around, the panic like a steel vest as she made her way back to the junction she'd just passed. She'd turned left here, hadn't she? It looked different from this angle, as if a giant had rearranged it. The tunnel on her right looked too narrow, the ceiling too low. Had she really come down that way?

"Kett?" she called out, her voice wavering. "Porter? Aaron?"

Nothing, just the keening song of the wind as it mourned her.

"Come on," she told herself. "Think."

It had to have been the right-hand passage, she was sure of it. She set off, head ducked, gripping the hammer so hard her fingers ached. It was taking too long, wasn't it? It hadn't been this far before. She stopped, looking back, wondering how she could have taken a wrong turn when she'd only been down here for twenty minutes. Her blood roared in her ears, the fear so big, so all-consuming, that she almost lost herself to it.

"Kett?" she called out again, her voice unbearably weak.

She kept going because she didn't know what else to do, one hand trailing the soft chalk wall, the other holding up the lamp. She hadn't been lying. There were hundreds and hundreds of miles of tunnels beneath the city, and some of them hadn't been explored for decades, maybe even centuries. You could get lost down here.

You could get lost down here forever.

She pictured it now, the lamp slowly dying, the dark creeping in, the cold settling inside her bones.

And she thought of Aaron, she thought of his smile, his goofy laugh.

She wondered if he'd remember to feed the dog.

"No," she said, and she wasn't sure if she was answering her question or refusing to give in. "No, no, no."

She pushed on, the tunnel snaking to the left, a curve she couldn't remember. She kept moving, step by step, until the walls peeled away and she found herself back in the circular chamber. She leaned against the chalk, closed her eyes for a moment, almost crying with the relief of it until she acknowledged the next problem.

She had no idea which tunnel to take to get back to the others.

You idiot, Kate, she said, walking to the middle of the room. *You absolute bloody idiot.*

It was the first rule of exploration, wasn't it? Hansel and Gretel had known it with their pocketful of stones. Theseus had known it when he entered the labyrinth with his ball of twine.

Always leave a trail.

"Kett?" she shouted. "Can you hear me? I'm lost."

No answer.

She dropped the hammer and pulled her whistle free. Three short, sharp blasts.

"Hello?"

Still nothing, other than a sudden roar of fury from deep inside one of the tunnels—a noise so loud and so relentless that it made her want to scream.

It's an angle grinder, she realised after a moment, the flood of relief almost euphoric. *That's all. They're coming to get you.*

She ducked down onto her haunches, her head in her hands. And despite everything, she couldn't help but laugh.

CHAPTER TEN

Kett twisted the angle grinder, wincing against the stream of sparks that blistered past his arm. The gate trembled and groaned, but the metal strut stubbornly refused to give in. He stood back, switching off the motor but feeling the vibration of it in every single cell of his body.

"Bloody thing," he said. "Won't budge."

"Want me to get one of the workmen down here, sir?" Porter asked. "They'll know what they're doing."

"*I* know what I'm doing, Pete," said Kett. "It's not rocket science."

Porter looked at the mangled midsection of the gate, pulling a face.

"I'll go get someone," he said.

He disappeared, leaving Kett alone in the chamber—Hay and her team had left as soon as the sparks had started flying. He'd managed to get almost all the way through the middle strut of the door, but the grinder's blade was seriously blunted and it didn't seem to want to go any further. He leaned through the gap, holding his breath and trying to hear anything past the ringing in his ears.

"Kate?" he called out. He hadn't heard from Savage in nearly half an hour and he was starting to worry. "Kate? You hear me?"

"Where is she?" came Duke's voice as the big PC traipsed down the stairs. He walked around the column, his face creasing into a giant frown when he saw the opening in the door. "She went in *there*?"

"She was the only one who would fit," said Kett.

Duke peered into the dark.

"She okay?"

"I hope so," said Kett.

"Kate?" Duke bellowed, louder than the angle grinder.

"Can't get through the door," said Kett. "Bloody thing won't budge."

Duke stood tall, lifted an enormous boot and drove it into the middle of the door. The strut cleaved free with a squeal, clanging to the floor.

"Wow," said Kett.

The PC pulled out his torch and ducked through the gap.

"Kate?" he roared as he lumbered into the gloom.

Kett leaned the angle grinder against the wall, scratching his head as he studied the broken door. He heard more footsteps and Porter reappeared.

"They've all buggered off," he was saying. "Can't see... Oh, you got it open?"

"I didn't," said Kett. "Duke did."

"Duke?" said Porter, clicking on his torch. Duke was almost at the end of the tunnel, a hulking shadow. "Didn't know he was smart enough to operate machinery."

"He used his boot," said Kett.

"His *boot*?" said Porter, and Kett could hear the pout in his voice. "I mean, *I* could have done that. Anyone could have done that. I just didn't think... I just didn't want to, you know, uh..."

"I know, Pete," said Kett. "Come on."

But stepping into that tunnel was easier said than done. The place was like something from a nightmare. All Kett could think about was the labyrinth where Hollenbeck had taken him, a warren of passageways and rooms filled with danger, promising nothing but violence and death. He closed his eyes and pulled in three deep breaths to centre himself, then he set off, Porter right behind him, both of them ducking beneath the low ceiling. Up ahead Duke was almost bent double, his broad shoulders scraping the sides of the passageway.

"Kate?" the PC shouted, the tunnel swallowing his voice, and then swallowing him as he took a left-hand turn.

"Aaron?" Savage's reply drifted back

Kett turned the corner and picked up speed, the tunnel widening into a circular chamber with a domed ceiling. Savage was there, already wrapped in Duke's big arms. Kett couldn't tell if she was laughing or crying—or a bit of both—but when she finally let go of him she had to scrub her eyes with her dirty fists. She looked exhausted, as if she'd been down here for years, not minutes, and she was absolutely caked in chalk dust. Kett had the uncanny notion they'd stumbled across her ghost.

"Good to see you, sirs," she said. "Managed to mess that one up. Got lost."

"Easily done," said Kett, counting the tunnels that led out from the chamber. He looked back, and even from here he couldn't be sure which passageway they'd entered through. He pulled off his overcoat and dumped it in the opening behind Porter in order to mark it, the freezing air wrapping him in an unwelcome hug. "What happened?"

"I saw someone, sir," said Savage.

"Who?" asked Kett.

"No idea. I didn't *see* them, as such. But I heard footsteps. They had a torch. Ran off when I called out. I followed them down that tunnel there." She nodded to a slab of darkness on the right. "Took a left at a junction, then... then bottled it. Sorry, sir."

"Don't be," said Kett. "You did the right thing. I had no idea there were tunnels like this around here."

"Hundreds of them," said Savage. "Some go back to the stone age. They mined chalk, obviously, and flint. They collapse sometimes. You remember the bus?"

"Bus?"

"Yeah, sir, the double decker that disappeared into the street. Famous, back in the 80s. That was a chalk mine."

"Vaguely," said Kett. "We'll need a map. And a search team. Pete, can you call this in to the Super?"

"Sure," said Porter. "But I can't see him sending a team down here, not for some old bones."

"Good point," said Kett, turning back to Savage. "You think the person you heard had anything to do with the cellar we found?"

She shrugged, her teeth chattering.

"Weird coincidence if it isn't," she said. "But that door's been cemented shut for four years, why would they be down here now?"

"Because they know we found it," said Kett.

"But if they know that, they'll know we've already cleared out the bones, right?" she said.

Kett popped his lips, the soft sound of it echoing off the walls.

"You remember which way you went?" he asked.

"Yeah," she said. "But I don't think we should go any

deeper, not without some rope, or at least some markers. It's a maze in here."

"I'll go," he said. "Duke, come with me, just in case whoever it was is still waiting down there."

"I can come," said Porter.

"Okay," said Kett. "But take Kate back first and let Clare know what's going on. And see if you can grab some paint or something so we can mark our way."

"Sir," said Porter, handing Kett his torch.

"I'm fine, sir," said Savage. "Honest. I'm okay."

"Well, if you're going then I'm going too," said Porter.

"Then who's going to get the paint?" said Kett.

"Duke," said Porter.

"I need Duke. He's got the Taser."

Duke patted the weapon on his hip with a look of profound self-importance. Porter grumbled something as he stomped away, treading on Kett's crumpled overcoat. The dark gobbled him up almost instantly.

"Okay," said Kett, steeling himself. He could taste the chalk dust on his tongue and he spat it out, turning to the passageway that Savage had pointed to. "That one?"

"Yes, sir," said Savage.

He made his way through the opening of the tunnel, holding the heavy Maglite like a lance. The beam was strong enough to light the walls all the way up to a distant junction and he made his way towards it as fast as the rough ground would let him.

"Left here, sir," said Savage, and he followed her instructions.

This new stretch of tunnel was even narrower, and after a dozen steps it split in two again.

"This is where I gave up," said Savage. "Whoever it was,

they knew I was here. They kept their light off. Couldn't see which way they went."

"Eenie meanie," said Kett. "Left or right?"

"Breeze coming from the tunnel on the right," said Duke, aiming his torch down it. "You feel that?"

Kett did. It was fresh air, no doubt about it. He glanced at the tunnel on the left, but it sat there like a dead man's lungs. He pushed into the right-hand passage. Almost immediately the floor began to rise, and after a minute or so it was so steep he was struggling not to slip as he climbed.

"Any idea where we are?" he asked. "Which direction this is?"

"No," Savage called back. "Too many twists and turns. Has to be north, though, because south is downhill. At a guess, I'd say we're beneath Bracondale somewhere."

The tunnel curved to the left, still rising. Kett braced his hands on the wall as he went, using the bone-like lumps of chalk to haul himself up the slope until it finally began to level out. His heart was thrashing, his breaths so heavy that he didn't hear Savage until she jabbed him hard on the shoulder.

"Huh?" he said, turning back to see her. Duke peered over her shoulder.

"I said hush a second, sir," she replied, holding her hand up. "Listen."

He turned back, aiming the torch down a long, straight section of tunnel ahead. For a moment he couldn't hear anything, then a soft voice lifted itself from the silence—not shouting, barely even speech.

It almost sounded like a song.

"What the hell?" said Duke. "Who's that?"

There was only one way to find out. Kett pressed on,

following the meandering tunnel to the left, then to the right. He passed three openings, one of which was secured by a heavy iron gate, but the voice was coming from up ahead—almost perfectly in tune with the groaning wind. The tunnel rose ever upwards, the air laced with the unmistakable aroma of piss and shit—a stench that grew worse with every step until Kett found himself standing outside yet another passageway that branched off from the main tunnel.

"Urgh," said Duke. "Smells like a toilet in here."

Kett poked his head through the opening, following the torchlight to see that the PC was bang on. A small, chalk-walled chamber sat there, maybe a hundred little mounds of shit growing from the floor like baby stalagmites.

"Oh God," said Kett, pulling his head free like he'd seen a snake and covering his mouth with his free hand. "Nope."

Whoever was singing the song didn't seem to have heard them coming, the man's voice louder now, reverberating down the tunnel. Kett glanced at Duke and the PC popped the stud on his holster, his hand resting on the Taser.

They moved slowly down the tunnel, rounding a final bend to see a small, low room ahead. Quiet rays of sunlight broke through the far wall, revealing a mattress on the floor almost lost beneath a bundle of quilts and blankets. Somebody was lying in it, a bare shoulder and a mat of dark hair, so still that she had to be unconscious.

Or worse.

Kett angled himself around the door, catching sight of the singer. It was a man in his forties, tangled dreads of greying hair hanging down almost to his waist and a scraggy, unkempt beard. He was wearing filthy jeans and a black puffer jacket, his feet bare. He was busying himself by a cluttered table, something clenched in his hand. The man angled his body and Kett caught sight of the knife gripped in his fingers, its crimson blade long and sharp.

Savage elbowed Kett, nodding to the woman in the bed and tapping her own elbow. It wasn't quite bright enough to see what she was trying to draw his attention to, but was that a rope tied around the woman's arm? Was she tied up?

The man belted out another few lines, his hands moving fast. There was something wet on the table in front of him, and now that the stench of excrement had left Kett's nose, he thought he smelled something else.

Blood.

He glanced at Duke again to see that the big PC had removed the Taser. He stood to one side to let him pass, then held up his hand, counting down with his fingers.

5, 4, 3, 2…

Duke charged into the room, the Taser up.

"Armed police!" he roared.

The man loosed a strangled scream, his body jolting so hard that the knife shot out of his hand and hit the low ceiling, clattering to the floor. He spun around, his face knotted into an expression of apoplectic rage, something clenched in his other fist.

"Drop it!" yelled Duke. "Now!"

The man screamed again, a perfect falsetto, then lobbed whatever he was holding at Duke. It hit the PC in the face and he lurched back, the Taser discharging but going well wide. The man was reaching for something else on the table and Kett rushed forward.

"Leave it!" he yelled.

The man's arm whipped out again and something wet struck Kett on the ear. He ducked low and charged, thumping into the guy hard enough to shunt him into the table. Savage was there in an instant, pushing her foot into the back of the man's knee and dropping him. He screamed again, and this time he was answered by another shriek, just as loud. The woman was clambering out of the mountain of blankets, the rope dangling from her arms.

"What are you doing?" she shouted. "Leave him alone!"

"We're police," said Kett, struggling to hold the man as he fought to get back to his feet. Savage snapped a pair of cuffs on one wrist, but his other arm was flailing wildly, slapping Kett repeatedly but weakly about the head. Kett grabbed it and held it tight. "Just stay still."

"No!" the man said, his voice breaking. "No, I won't! Get out of my house, get out!"

"Hang on," said Kett. The man's arm was bone thin in his hand, so fragile he was worried he might accidentally break it. "Just hang on a minute. Everyone calm down."

The man did as he was told, sinking into a squat and panting hard. Savage was still trying to get the other cuff on but Kett shook his head and they both stood back. The woman hovered by the bed, her fingers in her mouth, her body making small, erratic movements like a broken clockwork toy. She was wearing a nightie that might once have been white but which was now various shades of brown. Kett looked at the rope around her upper arm again, realising that it was actually a section of rubber tubing. Even though it was dark in here, he could make out the ugly, infected track marks on her arms.

Only Duke was still moving. He'd holstered the discharged Taser and was scrubbing at his face like a man possessed.

"What is it?" he said. "What the fuck is it? Acid? Is it acid? Get it off!"

"It's squirrel," said the man, craning his neck back. "Sorry."

"*Squirrel?*" squeaked Duke.

"Fuck you expect to happen?" the man said. "Jumping out at me like that? Give a bloke a heart attack."

Kett wiped his palm over his ear to feel the sticky wetness there, then he scanned the floor until he found the lumps of meat that had been thrown at them.

"Squirrel?" he asked.

"Yeah, for our supper. Nothing illegal about it, I can assure you. I catch 'em myself. Cook 'em outside. It's all good and proper. It ain't illegal."

"It's not," said Kett, catching sight of the addict's toolbox beside the bed, foil-wrapped heroin and a couple of needles that looked like they'd fallen off a production line sometime during the Second World War. "But that is."

The man and the woman exchanged a glance, and she seemed to remember the tube on her arm. She slipped it off, throwing it onto the bed and shrugging dramatically.

"Medicinal?" she said, more question than statement.

"Right," said Kett. He glanced at the man. "You gonna throw any more rodent guts at us?"

He shook his head, and Kett offered him a hand, hauling him up. He stood there like a scarecrow, skinny and bent, sniffing hard every few seconds. The handcuffs dangled from one wrist and Savage unlocked them, putting them back in her pocket.

"What are your names?" asked Kett.

"Lord Montague," said the man. "That's me wife, Lady Montague."

Kett waited for the man to add more information, but he just stood there, wide-eyed, waiting for the next question.

"Okay, Lord Montague," said Kett. "You live in here?"

Montague smiled, revealing more gums than teeth.

"Not bad, is it? Got a bed, got an *en suite* n'all, just

down the way there. Got to watch your feet, though. Bit of a minefield."

"Where are we?" asked Savage.

"Top of King Street," he replied. "By the old wall. Found a way in last year and we in't left since, have we?"

The woman shook her head so hard her hair fell in front of her face. It seemed to throw her off balance because she collapsed onto the bed, groaning.

"Nobody else knows about it," Montague went on. "People been scragging their way over these hills for months and ain't nobody knows we're down here. Can't see it, you know? From outside. Secret."

"You on your own in here?" asked Kett.

"Just us and the squirrels," Montague said. "But they don't say much."

He laughed, revealing those wet, pink gums again.

"You ever go deeper into the tunnels?" said Kett. "Past your *en suite*?"

The man's smile vanished like a startled mouse.

"Did once," he said. "But no good down there. Too deep, too dark, and too many choices."

"You weren't down there today?" asked Savage. "Half an hour ago?"

"No," said Montague. "We don't go down there."

The look of fear on his face would have been hard to fake, Kett thought. He seemed genuinely terrified.

"You ever hear anyone in there?" asked Kett. "Voices, footsteps?"

Lord Montague took his time before nodding.

"Rats," he said. "But not the furry ones. We call 'em that cause they're always scurrying around in the shit."

"People?" asked Kett, and the man nodded.

"Won't ever let you see 'em. But we hear them talking

sometimes, echoes. I don't mess with them, they don't mess with me. You're better off not messing with 'em either, you hear?"

"But you've never seen them?"

"They know the tunnels," he said. "They know where to hide. Folk say they lure you in with their lights if you're not careful. Lure you so deep you never find your way out."

"Then they eat you," said Lady Montague from the bed. The man nodded.

"Uh-huh," said Kett. "You know what these people are up to?"

"Not drugs," he said, a little too defensively.

"Not drugs. Right. They smuggle drugs in the tunnels? That would make sense, much safer than carrying them above ground."

"Wouldn't know anything about that," Montague said, scratching the ugly welts on his own arm. "Like I said, I don't mess with them, they don't mess with us. Got ways of trapping you down here, don't they?"

"They do," said Lady Montague.

"Rig the place up well and true, one big bang and you's buried forever, in't that right?"

"It is."

"Bombs?" asked Kett.

"Kinda," the man said, shrugging his skeletal shoulders. "Anarchist's Cookbook, innit? I've seen gas canisters set up ready to blow. You go after these people and they pop the tunnel and run." He mimicked an explosion with his hands. "Even if you don't die you'll never find them again."

"You ever use them?"

"Bombs? Fuck no, would blow me own balls halfway to kingdom come. But I got other means, my friend. Come after me and you'll look like one of these guys." He gestured to the squirrels. "That's a promise, right love?"

"It's a promise," echoed the woman, sounding like a parrot.

Kett scanned the room, seeing nothing else.

"You mind if we use your front door?" he said.

"Be my guest," said Montague, nodding to the far wall. "Right there, but there's a big drop, so watch you don't fuck over the edge."

He hesitated, twiddling his fingers.

"You, uh, going to arrest us?"

"No," Kett told him. "But you've got about half an hour before this place is crawling with coppers, so if I were you, I'd scarper."

"Scarper I shall!" the man said with a powerful salute that sounded more like he'd slapped himself in the face.

Kett made his way carefully through the detritus, the uneven floor doing its best to trip him. The far wall was pocked with holes, the crumbling chalk held up by twisted sinews of ivy. It took him a moment to find a gap big enough to squeeze into, pushing through a vicious curtain of brambles into the cold, wet day.

He knew where he was instantly, a valley of tall trees and thick vegetation that led past two guard towers that were all that was left of the city's medieval wall. A trail of steep wooden steps led down towards the river, the entertainment complex visible through the leafless canopies. The entrance to the cave was halfway up an almost vertical slope and the wet ground was treacherous. Kett's foot gave way and he snatched at the ivy to root himself in place. It worked for a handful of seconds before the leaves tore free and he fell, sliding on his backside all the way to the path below.

"Ow," he muttered.

"You okay, sir?" Savage called down.

He looked back to see her head poking from the slope, as if it had been severed and hung there. The entrance to the chamber was pretty much invisible, the cliff face stretching up another twenty feet to the street overhead. He stood, rubbing his aching arse.

"I'll live," he said. "Watch out, though, it's lethal."

Savage eased herself out and skipped lightly down the slope, managing to keep her feet until Kett caught her at the bottom. They both looked up to see Duke angling himself through the gap. He clung to the ivy like King Kong at the top of the Empire State Building.

"This isn't going to be pretty," Kett said.

"You kind of just have to let go and roll with it," Savage called up.

"I'm not..." Duke grunted. "I can't... Shit!"

His foot slipped, and he started running, so hard that Kett thought he could feel the ground tremble. By some miracle of physics and biology he managed to stay upright until he met the wooden path, where one foot gave way beneath him and he actually did the splits, the sound of tearing cloth filling the woods.

At least, Kett *hoped* it was only the PC's trousers that had split.

"I'm okay!" Duke wheezed, waving Savage away when she tried to help him. He struggled up in slow motion and stood there for a moment, his hands on his knees. There was indeed a tear down the seam of his trousers, his bright yellow underpants peeking through the gap as if startled by the sight of daylight. His entire face was streaked with the remains of an unfortunate squirrel, a lump of something dark and bloody stuck to his forehead. He looked like a Halloween decoration.

"You've got a bit of... red on you," Savage said.

Duke wiped his cheek with his sleeve, only making it worse.

"Is it gone?"

"Uh... yeah," she said. She turned to Kett. "What now, sir?"

He sighed, pulling a twig from his hair and throwing it away. He thought about the old bones, the cemented door, the person that Savage may or may not have heard in the tunnels. Even after all this, he still wasn't sure a crime had actually been committed.

"Honestly, Kate," he said. "I have absolutely no idea."

CHAPTER ELEVEN

Kett opened his front door to the smell of toast, and when he walked into the kitchen he found Billie at the counter halfway through a slice that was as thick as a hardback book. The kettle was rumbling gently behind her, a cup already waiting on the counter. Her eyes grew wide when she saw the state of his trousers.

"What on earth happened to you?" she asked, spraying crumbs. "You look like you've been mud wrestling."

"I have," he said, walking over and stealing the second slice of toast from her plate. "Part of our training now."

"Where's your coat? It's freezing out there."

"Left it in a hole," he said. He bit into the toast, butter dribbling down his chin. Billie always put about an inch of the stuff on. It tasted amazing, but it would probably contribute to both of their early deaths. He wiped it off his stubble. "Just came to get changed. Can't stay, sorry."

"It's okay," she said, checking the kitchen clock. "Going to get the girls in a mo, might walk them into town. Moira needs new shoes."

"Got feet like a bloody elephant, that one," said Kett. "Thanks for the toast."

"Never actually offered it," she said. "Might have to call the police."

"You need the car?" he asked.

"No, you can have it. You want tea?"

The kettle was coming to a boil and Billie reached out, snapping the switch before it could turn itself off. It was a strange quirk that she'd picked up after he'd rescued her from the Pig Man, one of two dozen or more obsessive rituals she had to perform in order to curb her anxiety. If she didn't click the kettle off in time, she'd told him, something bad *would* happen. It was inevitable. She'd managed to overcome it for a while last year, but ever since Kett had been taken by Hollenbeck she'd been trapped inside the impossible certainty of it once again.

"It breaks my heart to say it," said Kett, eyeing the cup mournfully, "but I don't have time."

He shrugged his clothes off upstairs and considered taking a shower just to warm up, deciding he'd save himself for a bath later. By the time he'd changed into another suit and walked back downstairs, Billie had made another round of toast. He swiped it from her plate as she was putting the butter back into the fridge, ignoring her cry of fury as he bolted from the house.

"Love you!" he called out, holding the toast in his teeth until he'd climbed into the car. A lump of butter slid free as he was reversing, splatting onto his clean shirt. "Oh, come on," he said, knowing full well he deserved it.

He devoured the toast as he made his way back into the city, trying to get his head around the case. It didn't feel like anything he'd worked on before, and he knew it was because there was no sense of urgency here. Most of the bones were a hundred years old or more, and what few were newer still related to a crime that would have happened—according to Franklin's first estimations, anyway—at least thirty or forty years ago. Assuming the bones hadn't just been pulled out of a graveyard, the chances of finding the person responsible for a decades-old murder was so slim that it didn't seem possible.

And yet here he was, a senior detective in the Norfolk Constabulary, chasing the coldest case he'd ever heard of. He wouldn't give up. He *couldn't*. Because in his entire career he'd only ever given up on one case—when Billie had been taken by the Pig Man, when he'd moved out of London just to get away from the horror of not being able to find her.

The shame of it made him feel sick even now, made him want to scream.

No, he'd never give up on a case again, even this one.

"So what now?" he asked himself, squeezing the wheel as he waited for the traffic to move.

He used his hands-free to call the Superintendent, Clare's voice filling the car like a wet fart.

"Where are you, Kett? I've tossed over the entire station and I can't find you anywhere."

"Right, sir," said Kett, grimacing. "Just had to pop home. Porter and Savage fill you in?"

"They did," said Clare. "Buggering about in some tunnels and eating squirrel dicks. You know, Kett, when I posted you to this arse-end of a case I didn't expect to lose my entire Extreme Crime Task Force to it. You're on your own with this one, is that clear? Leave them out of it."

"Yes, sir," he said. "I was just calling to ask whether anyone had interviewed Kitty Lewington yet. The woman who was protesting at County Hall. From what I can gather, she was the first one down in the cellar along with Geoff Wileman."

Clare didn't answer, and Kett heard him rustling through some papers.

"Sir?" he asked.

"How the toss should I know?" Clare replied eventually. "I'm not your bloody mother, Kett."

The Superintendent hung up and Kett called Porter instead. The signal was atrocious, Porter's voice broken into a thousand pieces.

"Pete?"

"Hello? Sir?"

"Where are you?"

"Back in the tunnel," he said, or at least something close to it. "I got paint."

"Do you know if anyone interviewed Kitty Lewington?" Kett said. "Properly?"

"Who's got proper tea?" said Porter.

"*Properly,*" said Kett, then he hung up with a grunt of frustration. He pulled over to the side of the road and grabbed his phone, texting the DI.

Text me Kitty Lewington's address, will you? Cheers.

There was no point heading off again until he got an answer, so he stared through the rain-soaked windscreen while he waited, seeing a parade of miserable people crushed beneath the oppressive grey sky. It was almost like being on the beat again, and as he sat there he spotted two women talking on their phones as they drove past, a truck with no rear registration plate, and two men hunkered by a brick wall passing something between them that was almost certainly illegal. He half wondered whether to make himself useful, but it was so cold outside, and wet, and after three minutes his phone vibrated with Porter's reply—an address to the east of the city.

He joined the traffic again, grinding his way through the gridlocked centre of Norwich, driving down the hill close to where he and Savage and Duke had emerged from the tunnel, then past the Riverside Entertainment complex and the train station. He wondered how many tunnels lay beneath him right now, how deep that honeycomb of passageways and chambers went. It was a wonder that the hollow-boned city hadn't vanished inside itself, swallowed whole.

Ten minutes later he parked the car halfway up a steep hill in Thorpe, double-checking the address on his phone with the impressive Georgian manor house that peeked over the top of a flint and brick wall. There were trees everywhere, enormous ones that must have stood in this spot for centuries, and through the gaps in their branches he could see scraps of the city laid out like a patchwork below, speckled with lights. For a place famous for having no hills, Norwich was putting on a pretty good show.

He got out, slamming his door and jogging through the drizzle to the electric gate that secured the house. He pushed the buzzer, expecting to have to announce himself, but almost immediately he heard the click of the lock as it disengaged. He made his way down a gravel path, past a garden that was immaculately tended, and by the time he'd reached the enormous front door it was already swinging open.

A woman in her seventies stood in the bright hallway, her white hair pulled back into such a severe ponytail it looked like she'd had a facelift. Her clothes were simple but obviously expensive, the way the Queen's always were. And she did look a bit like the Queen, he thought. She was small—not much taller than Alice—but there was a certain authority in the way she was standing. She looked up at Kett through a pair of silver glasses, her eyes fierce but not unfriendly.

"Good afternoon, Detective," she said, breaking into a smile. "I wondered when you'd show up. Come in, come in. Bedlam here, I'm afraid."

She stood to one side, revealing a tiled hallway that was wide enough to flank an enormous staircase on both sides. The ceiling was so high that Kett doubted he could have touched it even if he was standing on Duke's shoulders. He could hear children shouting from deeper inside the house, then a man's roar, then laughter.

"Is this a bad time?" Kett asked as Kitty ushered him inside, pushing the heavy door closed.

"Never," she said. "There's never a bad time for justice, young man, and justice is what we seek. Through here. Can I get you a tea? A coffee? Something stronger?"

"Tea would be great," he said. "Just milk, thank you."

"Don't tell me, I'll forget," she said. "Tell Muddle."

Kett had no idea what she was talking about until she led him through a tall archway into the biggest kitchen he'd ever seen. He could have fitted the entire footprint of his own house in it with room to spare. To the right was a maze of farmhouse-style counters, including two marble-topped islands and a twelve-foot dining table. To the left was a square of sofas, each of which would have comfortably sat six people.

There was currently nobody at all on the sofas, but in the gap between two of them was a man who looked like he was getting beaten to within an inch of his life. Two children sat on his back, pounding him with cushions. Neither of them even glanced at Kett as he walked through the door.

A woman in her fifties was doing her best to take the weapons away from the kids, but she wasn't having much luck—which was surprising, given that she was built like a brick outhouse.

"Chaos," said Kitty as she walked towards the bigger of the two islands, the word ringing from her mouth like she was on stage. "The best thing in the world, isn't it? If it's the right kind of chaos, that is. Muddle?"

The large woman left the man and the kids, walking over with the gait of a wrestler. She really was quite impressive, reminding him of Miss Trunchbull from the Roald Dahl book—in her tight-lipped face as much as her shot-putter's build. He wondered if this was what Duke would look like if he ever shaved his beard.

"Tea, my dear," said Kitty. "Detective Kett here will have milk with his, and sugar?"

"Just milk," said Kett.

"Told you I'd forget. I'll take an Earl Grey, Muddle. Thank you."

The maid picked up the kettle like she was going to hurl it through the window, filling it at the sink.

"Mrs Lewington?" Kett asked, and Kitty nodded. "How do you know my name, if you don't mind me asking?"

"Same way you knew mine, I suppose," she said with that same smile. "I do my research. And I've seen you on the news, of course. I thought you'd retired after that awful kidnapping thing."

Kett didn't bother to ask whose kidnapping she was referring to. He turned his attention to the man on the floor, who had managed to lift his head beneath the barrage of attacks.

"Did I hear you say you were police?" he whined. "I need help!"

The kids—one girl around Evie's age and a boy who was maybe a couple of years older—proceeded to pound the man with the cushions. They were only little but they weren't holding back, and the cushions weren't exactly small. The girl walloped the man on the back of his skull hard enough to make him headbutt the floor, and when he looked up again, his smile had gone.

"Ow," he said. "That's enough, Clara. You don't actually want to injure me."

"I do!" the girl yelled gleefully.

She thumped him another couple of times for good measure, then Kitty cleared her throat and glared at her.

"Your father said that's enough," she boomed in that imposing voice. "And this is indeed a policeman."

"I am," Kett told the children when Kitty paused expectantly.

"So if I were you, I would *run*."

Clara screamed and bolted out of a door in the side of the room, trailing the cushion behind her. The boy held on for a moment longer, looking at Kett with dark, curious eyes. Then the man started to push himself up and the boy rolled away, chasing after his sister with a joyful giggle.

"You'll never catch us!"

"This is Ronald," said Kitty. "My son. I'd wager you just saved his life."

The man finished getting to his feet and limped over with dramatic effect, one hand on the small of his back, the other clamped to a bird's nest of sandy hair. He was older than Kett had first assumed, closer to fifty, dressed in jeans and a black polo shirt. He was thin, but the tight muscles and prominent veins in his arms made it clear he was used to hard work. He took the hand from his head and offered it to Kett, who shook it. There was something strangely familiar about him, but Kett couldn't place it.

"Thanks," he said. "They don't know their own strength sometimes."

"Tell me about it," said Kett. "I've got three and I'm scared to death of them."

"Boys?" he asked.

"All girls," said Kett.

"Yikes. They're the worst. Clara's the ringleader for sure, Nathan will do whatever she says, although he'll pretend it was his idea. It's Ron, by the way. Only Mum calls me Ronald."

"Because it's your name," Kitty said, rolling her eyes. "I didn't write Ron on your bloody birth certificate, did I?"

"Ron," repeated Ron. "Listen, while you're here, and since you're a dad, I'm part of a group of fathers—most of us older, who started a bit later in life, no offence."

"None taken," said Kett, who found himself a little offended.

"We meet up every now and again to talk about... well, about how hard it can be sometimes. There's six of us. We're trying to grow our numbers. Just thought, you know, if you ever wanted to go out, grab a pint, have a moan about how awful our children are."

"Uh, no thanks," said Kett. "Sorry."

"Enough with your bloody group, Ronald," said Kitty. "In my day, men just got on with being men. They didn't feel the need to whine about it."

Ron's face fell. Kitty gestured to the dining table.

"Seat, Detective? Or you can take a sofa, if you like."

"Table's fine," he said. "Again, I'm sorry to interrupt."

"You're lucky you caught us," said Kitty. "We're just back from the city. There's a soft play place in the Castle

Mall, you know it? Absolute hell, I can't think of anywhere worse. But the kids like it. We spent a good few hours there today, didn't we, Ronald?"

"Hmm?" Ron replied. He was looking at the door the kids had escaped through with an expression of grave concern. Kett could hear the brother and sister screaming at each other. If he closed his eyes, he could have been back at home. "Right," the man said after a moment, returning his attention to the room. "Soft play. Yes. Hell. Sorry."

"No school?" Kett asked.

"They're homeschooled," said Ron. "By me and their grandmother."

"I teach history, of course," Kitty said.

"It was a Fun Day, good for the mental health. Theirs, not mine. Six hours in a soft play and bowling alley is enough to send a grown man to the madhouse."

"I don't think I could do the homeschooling thing," Kett said. The thought was enough to make him break out in a cold sweat.

He pulled out a heavy wooden chair and took a seat. The room really was impressive, the entire back half of it glazed like an orangery, revealing an impressive garden and those same views of the city. The walls were decorated with antiques—oars, vases, original oil paintings of sour-faced people, and maps, so many maps. He studied the biggest of them, an eight-foot-wide tapestry that showed the tangled web of Norwich streets as they had looked during medieval times.

"Nice, isn't it?" said Kitty, taking the seat opposite his. "Used to hang in the Castle Museum. My husband acquired it a decade or so ago."

"Your husband?" asked Kett, and she sighed.

"God rest him," she said. "Keith. He died in 2016."

"I'm sorry to hear that, Mrs Lewington."

She nodded her thanks, still lost in the tapestry.

"Had a fondness for cigars and single malt," said Ron, perching on the end of the table. "Amongst other things. All considered, he did well to make it to seventy-two."

"He liked his antiques, then?" asked Kett.

"Only knickknacks, really," said Kitty. "He liked history. It's how we met, through the Archaeological Society. He was the chair, I was the secretary. Those were some interesting meetings, if you catch my drift."

She wiggled her eyebrows.

"Mum," scolded Ron, pulling a face.

"You'd do well not to read the minutes, it's like Fifty Shades," she went on, and she put her hand to her mouth as if to catch the laugh that escaped. "Sorry. Ron would like to think his father and I didn't have a physical relationship, even though he's direct proof that we did."

Ron looked deeply uncomfortable, his pale face growing paler still.

"I really am sorry about her, Detective," he said. "That's him, by the way."

He was pointing to a large oil painting above the fireplace, a stout, serious man dressed in what looked like an old-fashioned Admiral's uniform. The painting could have been two hundred years old, and Kett was about to say as much when he noticed that the man was clasping a mobile phone in his right hand, one of the indestructible Nokia ones. His feathered boots also had a Nike logo emblazoned on them.

"He loved a good joke," said Kitty, looking longingly at the painting. "That thing was his pride and joy. Ronald painted it, you know?"

"Really?" asked Kett. Ron waved a hand through the air like he was chasing away a fly, blushing.

"Fine art at Oxford," Kitty went on. "Top of his class."

"I really wasn't," said Ron, apparently desperate to change the subject. "Dad was quite ill towards the end. He's in a happier place now, touch wood."

He knocked his knuckles twice on the tabletop.

There was a delicate clinking of porcelain as the maid walked over, a tray in her hands. She set it down gently and proceeded to pour tea from one of two steaming pots. She passed Kett his and he inhaled deeply, feeling positively euphoric. He tipped in a little milk and took a sip, even though he knew it would be far too hot.

"Thanks," he said, wincing. "Muddle?"

"Yes, Muddle," said Kitty. "It's an old nickname, we shouldn't use it, really. Muddle's been with us for thirty years, near enough, and when she started she always used to get in such a muddle, especially with the crockery."

Kett wasn't surprised, the maid had hands like shovels. Kitty was laughing again, this one edged with uncertainty.

"Sorry, Margaret, you know we'd use your real name if you asked us to."

"Quite like it," Muddle said with a shrug. "Been called worse things in my time, mostly by my own kids."

"Haven't we all," said Kitty, shooting Ron a mean side-eye. "Right, I'm sure we have more important things to discuss. Am I correct? Namely, why the council are doing their best to destroy this city's irreplaceable heritage. I'm assuming that's why you're here, Detective? You have finally decided to listen to us?"

"Not exactly," said Kett. "City planning isn't really my field. I'm more interested in what you found yesterday morning. The bones."

Kitty blew out a breath and seemed to deflate, suddenly a decade older.

"Ah, yes," she said. "Of course."

"All quite horrific," said Ron. "She was very upset when she came home last night."

"I'm sorry I have to ask," said Kett. "But we're trying to figure out where they came from, and who put them there. I hear you're the best person to talk to about all things historical."

This, at least, seemed to cheer her up a little.

"It's nice to be recognised. I'm chair of the Norwich and Outer Norwich Heritage Society, co-founder of the County Hall Crisis Team, co-director of the Fine City Conservation Trust and a Patron at the Museum Trust, amongst many other accolades. I've devoted my life to this city, pretty much, trying to protect it from the heathens in council and the morons in government, not to mention all the plebs."

"Mum!" said Ron, and she dismissed him with a wave.

"Tell me about the house that once sat on the site," said Kett. "The one the cellar used to belong to."

"Knucklebone Hall," said Kitty, picking up her tea and cradling it against her chest. "We don't know much, but we do know there's been a domicile of some kind or another there for around six hundred years. The hall itself is believed to be Jacobean, originally, then—"

"Hold up," said Kett. "Assume I know absolutely nothing about history."

"You do know what Jacobean means, though?" Kitty said, frowning like a disappointed teacher. Kett shrugged apologetically, and she tutted. "James VI, dear. 1603 to 1625. But we know much of that structure was lost to a fire. The manor was rebuilt several times but never lasted long. Some say it was cursed."

"Who says that?" asked Kett.

"Mum does," said Ron, rolling his eyes. "Nobody else."

"Well, it would make a good story, wouldn't it?" she said, smiling. "Probably just sloppy workmanship. The last incarnation was built around 1850, by a local family, the Filbys. No fires this time, just ruin. Nobody really knows what happened to them, but we think they fell upon hard times. The house was abandoned and over the years it was dismantled by the people of the city. Free stone. All that remains is an arch in the woods behind that monstrosity of a County Hall. Have you seen it?"

"No," said Kett. "So the basement, it was just left there when the house fell into ruin?"

"I expect so," she said. "Much like the nitwits we have today, people back then took the easiest and cheapest route. Better to cover it with a slab than fill it in."

"Did you know it was there?" said Kett. "Isn't that why you were protesting? To preserve the remains of the old house?"

"I was there for the trees, mainly. There's a history there too, isn't there? A living one. But yes, I knew there would be elements of an architectural and archaeological nature on site, things that it is our solemn duty to preserve."

Kett took a sip of his tea, the brew as close to perfect as he'd ever had. From deeper in the house he heard the girl scream something, footsteps pounding overhead.

"Sorry," said Ron.

"Feel free to go check on them," said Kett.

"It's nothing new, they're always fighting but they never really hurt each other."

He rapped his knuckles on the table again for good luck, the pained expression on his face so similar to the one Kett had worn over the years that he smiled.

"In all your years as a historian, have you ever seen anything like the collection you found in the cellar?" he asked Kitty after a moment. "A display of bones like that?"

"Yes," she said, her answer surprising him. "I've seen countless displays of bones and body parts. You only have to take a trip to the Castle Museum to find a full human skeleton on display, and there are countless more scattered across the region. We are a curious species, we like to know the history of our own bodies."

"But you don't think it's weird, the way they were arranged?"

She lifted her cup to her mouth but didn't drink, considering the question.

"I didn't say it wasn't weird. But I don't think it's criminal. Houses like that would have had a large cemetery on site, maybe even a crypt. What is criminal, Detective, is what those festering bureaucratic bungholes are doing to the woods. What are you going to do about that, eh?"

"I'm working on it," he said in an attempt to placate her. "I've spoken with Mr Foulger."

"Oh, Christ," she said. "He's the biggest fucker of them all. I wouldn't piss on him if he was on fire."

"Mum!" said Ron, but she waved him away.

"I wouldn't," she said. "I'd rather watch him burn. Wouldn't waste a thimbleful of my own piss, so help me God. He thinks he's lord of the city, that man."

"Foulger *is* lord of the city," said Ron. "Or was, anyway. Literally. Lord Mayor. Now he's the Governor, or so he tells everyone, even though there's no such position on the council. He's connected to everybody, he's a guild member, a freemason, probably an Illuminati. You name it, he's part of it. Dad absolutely hated him too."

"Guild member?" asked Kett.

"They call them guilds but they're not really," said Kitty. "They're not like the old societies, they're more like clubs for rich old wankers who like gambling and whoring."

"Mum!" said Ron, exasperated.

"What? You're saying I'm wrong? They're the kind of men you should be talking to. Digging up protected trees is the least of their crimes. But they can get away with it because they're rich, they're old, and they're men. The way the world has always been."

Kett made a point of looking around the enormous kitchen, then up to the portrait of Kitty's late husband. She followed his eyes and laughed.

"Yes, yes, I know. But we're talking a different league here. My Keith worked bloody hard and got lucky with the housing market, but Foulger's from old money. His family's been lording it over the rest of us for centuries. They pull a lot of strings. Always have."

"You think they're connected to the bones?" asked Kett.

"No," Ron answered, shaking his head. "Mum's putting it on a bit. Foulger and his cronies are not nice people, but they're not serial killers or anything."

Kitty waved him away again, like he was a bad smell.

"Who knows what goes on behind closed doors," she said. "But you only have to look at the city registry to know that Foulger's family owned a lot of land around that way, a couple of the manor houses on Bracondale too. Who knows what went on there? Maybe you can find out. It's about time Foulger finds out he's nothing special."

"We're speaking with him, don't worry," said Kett. "Is there anything else you can think of that might help us?"

Kitty glugged the rest of her tea like a builder, placing the cup delicately back on its saucer.

"You won't find a record of the basement room

anywhere," she said. "Not in any plans. Believe me, I've looked. That suggests to me that whoever built the house wanted to keep it quiet, which in turn suggests that possibly there was some nefarious purpose to the collection. I'm not suggesting murder, but grave digging was highly taboo in Victorian times."

"I'm pretty sure it still is," said Kett.

"Indeed. But I have no doubt it was a secret room, designed to do what secret rooms do best."

"Keep secrets," said Ron.

"That was hardly worth saying, was it?" she scolded him. "I think that was perfectly clear in my dramatic build-up."

He held up his hands like she was coming at him with a loaded teapot.

"Maybe it should have remained secret," she went on.

"I thought you wanted people to find these things," said Kett. "I thought you were worried about them being destroyed. Without the dig, you never would have discovered the room."

"All fair points, Detective," said Kitty. "I would hate to have seen that room destroyed. But that's not to say it needed to be found, either. I believe there are things that should remain buried."

"Why?" asked Kett.

"Like I said," she told him, her face deadly serious. "Some history is cursed."

CHAPTER TWELVE

"WATCH THE BLOODY SUIT, MATE."

Porter stepped back as the PC beside him splashed paint on the tunnel wall, bright red droplets exploding everywhere. It looked much like blood for his liking, especially against the pale chalk, and even more so in the harsh torchlight. But it was all he'd been able to find in the deserted building site overhead.

"Sorry, sir," grumbled PC Niven, wiping paint from her own uniform. "Hard to see what I'm doing."

They were in the fourth passageway that split off from the circular chamber where they'd found Savage, a long, narrow tunnel that had been sloping downwards for the last hundred yards or so and which had split three times. Porter didn't know how deep they were, but he swore he'd felt his ears pop like he was swimming to the bottom of a pool. He could almost feel the vast weight of the world over his head, the pressure of it. The air was stale with a hint of something chemical that had made his tongue go numb, and the panic was a white-hot furnace right in the middle of him.

He'd finally found something he hated more than trees: being underground.

At least he wasn't alone. As well as the constable by his side, who was doing her best to imitate Jackson Pollock on the chalk walls, two more followed close behind, and another six were currently exploring the other tunnels. It felt good to have company.

Yeah, so you can all be buried alive together when the ceiling collapses.

He tried not to think about that, but the fear of it sat heavily over everything else. How many tonnes of earth and stone and concrete were above him right now? How much weight was the crumbling roof of the tunnel holding up? If something gave way, if a prop snapped, if somebody so much as farted too loud, then it would come down like the fist of God and he'd be nothing but a smudge of jelly on the floor.

He looked over his shoulder, gripped by a cold sweat. He couldn't retreat now even if he wanted to, because of the two coppers behind him. The tunnel wasn't wide enough for more than one body at a time.

"There's another junction ahead, sir," said PC Niven, whose first name he had forgotten. "Left or right?"

"Keep going left," he said. "Make sure you mark it clearly."

"Sir," she replied, dipping her brush in the paint and marking an arrow on the left-hand wall of the tunnel, pointing back the way they'd come. Porter felt a droplet hit his cheek, and he scrubbed it off.

"Sorry, sir," she said again, and he tried not to growl at her.

"You two go right," he told the officers behind him. "If you hit a split, come back. Remember, we've painted every left-hand turn, so to get back to the chamber you have to..." He paused, trying to work it out. "You have to take every... Just follow the arrows."

Porter trailed the young PC to the left, relieved that the floor seemed to be rising here. The tunnel curved sharply, growing wider and taller. Porter's borrowed torch picked out a shopping bag on the floor—empty—then a few steps further on he flinched when he saw what looked like a small animal, a cat or something, sitting perfectly still.

"Just clothes, sir," said Niven ahead of him, shining her torch at it. "Looks like black jeans, maybe a jumper."

"Don't touch them," he told her. "You see anything else?"

"Some gas canisters," she said, shining the torch to the side.

There were four 13kg cylinders of Calor Gas there, one on its side. He didn't go near them, because he didn't want to think about what would happen if they decided to explode.

He focussed on the bundle of clothes instead, using the toe of his shoe to push them apart. There were no visible labels, and they were caked in dust, as if they'd been here for decades. He moved on, PC Niven a silhouette against her own torch, the tunnel a kaleidoscope of light and shadow around her, like something from a funhouse. He hated it down here, and the stress of it was making him hungry. He patted his pockets, but he'd eaten the last of the multipack of Boosts, and the jumbo Twix he'd bought was in the car. He'd left it there in case Duke saw him with it and started teasing him.

"It's all your fault, Duke," he muttered. "You bastard."

"What's that, sir?" Niven called back.

"Nothing," he replied. "You see anything?"

"Yeah, there's a door."

Porter hurried to catch up to her, seeing the metal gate that had been set into the rough walls. It looked almost like the doors they had in the cells in holding, solid steel with a small barred window at the top. He aimed his torch past the bars to see more tunnel up ahead, still rising. The PC gave the gate a solid shove but it didn't so much as rattle.

"Pretty solid, sir," she said. "There isn't even a handle or anything."

There wasn't a keyhole either. Porter pushed his face to the bars, angling his head to try to get a look at the other side.

"There's a padlock," he said. "Big one."

He gave the door a push and had just as much luck as the PC.

"Already tried that, sir," she said.

He did it again, just to annoy her.

"We need that angle grinder," he said. "Can you go grab it? And somebody who can use it?"

Niven stared back down the tunnel they'd just walked along. In her wavering torchlight it looked like some kind of intestinal tract.

"On my own, sir?" she asked.

"Just follow the paint," he said. "You left enough of it."

She didn't look happy, but she walked away, trapped in a halo of light until she disappeared around a corner. Porter leaned against the wall, patting his pockets again just in case a chocolate bar had magically appeared. Impatience gnawed at him, the exact same feeling he'd had when he'd been a smoker. Right now he'd have happily killed somebody for a Boost. He'd even eat a Bounty, if that's what was on offer. That's how desperate he was.

He checked his watch, then his phone, then his watch

again. Now that he was on his own, the silence down here was vast. It felt heavier than the rock over his head, and just as able to crush him if it wanted to. He pursed his lips and began to whistle quietly, just to chase it away. The only song he could think of was the Benny Hill theme tune, and he whistled it on repeat for what felt like hours before he heard footsteps again. When he checked his watch, he saw that only twenty minutes had passed.

There was a glow at the end of the tunnel as PC Niven appeared. Behind her was a man, the flash of a yellow fluorescent jacket and a red hard hat. Another constable followed.

"Bloody hell," the man said. "Is it much further? Creepy down here."

"Any luck?" Porter called to them.

"Yeah," said the PC. "Got the grinder."

"Don't call me that," said the man with a feeble attempt at a laugh. "Never used Grindr in my life."

Niven stood to the side to let the man pass. He was a young guy, his face covered with acne scars and a scraggly beard. In his gloved hands he held the same angle grinder they'd used before, and he held it up like a weapon.

"Where do you want it?"

"Where do you think?" Porter replied, gesturing to the gate. "Padlock's on the other side. I think we'll have to cut a chunk out around the lock or take it off the hinges."

"You got a warrant?" the man asked.

"What?" said Porter.

"A warrant. Looks like private property to me. Why would the padlock be on the other side? Think you need a warrant."

Porter glanced at the gate, then back at the man, who was probably right.

"Less thinking," he said. "More grinding."

The man shrugged, using his free hand to pull on a pair of ear defenders.

"I'd get well back if I were you. You'll be deaf otherwise."

Porter's ears were still ringing from the last time, so he moved down the tunnel with the two constables. The other was a guy he knew from the station, PC Wilkes.

"You got any snacks or anything?" he asked them. "Bloody starving."

"Got gum?" said Wilkes, offering a strip of Juicy Fruit. It was better than nothing, so Porter took it with a grumbled thanks and popped it into his mouth. The taste reminded him of being a kid for about fifteen seconds before disappearing completely, leaving him chewing what might as well have been a lump of earwax.

The angle grinder roared, then shrieked as it made contact with the gate, the tunnel bursting into a fireworks show of sparks. Porter checked his watch, then his phone again, even though he didn't know what he was checking it for because there was no signal down here. He thought about Allie and the baby and a wave of what might have been excitement and what might have been terror rolled over him. He used the time to think about names, whispering the ones he liked.

"Warrior Porter," he said quietly, liking the shape of it in his mouth. "Samurai Porter. Killer Porter."

The noise cut out, a section of the gate falling to the ground with a dull crash. Porter walked over as the man was removing his ear defenders.

"Should do it," the guy said. "You want me to try and open it?"

"I'll do it," Porter said. "What's your name, by the way?"

"Jordan," he replied.

Jordan Porter.

Porter pulled a face.

"What?" asked Jordan.

"Nothing."

He bent down and peered through the hole that the man had made. The bolt housing had been cut out completely, and when Porter gave the gate a shove it swung out effortlessly. The hinges didn't so much as squeal.

"Can I go back now, please?" said the man. "Shouldn't even be down here."

"Yeah, thanks," Porter said. "One of these officers will go with you."

Wilkes volunteered, leading Jordan down the tunnel.

"Hey," Porter called after him. "What's your name?"

"PC Wilkes," the man replied.

"I know that. I mean your first name?"

"Gerald," he shouted back.

"Jesus Christ," muttered Porter when they'd gone. "Why would anyone call their kid Gerald? He only looks about thirty years old."

"Sir?" asked PC Niven.

"What's your first name?" he asked her. "Geraldine?"

"Flick," she said.

"*Flick*?" he echoed. "The whole world's gone insane."

She laughed.

"Short for Felicity, sir."

Porter chewed on it.

"Quite like that," he said. "Felicity Porter."

"Oh, uh..." The woman looked horrified. "I'm not planning on marrying you, sir. Sorry."

"It's for my *baby*," he spluttered. "Bloody hell. Come on."

He led the way this time, peeling apart the darkness with his torch. The tunnel kept climbing as it rounded a bend, growing into a wide chamber that had been propped up with wooden struts that looked about as reliable as toothpicks. There was only one exit, and Porter could make out a set of stairs there. He was halfway to them when his phone chirruped to announce a text. Six more had arrived by the time he'd pulled it out of his pocket.

"Must be close to the surface," he said, feeling the immense relief of it. The first text was from Allie, asking him to pick up some more paracetamol on the way home. The rest were from Superintendent Clare, each one angrier than the last, along with four missed calls.

Porter, where are you?

I need you back here on the Hopper case, tell Kett to leave you alone.

Why aren't you answering my calls? You'd better not be in those tunnels.

Stop tossing about when you're on duty!!!

Do you have any idea how painful it is to be CASTRATED???? Because you're about to find out. GET BACK TO HQ NOW!!

"Shit," said Porter.

"You in trouble, sir?"

"Always."

He reached the opening in the wall, leaning through in order to peer up the steps. They were made from wood, and they were riddled with damp and rot. Porter counted twenty of them, and at the top was a wooden door.

"Weird," he said.

As carefully as he could, he started to climb, the stairs creaking and groaning beneath him like they were crying out in pain. Niven followed close behind, her torch casting Porter's enormous shadow ahead.

"Do you want me to go first, sir?" she asked. "Just to test the stairs?"

"What are you saying, *Flick*?" Porter asked, sucking in his gut. "I'm fine. I'm light as a fairy, so—"

The step splintered beneath him and his words became a squeal. He braced his hands on the wall, gritting his teeth, but the stubborn staircase held firm. He took the last few stairs even slower, reaching a short landing. The door was a four-panelled internal one and it, too, had been ravaged by the damp. It looked flimsy enough to kick down, but he turned the handle instead and gave it a gentle shunt with his shoulder. It opened without a sound into more darkness, but a quick sweep with the torch told him he was no longer in the tunnels. Ahead was a small, cement-walled room, the ceiling made up of wooden slats. Piles of dust-covered junk sat against every wall, and more stairs waited for him up ahead.

"Looks like a house," he said to Niven, who was standing so close he could feel her breath against his neck. "Hello? It's the police."

The boards overhead creaked softly, dust raining down. Porter wondered whether he should head back and ask for a warrant, but he didn't even know which part of the city he was in, let alone an address, and the last thing in the world he wanted to do right now was traipse back into those airless tunnels. He entered the dank basement, calling out again.

"Police. If anyone can hear me, please make yourself known."

Nothing, just the rattle of his own breaths. He turned to the PC and nodded to her baton, and she flicked it out.

"Just in case," he said.

He moved to the second set of stairs, these in better nick but only just. There was another door at the top, this one already open, and Porter was relieved to see splashes of pale, grey sunlight through the gap. He pushed it all the way to see a large room. It was almost entirely derelict; the walls black with mould, the ceiling sagging, the floor covered with a dandruff of chalk and plaster. Two of the three windows were boarded up from the outside, the third missing entirely, strips of shredded curtains hanging like peeling skin and shifting nervously in the wind. The smell in here was something else, and Porter put his free hand to his mouth before remembering how filthy his fingers were.

"Why does crime always have to be so grim?" he said.

"Beats me, sir," replied Niven.

Porter took a deep breath, then bellowed.

"Police! Is anybody here?"

There was no reply. He crossed the room carefully, opening the door to find himself in a short, dark hallway. To his left was what had to be the front door, its glazed panel boarded up. To the right was a staircase, and past that two more doors. He hesitated a moment, listening to the currents of air the way Kett always did, trying to figure out if the house was empty or not.

"You think anyone's here?" asked Niven.

"How the bloody hell would I know?" he replied, giving up. "Can you—"

He was cut off by his phone, and he knew who it would be before he'd pulled it out of his pocket.

"Sir," he said when he answered. "Sorry, I—"

"Just so you know, Porter," said Clare, "I've got my shears on standby. I hope you're ready to be de-tossed."

"That's a new one, sir," said Porter, fighting to shake off the mental image. He watched as Niven made her way down the corridor, her torch in one hand and her baton resting on her shoulder. "I'm sorry, I was underground."

"I bloody knew it," said Clare. "This is Kett's case, Porter, and I only bloody gave it to him because I didn't think it would involve any work. I just wanted him back through the door. I wanted him to remember how much he loves the job. We don't need the whole Extreme Crime Task Force on a cold case. I've got three people waiting to be interviewed for the Hopper thing. Who's going to do it, Porter? Me? A *superintendent*? Shall I wipe their arses for them while I'm at it?"

Flick had pushed into the room to the left of the stairs, the door opening with the gentlest of creaks. Porter watched her walk inside, hearing the groan of the floorboards.

"Kett asked me to help search the—" he started.

"Oooh!" said Clare, a long, low moan of fury. "So *he's* your boss now, is he? Well thank you very much for letting me know I've been demoted. I'll go pack up my stuff, cash in my pension, move out to Honolulu and spend the rest of my days drinking coconut margaritas out of a stripper's cleavage."

"What, sir?" said Porter. "Sorry, I'm—"

"Well, you're wrong, Detective," said Clare. "I haven't actually been demoted."

"I never said—"

Clare was in the middle of yelling something else, but Porter pulled the phone away from his ear when he saw PC Niven retreat from the room she'd entered. Her shoes hit a loose board and she staggered back, caught by the wall. When she turned around, the look she gave him almost froze his blood solid.

"Sir?" she said.

Porter walked swiftly over to her, Clare's voice still

ringing in his ear. She was pointing her torch through the open door and the expression on her face was like something from a horror film. He almost couldn't bring himself to move, almost couldn't bring himself to push the door all the way open with his fingertips and step inside. There were more stairs here, dropping into a second basement, and the nausea churned in his gut as he descended them.

"... and that's final," yelled Clare, his voice breaking up. "I won't have any more resources tossed down the drain because of some old bones. Clear?"

"Clear," said Porter, although the word was little more than a breath.

He looked at what waited for him down here, but only for a second before closing his eyes. He clutched the phone to his ear with trembling fingers, took a shaky breath.

"But what about some new ones?"

CHAPTER THIRTEEN

Kett drove down Bracondale at five miles per hour, serenaded by a chorus of horns from the vehicles that followed him. Two or three overtook his Volvo, almost hitting oncoming traffic as they did so, but he ignored them, searching for a break between the tightly packed houses that lined the road.

There, almost lost behind a curtain of sorry-looking, flowerless buddleias. Kett waited for a cyclist to zip past on the pavement, then pulled in, the track so narrow he almost lost his wing mirrors. The trees loomed overhead, cutting out so much of the late afternoon light that the car's satnav screen dimmed into night mode. The headlights picked out a PC standing halfway down the track, her arms waving to him like she was worried he wouldn't see her in the dancing, wind-shifting shadows. He pulled up next to her and wound down the window.

"Niven," he said, looking at the splatters of red on her face and her uniform. "You okay?"

"Yes, sir," she said. Despite the cold, her face was covered with a sheen of sweat, and her eyes were puffy, like she'd been crying. "It's just paint, sir. But..." She swallowed hard. "The house is further up. You can't get close because the road's torn to pieces, but you'll see it around this bend."

"Thanks," said Kett. "You sure you're okay?"

"Yeah," she said, but her head told the truth, moving rapidly from side to side. "Sorry, sir, it's..."

She shrugged, and Kett took pity on her.

"Backup's on the way. Soon as they're here, you head off, get a cup of tea."

He drove the rest of the way along the track, rounding a bend to see that the asphalt had been almost completely broken up, as if somebody had taken a sledgehammer to it. The remains of the road wound up a shallow hill to a house that would have been stunning when it was first built. It was an enormous Regency property with a two-storey bow-fronted bay, topped with a pair of chimneys that made Kett think of a devil's horns. Now, though, it was a shell of its former self, the windows covered with plywood boards and half of the roof caved in. The gardens had done their best to reclaim it, ivy growing over the door like a hand over a mouth.

Kett drove the car as far as he could, then climbed out, navigating the cracked path on foot. Crows chuckled at him from the knotted branches overhead, accusing him of trespassing. There were hundreds of them.

A bad omen, for sure.

Porter hadn't said much when he'd called fifteen minutes ago, so Kett had no idea what to expect. But the way the DI's voice had trembled made it clear nothing good waited for him in the house at the top of the hill.

He was almost at the front door when Porter stepped out of it, his face ashen in the tree-smothered light. He flinched when he saw Kett, putting a hand to his heart.

"Shit, sir," he said. "Scared me."

"Never known you to be jumpy, Pete," said Kett, out of breath from the climb. "What's up?"

"Gonna let you make the call on that one," said Porter. "Don't want to ruin the surprise. You got gloves?"

Kett was about to reply with, "*What do you think?*" but Porter was already holding some out. He took them, fumbling his hands into them like a blind butcher trying to make sausages.

"Bloody things," he said. "Booties?"

"Just don't step in the blood, sir," said Porter.

Kett looked at the door, seeing that somebody had forced it open—not that it would have taken much effort, the wood powdery with rot.

"What led you up here?"

"Following the tunnels, sir," Porter said, clicking on his torch and walking back inside. "One led to a locked gate. We cut through it and found ourselves in the basement of this place."

Kett entered the house, the stench of mildew sitting right at the back of his throat like dirty fingers against his tonsils. The interior of the property was brutally dark, thanks to the boarded windows, and Porter's torch barely made a dent. Kett pulled out his phone and switched on the light, but he may as well not have bothered. The shadows snuffed it out effortlessly. This was a house that had grown used to getting its own way.

"Came up the basement steps," Porter went on as he led Kett past a wide central staircase, the boards creaking beneath his weight. "Flick was—"

"*Flick*?" said Kett.

"Constable Niven, sorry," Porter said. "She was searching the back of the house, and she found..."

He faltered as he reached an open door, hanging back. Kett could hear something inside, the steady beat of water dripping.

"Well, you'll see, sir. There's a second basement back here. Brace yourself. It's bloody."

"Bloody what?" he asked when Porter stopped talking.

"Just bloody, sir," the DI said quietly, offering his torch.

Kett pocketed his useless phone and took it. There was no point in waiting any longer. He took a deep breath of air that wasn't just damp anymore, but *meaty*. He knew that smell all too well, just like he knew that if this was the summer, and not February, he'd be walking into a storm of flies. He took Porter's advice and braced himself for the worst.

Then he walked through the door, down thirteen rickety steps, and realised he wasn't even close.

"Holy shit," he said, feeling the blood leave his head. He put his free hand to the wall, his fingers sinking into a mush of plaster, and stared at the floor. Only when the rush of dizziness had passed did he look up again, did he force himself to see what waited for him in this basement room.

It was a body, that much was instantly clear. But Kett couldn't make sense of what had happened to it. It was in pieces, and most of those pieces had somehow been fixed to the crumbling wall. There had been no attempt to put anything back in the right order, the arms and legs arranged in a crude spiral around a skull that had been so badly mutilated that Kett couldn't even see where the face had been. Only the trunk remained on the ground, sitting in a puddle of blood that seemed to stretch from wall to wall—too much blood, surely, for one person.

"Holy shit," he said again, putting his hand to his mouth. The smell of it had cornered him now, the stench of somebody turned inside out. He had to look away again because, for an awful second, he thought he was going to pass out.

"Yeah," said Porter, quietly, but he didn't follow it with anything.

Kett counted to three, breathing through his mouth. He swung the torch around again, finding that twisted artwork that had once been a living, breathing human being. He stepped robotically towards it, stopping well short of the crimson lake but close enough to see the enormous screws that held those portions of rendered flesh in place.

"Coach screws," he said, his voice thick. "Twenty, thirty centimetres long."

He forced himself to look at the cuts, seeing the ragged sections of torn skin, the splintered bone. Nothing about this had been delicate, or surgical. It had been raw and brutal and quick.

"That's from a chainsaw," he said with a groan. "Right? Has to be."

"Right," said Porter, who had followed him in. "That's what I thought. You can see the grooves in the floor where it cut right through him."

Kett aimed his torch earthwards, finding four or five long scars in the wood, almost hidden by the blood.

"Went straight through the... the victim and into the boards."

"Happened right here," Kett said. "Jesus."

"Recently, too," said Porter. "It's still..." He swallowed noisily. "Still dripping."

That was the sound he'd heard, he realised, the slow *pat-pat* of blood falling from the corpse into the puddle below. It had to have been *really* recent. Just hours ago. Kett checked his watch to see that it was coming up for four.

"Franklin coming?" he asked.

"I've called her, left a message," said Porter.

"Call her again."

Porter retreated, his phone to his ear. Kett turned his attention to the body, to the limbless trunk that sat below the butcher's spiral. A number of long screws jutted out of this, too, reminding him of images of Saint Sebastian riddled with arrows. The killer had tried to fix it to the wall, he realised, but it had been too heavy.

From where he was standing, Kett could only make out the victim's back, but judging by the second skin of thick, black hair, it was pretty obvious it was a man. He'd been savaged so remorselessly that Kett could see the glint of spine, and beyond that something darker, slicker.

"Fuck me," he said, doubling over and belching acid.

"Got her," said Porter. "She's leaving now. She sounded quite excited."

Kett nodded.

"You see any distinguishing features?" he asked.

"Can't see anything," said Porter. "They cut the face off, I think. Or just..." He made a slashing motion with his hands. "You know. We can print him, though. Hands are still there. But..."

He was frowning, and Kett followed the direction of it to the corpse's legs. He saw what Porter was thinking just as the DI said it aloud.

"No feet."

The man's legs ended just above the ankle, more yellow bone peeking through the mangled flesh. Kett swung his torch around the room, peeling open the shadows.

"Can't see them," he said. "Killer took them with him?"

"Why the fuck..." said Porter, swallowing again, "would you do that?"

Kett shook his head. The darkness and the smell was starting to suffocate him, the panic a stew of heat in his stomach. Porter gagged and Kett echoed it.

"Not much more we can do until Franklin gets here," he croaked. "Should we go?"

"Yeah," said Porter. "Definitely, yeah. We should wait outside. In the light."

"In the fresh air," Kett groaned. "Definitely."

"Definitely."

The DI climbed the stairs at some speed and Kett started to follow, hesitating for a moment. He didn't look at the body again, but he rested his gloved hand on the open door, broadcast his silent words into the basement.

I'm sorry this happened to you.

Then he chased Porter out into the day.

"ONLY *YOU,* Robert Kett, you giant poodle's foreskin."

Superintendent Clare stood in the shadow of the house, braying like an angry donkey. Pieces of coconut sprayed out of his mouth, hard enough for one to hit Kett's neck even though he was standing a good six feet away. He resisted the urge to wipe it away, knowing that any movement would only rile the Super even more. Evening had fallen, as if trying to scrub all evidence of the house from the day. Even with the headlights of half a dozen police vehicles blazing, it was impossible to see anything past the front line of trees.

Clare pointed his half-eaten Bounty at the house.

"Only *you*, you racoon's rectum, could turn a simple cold case into *this*!" he spat. "How the toss did you manage that? How the toss could you turn a bunch of old bones into a dismembered corpse with missing feet?"

"To be fair, it wasn't me who killed—"

"I know you didn't bloody do it," Clare roared, waiting for a forensic technician to skip nervously past, heading for the front door. "But what *you* did is worse. What *you* did is bloody find it, so now it's my bloody problem, you god-awful gopher's gonad."

Clare waved the Bounty like a club. Kett glanced at Porter, who was watching the Super's chocolate bar with a hawkish expression, like he meant to swoop down and snatch it.

"Technically, it was Porter who found it, sir," Kett said.

"Yes, because he was working *your* bloody case, Kett, you kangaroo's cockhole, which I told him not to do."

He stuffed the last chunk of chocolate into his foaming mouth, never breaking eye contact with Kett as he chewed furiously. Porter's shoulders slumped as the last of the Bounty disappeared with a gulp.

"I mean, somebody would have found it eventually, sir," Kett said.

Clare closed his eyes and took a deep breath. He looked like he was going to say something else of a zoological nature, but the powerful roar of a car engine cut him off. Everybody turned to see a powder-blue TVR Tuscan struggle past an IRV and the forensics van, its undercarriage almost grating on the broken asphalt. It growled to a halt, Emily Franklin waving to them from the driver's seat. The passenger door opened first and, to Kett's surprise, he saw Savage clamber out. She nodded gravely to him, but there was no denying the smile she was trying to hide.

"About bloody time," said Clare. "Body's inside, Emily. It's horrible."

"Oh goodie," said Franklin as she walked over. "Who's going to take me there?"

"He can," said Clare, pointing the limp, empty Bounty wrapper at Kett. "It's all his bloody fault. Porter, I need a word."

Porter grumbled his way over. Franklin had opened her bag and pulled out a full-body forensic suit, tugging it on over her pink, koala-covered dungarees. Kett moved away from the door to let her pass, waiting for Savage to catch up.

"You okay?" he asked her. "You look... sweaty."

Savage laughed.

"Emily drives like an absolute loon, sir," she said quietly. "I mean, if she wasn't working for us, I'd have had to arrest her. That car is something else. It's brilliant."

She turned her attention to the door and her smile vanished.

"On a scale of one to ten, how bad is it?" she asked.

Kett followed her gaze into the throat of the old house, thinking of the horror that lived there.

"Not sure I can count high enough to answer that, Kate," he said, ushering her inside.

CHAPTER FOURTEEN

They gathered around the dead man like it was his funeral, the atmosphere of the house so oppressive that for a good few minutes nobody spoke. Even Franklin, it seemed, was lost for words—or so Kett thought until she uttered a soft whisper.

"Chuffing Nora."

Kett raised an eyebrow.

"Chuffing Nora?"

"Nora is indeed well and truly chuffed," she said, dropping her bag to the basement floor in one of the few patches that were clear of blood.

The room had been rigged with portable lanterns in the hour or so since Kett had arrived, six of them casting their harsh light on the carnage, revealing every cut, every slice, every piece of sundered flesh in such fine detail it didn't look real. Kett could have convinced himself he was looking at a Halloween display if it hadn't been for the smell. It scoured its way inside his nostrils, sat heavy in his throat and his stomach. It seemed to cling to every inch of him.

"No doubt at all it happened right here," Franklin said,

snapping on a pair of gloves. "That's about eight pints of blood on the ground, give or take. Victim has been completely drained."

She glanced at the floor.

"Cara been in yet?"

Kett nodded. Hay had done a preliminary examination of the room, but there hadn't been much to find. She and her team were elsewhere in the house now, chasing ghosts.

"No bloody prints," said Franklin. "Killer must have taken their shoes off, maybe wore some kind of protective gear."

"He was prepared," said Kett, and Franklin held up a finger.

"We don't know it's a he," she said.

"Sorry," said Kett. "Force of habit. But yeah, killer brought a tool kit. They'd have needed a battery-powered drill to drive those screws into the wall, and whatever they used to cut him up must have been mechanical."

"Chainsaw for sure," said Franklin. "Chewed the skin and the muscle to pieces. I've done experiments on pigs. The tracks a chainsaw leaves in flesh are unmistakable."

"Pigs?" asked Savage.

"Dead ones, obviously," Franklin added.

"Cara said the same," said Kett, pointing to the arcs of blood that had hit the walls, the floor, even the ceiling. "Spatter pattern belongs to a chainsaw."

"They wanted it to be quick," Franklin said. "Time was of the essence. This is a rush job."

"Not that rushed," said Savage. "Whoever did this took the time to arrange the body parts like this. It's a... display. And it's almost identical to the bones we found, isn't it?"

Kett nodded.

"Skull in the middle, limbs arranged around the outside in a kind of spiral," he said. "I was thinking exactly the same. Only difference is that these bones haven't been stripped of flesh."

"Not all of them, anyway," said Franklin. She had waded through the sticky blood, her shoes protected by plastic booties. "But they tried. Look at this leg."

Kett and Savage craned forward.

"Skin's been hacked back, I can see tendon here, and the surface of a shinbone. They've made an attempt to peel everything else away. Bloody hard, though. You ever skinned an animal?"

"No," said Kett.

"Yeah," Savage said at the same time. "Used to hunt rabbits sometimes, when I was younger. Had a mate, Malcolm, taught me how to prepare them and cook them. I ate everything I shot, mind. Taught me the value of what we eat."

"Conscious carnivore," said Franklin, with a nod of approval. "I like it. So you know how hard it is to actually get the meat off the bone of a fresh kill. It takes a lot of time and a lot of patience, and a very, very sharp knife or a big pan of boiling water."

Kett's stomach turned and he belched into his hand.

"So they wanted to display the bones?" he asked. "That's what mattered to them?"

Franklin shrugged, pulling a thermometer from her pocket and inserting it into the trunk that sat against the wall.

"I have no idea what mattered to them," she said. "Because I have no inclination to enter that state of mind. I'm just reporting what I see. The peeling of cutaneous and subcutaneous tissue is a separate injury to the one that killed the victim, and to the dismemberment. It's a subsequent act. They wanted to at least see the bones."

"That's too much of a coincidence to ignore," said Savage. "We find a collection of bones arranged in a specific pattern inside an underground chamber, and the very next day somebody is murdered and nailed to the wall in almost exactly the same way, in another underground room. Just fewer bones, obviously."

"Technically *more* bones," said Franklin. "We found sixty-four in the cellar, and there are almost 200 here, if we accept that the feet are missing."

"And all connected by the same tunnels," said Kett. "Do we know anything about this house?"

"I'll make some enquiries, sir," said Savage. "If you're okay for me to go?"

"Just hold on a few minutes," said Kett. "I need your brain on this."

Savage didn't look too pleased with being asked to stay, but she rooted herself in place, her teeth gritted as she studied the corpse. Franklin had pulled out the thermometer and was studying it.

"Going by this, I'd say death occurred four hours ago. Roughly 2 PM."

"Shit," said Kett. "Seriously?"

"It's harder to tell when the body has been dismantled like this; it loses heat faster. But yes, I'm fairly confident. The blood is still congealing, rigor mortis hasn't set in yet."

"It was still dripping when we got here," said Kett.

"The cold helps," said Franklin. She checked her watch. "Let's say between midday and three, just to be on the safe side."

"Porter must have only just missed him," said Kett. "Sorry, *them*. The killer."

"I'll start checking the street for security cameras," said Savage. "But they might have escaped through the tunnels."

"They didn't," said Kett. "There's a gate. Porter said it was padlocked from *this* side, no way of doing that from the tunnel. They had to have left through the front door."

"Either that or they're still here," said Franklin.

"PCs have searched the house," Kett said, shaking his head. "Nowhere to hide."

Franklin pulled out her phone and took a handful of photographs of the victim's trunk. Then she picked it up beneath the stumps of its missing arms and hefted it back through the puddle of blood.

"Little help?" she said.

"Uh... no," Kett told her. "Sorry."

"Not with this, with the plastic sheet. There's some in my bag."

Savage opened Franklin's holdall and pulled out a sealed plastic bag. Inside it was a roll of sheeting and she flapped it open like a bedsheet before laying in on a clean patch of floor. Franklin lugged the body the rest of the way and laid it on its back.

"Definitely a man, then," said Kett.

"Got ink there," said Franklin, prodding a tattoo on the man's left pectoral. There was so much blood that Kett couldn't work out exactly what it was. Some kind of tribal marking, maybe, the size of a plate.

"A bird, I think," said Savage, tilting her head. "Phoenix, maybe?"

"Ironic," said Franklin. "Given that he won't be rising again."

She moved her hands around the body, squeezing the flesh so hard that bubbles bulged through the various wounds. Kett had to look away again, staring at the ceiling and counting slowly to ten.

"This fucking job," he muttered.

"I don't think anything's missing from inside," said Franklin. "Good muscle tone, not much flab. Hard to put a pin in it but I'd guess twenty to forty. Head's not got a lot of grey on it."

"Hasn't got much of anything on it," said Kett without looking.

"Yes, I saw," said Franklin. "Your killer didn't want him to be identified. I saw three big vertical gashes from the forehead to the chin. But they left the fingers, which is weird."

"Took the feet," said Kett. "That's weirder."

"I'll come back to them," she said. "Your man's had an old-school appendectomy, he's got another scar on his back. Very small. Probably a nephrolithotomy, a kidney stone maybe. I'll know more when I get the bits and bobs over to my table."

"Let us know," said Kett, retreating to the door.

"Leaving so soon?" asked Franklin.

"It's either that or risk some serious crime scene contamination," he told her, belching again. "Sorry."

"Just give me another minute," she said, standing up and returning to the wall. "The feet, have you found them anywhere?"

"No," said Kett. "No trace of them."

Franklin pushed her finger into the bottom of a leg, feeling for something.

"Severed the base of the tibia and fibula, ripped right through them. I can feel splinters. And that, Detectives, is very, very interesting."

"Why?" asked Kett.

She turned back to them, her brow furrowed.

"I've been cataloguing the bones we found in the cellar room. There were sixty-four of them, far short of the 206 we find in a regular adult body. All human, except for the single one I found a section of and still haven't identified. But there was a method to the collection in that there were bones from pretty much every part of the body—from toes all the way up to the skull. But one bone I didn't find anywhere was the talus."

"The ankle bone," said Savage before Kett could say he didn't have a clue what she was talking about.

"Uh-huh," said Franklin. "Otherwise known as the astragalus. I thought it odd at the time that I couldn't find one."

"That's what's missing?" asked Kett. "The talus?"

"It's part of what's missing. But to get to it, you'd need to sever the entire foot."

Kett sipped air, trying to get his head around what the young pathologist was driving at.

"What makes you think that's what the killer was interested in? That particular bone?"

"Because it's significant, isn't it?" asked Savage. "It means something."

"Right," said Franklin. "These bones have history. For centuries—for millennia, really—humans have used these bones to make dice."

"Dice?" said Kett.

"Yes, it's why we call dice *bones*. There are all sorts of games that can be played with them, they're really quite versatile."

"You're saying somebody killed this man, cut his corpse into pieces and arranged him on the wall like some kind of tapestry just so they could use his... his whatever bones as *dice*?"

“Not at all,” said Franklin. “I’ve told you, speculation isn’t my field. I’m just saying that your killer would have had an easier time of it sawing through the ankle joint, but they deliberately made the cut higher on both legs. Why do that unless you’re after something special?”

“Hang on,” said Savage. “The games you’re talking about. The dice. They have a name, don’t they?”

Franklin nodded, waiting for Savage to say it.

“They’re called knucklebones.”

CHAPTER FIFTEEN

Kett waited until he'd walked at least twenty paces from the room—until his lungs felt like they were about to burst—before daring to take a breath. The air at the front end of the house was fresher, but he'd carried the stench of the corpse with him, on his clothes, in his hair. There was no escaping it. He walked to the open front door and stood there for a moment, watching forensic technicians and uniformed police dance around each other outside. It was full-dark now. He'd spent more time in that basement of butchery and bloodshed than he'd realised.

Savage pushed herself in next to him, close enough that he could feel the vibrations that ran through her.

"That's the worst I've ever seen, sir," she said.

"Me too, Kate," he replied.

"Who could do that to somebody? Who could pull somebody apart like that, and then *arrange* them? It's so... so alien."

He nodded.

"They didn't want to do it," Savage went on.

"What do you mean?"

"I don't know," she said, suddenly bashful. "Forget it, just thinking aloud."

"Don't do that to yourself," he said. "What are you thinking?"

Savage glanced back down the corridor, then turned to Kett.

"It's one thing to dismember a man like that," she said. "Cutting off the arms and legs, screwing them to the wall. That feels like a ritual to me, something the killer has done before, something they feel they *need* to do. Right?"

He didn't respond, he just waited for her to carry on.

"It's the face that gets me," she said. "Why mutilate the face like that? The body was cut up, but it wasn't destroyed. The face was... it was obliterated, sir. You wouldn't have even known where it was. Why do that, unless you feel bad? Unless you don't want to be seen? I think maybe the killer..."

She faltered again, chewing on a nail for long enough to remember the dirt on her hands. She slapped her arms to her sides, spitting.

"You think they don't want to think of themselves as a bad person?" Kett asked her.

"Exactly," she said. "That's exactly it, sir. They took off the face so their victim couldn't see them, couldn't judge them. I don't know, sorry. It's probably not that at all."

"Better than anything I was thinking of," he said. "It's good, Kate."

She smiled, nodding her appreciation. Kett spotted movement behind her, Cara Hay descending the house's wide central stairs in her forensic overalls. She looked a hundred years old, and she turned her weary eyes to Kett and Savage.

"You okay?" Kett asked her when she'd reached the

bottom. The newel post groaned as she leaned against it, dust raining from the cracked ceiling.

"I am thinking I like this job less and less with every passing day," she said. "The house has seen very little use, but that isn't to say it has lain empty. Nothing has disturbed the dust upstairs for some time. I think there were squatters here a while ago. I found a sleeping bag, some clothes. But we're talking weeks, maybe months."

"What about down here?" Kett asked.

"Peter Porter did a good job of kicking up the dust and erasing any footprints," she said with a reproachful look towards the front door. "I've dusted for prints, but it looks like the door furniture was wiped clean, and I'm guessing the killer used gloves. He was careful, and he was prepared."

"Not necessarily a *he*," said Kett, but Hay waved him away.

"You and I both know it, Detective. No woman expresses her rage this way, as much as we sometimes would like to."

"A chainsaw's a pretty good leveller," said Savage. "A woman could do just as much damage with it as a man."

Hay conceded the point with a nod.

"Come this way, there's something I want to show you."

She walked across the creaking boards of the hall and through a wide doorway, holding up her lamp to illuminate what would have been an enormous living room or dining room. A pile of black fabric lay in the middle of the room like a puddle of pitch, surrounded by scraps of what might have been old meat. The room carried a different kind of scent, one older and fouler but no less dead.

"What is that?" asked Kett, the back of his hand to his nose.

Hay answered the question by picking up a thick swathe of black cloth, holding it aloft with some effort. Dust poured off it, thick enough to look like liquid.

"A cloak?" said Savage, and she nodded.

"Thirteen of them, all identical, as far as I can see. Heavy duty hessian, dyed black. I've retrieved hairs from two or three and will likely find more back in the lab. But don't get your hopes up, they haven't been touched for a long, long time."

She gently dropped the cloak, creating a tsunami of dust, then smudged her gloved hand on her overalls.

"And the meat?" asked Kett, ducking down to get a better look at the nearest piece. It was the size and shape of a large dice, the edges far too neat for it not to have been cut that way. It was still red in places, but most of the colour had been lost behind a cape of white mould. As far as he could tell, they were all roughly the same.

"Your guess is as good as mine at the moment," said Hay. "There's a piece on the way to the lab right now."

"It's not good, though, is it?" asked Kett.

"Random meat in a murder house rarely is," said Savage.

"Only place I haven't been yet is the tunnel," said Hay. "You coming?"

"Wouldn't miss it," said Kett as they returned to the hallway. "You okay to find out more about the house, Kate? See who owns it?"

"I'm on it, sir," said Savage, visibly relieved to be heading out the front door.

"After you," Kett said to Hay, gesturing to the door on the right.

Hay called a name and a moment later a second technician appeared, a lamp in her hand. Kett waited for them both to walk through the door to the primary basement before following them. The steps were warped by age and damp and they bent alarmingly beneath his boots as he walked down them. He made it to the bottom in one piece, only to find himself staring across a cramped room at yet another set of stairs. These looked far worse, and even with the technician's lamp Kett couldn't see far. Darkness pooled at the bottom like ink. There could have been anything down there.

Or any*one*.

Hay didn't hesitate, stepping carefully downwards. The other technician went next, both of them lurching over a missing step. The stairwell had been cut into the rough chalk wall, which widened out at the bottom into a tunnel. A cool wind welcomed them, and Kett had to bite down on the same claustrophobic panic that had almost swallowed him whole the last time he'd been underground.

"There it is," said Hay.

Kett followed the light of the lamp to see where the tunnel had been sealed with a solid metal gate. It was open, nothing beyond it but those same tight white walls, that same grave-deep dark. The wind sang to him as he followed Hay, the melody uncannily lifelike. The air down here was brutally cold, and he flexed his numb fingers in his gloves until he got some feeling back into them.

"I'll dust it for prints," Hay said. "But it's painted, and flaky. I'd say the odds of getting something are 50/50, and they'll probably be Porter's. The padlock, on the other hand, looks brand new. Not a scrap of dust or rust on it."

The technician passed Hay a tool kit and she set to work, but after a minute or so she tutted her disappointment.

"Wiped clean," she said. "I can see where they rubbed it, and I can smell the bleach too."

She eased the gate away from the wall. It didn't make a sound.

"Hinges are oiled," she said, crossing the threshold to get a better look. "Extremely well-oiled. Somebody wanted to keep this gate functional."

"But what was its function?" asked Kett. "I mean, other than keeping people out, obviously. Why have a tunnel underneath your house?"

"Smuggling, maybe?" said Hay with a shrug. "I heard these passages lead all the way down to the river. Good place to bring illicit goods. And illicit people. Nobody would ever know."

She opened the gate a little more, bringing her lamp up.

"This mean anything to you?"

Kett stepped up to her side, pulling out his glasses and ducking down. Something had been carved into the back of the gate, a crude circle lined with what might have been feet —as if the entire thing was running. Maybe twenty of them around the circumference. In the middle of the circle was a wide eye wearing a crown. The lines were small, but it had to have taken some effort to carve them into solid iron.

"No idea," he said. "They're feet, right?"

"Could be," said Hay.

Kett pulled out his phone, realising the torch was still on. He turned it off and took a couple of photographs of the image.

"The body we found didn't have its feet," he told Hay.

"I remember vividly," she said. "Some coincidence."

"Or not," he said as he straightened. "Do what you can, but don't go too far down these tunnels because you'll never—"

He stopped, because he had the sudden, uncanny notion that he was being watched. His skin seemed to fold into goosebumps, his scalp growing as tight as a swimming cap. He stared into the darkness at the end of the tunnel, and it seemed to stare right back.

"Give me the lamp," he said quietly, clicking his fingers. Hay passed it over and he held it up, walking through the open gate. "Hey, who's there?"

There was a groan.

"Hello?" said Kett.

"Sir?" came a voice, one that was laden with fear. "Is that you?"

The darkness peeled away and a shape lumbered out of it, so tall it barely fit beneath the ceiling. It staggered down the tunnel like something from a monster movie, a clumsy march that was instantly recognisable.

"*Duke*?"

The PC staggered out of the dark, his face, helmet and uniform absolutely caked in chalk dust. He could have been a phantom, some long-forgotten Norwich spectre, the illusion not helped by his long, low groan.

"What on earth are you doing?" asked Kett.

"I was looking for Porter, sir," he said. "He told me to meet him down here. I was in the tunnel and..."

"Where's your torch?"

"I didn't have it," said Duke. "I was using my phone and then the battery ran out and then... I thought..."

Kett had never seen the big PC look so scared. He wasn't sure whether to give him a hug or a clip around the ear.

"I thought I was going to be stuck down here forever."

"You're bloody lucky you aren't," said Kett. "Of all the stupid..."

Duke actually looked like he was going to cry.

"I heard your voice, sir," Duke said. "Thank God. Thank you."

"Get upstairs," Kett told him, standing out of the way so that Duke could squeeze past. "I'll come with you so you don't get bloody lost again. Hay, can you see what you can find?"

"Of course," she said. "I'll let you know if anyone else comes wandering out of the dark."

Don't even joke about it, he thought.

Duke crunched his way up the steps, the wood literally splintering beneath his boots. By some miracle they made it through the basement and up into the house without incident, and only there did the PC seem to relax. He leaned against the wall, shivering like a lost dog in a storm.

"That was stupid, Aaron," Kett said again. "But I'm glad you're okay. You see anything when you were down there?"

Duke shook his head.

"Why did Porter ask you to come that way?"

"Wants to get rid of me, sir," said Duke. "Because of all the photos."

Kett shook his head, turning to the door as Savage walked through it. She did a classic double take when she spotted Duke standing there, caked in dust.

"Aaron? What happened?"

"Don't ask," said Kett. "You get anything?"

"Yeah," she said. "House is owned by a limited company, DeGrasse Holdings. They bought it sixteen years ago from the estate of a man called Morris Foulger. The Foulger family built the place all the way back in 1814."

"Foulger?" said Kett. "Any relation to Derek Foulger, the council guy?"

Savage shrugged.

"Couldn't say for sure, sir. But it's a weird coincidence if not."

"Kitty Lewington told me he owned property around this part of the city. Find out for me, will you?" He pulled his phone from his pocket, locating the photograph of the wheel of feet and the crowned eye. "You have any idea what this means? It was on the gate that led into the tunnels."

Savage studied it for a moment, then shook her head.

"The Superintendent is outside," she said. "He might know."

She walked through the door, Duke and Kett following, all three of them sucking down the sweet night air like it was a drug. Clare was standing by the forensic van, Porter by his side. Kett wasn't sure which of them looked more miserable, although Porter's face lit up when he saw Duke.

"Bloody hell, mate," he said. "What happened to you?"

Whatever Duke said in return, it was lost beneath his breath.

"Any luck?" said Clare, pulling his Big Tossing Jacket closer to his scrawny neck. "My tosspole's like a bloody freeze pop out here."

"Nothing solid yet," said Kett, wishing he had some bleach to wash away the mental image Clare had just planted in his head. "Killer knew how to hide their tracks. We've got thirteen cloaks. Not sure if they're connected to the body, but something weird's been going on. Found this on the gate. Does it mean anything to either of you?"

He held up his phone and both men leaned in.

"*That* was on the gate?" said Porter, frowning. "I never saw it, sir. Are you sure?"

"It was on the back," said Kett.

Porter's frown deepened as he mimicked opening a gate. "Oh, right. Never even looked."

"You sure you're okay, Pete?" asked Kett.

"I'm fine, sir," he grunted. "Just... just need..."

He licked his lips, one hand to his stomach.

"He's hangry," said Duke. "You're not yourself when you're hangry. Just needs a Snickers."

Porter pointed a gloved finger at him.

"I'm going to eat you in a minute, you piece of—"

"Enough," said Kett, before they could start slapping each other like a couple of kids in the playground. "The picture."

"Could almost be an emblem of some kind," said Clare. "Tradesman's symbol or something. I've seen feet like that before."

"House belonged to the Foulger family," said Kett. "Did Savage tell you?"

"Foulger?" said Clare, pulling a face. "As in Derek Foulger?"

"She isn't sure," said Kett.

"I wasn't," she replied, walking over from the house. "But I am now. Foulger's married to a woman called Nora DeGrasse. They're both shareholders in the company. Morris Foulger was his father, and when he died, Derek Foulger sold the house to his own limited company. He still owns it. And there's something else, sir."

She held up her own phone and Kett saw an image on the screen: a wheel lined with feet, and in the middle of it a crown positioned over a watchful eye. It wasn't identical to the one he'd found on the gate, but it was mighty close.

"What is that?" he said.

"It's the symbol for a group called the Harford Guild," she said. "Derek Foulger is the current chairman. I got this off his website."

"No way," said Kett.

"Now hang on," blurted Clare, his hand up as if to stop a herd of stampeding bulls. "Hang on. I do *not* want you tossing over that man until I've spoken with the Chief Constable. Is that clear?"

"Wasn't planning on—"

"I said, is that clear?" Clare demanded. "If we get this wrong, we all lose our jobs. Let me make a call."

He gave them all another furious, bug-eyed look, then spun around and stormed off.

"What now, sir?" asked Savage when he was out of earshot.

Kett looked at her, then at Porter, and finally at Duke.

"He said not to toss over him," he said, the faintest of smiles on his lips. "Didn't say anything about a conversation. Who's in?"

CHAPTER SIXTEEN

Kett's Volvo was blocked in by a fleet of IRVs and forensic vans, and so was Porter's Mondeo, but fortunately they didn't have far to go. It was a five-minute walk back down the hill to the entrance to County Hall and Kett led the way, the chill magnified tenfold by the thin layer of drizzle that clung to his skin. Bracondale was choked with cars as people tried to get out of the city, a dazzling display of taillights against the frozen night. He crossed the road where he could, Porter, Savage and Duke following him like ducklings chasing the mother duck.

"Doesn't seem possible," said Porter as they neared the bottom of the hill. He was devouring the giant Twix he'd liberated from his car, which seemed to have gone some way to cheering him up. "How's the house so close to the cellar? Felt like we were in those tunnels forever."

"I was thinking the same thing," said Savage. "This is, what, half a mile? We definitely walked further than that."

Kett pictured those passageways now, cut into the soft, chalky rock under his feet. He wondered whether, if he stamped down too hard, the ground would open up and swallow him whole.

"Time runs differently when you're underground," said Duke with a nod of wisdom. He was still absolutely covered in chalk dust, the soft rain cutting rivulets into it and making it look like he was wearing war paint. More than ever he could have passed for a Viking Berserker. "Saw a documentary about it once."

"*You've* watched a documentary?" said Porter.

"It's a fact, sir," the PC went on. "Something to do with the quantum universe. Or relativity. Or something. Same way it's different if you're on a plane."

"I actually think that's right," said Savage, raising her eyebrows.

"Definitely not right," said Porter, stuffing the last of the Twix into his mouth.

"Saw another documentary about carbohydrates and waistlines, sir," Duke added with a sly look at the DI. Porter tried to shout something back but his mouth was too full, making him sound like a bear that had swallowed a beehive.

By the time he'd gulped down the last of the chocolate they'd reached the booth that guarded the car park, and the man opened his window to talk to them. He made a show of leaning out and frowning down the street.

"You fellas lost your car?" he asked.

"Something like that," said Kett. "We were wondering if we could have a word with Derek Foulger."

He pulled out his warrant card but the man waved it away.

"Know who you lot are," he said, studying his fingers like he'd just had a manicure. "I'm not that forgetful. Mr Foulger's not here; he left this afternoon. He's usually away by four."

Kett popped his lips, looking up at the enormous main building. Against the brutish dark it looked bigger than ever, as if it had swollen in the rain. It looked far too much like Hell House, the building where Hollenbeck had held him prisoner, and he had to clench his jaw as the panic washed through him.

"Thanks," he grunted after a moment.

He pushed past, heading up the road.

"Hey," the man called after him. "I said he's not here."

"He might not be," Kett said without looking back. "But as far as I know, this is still a crime scene. You got a problem with that, call the police."

They made their way down the side of the building, their footsteps echoing off the walls. A couple of people scurried out of the doors, heading for their cars and offering tired nods, but it really was quiet.

"You thinking what I'm thinking, sir?" asked Savage.

"Depends," he said. "If you were thinking that man was full of shit."

"Yeah, exactly. He seemed very interested in his fingernails for somebody who was pushing fifty."

There was a line of three vehicles parked up ahead on the access road, all of them expensive. A sign announced that the area was reserved. Kett walked past a BMW X5 with a matte black paint job, then a Mercedes, stopping at a metallic blue Jaguar XJ40—a hulking old-school model that had to have been from the 1980s. He glanced at the number plate, reading it aloud.

"DE11 REK."

"Delrek?" said Duke, and everybody looked at him. "Oh, wait, *Derek*."

"He might have walked home?" Savage said with a shrug.

"I've met him," said Kett. "I'm guessing he doesn't do much walking."

"So he's here, but he doesn't want to see us," said Porter.

The DI pulled out his phone, taking a photograph of the car. Kett cupped a hand to the window to see an immaculately kept interior. Then he looked up at the building again.

"Let's not give him a choice."

He tugged on the handle, hard. Then, when that didn't work, he rammed his backside into the car hard enough to rock it. Immediately, a shrill alarm filled the air, the Jaguar's headlights blinking in a mad panic.

"Not sure that's protocol, sir," said Savage, worried. "The Super did say not to rock the boat. Or the car."

"I tripped," said Kett. "Thank God the car broke my fall. Listen, Kate, while we're here, can you and Duke pop round to the dig, see if there are any updates from the cellar?"

"Sure, sir," she said.

She set off, the big PC treading on her shadow.

"Try not to fall in any holes, Duke," Porter called after them.

"Try not to eat anyone," Duke shouted back. "*Sir*."

Porter scowled, and Kett had to conceal his laugh behind a cough. The main doors were opening and a woman appeared, looking over her half-moon spectacles and down the steps.

"Not sure what happened, sorry," Kett said.

"Oh, it's Mr Foulger's," she replied. "I'll fetch him. Can I help you?"

"We're fine," said Kett, and she vanished back inside the building.

"You think he's got anything to do with this, sir?" Porter asked, stamping his feet in an attempt to stay warm.

"Foulger?" Kett blew out a breath. "I have no idea. A fair bit is starting to point to him, but my gut still says no. What about yours?"

"My gut's telling me it's hungry," said Porter with a sorry look.

"You doing okay?" Kett asked him. "You don't seem yourself, mate."

Porter chewed on his answer for a moment, his eyes scrolling back and forth as if reading an invisible book.

"I'm... Yeah, I'm... I don't know what the word is. It's the baby, it could be here in like a month and..."

He turned to Kett, his eyes full of doubt.

"I have literally no idea what I'm doing, Robbie. I mean zero. I'm standing on the edge of this cliff and life's about to throw this thing at me and I'm supposed to what? Look after it? Forever? And it can't even walk or anything, can't talk, can't feed itself. I mean, how the hell am I supposed to keep it alive? Let alone all the other stuff. What am I supposed to do?"

Kett dropped a hand on Porter's shoulder.

"Pete, that's the miracle of being a parent. You have no idea what you're doing, but you do it anyway. You do enough. I'm not going to lie, it's terrifying. Every single day is terrifying. But take a breath, because you're going to be amazing. That kid's going to be the luckiest child on the planet."

Porter took Kett's advice, breathing deeply and holding it. He nodded, some of the fear leaving his eyes.

"Just worried they're going to pass me the baby and it's going to explode or something," he said.

Kett laughed, letting go of the DI.

"Pretty unlikely," he said.

"Or they'll pass it to me and *I'll* explode."

"That's less unlikely," admitted Kett. "Heads up."

Foulger was limping through the reception door, bracing himself on his stick. The big man was so intent on not tripping that he'd made it halfway down the stairs before he noticed who was standing beside his car. He stopped, wheezing like an asthmatic accordion, and aimed his key fob at Kett like it was a pistol. He pressed the button and the car chirruped, then he turned his obese body around and lurched back up the steps without a single word.

Kett slammed his hip against the side of the car again, hard enough to hurt, and the alarm resumed its manic call. He thought he could see every single hair on Foulger's balding head bristle before the big man performed another slow, difficult one-eighty.

"You're on thin ice, Kett," he said, his deep voice carrying effortlessly. He switched off the alarm again, but this time he stood there, halfway up the steps. He put the key fob back into his pocket and grasped the metal bannister with some force. "Do I need to call my friends in the Force? I have a lot of them."

"Feel free," said Kett. "But I think they'd want to know the answers to my questions as much as I do."

"Yeah?" sneered Foulger. "What questions are those? What job can I qualify for after I'm fired from the police? How do I sign on? What do I do when my wife initiates divorce proceedings against me because I'm broke? Why am I such a limp-dicked weasel?"

"No. More like, why is there a very mutilated, very dead body inside a house that you own?"

Foulger's mouth opened and he made a noise like he was trying to cough out a hairball.

"A house just up the road from here," Kett went on. "On Bracondale. Connected by tunnels to the chamber where we found the bones of dozens of other bodies—a chamber that lies right here in the place where you work. How about that for a question, Mr Foulger?"

Foulger's mottled, psoriasis-scabbed cheeks had turned purple, flecks of white foam hanging from his lips. He looked every bit the ogre, thought Kett, even more so when he lifted his heavy walking stick off the step and thrust it forward.

"I don't own any property around here."

"Wrong answer," said Porter.

"There's a house halfway up Bracondale," said Kett. "Tucked away on the hill. I wouldn't have even known it was there if the tunnels hadn't led us right to it. It's your house, Mr Foulger. Owned by a company you formed with your wife, DeGrasse Holdings. But I think it's been in your family for a lot longer."

Foulger glared at him, as if he was trying to stop Kett's heart with the sheer power of thought. The walking stick clacked back to the step like a wizard's staff.

"Want to take a guess at my next question?" Kett asked him. "Why wasn't your reaction to my *last* question not, 'Whose body have you found?' I don't know about you, Pete, but I think I'd want to know."

"Me too, sir," said Porter. "That's definitely the first thing I'd ask, unless I already knew the answer."

"You're full of shit," said Foulger, some of his smugness returning. "I don't know anything about a body. I don't know anything about a house. I own a lot of property, Kett, because I'm first and foremost a businessman. I get things done. Last time I checked there were nearly a hundred buildings registered with DeGrasse, all over the country. I've visited less than a tenth of them, if that. Some, like the Bracondale place, are derelict, and I've never set foot in there because the whole thing might come down around me. Am I responsible if some deadbeat breaks a window and pops his clogs inside? I think you'd find that very difficult to prove in court."

"That depends," said Kett. "Where were you this afternoon, between twelve and three?"

He thought he saw a flicker of something pass over the big man's face, a crack in his flabby armour.

"I'm giving you one more chance to fuck off, but after that, no mercy."

"Between twelve and three," Kett said again. "You can tell me here or you can tell me at the station."

"I wasn't even in the city," said Foulger. He lurched down a couple of steps, his confidence back. "You know what I think, Detective? I think you're a limp-dicked weasel with an itch you can't scratch because you don't like me. But you know what will happen if you keep walking this road?"

Kett didn't give him the satisfaction of an answer, and Foulger jabbed a finger into his own chest.

"*I* happen," he said, his booming voice almost operatic. "And I promise you I will rain down the wrath of God Almighty!"

"He's bloody nuts," muttered Porter, too low for Foulger to hear him.

Foulger smiled, and there wasn't an ounce of kindness there. His teeth jutted from pale gums like horse's teeth, big and yellow and blunt.

"You're fucked, Kett," he said, spinning himself around

and beginning the arduous climb up the steps again. "You'll be hearing from my lawyer, and from the Chief Constable."

"I'll look forward to it," Kett shouted. "In the meantime, can you tell me if all of this has anything to do with the Harford Guild?"

Foulger missed a step, but he kept his balance, hauling himself up the stairs with considerable effort.

"Whatever this is, Derek, we'll find the truth," Kett said. "You can't hide it."

Foulger grabbed the door with his free hand, but he didn't open it. He looked over his shoulder, that grin still sitting on his face.

"I wouldn't be so sure about that," he said. "It's already buried."

Then he opened the door and walked inside.

"Limp-dicked weasel is a new one," said Porter. "What do you think he meant by that?"

"By the insult?" said Kett. "I think it's pretty self-explanatory."

"No, sir, about being able to bury the truth."

"No idea," said Kett. "Come on."

He started walking down the building's flank, making it a couple of steps before doubling back. He gave the Jaguar one more shunt with his rear end, setting the alarm off for a third time. Then he jogged after Porter, both of them snorting with laughter as they rounded the corner.

"He deserves it," he said when Porter lifted an eyebrow. "You see Savage anywhere?"

"There, sir."

The grounds of County Hall basked in the glow of half a dozen portable lights, the purr of their generators strangely comforting. The enormous, excavated pit sat right in front of them, its diggers still and silent. Past them was the second, smaller pit where the cellar had been found. Kett could just about discern two shapes moving beside it, and by the time he'd skirted the main dig the shadows had solidified into the outlines of Savage and Duke. They were standing at the top of the slope, looking down to where the entrance to the underground room lay.

Or rather where it had *once* lain.

"They've filled it in, sir," Savage said when Kett was within earshot.

That gaping mouth in the dirt was now a plug of concrete, the cellar obliterated.

"Unbelievable," said Porter. "What the fuck's he playing at?"

Kett studied the pit for a moment before turning to the building that loomed over them. Half the windows were lit, the rest as black as a spider's eyes. He knew Foulger was watching them, though. He could feel his gaze, he could feel that arrogant smile burning a hole in the night.

"He's doing exactly what he told us," he said. "He's burying the truth."

He turned to the others, three faceless statues in the dark.

"But he can't bury it all."

CHAPTER SEVENTEEN

SUPERINTENDENT CLARE WAS WAITING FOR THEM when they got back to the murder house, and despite the bitterly cold wind and the icy rain, Kett could feel the heat coming off him from the other end of the long, wooded driveway. He pointed a long finger at Kett, glaring down it like it was a rifle. If it *had* been a rifle, Kett knew, he wouldn't have hesitated in pulling the trigger.

"Sir," he started.

"Don't," barked Clare. "Don't you dare open your mouth, Detective, because if you do, then I am liable to shove my foot right down your throat and give you a good hard kick in your kidneys. Do you know who I've just had a very unpleasant talk with? Hm? Can you guess?"

Kett started to reply but Clare waved his hands in the air like a deranged child.

"I said don't open your mouth, Kett. The Chief Constable, that's who. And do you know who *he* just had a very unpleasant talk with?"

Kett kept his mouth shut.

"Well?" Clare insisted.

"Uh..."

"Zip that facebag, Kett. Derek Foulger. You directly went against my orders and spoke with him. Do you know how that makes me look? It makes me look like a man who can't control his bollocks, Kett."

"Not sure I'd—"

"My bollocks!" Clare roared. "They're ping-ponging all over the place asking insane questions and I have absolutely zero ability to make them do what I say. So what I'm going to need you to do is make a call of your own, a very sincere one, to Derek Foulger. I want you to tell him that you're a man who temporarily lost his mind. And I want you to apologise. Is that clear?"

"With all due respect, sir," said Savage. "We found a dead man in Foulger's house, and the bones we found are right outside his workplace. I think..."

She tailed off because it looked like the Superintendent was having some kind of medical episode. He stood almost perfectly still, one eye twitching.

"He's buried the chamber, sir," Kett chanced. "They've filled it in, on his orders."

The Super was making a soft whining noise that grew in volume like a boiling kettle.

"Sir," said Kett. "You once told me it didn't matter who the suspect was. It didn't matter if they were a peasant or royalty. If you have evidence to question them, then you question them."

"Not if it puts my knob in a vice, Kett," said Clare, finally waking from whatever furious trance he'd been in. "And not when Foulger's the man twisting the handle. I didn't say don't question him, I said tread carefully. You walked all over him. Foulger's a big bear. He's going to make you pay for that, and more importantly, he's going to make me pay too."

"Sir," said Savage.

"Enough," he said. "Enough. I'm not saying you're not right, I'm just saying that with people like that, we need to do things in a different way. Foulger's a piece of shit. Do I think he could cut a man to pieces with a chainsaw and hang them on the wall?"

He looked up at the house.

"Probably. I wouldn't put anything past him. But do I think he *did* it? No. Foulger's mean, but he's not stupid. He wouldn't shit on his own doorstep. He's also infirm, I've seen him bugger over a dozen times without that stick, practically watched him roll down a hill once. He's not a strong man. Let me deal with him. You lot have done enough, so toss off for the night. Let Franklin and Hay make their reports. We'll convene in the morning. But I mean it, Kett. You're going to call Foulger and you're going to apologise."

"Fine," grumbled Kett.

"What?"

"I said fine, sir. I'll do it."

Clare eyeballed him for a moment more before walking back to the house.

"What now, sir?" asked Savage when the Super had gone.

Kett checked his watch. Clare was right, until the forensic and pathology reports were in there wasn't much they could do, and they'd spotted Uniforms doing door-to-doors along the street on their way back up the hill. The weather was worse than ever, the drizzle now a steady rain.

"Head home," he said.

"Good plan," said Porter, who was texting on his phone. "Allie's not feeling too good, I need to pick up some stuff for her, was supposed to do it hours ago."

"If it's all the same, I might try and get some of this on the board," said Savage. "While it's fresh."

"Do I have to come too?" Duke asked her.

"You're a free man, Aaron," she replied.

"That means yes, mate," said Porter. "I'll give you both a lift back to HQ."

Kett watched them walk to Porter's Mondeo, and he called out after them.

"Remember, you've got this, Pete. You're going to be great."

Porter saluted a thanks and Kett made his way back to the Volvo, switching the heat on full blast and basking in it for a few minutes before carefully reversing to the road. He paused there, thinking of his house, thinking of a hot meal and dry clothes and the comfortable sofa. Thinking of his wife, his girls.

Then thinking about the dead man, ripped to pieces and displayed like a work of art. There had been something familiar in the circular design of his ruined body. It had resembled the bones they'd found, for sure, but the pattern didn't end there.

Kett pulled out his phone and found the photo he'd taken of the seal on the back of the tunnel door. That wheel of feet, a single boiling eye in the middle topped with a crown. It reminded him of images he'd seen of the Illuminati, that pyramid topped with an eyeball that still sat on dollar notes in the US. Surely the victim's missing feet couldn't be a coincidence, could they? And the eye, was it all that different from a skull?

He had no idea what it meant, but he knew somebody who might.

He waited for a bus to rumble past, spraying rainwater, then pulled out onto the road.

HE WAS on the right side of town for the Lewington place, a ten-minute drive over the river and up the hill. Brightly lit windows peeked over brick walls like nervous giants, occasional pockets of city light visible in the gaps between them. It could have been another city entirely up here, Kett thought. Another world.

He parked in the same place he had earlier that day, wondering whether it was too late for a house call. But he was here now, and it wouldn't take long. He ran through the rain to the pedestrian gate, ringing the buzzer. This time it didn't open automatically, an abrasive voice exploding from the speakers—Muddle, the maid. Kett was ashamed to admit he couldn't remember her real name.

"Who's calling?"

"Oh, hi. It's DCI Kett. I popped by earlier. I was wondering whether I might be able to have a quick chat with Mrs Lewington?"

"One moment."

The speaker fell quiet and Kett stamped his feet, feeling freezing fingers of rainwater explore his neck and run down his back. He was again wondering whether he should just jump back in the car and head home when the gate buzzed. He pushed through, running to the front door. When it opened, it wasn't Muddle he saw there, or even Kitty. It was Kitty's son, Ron, and he had his daughter in his arms.

"Hi," he said. "I—"

He was cut off by Clara, who looked at Kett and issued a long, wet raspberry. Both men waited patiently for it to finish.

"I'm so sorry," said Ron. "Please don't—"

She did another one, and Kett couldn't help but laugh at the look of utter exasperation on Ron's face.

"Don't worry," he told him, smiling at Clara. "That's a pretty impressive raspberry."

"It's a fart," she said. "Daddy, I'm cold."

"Sorry," said Ron, standing to one side. "Come in. Mum's upstairs. She heads to bed early these days. Earlier than the kids. But she knows you're here, and she's coming down."

"Oh, it's no trouble, really," said Kett. "I can come back tomorrow."

"Nonsense," said Ron, closing the door behind him. The house was big and old, but it was as warm as a freshly drawn bath and Kett shuddered with the delight of it. Ron put Clara down. "Go fetch Nanny, sweetie. Can I take your coat, Detective?"

Kett shrugged it off with a thanks, and Ron hung it on the newel post of the wide stairs. He set off towards the kitchen, talking over his shoulder.

"Have you got anywhere with the bones?"

"Honestly, I'm not sure," he said. "The case has got a little more... complicated."

"How so?" asked Ron as they entered the vast kitchen diner. He caught Kett's expression and tapped his nose. "Ah, I see. Confidential. I won't ask."

Clara was bouncing on one of the sofas, her eyes glued to the TV where *Moana* was playing. The boy sat next to her, although Kett had forgotten his name too. He gave Kett a suspicious side-eye, then returned to the screen.

"Please, Clara," Ron said. "No jumping. You'll wreck the couch."

If she heard him she paid no attention, jumping off the

sofa and then leaping right back on again. Ron looked like he might actually cry.

"She has ADHD," he said. "I know it's not always her fault."

"I know exactly how you feel," Kett said. "Our oldest, Alice, she has it too, and she's autistic. The most wonderful girl in the world, until she's not."

This brought a gentle smile to Ron's face.

"You really should think about the group, uh..."

"Robbie," Kett said.

"Sorry, I'm useless with names. But you should. It's just a few of us dads having a good old moan, setting the world to rights. I'm heading off there in a little while, you'd be more than welcome. Mike, he has a daughter with autism too. Non-verbal. Lovely girl, but it's hard work. He and his wife have really struggled this year."

"Maybe," said Kett. "But probably not."

"Understood," said Ron. "You know where I am if you change your mind. Clara, did you get Nanny for me?"

The girl didn't reply, but there was no need. The door on the side of the room opened and Kitty Lewington walked out, dressed in a Victorian nightie that reached her ankles. Muddle followed, looking more like a bodyguard than a maid.

"Put the kettle on, dear," Kitty told her, beaming at Kett. "It's good to have you back, Detective. I hear there is something you need my help with?"

"I'm sorry to call so late," he said, and she waved his words away as she sat down at the dining table.

"Matters of history pay no heed to time," she said. "Ironically. Do take a seat. Tea?"

"You know, this time I won't," said Kett, surprising

himself. That was twice today he'd refused a cuppa. "I really don't want to impose."

He took a seat opposite Kitty, glancing up at the portrait of her late husband.

"You're not imposing," said Kitty. "But I am very tired. We went to the soft play today, the one in the mall. Me and Ronald and the grandkids. It was exhausting."

"You said that already, Mum," said Ron, and her forehead creased into a frown.

"I did? Oh. Well, that's what you get for bringing me out at this time of night. I love the grandkids but gosh, they don't half drain the sauce out of you."

Kett pulled out his phone and found the photo of the markings on the back of the tunnel door, then slid it across the table.

"I was wondering whether you might be able to look at this for me."

"Oh, I'll need my glasses. Muddle, dear?"

The maid stomped out of the room, returning a few seconds later with a pair of sturdy tortoiseshell reading glasses in her hand. Kitty put them on, squinting at the screen.

"I can still barely see the bloody thing," she said. "I'm going to need new ones. I'm sorry, Detective, I have no idea what I'm looking at."

"We found that symbol engraved on a gate in the tunnels," he said. "I just wondered if you recognised it. We think it's a seal of some kind, maybe—"

"Looks like Harford," said Ron, who had walked to his mum's side. "The guild emblem. That's an eye, a crown. Maybe."

"I was just going to say that, Ronald," said Kitty, glaring

at him. "The wild impatience of youth, eh? Yes, it's the insignia for the Harford Guild, I'd stake my eye teeth on it."

"Can you tell me something about it?"

"I could tell you a great deal," said Kitty. "If you had the night to spare."

"Uh... I don't."

"Then I shall stick to the pertinent facts," she said, her voice booming. "It was a medieval guild that began here in the city, and which—like all the guilds, I suppose—grew to be extremely powerful. Unlike the trade guilds, Harford was a union of like-minded people blessed by fame, fate and fortune."

"Hang on," said Kett. "Can you dumb it down even more? Sorry."

"Rich bastards," said Kitty. "Landowners, nobility, even royalty. You see, a guild's primary focus was to look after its members, but when the trades began to get powerful—you see this happening towards the Renaissance—they were even able to challenge the hierarchy of the old rich, the nobility and the aristocracy. So these wealthy families—"

"The rich bastards," said Ron.

"Yes, they banded together to form their own guild. They called it Harford, after the family who had the idea. They met for a long time in Harford House, over by Town Close. Mansion Row, as we call it."

She pulled a face like she didn't approve, and Kett once again took in the enormous kitchen he was sitting in, the palatial house that surrounded it.

"They were accused of all sorts of shenanigans, back in the day. Murder, mayhem, even witchcraft at one point."

"Really?" asked Kett, and Kitty nodded with great enthusiasm.

"I wouldn't put it past them, either. They must have

been guilty of something, Detective, because they were able to subdue the guilds, even dismantle some of them. That's no mean feat. Guilds are powerful societies."

"And they're still going, the guilds?"

"I imagine they'd like to believe they're still going," she said. "But like all great power structures from the Middle Ages, the influence of these collectives has been lost. It's mostly ceremonial now. You'll see them strutting their stuff down at the cathedral sometimes."

"But they must still mean something," said Kett. "Derek Foulger has—"

"Wanker," spat Kitty, taking Kett by surprise.

"Uh, he has the emblem of the guild on his website, and we found those markings in a tunnel that led to a property he owns."

"Like I said, he's a wanker. One of the biggest I've ever met. It's not surprising he waves that symbol around like an extra cock. His family were instrumental in creating the guild, along with the Harfords. They're old Norwich, and for a long time, for centuries, there wasn't much that happened in the city without their say-so. Foulger would give anything for it to be that way again, but fortunately for the rest of us he's as impotent in local government as he is in bed."

Kett's eyes widened and she laughed.

"That's hearsay, Detective, I've never felt the need to confirm it myself."

This time it was Kett who laughed, although Ron looked mortified.

"One more thing," Kett asked. "The symbol, what does it mean? All those feet and stuff?"

"Oh, not much," said Kitty. "All the guilds had a secret language of symbols to help them protect and identify their members. All a lot of hocus pocus, if you ask me, but it led to some beautiful imagery. The crown, in this case, was a symbol of divine right, because these people believed the rest of the world was obliged to bow to them. From my dealings with old Wankstain Foulger, absolutely nothing has changed there."

"The eye was along the same lines," said Ron. "It's a warning, really. 'We see all.' You see eyes in all sorts of iconography from the golden age of the guilds."

"Like the Illuminati?" said Kett, and both Kitty and Ron laughed.

"Oh, you dear boy," said Kitty, and Kett got the feeling that if she could have reached him she would have pinched his cheek. "These feet appear quite often too, a symbol of reach."

"Reach?"

"Yes. It's another warning, I suppose, that the guild travels far and wide, and at speed. There is nowhere you can hide from them. They will crush you. But like I say, it's history. There's no need to fear them now. The only danger of being crushed these days is if that fat bastard falls over and you happen to be in the way."

"Sorry," said Ron.

"Don't you apologise for me, Ronald," Kitty told him. "I'm old enough now that I say what I think, and I wouldn't wipe my arse with that man or any of his cronies."

"Are there many of them?" asked Kett. "Harford members?"

"A handful," said Kitty. "From what I know. Maybe twenty, and some you wouldn't expect, either. I know a local TV presenter who's sworn his allegiance, believe it or not. Most are just rich old farts with nothing better to do. When the guild lost its power most people left, just a few dry old dangleberries clinging onto the hairy vestiges of their heritage."

"Dad was a member," said Ron, looking up at the portrait. Kett saw the look Kitty gave him, a sudden flash of anger—gone before he could even be sure. "But he didn't take it seriously."

"He didn't even attend the meetings," said Kitty. "He couldn't stand Foulger either."

"How did he become a member?"

"It's no mystery," Kitty replied. "Keith made a lot of money, he bought this place, he held a seat on the council for a while. He wasn't old money, but who is these days? He was just the sort of person Foulger wanted around his table. But like I say, Keith couldn't stand to be in the same room as him. He resigned from the guild after a short while, blamed his poor health."

She yawned, although Kett didn't think it was entirely genuine.

"You must excuse me, Detective, it's getting late. Can I help you with anything else?"

"No, and I apologise again, Mrs Lewington." Kett pushed himself up. "Thank you. That was very helpful."

"Ron will see you out," she said. She made a clicking noise, like she was calling a horse. "Muddle, with me."

The maid took her arm, practically carrying her from the room. Ron watched her go, his cheeks still blazing.

"She's quite something, your mum," said Kett.

"She's certainly one of a kind," he replied, checking his watch. "Right, I'd better go. Are you sure I can't tempt you? It's only down the road, one beer and you can make your excuses."

"No, Dad!" wailed Clara, vaulting off the sofa and careening across the room. Ron scooped her up and she grabbed his shirt so tightly it almost throttled him. "You're not allowed to go."

"Don't go," echoed the boy. "You're not allowed."

Ron tried to open up the noose of his shirt, pulling the girl's hands loose.

"It's just for an hour," he croaked. "I'll bring you something nice back. How about some Smarties?"

Kett laughed.

"The universal bribe," he said. "I do the same with mine."

Clara dropped off him, giving both men a serious look.

"Two packets," she said. "Each."

"Deal," her dad replied. "Now, be good for Muddle."

The wild shriek that Clara replied with as she flew back onto the sofa didn't fill Kett with hope. Ron rubbed his neck, wincing. Kett thought about his own kids, how much he loved them, how wonderful they could be, and how infuriating too. He knew the minute he opened the door they'd be all over him just like Clara and her dad, he knew just how relentless they could be. And he knew how difficult it was, sometimes, to be a dad.

"You know what," he said, checking his watch again, "a pint might be nice."

CHAPTER EIGHTEEN

Kett closed the front door behind him, almost floating into the sweet smell of whatever Billie was making for dinner. Just as he'd predicted, he heard a volley of shouts rise up from the back of the house and seconds later all three girls came barrelling down the hallway, a tsunami of noise and movement that almost made him scream.

"Daddy!" shouted Evie. "I got a house point for my art."

"Daddy!" Moira said at exactly the same time. "I played with Sophie today and she fell over and banged her—"

"Dad!" Alice yelled, louder than both of them. "Can I have a horse?"

"Hang on!" he said, trying to wrestle them away as they all leapt at him. "Hang on, just let me change."

"I drew a picture of you," Evie said. "It's really—"

"So I can go riding, because Sophie goes riding and I want to—"

"Nobody speak!" Moira roared. "Just me!"

"No, it's my turn!"

"He's *my* Daddy!"

Kett made a break for the stairs, the girls giving chase as

they yelled over each other. He ran into the bedroom and closed the door, grateful for the lock the previous owners had installed. The battering of fists was like hail.

"Give me one minute," he said. "I just need to change. One minute."

Outside, the girls began a frantic countdown.

"You cannot be my children," he told them. "Go away, or I'll take you back to the bin where we found you."

He took a breath, strangely grateful for the hour he'd just spent with Ron and his friends in the Rushcutter's Arms down by the river. There had been five other men there, from a young dad called Rob to an older man called Mike, who'd spent the first ten minutes hunched over the table in tears. It had been awkward, at first, because Kett had felt like an intruder. But the men had been so kind, and so welcoming, and their stories of chaos and love and responsibility and guilt resonated so effortlessly in Kett's mind that before long he'd felt like he'd known them forever.

Ron had been a constant, reassuring presence, creating an air of friendship and openness. By the end of the session, Kett had found himself speaking about his own girls, about the good things and the bad, and Ron and the others had listened without judgement. It had lifted a little of the weight from his heart that he hadn't even known was there.

"Every week," said Ron as he'd got up to go. "You'll be amazed how much it helps."

He stripped, jumping into the shower in the *en suite* and rinsing off the chalk dust under a trickle of lukewarm water—the shower was the only thing in the house that didn't seem to work, the head caked in limescale. Outside, all three girls were making an alarm sound to let him know his minute was over. He laughed to himself, because despite the unbearable noise it was still great to hear them. As he'd told Ron and the others, his children were life, and goodness, and love. They were the perfect antidote to the horrors of his job.

They were the *only* reason he could survive his job.

He pulled on some pyjamas and his tattered blue dressing gown. Then, taking a deep breath, he opened the bedroom door.

"Come here, girls," he said as they flew through, and he gathered them all in a hug that made them squeal with laughter. He held them tight until they were all squirming to get free. "What's wrong? Come back for more hugs!"

They bolted, chortling their heads off, Moira nearly falling down the stairs as she ran away. He chased them with a selection of his best monster noises, catching them every now and again and giving them giant cuddles before letting them escape. The pursuit continued downstairs, and after five minutes of it he was panting for breath and ready to collapse. He fell onto the sofa and the girls, seeing their chance, pounced on him, their belly laughs the best sound in the world.

"You win," he told them. "You win. I surrender!"

He waited for them to clamber off him, then he sat up, the room pulsing bright with every beat of his heart. Evie fell onto the sofa next to him, her face flushed. Moira was even sweatier, her hair plastered to her cheeks. She sat on the other side of him while Alice stood in the middle of the room.

"Please, Dad? Can we get a horse?"

"Why on earth do you want a horse?" he said, and she shrugged like she hadn't quite thought it through.

"So," said Billie, putting her head around the door. "I see you're getting them all calm for bed, then."

"Sorry. They started it."

"Did not," said Evie.

"Dad told us we can have a horse," said Alice.

"Yay! A horse!" added Evie.

"Whoa, I did not," he said. "Where would we even keep it?"

"My room," said Moira matter-of-factly.

"No, mine," said Alice. "It can share my bed."

"Why?" chimed Evie. "Are you going to marry it?"

"No!"

"Alice and a horsey, sitting in a tree."

"Dinner's nearly ready," said Billie, stopping Alice in her tracks as she charged at her little sister.

"Sorry I was so late. You could have eaten without me."

"It's okay," she said. "You okay? Good day?"

He'd almost forgotten it, he realised, by being with the girls. They'd obliterated those old bones and wiped that mutilated corpse from his head. He nodded, but Billie saw the truth of it in his face the way she always did.

"Already?" she said, and he nodded. She gave him a sympathetic smile. "Come on then. Some stew and dumplings will help."

"Amazing," he said, holding out his arms to the girls. "Help your old dad up, will you?"

Together, the three of them managed to lever him out of the sofa and they made their way into the kitchen diner. The smell was so good that Kett was salivating by the time he got to the table, and when the steaming bowl appeared in front of him it took every ounce of willpower he possessed not to tip the whole lot straight into his mouth. He ate it slowly, content to listen to the girls as they told him about their day. When they'd finished, Evie ran off to get the picture she'd drawn of him at school, slapping it down onto the table for him to look at. He almost regurgitated his dinner.

"That's... *me*?" he asked, doing his best to smile. "Wow!"

The picture did bear a crude resemblance to a human, but only if you squinted.

"What's that long thing?"

"Your nose," said Evie, as if he'd asked the stupidest question in the world.

"And that thing that looks like a bum?"

"Your chin," she said.

"Why is my nose touching my chin?"

"Perspective," she said, wisely.

"Right... It's brilliant, Evie, thank you. Go on, brush your teeth."

She beamed at him and ran from the room, leaving just him and Billie. He started to collect the bowls from the table, carrying them to the dishwasher.

"My nose doesn't really look like that, does it?"

"Like a ding-a-ling?" Billie said with a smile. "Well, only a little."

She kissed him on the end of his nose.

"You ever hear of a game called knucklebones?" he asked, as he rinsed off the gravy.

"Sure," she said. "We used to play it when we were kids."

"With *bones*?"

"No, with scatter jacks. The metal ones. We've got some somewhere."

"What were the rules?"

"Honestly, I can't remember," she said. "It was something to do with throwing them in the air and trying to catch them on the back of the hand. Kept us entertained for a couple of hours on holidays and stuff. Why?"

"No reason," he said. "I've never played it."

Billie paused halfway to the dishwasher, thinking.

"My mum never called it jacks or knucklebones," she said. "She called it snobs. I remember that, because she didn't like me playing it."

"Snobs?" said Kett.

"Yeah, I can't remember why, though. Something to do with the fact that only rich people could afford joints of mutton or lamb, to get the bones. Poor people didn't have knucklebones, they had to use stones. Mum hated all that stuff, snobbery. She grew up poor."

"Weird," said Kett.

"Yeah, but then we already knew she was weird. Does this have anything to do with the case? The bones?"

The image of the dead man floated into his head on a river of blood, the stumps of his ankles, his missing feet.

"Maybe," he said. "I don't know."

"Don't think about it," she told him, loading the last of the cutlery into the dishwasher and closing the door. "Whatever it is, it doesn't belong here, not in our house."

He nodded, and when she opened her arms he walked to her and let her hold him, hugging her back with just as much force.

"There are other jobs out there, you know," she said, whispering the words into his shoulder. He could feel the heat of them through his dressing gown. "Milkman. Astronaut. Goat herder. You could take your pick."

"How did you know I've always wanted to be a goat herder?" he asked.

"You talk about it in your sleep."

They parted, and Billie opened the fridge and pulled out a bottle of wine. She proffered it to him.

"We can drink it in bed," she said. "Watch some TV upstairs with the hot blanket on."

"Sounds like heaven."

They did exactly that, after putting the girls to bed, although Kett only managed half a glass of wine and an hour of whatever BBC sitcom Billie had chosen before he couldn't keep his eyes open.

"Sorry," he told her. "Getting too old for this."

"Yeah, mid-forties, I'll order you a Zimmer frame."

She leaned over and kissed him, running her hand through his hair.

"I mean it, Robbie. Whatever happens out there, it has to stay out there. It cannot come through that door. You won't survive it. Neither of us will, not after everything we've been through."

"Deal," he said. "I promise."

It was a promise he couldn't keep, though, because in his dreams he was right back there in those tunnels, running from a force that he couldn't see but whose laughter roared like chainsaws in the dark. And when he was woken, at just after five the next morning, it was by a text from Clare.

Get your arse in here, Kett. We've ID'd our dead guy.

CHAPTER NINETEEN

Friday

By the time he'd parked the Volvo outside the morgue it was pissing it down, the world so dark it was like it had been plunged underground. Kett ran to the main doors and practically fell inside, shaking himself like a wet dog before making his way down the corridor. He turned the corner and almost walked into Superintendent Clare, who was pacing back and forth from wall to wall.

"Morning, sir," he said. "What have we got?"

"A headache, a toothache and a bad case of constipation," Clare replied. "Not to mention the fact that I had another very angry call from the Chief Constable last night reiterating how upset he was at your indiscretion."

"Sorry, sir."

"You called Foulger to apologise?"

"Um..."

Clare grunted, pushing through the double doors into the autopsy room. Franklin and Savage stood by the steel table, talking quietly. Thankfully, they did a good job of blocking the view of what sat there, but Kett caught flashes of crimson in the gaps between them. He sipped air through his lips.

"Right, Kate, tell us what we know," said Clare, perching against a bench on the side of the room.

Savage lifted a piece of paper from the desk, then stood to one side. The man from the house lay on the slab, assembled much as he would have been before he'd been attacked. It was almost worse seeing him like this, Kett thought, as if the more human they tried to make him, the worse his mutilation became. Fixed to the wall, he had been a sick piece of art.

Here, though, he was once again a man.

"Couldn't sleep last night," Savage said. "So I went on the hunt. Prints came up blank, and the chainsaw..."

She hesitated, licking lips that had been chewed to pieces.

"The chainsaw had removed most of his teeth, making a dental match impossible. We're still waiting for DNA but I'm not overly hopeful. The only identifiable thing on the victim's body was this."

She gestured to the tattoo on the man's chest. Franklin had cleaned the body to the best of her ability, but even though the blood was gone his skin was a patchwork of cuts and bruises. Kett stepped closer, trying to make sense of the dark ink. It was definitely a bird, standing on two thick legs and staring back at Kett with a beady eye. It held something in its mouth.

"Recognise it?" Savage asked.

"A stork of some kind?" Kett said, and she shook her head.

"It's a Liver bird," she said. "It's not real, it's the mythical bird on the Liverpool Football Club logo, although I tracked this image down to a museum in Liverpool, from an old sailor's home. He must have used it as a template."

"Good job," said Kett. "I'd never have guessed. So he was a Scouser?"

"That's what I was thinking," said Savage. "There's more. Emily?"

"There was a lot of dirt on his hands," said Franklin. "I mean a lot. Old dirt. It was ingrained in his skin beneath the blood, and there was more beneath his fingernails."

She pointed her metal ruler at the man's hands and Kett saw the long, yellow nails caked with filth.

"Dirt on the knees, behind the ears. It's everywhere."

"So without wanting to make any assumptions," Savage took over, "I guessed that maybe the victim didn't have easy access to washing facilities."

"He's homeless?" said Kett.

"It was one theory. Another was that he was a worker, maybe even somebody from the County Hall dig. Those guys can get filthy. But I went with the homeless theory first because, well, it was the middle of the night."

"You really didn't sleep?" asked Kett.

"No, but it worked out. You remember the CI we used to use over in Anglia Square, Paul?"

"Gummy Paul?" said Kett.

"No."

"Pervy Paul?"

"No, the other one, the one with the hair."

"Oh," said Kett. "*Bald* Paul."

"Yeah," said Savage. She caught Clare's questioning face. "It's an ironic nickname, sir. Anyway, he's living in a bedsit on Cowgate, was still up when I called by. Asked him if he knew of any Scousers in the city with a tattoo of a Liver bird on their chest. Turns out he knew quite a few."

"It's a bit of a rite of passage up North," said Clare. "Although I wouldn't know because obviously cricket is the king of sports. Football is for the lower classes."

"Sir!" said Savage. "You can't say that."

Clare held a hand up in apology.

"Bald Paul told us two of the men he knew had moved back up to Merseyside, and three didn't have dark hair, like our victim. He told me he knew one more man who might fit the bill, a labourer who came to Norwich looking for work about ten years ago. Big LFC fan, used to hang out at the Murderer's Pub in the city to watch the games."

"That's horribly appropriate," said Franklin.

"It is. Anyway, he didn't know his surname, but he went by the nickname Wee Pete."

"What is it with ironic nicknames?" grunted Clare. "He's not exactly small, is he?"

"It was more that he used to urinate down the back of the old cinema, according to Bald Paul," said Savage.

"Surely *Peepee* Pete would have been better?" said Clare. "Alliteration is not an entirely lost art, is it?"

Savage shrugged.

"I'm not sure, sir. I guess so. But anyway, Wee Pete—"

"Petey Pisspot?" Clare went on, ruminating.

"Uh, that's not really... So anyway, Wee Pete was working with a construction crew, under the radar kind of stuff, mainly Eastern Europeans. Told me they do a pickup every morning off Whitefriars, early. Thought I'd chance it this morning and there were a couple of guys living there in tents by the old car park. Friendly enough. They knew Wee Pete, and when I showed them the photo of his tattoo they told me it was almost certainly him. Right hair colour, right height, right sort of build. They told me Pete—"

"Savage," said Clare, stifling a yawn. "You know at school when they always tell you to show your working when you do a sum?"

"Yes, sir?"

"Don't. Just tell us who he is."

Savage looked crestfallen. She held up the piece of paper to reveal a photograph of a man in his late forties wearing the expression of somebody who'd seen the world and found nothing but suffering. His dark eyes looked haunted, his face covered in a scraggly beard, his nose broken. Kett looked from the photo to the corpse on Franklin's table, wondering again at the savagery and violence it would take to turn one into the other. And once again he found the silent words leaving his head.

I'm sorry this happened to you.

"Long story short," said Savage.

"Too late," muttered Clare.

"I'm almost positive that our dead guy is Peter Carran. One of the men by the river took me to Carran's girlfriend's house and she confirmed that the tattoo belongs to him. She gave me this photograph, it's about six months old. She hasn't seen him for a couple of days but she said that's not abnormal for him. He has a habit of taking off. But get this, Wee Pete had a side hustle doing garden maintenance, his girlfriend—Kelly Haworth, her name is—gave me his business card."

She pulled it out of her pocket with her free hand and

Kett took it, seeing a clip-art image of a lawnmower and reading the printed text aloud.

"*Pater*—Pater? He's spelled his own bloody name wrong —*Pater Carran Yard Services and House Clearances, All Work Considered, Free Quotes Just Call.* You've checked the phone number?"

"I have," said Savage. "Phone's off; I've put in a request for call records. I was thinking, though, that if you wanted to lure somebody to a secluded house to murder them, then this is a great pretence, right? You ask them to come and take a look at the garden. A big old house like the one on Bracondale, that overgrown garden. It would have been good money, too good for him to refuse."

"Plus, if he was a gardener, he may have had his own chainsaw," said Franklin.

Kett nodded, turning the card over to see nothing on the other side before handing it back.

"If we're lucky," Savage said, "then our killer will have called this number at some point before Peter Carran was murdered."

"That would be some luck," said Kett. "But that's amazing work, Kate, well done. I can't believe you found that out in one night."

"Might be wrong, sir," she said. "There's no way of knowing for sure without DNA or prints."

"Or a face," added Franklin.

"No, it feels right," said Kett, taking the photo from Savage and looking at it. Carran stared back at him, his jaw set, the tendons in his neck tense. Kett had met a thousand men with the same look, aggressive, quick to violence. Carran had been a big guy, and he was in shape. It wouldn't have been easy to take him down, even with a chainsaw.

"Did his girlfriend mention any grudges?" he asked. "Any enemies? Some of those work crews operate for the gangs and dealers."

"I asked, and she didn't say much. Mentioned a couple of brawls outside the pub, and the men by the river told me he wasn't somebody they'd mess about with. But everyone said he was a good man, kept his head down, kept his work honest. No gang connections that I can see, no arrests, no evidence of drug use. I don't think he was killed because of anything personal."

"No?" said Clare. "Why?"

"Uh..." Savage said. She looked exhausted, her eyes red-rimmed.

"I'm thinking the same thing," said Kett, saving her. "This feels like a random act of violence. The timing is too close to the discovery of the old bones to be a coincidence. The arrangement of the body is too similar. I think that whoever killed Carran did it in a panic. I think they heard about the cellar being uncovered, heard about the bones, and killed the first person they could."

"But why?" snorted Clare.

"Why arrange a bunch of old bones on the wall?" Kett replied. "Why keep them buried in an underground room?"

"It can't be the same person, though, sir," said Savage. "Those bones have been down there for too long. The killer would have to be a hundred years old."

"Not strictly true," he said. "The bones are old but the display in the cellar might not be. Somebody's been down in those tunnels, but the door that led into the hidden cellar was concreted shut, nobody's been in there for three years. It doesn't mean that this same person wasn't the one who made the display of bones in the first place. Maybe they built up a collection of bones for whatever reason, then sealed them inside that room knowing that they'd be there forever, nobody would ever find them. Maybe just knowing that they were there was enough for them."

"But somebody did find them," said Savage. "And we moved them. So whatever meaning those bones had to the person who put them there was, I don't know, gone?"

"Exactly," said Kett, looking at the body, at the places where the killer had tried to peel off Carran's flesh and expose the bones beneath. "The killer was prepared—they knew what they were doing—but there's no doubt this was a rush job. They were panicking, they were under pressure."

"They had a deadline," said Savage.

"This is a great big bucket of toss," said Clare.

"Sir," said Savage. "I really think—"

"Not your theory, Kate, but this case. This job. My life. One great big steaming bucket of absolute toss. I can't deny you're onto something, and my gut is telling me to tell you to follow it. I'll expedite those call records and we'll see if we can pin down any of Carran's contacts. Anything else?"

"I checked," said Franklin. "Your victim is definitely missing his astragalus bones, in both legs, and there were no knucklebones at all in the collection we found in the cellar. Either they meant nothing to the killer, and were discarded, or they meant everything."

"And were kept," said Savage.

"Billie was telling me she used to play knucklebones when she was a kid," said Kett. "Not with actual bones, the metal ones. Jacks."

"The game goes back centuries," said Savage. "More, maybe. I think the ancient Egyptians used to play it. They used the ankle bones of sheep and goats, I think."

"I don't believe this is a game," said Clare. "If these bones mean anything to our killer, it's something else."

"Billie told me it's also called snobs. Harks back to a time when only rich kids would have access to real sheep bones."

Clare stared at him, his eyes so wide they looked ready to pop.

"So?" he said after a moment.

"Uh, I just... Just thought it was worth mentioning, sir."

Clare pushed himself off the desk, traipsing towards the door.

"Get on with it," he said. "This will hit the papers today, I need to have some good news for the press release."

He hit the doors like he was rugby tackling them, stomping out of sight.

"He seems even grumpier than usual," said Franklin.

"Told me he was constipated," said Savage, pulling a face. "Hasn't been for a number two in four days, apparently."

"That's far too much information, Kate," said Kett.

"That's exactly what I said to him, sir."

"Well," said Franklin, slapping her hands together. "As fun as this conversation is, I'd better crack on."

"Okay, thanks, Emily," said Kett. He walked to the door, holding it open for Savage. "Let me know if you find anything else."

He was halfway into the corridor when Franklin's voice called him back.

"Wait, I completely forgot," the young pathologist said. "You know the meat we found in the murder house, next to all those cloaks? The weird cubes?"

"Yeah," said Kett.

"Well, I don't have an official report back yet, but I took a closer look. A couple of them still have the skin and the hair attached. I'm not 100% sure, but it looks like squirrel fur to me."

"Squirrel?" said Kett.

He caught Savage's eye, both of them realising it at the same time.

"Shit!"

CHAPTER TWENTY

"They go by the name Lord and Lady Montague," said Kett, leaning over the front seat so that Clare could hear him over the roar of the BMW's engine. Savage was driving the IRV, the siren wailing as they blasted back into the city. The dual carriageway was clear of traffic other than them and the two other police cars that followed, dawn a soft, grey blur through the windscreen.

"That's not their real names," said Savage.

"That's not exactly very helpful, then, is it?" said Clare, holding onto the strap above the door. "You saw them yesterday?"

"Yes, sir," said Kett. "When we found them, Lord Montague was skinning a squirrel, said he ate them. Evidence of a lot of drug use, heroin."

"And you didn't arrest them?" said Clare.

"Didn't warrant it," he replied. "We were chasing a different bone, so to speak. This was before we'd found Carran, obviously."

"You really think it's them, sir?" asked Savage.

"I don't know," said Kett. "But it's a possibility. They

live in the tunnels, they have done for years. There's a chance that at some point they stumbled across the bones."

"Or brought them there," said Clare.

"Maybe. Either way, they'd have known about them. Montague told us other people used the tunnels, maybe for moving drugs. He said these people knew not to mess with him."

"So maybe they did," said Savage.

"Right. Maybe there's a conflict, an argument over drugs or territory. Maybe Carran just wanted to use Montague's *en suite*, I don't know. Montague kills Carran, he arranges him on the wall so that we think there's a connection to the bones. It's a diversion, a way of throwing us off the scent."

Savage slowed as she approached the Thickthorn roundabout, easing through a red light, then accelerating hard.

"I think you're giving Montague and his wife a lot of credit, sir," she said. "That's some serious planning. I'm not sure they seemed capable."

"Never assume," said Clare. "It makes an ass out of you and me."

"What?" said Kett.

"Assume," the Super said. "Ass. U. Me."

"*What?*" Kett repeated, oblivious. "Anyway, there are too many pieces here to ignore. They live in the tunnels, they're addicts, and they've had run-ins with whoever else is down there. And when we met them, Montague was using a very big, very sharp knife to butcher some squirrels."

"It's enough for an arrest," said Clare. "You know where he is?"

"We know where he was," Kett said. "But I told him to scarper."

The Super gave him a withering stare. Savage left the

A11 and joined the A47, overtaking the trucks and the delivery vans before pulling off a few minutes later. The ugly bulk of County Hall appeared on the dark horizon, a monolith that seemed to look down on the city—not protective, but aloof.

If Derek Foulger was a building, thought Kett, *that would be it.*

They drove alongside its sprawling grounds before sling-shotting around the roundabout and heading up the hill. There were more flashing lights ahead, two IRVs waiting for them at the junction with King Street. Savage eased past them, then pulled over at the side of the road. A huddle of soaking wet uniformed constables greeted them as they climbed out, illuminated by the car headlights and by the first haze of dawn.

"Any sign of him?" barked Clare.

"We can't find the place, sir," said one. "You sure this is the right location?"

"It's invisible from out here, unless you know where to look," said Kett, pushing past them and entering the steep, wooded hillside. "Especially in the dark. Follow me."

He ran down the uneven path, past the two medieval towers that had once been part of the old city wall, scouring the slope that rose overhead as half a dozen torches crawled across it. Even though he'd only been here yesterday, even though he'd fallen down the same bloody hill less than twenty-four hours ago, he couldn't see any trace of the opening to Lord Montague's lair. It was as if the dense foliage had grown over it, sealed it shut like a wound.

"Shit," he said. "It was up there somewhere."

"There," said Savage, pointing to the tiniest sliver of broken rock beneath a monstrous bush. Kett wasn't sure that was it, then Savage directed her finger to a deep scar that ran from the bush all the way to the ground. "That's the track your backside made on the way down, sir."

"Oh, yeah," he said, turning to the officers. "Not much use shouting a warning as there's a back door. Can you get up there, sharpish?"

Nobody looked too happy about the prospect of trying, but they threw themselves up the slope as best they could, grabbing great handfuls of weeds and tree roots as their boots slipped and slid in the mud. Their torches swept wildly through the air, reminding Kett of searchlights looking for planes. Two coppers came sliding back down on their bellies before they'd made it halfway, Clare roaring at them like a drill sergeant on an assault course. Past the sound of his fury, Kett heard laughter, and he turned to see Porter walking down the path.

"This is amazing," said the DI, pulling out his phone and holding it up. "Look at them go!"

Another constable lost her grip, slipping all the way down from the top of the slope and losing her hat in the process. Clare glowered at her, then at Porter.

"If you're filming this, Porter, then I'm going to ram that phone so far up your tosshole you'll need a catheter if you ever want to make a call."

Porter's face blanched as he slid the phone back into his pocket.

"Wouldn't dream of it, sir."

With a Herculean effort, one of the constables made it to the top of the hill and penetrated the thick fortification of foliage. Kett could hear him announcing himself with a fierce shout, but after thirty seconds his head appeared again.

"No sign of anyone," he said. "There's a tunnel leading out the other side, you want me to follow it?"

"No," said Kett. "Can you have a look around the cave? See if they left any clues. And be careful, there will be needles."

The copper nodded, helping another couple of Uniforms inside before disappearing again. The rest of the officers slumped back down to the path, caked in mud and leaves and looking more than a little sorry for themselves.

"Shit," said Kett. "He's flown."

"Well, you did give him plenty of warning," said Clare. "Have a look for him out here, he might be hanging around."

The Superintendent stomped back towards the street and Kett made his way down the slippery wooden steps that had been set into the hillside. Fingers of weak sunlight had started probing the trees, peeling apart the scraggy canopies like a curious giant. Traffic flowed on the road below as the city started to wake up, red lights dancing over the bridge that led to the football ground.

"How was your night?" Kett asked Porter as the DI traipsed after him.

"Nice," he said, his face lit up by his phone screen. "Quiet. You, sir?"

"Ended up going out with Ron Lewington," he said. "For a pint."

"Lewington? You mean Kitty Lewington's kid? Why?"

"He's not a kid, Pete. He's a couple of years older than me. Got kids the same age, him and a few others have a support group for... I don't know what the word is. Exhausted? Yeah, exhausted dads. There's six of them. It was..."

He shrugged as they neared the bottom of the steps.

"It was good, you know? Nice to have somebody to moan to. You should come along next time."

"Haven't actually got a kid yet, sir," said Porter, shining

his torch into the trees. "How come you never go for a pint with me?"

"With you? I mean... You've never really asked."

"I have," said Porter, shining the torch at Kett like he was interrogating him. "I ask all the time. 'Fancy a drink, sir?' 'Want to nip out for a curry after work, sir?' 'Come over for a beer at the weekend, sir.' I say it all the time."

Kett gently pushed the DI's torch away, blinking the fire from his eyes. Porter looked like he was pouting.

"I literally can't remember you ever asking me," said Kett. "Sorry, mate. I'll say yes next time, I promise."

"Okay," said Porter. "So a drink after work today, then?"

"Uh..."

The look of anticipation on Porter's face was so sincere that there was only one answer he could give. He'd only just opened his mouth, though, when something exploded from the thick bushes like a charging boar and slammed into the DI's back.

Porter fell into Kett with a cry of pain, both of them tumbling down the last few steps onto the dirt path below. Kett landed first, Porter dropping hard on top of him, his knee landing in Kett's stomach. Through the fireworks show of agony, Kett saw Lord Montague leap over the wooden handrail and vanish back into the bushes.

"Motherfuckers!" the scrawny man shrieked.

"Shit," said Porter, hauling himself up and offering Kett a hand. "Oi, stop! Police!"

They went after him, climbing the steps. The fall had knocked the air out of Kett's lungs but Porter's voice was loud enough to wake the dead.

"Police! Stop fucking running!"

Porter vaulted the handrail with ease but Kett didn't fancy his chances, ducking underneath it. Montague was invisible as he climbed the slope, the bushes shaking violently as he cut through them. Coppers had appeared at the top of the steps, careening this way. Kett pointed into the bushes in the hope they'd follow the direction of his finger.

"Where is he?" Porter growled, kicking a bush.

Kett pushed into the vegetation, branches whipping at his face, leaving welts on his skin. Every step was a struggle, roots catching his feet and bringing him down. Montague had to be used to the terrain because he was as quick as a mountain goat. Only his haggard breaths gave him away, and the occasional crack of a branch beneath him. It was still too dark, the crazed beams of torchlight making things harder rather than easier.

"You go that way," he said to Porter. "Flush him."

"Like a turd, sir," said Porter as he scampered away.

Kett pushed on alone, his legs burning from the steep climb. The hillside was chaos as the coppers pushed through the bushes, the air alive with shouts that did a perfect job of concealing the sound of Montague's movements. Kett stopped, his hand on the slim trunk of a sapling, his breath held tight in his lungs as he listened for movement.

There, up and to his left. He used the tree to haul himself higher, his boots slipping in the mud, rain dripping into his eyes. There was a section of hill ahead that was too steep for anyone to climb, but Kett thought he could see movement there, something hiding in a tangle of cow parsley and bramble. Sure enough, when torchlight sliced down the hill it caught two white eyes that seemed to burn with panic.

"Montague," said Kett, his voice struggling to carry over the shouts of the police. "Give it up, there's nowhere to go."

"You sure about that?" came a reedy reply, and Montague broke his cover, running.

"For fuck's sake," Kett grumbled.

He threw himself after the man, momentum the only thing keeping him going on the ridiculously steep slope. His feet caught on the stump of something and he started to fall, but with a roar of defiance he hurled himself at Montague's back, landing on him like a rucksack and clinging on for dear life. The man snapped like a twig, and before Kett could do anything about it they were both rolling down the hill, through needled tangles of blackberry and over knuckled roots—tumbling over each other for what felt like an eternity before they finally came to a stop at the bottom.

"Ow," Kett groaned, shaking stars from his eyes. He was lying on his back, Montague right next to him, the other man making a noise like he was about to vomit. He wasn't sure if anyone had seen them fall because the police were still scattered across the hillside overhead, none of them pointing their torches this way. Kett opened his mouth to call them down.

Then stopped dead when he felt something sharp against his throat.

Oh no.

"Don't move," said Montague in a hoarse, panting whisper. "Don't even breathe, or I'll push this thing until it comes out the other side. Hear?"

Kett didn't dare nod, the point of the knife right under the ridge of his windpipe.

"I'll fucking empty you, pig," Montague went on. "Why are you after me?"

"Kett?" Porter called out, sounding too far away. "Robbie? Where are you?"

Montague pushed the knife a little harder and Kett felt

the tickle of blood as it wound down his neck. It was excruciating, but he didn't dare move. In the time it would take him to lift an arm or roll away Montague would end him.

"Why?" the skinny man said again.

"We found a body," Kett told him. "A man. Peter Carran. You know him?"

"No," said Montague, leaning in. His breath was rancid, the smell of old meat. "What's it got to do with me?"

"We found the body in a house just up from here, on Bracondale. Run down place, falling apart but massive. You know it?"

"Yeah," Montague said after a moment.

"You've been there?"

The other man licked his lips. There were more shouts from the hillside, Porter's voice rising above them all. How the hell hadn't they found him yet?

"We found squirrel meat inside the house, Montague," Kett pressed, trying to twist his neck away from the blade only to feel it dig deeper, worrying its way beneath his skin. "Neatly cut. Bit of a coincidence, isn't it? There's a tunnel there that leads right to your place."

"Tunnels lead to every fucking house in the city if you look hard enough. I been there, so what? Didn't kill no one. Not a violent bone in my body, mate."

"You've got a knife to my throat right now," said Kett.

"Self-preservation, that, innit? I got to preserve myself from all you fuckers."

Some of the torches were starting to explore the bottom of the hill now. They'd find him in seconds.

But that might not be quick enough.

"You been worried about your self-preservation before?" Kett asked. "You ever needed to defend yourself, with force?"

Montague sniffed, but he didn't answer.

"Come with me now," said Kett. "Give yourself up and we can forget all about this. I mean it, there's nowhere to go."

"You're wrong," he replied, leaning in. "You just watch. Man like me can disappear, and they'll be too busy trying to save your life to even look."

"Don't."

The knife slid deeper and Kett's heart roared, almost loud enough to mute the thunder of approaching feet. Then a giant shadow ploughed into view, a solid kick to the head that sent Montague tumbling back into the bushes. Kett rolled away, somehow making it to his knees, one hand to his blood-slick throat. Porter dropped onto Montague's stomach and hit him so hard that the ground seemed to shake with the force of it.

"Knife!" he yelled, ripping it from the man's grip and hurling it into the bushes.

Two uniformed constables bouldered down the slope, one of them almost landing on Kett. They piled onto Montague like a pack of wolves. In seconds it was over, Montague on his belly with his hands cuffed behind his back, his entire body bucking and his mouth frothing like somebody had plugged him into the mains.

Porter turned to Kett, who was still on his knees.

"Shit, sir, are you okay?"

He offered his hand, and for the second time that day Kett let himself be hauled up by the big DI. He touched his neck again and saw blood on his fingers, but the wound was already starting to heal. The knife hadn't gone as deep as he'd thought.

It still stung like a bastard, though.

"Yeah," he said. "Thanks, Pete."

“Was he actually going to *stab* you?”

Kett shrugged, the pain flaring. The adrenaline rush was starting to fade, making every cell in his body pound. The woodland was spinning, and he wondered whether he’d be better off back on his knees until the vertigo passed. Luckily, Porter held onto him.

“Absolute prick,” said Porter, directing the words at Montague. He turned to the constables. “Can you get that piece of shit out of here? Take him down to the road, we’ll pick him up there. And nobody’s going to cry if he rolls down another hill, if you get me.”

They heaved Montague up, doing their best to carry him to the wooden fence that separated the hill from the street that lay at the bottom of it. He still had no plans to go lightly, thrashing with every ounce of strength he possessed, his long dreadlocks thrashing like a nest of angry snakes.

“You okay to walk?” asked Porter.

“I’m fine,” said Kett. “It was just a nick. Thanks again, mate, I owe you one.”

Porter nodded grimly, then broke into a smile.

“You do,” he said as he steered Kett down the slope. “So first round’s on you. Tonight. After work. When we go for a drink.”

CHAPTER TWENTY-ONE

KETT RINSED HIS FACE IN THE SINK, THE COLD WATER numbing his already frozen skin. A trickle of blood circled the drain, but when he checked his neck in the mirror there was only the tiniest of scratches there. It was impossible not to notice how close it was to the cord of his trachea, though, and he tried not to think about where he'd be now if Montague had pressed a bit harder. In the back of an ambulance, maybe. Or in a hospital bed.

Or on Emily Franklin's table in the morgue.

"Idiot," he told himself, although he couldn't quite work out how, in the middle of all those coppers, he'd ended up alone with the man.

He shook the water from his hands and held them under the drier, which wasn't working. Cursing it, he made his way out of the toilets into the brutal chill of HQ. Whatever the problem had been with the heating yesterday it clearly hadn't been fixed, the cold enough to crack his bones. He walked through the bullpen to collect his jacket, which was still caked in mud, then headed up the corridor to the interview rooms. Clare and Savage were waiting for him there.

"Are you okay, sir?" asked Savage, studying the wound. "Looks painful."

"He'll live," Clare replied. He'd given Kett a proper bollocking as soon as he'd caught up to them, of course, one that had stung as much as the knife wound. It was fair enough. They'd had almost twenty officers on site, half of them armed with Tasers. There had been no excuses for a tumble in the mud. "Important thing is we've got the arsehole in cuffs. Whether he's guilty of the murder or not, nobody gets away with putting a knife to a copper's neck."

He eyeballed Kett.

"Even one as annoying as you. You up for this? Kate's happy to stand in."

"I'd like to talk with him," said Kett. "He lawyered up?"

"Representing himself," said Clare with a grim smile. "But we've nabbed his girlfriend, too. Or wife, whatever she is. She's on her way in, and she wants a brief."

"She'll roll on him, no doubt," said Savage. "She gave us his real name, too. Philip Merritt. She sounded furious with him."

"Where's Porter?" asked Kett.

"Sent him back out," said Clare. "You're lucky he was there, Robbie."

Kett nodded.

"Ready?"

"I am," said Clare. "Let's tear him a new tosshole."

Kett opened the door, instantly assaulted by an overpowering combination of aromas. The worst of them was the stench of Montague's body odour, which was ripe enough to make the air shimmer. This was mixed with a hint of mud and old vegetation and the unmistakable aroma of fresh piss.

Sure enough, when Kett looked to the corner of the room he saw a puddle there, staining the carpet. The expression of satisfaction on Montague's face made it very clear he'd been happy to mark his territory. He leaned back, his cuffed hands behind his head, his dreadlocks so long they were almost on the floor. There was an ugly bruise on his temple where Porter had kicked him.

"Took a leak," he said. "Hope you don't mind."

"We don't," said Clare nonchalantly, taking a seat on the opposite side of the table. "Had a guy here once who stuffed a handful of his own shit into the tape recorder. Now that was proper rebellion. Everyone and his mother has taken a piss in here, it's nothing special."

Some of the smugness left Montague's face and he sniffed, wiping the back of his hand over his mouth.

"I'll happily take a shit in—" he started, but Clare cut him off, pressing the button on the recorder and announcing the interview.

"Don't interrupt me," said Montague, the cuffs rattling as he pointed both forefingers at the Super. "You don't get to—"

"So, *Phillip*," Kett said, cutting the man off again. "You want to tell me why you just tried to kill a police officer?"

"Stop being so dramatic," the other man said, a smile flashing those pink gums. "Just poked you a bit, can barely even see it from here. I've had bigger cuts shaving."

"Luckily another officer stopped you from seriously hurting me," said Kett. "But this is still attempted murder, Phillip, don't be in any doubt about that."

"That's life," said Clare. "Forty years. How old are you, Phillip?"

"My name's Lord—"

"How old," Clare demanded, and there was no denying the violence in his voice. Montague swallowed noisily, looking back and forth between them.

"Forty-eight, I think," he said. "Near enough, anyway. Don't know for sure."

"You'll die in prison," said Clare, and this robbed the last trace of confidence from the man's face. "So before we take this any further, think very, very hard about how you want to answer these questions."

"The body in the Bracondale house," Kett said, pulling out a photocopy of the picture they'd received from Carran's girlfriend. "It's a man called Peter Carran. I asked you before, on the hill, but I don't think you were paying attention. Do you know him?"

Montague stared at the photo, his tongue darting across his lips like a lizard's.

"Look," he said after a minute. "I know what you want me to say, and I am going to say it, and it's going to make me look guilty, but I swear on my mother's life I didn't kill him."

"You knew him?" asked Kett.

"Long time ago. I'm talking years back, when I had a job. I worked down at the quarry and so did he. I swear, I didn't even know his name. Scouser. He was an arsehole, he had a temper. He got fired, I think, for losing his rag with the foreman or site manager or whatever. I wasn't there, just heard about it. But I swear, I never saw him again."

"When was the last time you were in that house?" asked Kett.

"Years ago," Montague replied. "Two, three. Me and the missus camped out there for a while. We found the way in through the tunnels, you know? We've moved about down there for years, you find your way into all kinds of places.

Used it for a night and then left cos somebody else was living there, some fucker, he chased us out. Said he was gonna kill us."

"Who?" asked Kett, and Montague threw his cuffed hands into the air.

"Fuck should I know? It was dark, he was wearing a coat, he had his hood up. Shit myself, mate. And that's not an exaggeration. I *actually* shit myself, fell right down me trouser leg into my flip flop."

"You never went back?"

"Never," he said. "Swear to the lord in heaven. That house is cursed, bad shit happens there."

"You're not the first person to use that word," said Kett. "Cursed."

Montague shrugged again, less dramatically this time.

"Some places just fuck you over," he said. "It's right there in their bones. They just want to hurt you."

"You said he was wearing a coat, this man," said Kett. "A hood. Could it have been a cloak?"

"A cloak?" Montague echoed. He tilted his head, his eyes rolling up. "No. I mean, I don't know. Maybe? It was years ago, and I was... well, I was baked. That's why I shit myself, not the fear. Not *just* the fear. But yeah, could have been, I guess."

"Would your girlfriend remember?"

"She can't remember where her own fanny is half the time."

Kett rubbed the wound in his neck, which had started to itch. He'd used an antibacterial wipe on it, found in a first aid kit from one of the IRVs, and he was trying not to think about where the blade might have been before it had cut him.

"There was squirrel meat in the Bracondale house," he

went on. "Cubed, just like we found at your place in the cliff. Can you explain that?"

"Half the city eats squirrels," he said. "Fresh meat on your doorstep, I've lived off them for years. Can't pin all those dead squirrels on me."

"I don't need to," said Kett, leaning across the table. "Because all I need is for a jury to see the links. You've been in the house before, you know the way in through the tunnels, you used to work with the dead man, and we found the same snack-pack of squirrel meat. When we came to question you, you ran, then you stabbed a police officer in the throat with a very sharp knife, the kind of knife you butcher squirrels with, the kind of knife you can joint much bigger animals with. You own a chainsaw, Phillip?"

"No! I didn't—"

Kett slammed his fist onto the table and Montague almost leapt a foot in the air.

"I don't actually give a shit about you," he growled, the exhaustion finally catching up with him. "I think this city will be a better place without you in it, whether you're a murderer or not. You're going to prison, Phillip. It's up to you for how long. Did you kill Peter Carran?"

Montague met Kett's eyes and held them.

"No."

There was no lie on his face, not even a hint of one.

"Tell me something useful and I'll see what I can do to reduce your sentence," Kett said.

"I think maybe I want to call my—"

Kett hit the table again, harder.

"Don't you dare," he said. "Tell me something useful, Phillip. Right now."

It looked, for a moment, like he was going to cry, his eyes glistening in the harsh light of the room.

"I don't know who did it," he said, his bottom lip quivering. "I swear on my life."

"Tell me more about the man in the cloak," said Kett. "It was a man, right?"

Montague nodded.

"Tall? Short? Fast? Slow?"

"He was big. Tall, but fat too. Fat bastard, for sure. Was out of breath from chasing us. That's all I remember, he was fat and he had a hood and..."

His eyes brightened.

"He had a limp," he said. "I remember now, a limp, cos he almost buggered over on the steps. He was proper raging, and he definitely had a limp."

Kett glanced at Clare but the Super wouldn't meet his eye. His fists rested on the table, clenched so tightly that his knuckles were bone white.

"What about his voice? You said he was swearing at you. What did he sound like? Did he have an accent?"

"Like a bloke," Montague whined. "Like, I don't know, like an angry fat bloke. He was local, though, proper local boy. Told me I was a fucking koala, a koala with a small cock or something. Or maybe it wasn't a koala. I don't know. Weasel maybe? Told me I was a dead man."

"Did he call you a limp-dicked weasel?"

"That's enough, Kett," said Clare, his voice low and cold.

"You're absolutely sure those are the—"

"I said that's enough," Clare repeated, pushing his chair back and standing up. "This interview is terminated at 09:14."

He clicked off the recorder.

"Sir?" Kett said to the Super's back.

"With me, Detective," Clare said, opening the door and holding it. "Now."

A soft laugh slipped out of Kett's lips, but only because he couldn't work out what was going on. He stood up and walked to Clare, looking back.

"Phillip," he said. "One more question."

Clare actually took hold of his arm, but Kett shook him off.

"Back there on the hill. Were you going to kill me?"

"No," Montague said, the same answer he'd given when Kett had asked him about Carran. Only this time his eyes were locked on the top of the table, his hands scratching at his head, his feet scuffing the floor.

The lie was right there.

CHAPTER TWENTY-TWO

"What the hell was that, sir?"

Kett shot the words at Clare's back as the Superintendent barged through the doors that led to the bullpen. There was no sign of Savage, no sign of anyone in the dark, cold corridors, which is what gave Kett the courage to reach out and grab hold of Clare's shoulder.

"What's going on?"

Clare whirled around, looking angrier than he had ever seen him—his face so warped with fury that Kett actually took a step back.

"Leave it, Detective," Clare spat. "Whatever you think this is, you leave it alone."

"*What?*" Kett said. "You heard Montague, sir. He said he was chased out of the house by a fat guy with a limp, a man who used the insult limp-dicked weasel—or close enough. Foulger called me the exact same thing yesterday. I can't be the only one who's making a connection."

"It doesn't matter, Kett."

"Doesn't matter?"

The door at the end of the corridor opened and a

uniformed sergeant walked through, nodding to them both. Kett waited until she'd gone before he spoke again, keeping his voice low.

"It's Foulger's house, sir. He owns the property where Carran was murdered. He has a limp, he has a local accent."

"It doesn't mean a damned thing," said Clare. "It doesn't prove anything. It's not enough to bring him in."

"It's proof Foulger has been in the house," said Kett. "Proof he was lying, because he told me he's never set foot in the place. It's enough to bring him in and ask him some proper questions."

Clare shook his head, walking away again.

"We brought Montague in on less," Kett said quietly. "Why's it any different for Foulger?"

The Super stopped, his body deflating with a sigh.

"You know why," he said.

"Because Montague's poor, because he's homeless, because he's an addict, right?"

Clare didn't reply, but that was answer enough.

"And because Foulger's wealthy, he's connected, he's got friends in high places," Kett went on. "I thought nobody got to do that, sir? I thought nobody got to be above the law."

"Then you're an idiot," said Clare, although there was no malice there. "Because some people are."

He walked on, opening the door.

"Hollenbeck thought they were," Kett said. "They thought nobody would ever stand up to them. How much did they get away with because of that? How many people died?"

Clare paused, framed in the doorway.

"I'm not saying it's not him, Kett. I'm not even saying don't go after him." He sighed again. "I'm saying don't make it obvious."

THERE WAS nobody in the bullpen, so Kett made his way to the Incident Room, finding Savage and Duke perched shoulder to shoulder on one of the desks—looking every bit like a couple of giddy teenagers. They were laughing as Kett stepped through the door, and both of them tried to cover it with a cough, Savage hopping off the desk and flapping her arms like she was trying to take off.

"Right," she said.

"Right?"

"Right."

"Right," echoed Kett. "I'm not going to ask. Porter around?"

"Making tea," said Savage.

"As if this week couldn't get any worse."

Somebody had already got some things up on the boards that covered the far wall. In the centre of the display were two images, so similar and yet so different. On the left was a photograph of the skeletal display they'd found beneath the ground, that gruesome spiral of yellow bones arranged around a silently screaming skull.

Right next to it, like a distorted mirror image, was the corpse they'd found in the Bracondale house, the brutalised, faceless head of Peter Carran caught in a web of severed limbs. Scraps of bone peeked out behind fleshy curtains, the sight of them making Kett's stomach boil.

A handful of photographs had been printed and pinned. Carran was there, that same dead-eyed image that Kett had in his pocket. Lord Montague's mugshot hung next to it, and beside that, a snapshot of his girlfriend. On the other side, next to the bones, was a photo of the site foreman, Geoff Wileman, and a picture of Kitty Lewington too—only, he presumed, because they'd been the first people to enter the room when it had been found.

"Not much to go on, sir," said Savage.

"Don't suppose you've checked alibis for Wileman, have you?"

"Yeah," said Savage. "He told Duke he was on-site all day yesterday managing the shutdown, and a couple of lads from the crew confirmed it, not that they're the most reliable lot. Haven't checked with Lewington, should I give her a call?"

"No," said Kett. "I spoke to her yesterday. She was in the city with her son and his kids all day. Just wanted to rule them out. Like you say, there's not much to go on."

"How'd it go with Montague?" she asked.

"I don't think it was him. But he did know Carran."

"Really? That's a lot of connections, sir. Why don't you think he did it? He tried to take a slice out of you."

Kett didn't answer, rubbing his neck so hard that he felt the blood start to flow again.

"Shit," he said.

"I'll get you a plaster, sir," said Savage. "Hang on."

She left the room, abandoning Duke at his desk. He'd woken the computer and was logging into Facebook.

"What are you up to, Duke?" Kett asked.

"Just got to check my latest Facebook post, sir. Official business."

Savage returned, holding the door open for Porter, who held three mugs of tea in his big hands.

"Oh, sorry sir," he said as he dropped them onto the nearest table. "I didn't realise you'd finished. I'll make you one."

"There's no time," said Kett.

"You can have mine," said Duke and Savage, almost perfectly synchronised.

"I'm really okay," said Kett.

"Won't hear of you going without, sir."

Porter picked up a mug and dropped it on the desk next to Kett. The tea was the colour of bone, and there were so many oily black things floating on the surface it looked like the Exxon Valdese had sunk in there.

"What are you doing, Duke?" asked Porter, spotting the PC on the computer. "You better not be posting more photos of me."

He walked over, and while his back was turned Kett tipped his drink into the potted yucca in the corner of the room.

"You do realise that's not a real plant?" said Savage, opening the plaster and using her fingertips to tilt Kett's head back. She gently secured it to the wound, pressing down the edges.

"Just as well," said Kett. "Because Porter's tea would kill it. Thanks, Kate. Porter, Duke, can I have your attention?"

They didn't seem to hear him, the two men bickering about whatever was on the computer. Kett peered past Porter's head to see a photograph of Duke on the screen, the one that had been taken when he'd emerged from the tunnel beneath the Bracondale house. The chalk dust had stuck to the sheen of cold sweat on his face, so much of it in his beard that he looked like Santa. His eyes were wide and still full of fear, his terror seeming to flow from the screen.

"Let's have a look at the comments, then," said Porter, wrestling the mouse away from Duke and scrolling down. "Here we go... What the hell?"

"'*He's so brave,*'" Duke read aloud with a grin. "'*He's a credit to the force, and handsome too.*'"

"'*Makes me want to get arrested,*'" read Savage, who had joined them. "'*Somebody call 999 and tell him where to find me. He can bring his cuffs.*' Oh my God, Aaron."

"'*Is there a photo of his truncheon anywhere?*'" said Kett, trawling the comments.

"What?" said Porter, disgusted.

"'*What's his address?*'" Duke read on, his smile growing even wider. "'*123 Letsbe Avenue? Let's be 'aving him, more like!*'"

"You wrote these, didn't you Duke?" Porter said, furious. "I bet you sat up all night doing it."

"'*He can explore my tunnels anytime he likes?*'" Savage said, reading the comment with a snort of laughter. "Bloody hell, Aaron, you've got some fans, that's for sure."

"Yeah, well, let's have a look at my post then," said Porter. "Go on, I bet I've got fans too."

"You probably shouldn't look, sir," said Duke.

"Now, *Constable*."

Duke clicked back, then selected the photo of Porter mid-sneeze. He scrolled down to the comments and even Kett couldn't keep the smile off his face.

"'*He looks like one of my haemorrhoids,*'" Porter said quietly, reading it off the screen. "What's that supposed to mean?"

"Fairly self-explanatory, sir," said Duke.

"'*My Uncle Albert had a face like that,*'" read Savage. "'*But he was a pug.*'"

"Here's a good one," said Duke, tapping the screen. "'*Good to see the police trying new tactics to fight crime. If this guy tried to arrest me, I'd throw myself off...*'"

He grimaced.

"Okay, maybe that one's not so good. But I'm sure there's a nice one here somewhere."

He scrolled down the page.

"Uh..."

He scrolled further.

"Forget it," said Porter, backing away. "Unbelievable."

"You don't *normally* look like a haemorrhoid, sir," said Savage. "It's just a really bad photo."

"Enough," said Kett. "I need your heads back on the job."

Everyone turned to face him.

"Montague's going away, but I don't think he killed Carran. Can't say for sure yet, but my gut's telling me this is somebody else."

"Any idea who?" asked Porter.

"Maybe, but for now, this is just between us, okay? Nothing leaves this room, and we don't put anything on the board."

"Derek Foulger," said Savage, and Kett nodded.

"Montague told us he'd been in the Bracondale house before, he squatted there for a night until somebody found them and scared them off. Didn't see the man's face, but he said he was a big guy with a limp, and that he called Montague a limp-dicked weasel."

"That's a pretty specific insult," said Porter.

"He also said he was wearing a hood."

"The cloaks we found in the house had hoods," said Savage. "Did you see Hay's report?"

Kett shook his head.

"She's taken hairs from all of them, but it'll be a while before we get DNA back. There was blood, too. Human. Not much."

"Good to know," said Kett. "This is Foulger's house, his family built the place and he sold it to a holding company owned by him and his wife. He knew it was deserted, and he had ample means to access the property."

"He would have known about the tunnels, sir," said Savage.

"Right," said Kett. "And let's not forget that the symbol for his guild was found engraved on the property—a crowned eye surrounded by a circle of feet. It's too close to our arrangement of bones to be a coincidence, I'm sure of it. Kitty Lewington told me the Harford Guild had a history of arcane ritual. Occult stuff. Stretches back centuries."

"Seriously?" said Duke, and Kett nodded.

"There's too much here to ignore," said Kett. "But the Boss doesn't want us going after him. Foulger's too well connected. He needs evidence, he needs something concrete, and we're going to find it. Whatever it takes. First thing we need to do is work out where he was yesterday afternoon between twelve and three, when Carran was murdered."

He rubbed his throat again, thinking about Montague, thinking about the knife that had almost ended him—that *would* have ended him, if Porter hadn't intervened.

"You're sure about Montague?" said Savage, reading his mind. "Because a lot of pieces fit. There's enough here to charge him."

"I'm not sure, no," Kett confessed. "We pursue both angles. Montague isn't going anywhere, we've got time. Kate, Duke, can you guys check his alibi, see if you can pin together his movements yesterday. Pete, you and I will go after Foulger."

"Yes, sir," said Porter. He looked at the empty mug on Kett's desk and broke into a surprised grin. "You drank your tea!"

"I did," said Kett, clearing his throat and trying not to

look at the puddle of milky liquid that was seeping out of the bottom of the plant pot. "It was great."

He glanced at the boards again, seeing those twisted sculptures of flesh and bone.

"We're the Extreme Crime Task Force," he said, opening the door. "And it doesn't get any more extreme than this. So let's get to work."

CHAPTER TWENTY-THREE

Porter sat in the passenger seat of Kett's Volvo as the DCI drove them to County Hall. Every now and again he would glance into the back, at the sea of crisp packets and chocolate wrappers and plastic bottles that had washed up there. It resembled the city tip so much that he half expected a seagull to appear, battering the windows with its wings.

"I know, I know," said Kett. "I've been meaning to clean it."

"Never said a word, sir,"

"There's just no time," said Kett as he pulled off the roundabout. "I don't know how it happens but kids change the laws of physics. They take whatever time you have and just... I don't know, they just eat it. You think you've got all the time in the world to do everything you need to, but then you check your watch and you realise you're already late and nobody is ready. Every single time."

"Looking forward to it," said Porter, a not-entirely pleasant shiver of fear running up his back and settling in his scalp.

"It's different when they're babies," said Kett. "Time doesn't really seem to exist at all when they're first born. You float around in a sort of daze, nothing's real. *You* don't feel real."

"Sounds... weird," said Porter.

"But you'll be great," said Kett. "That's the thing I keep telling myself, it'll all be okay in the end so stop worrying about the little things. You'll get to where you need to be, the rubbish will get cleared away. The important thing is spending time with them, because when they get to eighteen or whatever and they leave the house, you won't be kicking yourself for playing with them every day instead of tidying up. You'll never regret deciding to spend time with them."

Porter nodded, looking into the back seat again. Kett had misunderstood his thought process, because he wasn't at all interested in the mess. He'd just spotted what looked like a multipack of Fudge that still had one left in it. He wondered whether he should wait until they'd arrived before surreptitiously fishing it out of the mess.

Sod it.

He craned his arm back, grabbing the pack and shaking the last Fudge free. To his immense disappointment it had been opened, half of it gone and the rest smooshed at the bottom of the wrapper.

"Don't eat that," said Kett. "I can't guarantee it's safe."

"It's probably fine, sir," said Porter.

"It'll have been stood on and all sorts," said Kett. "Probably been in one of their noses too. I really wouldn't chance it. Things can't be that bad, mate, surely."

Porter sighed, dropping the Fudge into his lap. Kett steered the big car up the hill towards the booth, winding down his window to flash his warrant card at the security guard who sat there. When the barrier opened he drove along the face of the giant building to where Foulger's Jag had been parked the night before. There was no sign of it.

"You reckon he's off sick?" said Kett.

"Bit of a coincidence if he is, sir," said Porter.

"Go find out. See if you can confirm his alibi, find out where he was yesterday."

"Yes sir," said Porter. "Where are you going?"

"To check out his house," said Kett.

Porter opened his door, the cold, wet air flooding the car. He shivered his way out, clutching the Fudge to his chest.

"Leave it, Pete," said Kett.

"I'm going to put it in the bin, sir."

The hard stare Kett gave him was one he'd seen him give his kids countless times.

"Leave it."

Porter gazed at the chocolate for a moment, inhaling the smell of it, then chucked it onto the seat and slammed the door. Kett nodded his approval and pulled away, doing a U-turn at the end of the road and doubling back. His window was down.

"Under the radar, Pete," he said, before roaring away.

Porter glanced down the flank of County Hall, wondering whether he should start by checking out the building site. But he couldn't hear diggers, and there were no vans parked on the side of the road, no men or women in fluorescent jackets and hard hats. Even if they were back at work there wasn't much more damage they could do—they'd already filled in the crime scene.

He climbed the stairs instead, using the railing to haul himself up and finding that he was short of breath at the top. This was ridiculous. Just a year ago he'd been in the best shape of his life, pretty much. Since his twenties, anyway. He'd fallen apart in the few months he'd known Allie was pregnant, and he wasn't even sure why. Yes, he was eating more to try and make *her* eat more, because she'd been off her food. And yes, in those times where she'd recovered her appetite, he'd eaten more to make her feel better about eating more.

But all the times he was eating on his own?

He had no idea what that was about, other than stress. He felt it gnawing at him now, the fear of what might happen in a few short weeks when Allie gave birth, the worry of whether it would all be okay, the terror of those early days, then the later ones, and then the hundreds and thousands that would follow that.

"Fuck," he said, swallowing the panic down where it stewed unpleasantly in his gut.

He pushed through the door into the enormous reception area, a handful of people waiting on couches while others busied themselves behind a wide desk. The space felt cavernous thanks to the high ceilings, everyone's voices muted, sound doing that weird, muffled thing it always did in places like this. He walked to the desk, offering a nod to the woman who sat there—the same woman who'd come to check on Foulger's car when they'd set off the alarm yesterday. She glanced over the top of her spectacles, frowning when Porter held up his warrant card.

"Detective Inspector Peter Porter, Norfolk Police," he said. "Is Derek Foulger around, by any chance?"

"Do you have an appointment?" the woman asked. Porter jiggled the warrant card.

"Uh, no. Generally, we don't need one."

"Well, here you do," she said. "Mr Foulger isn't in today. Can I take a message?"

"He's at home?" asked Porter. She didn't answer, still staring over the top of her glasses like an irritated schoolmarm. Porter kept the warrant card open. "You know, I can stand here like this all day until you look at it."

She huffed a breath as she glanced at the warrant card.

"I can't magic him out of thin air, I'm afraid," she said. "So if you'd like to leave a message?"

Porter folded the warrant card and put it back in his pocket.

"Is his PA here?" he asked. "Secretary, whatever. I have a couple of questions for them."

The woman huffed again, picking up the phone. Porter turned away while she made the call, scanning the lobby for a vending machine or a café. There had to be one in a place this size, didn't there?

"She's on her way down," said the receptionist. "Take a seat."

Porter didn't do as he was asked, walking past the waiting area to the far wall. Dozens of portraits of austere-looking men and women hung there alongside old maps and bright, newer-looking artworks that could have been made by children. He made his way along the wall, peering through the doors as he passed them and almost squeaking with delight when he spotted a vending machine through the glass. He tried the handle but it wouldn't open, a card reader mounted to the side of the door.

"Come on," he said, jiggling the handle again, just to make sure.

"You need clearance," said a voice behind him, close enough to make him jump. He turned to see a young woman standing there, a sheaf of papers clutched to her chest. She was in her early twenties, if that, and she looked like she'd stepped out of the pages of a fashion magazine. Her accent was European, French maybe.

"You're the policeman?" she said without offering a hand.

"Yes, DI Porter. Pete. You work with Mr Foulger?"

"I do," she said, and the look on her face made it clear she didn't particularly like it.

"You mind if I ask your name?"

"Oh, yeah, sorry. Flossy. Florence."

"Flossy Porter," Porter mumbled under his breath. It had a ring to it.

"I'm sorry?"

"Nothing. Is Mr Foulger in today?"

Flossy shook her head.

"He doesn't come in every day, works from home sometimes and he has a tonne of meetings. It's a nightmare to keep track of them all."

"That's weird, isn't it? Somebody told me his job title isn't even real, he just keeps hanging around. Why's he so busy?"

The young woman shrugged.

"Where is he today?"

"Uh," she pulled the papers away from her chest and studied them. "He had a meeting this morning with the Young Farmers, and this afternoon he's in Overstrand to open a fish and chip shop. He's cutting the ribbon."

"Why?" said Porter. "He's not exactly Jamie Oliver, is he? Or The Rock."

"We tried them both and they wouldn't come," Flossy said, the first hint of a smile on her lips. "He's the Governor here, and he was Lord Mayor at one point. He's a name."

"He's something, alright," said Porter. "That his schedule?"

She nodded, handing it over.

"He told me you might stop by today and ask for it, so I printed it out."

Porter found the column for the previous day, seeing that it was absolutely jam-packed.

"He had meetings in the chamber here all morning, then more meetings after lunch," said Flossy.

"Where?" asked Porter.

"The first was at one, over in Yarmouth. The second was back here, at five."

"You were with him?"

"No, I don't tend to accompany Mr Foulger. I stay here."

"Was anyone with him?"

Flossy shook her head.

"But he also asked me to give you this," she said, pulling a sheet of newspaper out from the bottom of the pile. Porter took it, finding a picture of a grinning, mutton-faced Foulger with four young people in tracksuits. The headline read: *Council Gives Go-Ahead for Marina Centre Renovations.*

"This was yesterday? In Yarmouth?"

"Yeah," said Flossy.

"What time would he have got there?"

"He left here before twelve, called me from Yarmouth half an hour later as he was walking into the leisure centre. The staff there will confirm it. He didn't get away until after three. Again, he called me while he was driving back. He wasn't happy he'd been delayed. Can I ask why you need to know?"

"No," said Porter. "Sorry. He ever mention any bones to you? The ones they found in the grounds? Anything like that?"

"No," she said. "I haven't been in the job long, he tends

to go through us PAs like... Like, I can't think of anything. But you know, we don't last long."

"There a reason for that?"

She shrugged again, looking uncomfortable.

"I don't want to say. But best not to be left alone in a room with him, you know?"

"Gross," said Porter. He fished a card from his wallet. "If he gives you any trouble, let me know, okay? There's no excuse for it, not now, not ever."

She took it gratefully.

"He's never actually done anything to me," she said hurriedly. "Nothing bad, you know? He's just..."

She checked to make sure the coast was clear, then leaned in, speaking softly.

"The girl who was here before me said that if he ever invites you into the tunnels, don't say yes."

"Tunnels?"

"Yeah, there are loads of them around here, apparently. He likes to give tours, and... Well, you know."

"I know," said Porter. "Like I say, you give me a call anytime, you or anyone else around here who feels threatened by him."

"I will," she said. "He's not, like, a *bad* man. He's just..."

"A man," said Porter. "I get it. Thank you. Hey, any chance I could take a look at his office while I'm here?"

It was a long shot, and it didn't pay off. Flossy shook her head, her lips clamped tight. Porter offered her a gentle nod of thanks then made his way back to the main door, enjoying the last few moments of artificial heat before stepping into the freezing rain. He clattered down the steps, wondering what the hell he was supposed to do with himself now without a car.

With no better ideas, he turned and made his way

around to the back of the building, the vast construction site stretching out before him, as big as a football pitch. The rain had churned it into a quagmire, the mud treacherous. There was no point in crossing it, so he skirted around the edge, heading up the hill towards what was left of the woodland. If he remembered right there was a track here that led to some houses, and maybe a shop. His nose began to tickle as soon as he'd entered the trees, and he launched a volley of sneezes as he went.

"Urgh," he said.

He pulled out his phone, Googling the number for the Marina Centre in Yarmouth. He'd almost made it to the top of the hill before somebody eventually answered.

"Hi," came a breathless voice. "Sorry, this is Joe at the Marina. How can I help?"

"Yeah, hi," said Porter, who was just as breathless, he realised. He stopped walking, looking back down the hill to County Hall and sucking in a couple of lungfuls of air. "This is DI Peter Porter, Norfolk Police. Can I just check something with you?"

"Sure," said Joe, his young voice full of excitement.

"You had a visit yesterday from Derek Foulger, from the Norfolk County Council. Can I check what time he got there, and when he left?"

"Sure. We were all here, I got my photo in the paper. My nan thinks I'm famous. Uh..." There was a brief pause, the line full of static. "He got here about twelve. I know because I had to show him where to park his car. Classic Jag, blue one, it's lush. Left about an hour later."

"At one?" said Porter. "You're sure?"

"Yeah, because the reporter guy didn't arrive until about 12:45, and he only stayed for the photo and a quick chat. Derek took off quite sharpish after that."

"In his car?"

"Yeah."

"He say why?"

"Not to me," said Joe. "Soz. Look, I've got to run. We're short-staffed today and I'm doubling as a lifeguard. I can call you back?"

"No need," said Porter. "Thank you."

He hung up and called Kett. The DCI answered after two rings.

"It's me, sir," Porter said, struggling up the hill again. "Foulger's alibi doesn't work out. He left Yarmouth at one, could have been back in Norwich for half one, two at the latest. That puts him easily inside the window for Carran's murder."

"Good to know," said Kett. "You spoke to him?"

"No, sir, he's not here. His PA says he's in Overstrand doing some opening thing, a chippie."

"Right."

"The PA also told me he has a reputation for giving guided tours around the tunnels, too. Though she made it sound like the only thing he was showing them was his knob."

"Seriously?"

"Yeah."

"You sound knackered, Pete, you running?"

"Walking, sir, but it's a hill."

"Where are you going?"

"No idea," said Porter.

"You're looking for a shop, aren't you, Pete?"

"No," he lied. "I was... I just thought..."

Panicking, he hissed into the phone, made a crackling noise, then ended the call. He slipped the phone back into his pocket as the path entered the woods, the canopies stealing the light like they meant to cage him. He didn't blame them, he could see the holes where their friends had been ripped out, roots and all, as big as bomb craters. He could see the damage that had been done to this ancient piece of woodland.

Serves them right, he thought, *for being stupid bastard trees*.

He ignored the fury of their swaying branches, keeping his head down as he followed the path up the hill. A few minutes later it spat him out on a residential street barricaded by squat blocks of flats and he set off up the road, trying to figure out how to get back onto the main street. The weather was worse than ever, the clouds so low and dark and the air so wet he might as well have been at the bottom of the ocean. There was absolutely nobody here, either, the street deserted, the windows dark and most with their curtains still drawn. It was so quiet, in fact, that when a dog started barking at him from the garden of a house he almost screamed.

The fright didn't last long, though, firstly because he wasn't entirely sure the little bag of fur was a dog, and secondly because he realised he knew the animal. He'd met him yesterday on the same path he'd just walked up.

"Chainsaw," he said, and the dog stopped barking, cocking its head like it was trying to remember who he was. "What are you up to?"

The dog pushed its head against the knackered wire fence and Porter let it sniff his fingers. Somewhere on its shaggy rump, a tail started to beat.

"Yeah, I bet you're happy to see me, aren't you? I bet you just want to piss on my shoes again."

The dog made a noise that was more squeak than bark, standing up and planting his paws on the fence. Porter looked past it to the house—flat, he realised, seeing the two front doors—which was more than a bit run down. The door on the right was open, and Porter could hear a familiar voice from the dark interior.

"I will, Mum, stop asking me."

Daniel, the teenage boy he'd met yesterday, stepped out, dressed in torn jeans and the same faded windbreaker, which didn't look anywhere near thick enough to counter the cold air. He was fussing with a Sainsbury's carrier bag, so engrossed in whatever was inside it that it took him a moment to see Porter. Just like their meeting yesterday, he nearly screamed.

"Jesus," he said when he'd recovered. Chainsaw had run over to him, making clumsy leaps as he tried to snatch the bag. "If it isn't PC Creepo McStalker. What are you doing here?"

Porter held his hands up innocently.

"It's a coincidence," he said. "I swear."

"That you're standing outside my door the minute I'm leaving?" said Daniel with a smile. He pulled the door to but it jammed, and it took him a few attempts before he was successful. The entire building seemed to rattle as it finally slammed shut. He clutched the bag in one hand and put the finger and thumb of his other together so that they were almost touching. "Seems a teeny-weeny bit stalkery to me, mate."

Despite himself, Porter laughed, opening the gate as the kid walked down the path. If anything, he looked even worse today than he had yesterday, his skin waxy, his eyes red. The clothes he was wearing weren't particularly big, but on him they looked positively enormous, like he'd dressed in his father's coat. Chainsaw scampered behind him, still nipping at the bag.

"You do realise you holding the gate open for me isn't exactly reassuring," the kid said as he stepped onto the pavement. "Mum'll think I'm going on a date or something."

Porter didn't know what to say to that.

"You not worried about somebody nicking your dog, leaving him in the garden like that?" he asked.

"Who's going to nick *that*?" Daniel replied, and both of them stared at the creature at their feet. The dog's eyes were bulging so much they looked like googly eyes that had been glued on a ball of tumble drier fluff, and there was a line of dribble leaking from Chainsaw's mouth.

At least, what Porter *hoped* was his mouth. It really was hard to tell.

"Looks like a bloody merkin," said the kid, and Porter laughed again.

"Fair point. You off anywhere nice?"

"Why do you care?" Daniel said, his face suddenly growing tense. "*Are* you actually following me? Because it's pretty weird, this."

"I'm not," said Porter. "I was down at County Hall, wandered up here looking for... clues."

"Clues," said Daniel, his brow still furrowed. "Sure."

"Fine," said Porter. "I was looking for a shop. I'm hungry."

Daniel glanced at Porter's belly and the DI sucked it in.

"Keep on walking that way and you'll get to some shops," the kid said. "Turn right, just up by the school."

"Thanks," said Porter. He studied the kid for a moment, at his almost bald head, at the darker rings around his eyes. "You okay? You don't look well."

"Bit rude, mate," Daniel said, pulling a face. "It's not as bad as it looks, probably won't kill me. Not today, anyway."

He looked like a stiff breeze might have knocked him

over, and there *was* a wind. It kicked up the street, making Daniel's windbreaker billow like the sail of a boat. Underneath, he was only wearing a T-shirt. He pulled a face like the cold had cut right through him.

"You walking that way?" Porter asked, hoiking a thumb at the road that led to the shops.

"Nah," he said. "Taking the dog for a shit in the woods."

"You want some company?"

"To watch him shit?"

Porter shrugged.

"Got to be more entertaining than the day I've had so far."

Chainsaw uttered a wheezing whine, as if agreeing with them.

"You sure you're not a creep?" said Daniel. "You're sure you're even a copper?"

Porter pulled out his warrant card again and the kid squinted at it.

"I don't even know what that is," he said.

"Come on," said Porter, putting it back. "I'll walk down the hill with you. I probably shouldn't bother with the shop."

"You think?"

"You cheeky git," Porter laughed. "You in those woods a lot, then? You ever see anything weird? Any*one* weird?"

"Yeah, you."

"I asked for that," he said. "What about the tunnels, you ever been in them?"

They passed the treeline, the road giving way to the same dirt path he'd walked up on. The trees shivered in the wind, excited, and Chainsaw watched them nervously from Daniel's heel, his pink tongue flopping out of his mouth.

"Nah," he said. "Not my thing. Claustrophobic. No

idea why anyone would want to go down there. What if you can't get out?"

"I agree," said Porter. "Nightmare."

"I've been down a couple of times, though," he went on. "You don't grow up here without messing around in them a bit. Most of the entrances have been sealed off now, but they weren't when I was a kid."

"How old are you again?"

"Seventeen," he said with a sniff.

"Still a kid, then," said Porter.

Chainsaw was running in tight circles and he suddenly squatted, his eyes almost bulging from his little head and staring right at Porter.

"That's not unsettling at all," Porter said.

The dog strained so hard he looked like he was going to explode, then he broke into a celebratory run, leaving behind something that was the size, shape and colour of a Cadbury's Button—and not a giant one, either. Daniel handed Porter an empty bag and he took it with an exaggerated groan of protest. There was barely anything to scoop up but he did it as best he could, tying a knot in the bag and handing it back.

"I don't want it," said Daniel. "Keep it, a souvenir."

"Thanks," said Porter.

They were reaching a split in the track, the left-hand path dropping down towards County Hall, the other leading deeper into the woods. Porter stopped, watching Chainsaw dart into the bushes.

"I'm heading back," he said. "You look after yourself, okay? And thanks for the poop."

"You're welcome, treasure it always," said Daniel with a genuine laugh. He broke into a cough, almost doubling up.

"You sure you're going to be okay?"

Daniel nodded.

"Like I say, it won't kill me today."

There was something in the kid's posture, in the way he made such an effort to stand up straight despite the tremor that rocked through him, to jut out his jaw, that made Porter's heart hurt. He gave him a nod and turned to go.

"Hang on, PC McStalker," Daniel said.

The kid opened his carrier bag and Porter saw a bunch of flowers inside it—so bright that he thought they might not be real until the scent of them broke free. He had no idea what any of them were except for the white lilies that dominated the bunch and a single bright red tulip. But he'd seen them before, littering the stone arch on the other side of the grounds. A rotting memorial to somebody, or something.

"Where are you taking them?" he asked.

"Oh, just down the path," Daniel said, like it was the most normal thing in the world to do.

"Any reason?"

"No," he answered, a little too bluntly. Daniel removed his hand from the bag, holding three chocolate bars. "Go on, take your pick. It's on me."

Porter studied them, his stomach contracting painfully. Under any other circumstance he'd have picked the Snickers, of course, which was his absolute favourite. You couldn't find a more manly chocolate bar than that, especially a big double one like this. He might even have gone for the Lion bar, because he was a sucker for caramel.

In the end, though, even though he couldn't stand them, he pulled the Double Decker from the boy's grip.

"Thanks," he said, and Daniel gave him another cryptic smile before limping down the path.

CHAPTER TWENTY-FOUR

"Your destination is ahead," said the satnav, as Kett eased the Volvo around a sharp corner, slowing down to check the long, empty road.

"Yeah," he replied. "A dickhead."

There was nobody in the car to hear his joke, and there was nobody outside, either. He was in the middle of the countryside here, about five miles north of Dereham; a barren field to his left half-hidden behind a scraggly hedge, and a thin strip of woodland to his right edged with an old brick wall. Through the sweeping windscreen wipers, the road dropped before rising again, stretching towards the grey horizon.

He drove on, scanning the trees until he saw the house that sat beyond the wall. It was positively palatial, a huge Georgian brick and flint rectory that sat at the top of a sloping, manicured garden.

He spotted the break in the wall ahead and slowed down, stopping outside a wide wrought-iron gate supported by two immense brick posts. A carved wooden sign read 'Oustings House', and next to that was an electronic key panel and a small security camera directed at the road. Through the bars of the gate he had a perfect view along the sweeping driveway to the house. The front door was open, a figure walking out of it—too far away for Kett to identify. There was a triple garage to the left of the main building, its doors closed, and no cars in sight—just a white van parked alongside an annex to the right.

Kett tapped out a gentle rhythm on the wheel, trying to work out what to do next. He had no doubt at all that if he pressed the button on that intercom and asked to speak with Derek, he'd be told to leave—and he doubted they'd say it so politely. Either that or they'd release the hounds. What, then? Why had he come all the way out here?

Because he was convinced that whatever was going on, Derek Foulger was at the heart of it. There was too much pointing his way: the fact that the bones were found outside his place of work, that he took young women into the tunnels, that the murder was committed inside a house that he owned and the body arranged to resemble the emblem he used for his guild. But even that wasn't enough. Clare wasn't going to bring him in unless they had something solid, something even the Chief Constable couldn't dismiss.

"So let's find it," he told himself.

He put the car in gear and drove on, following the low wall until it angled to the right. Here, a narrow dirt track traced the perimeter into a more sickly-looking woodland. He pulled off the main road, the car thumping its way over an obstacle course of potholes before he took pity on it and stopped. He was far enough away from the road for the car to be invisible—even with its bright orange paint job—and he couldn't see the house from here over the wall. He was as hidden as he was ever going to be.

He cut the engine, a sudden silence dropping hard,

making him feel like his ears were blocked. The wind had died down, the thick canopy overhead doing nothing to keep the rain away. To his left, the leafless trees stretched for what seemed like forever, shadows dancing between their trunks. He saw a pair of bright eyes, a deer, perhaps, gone before he could make sense of it.

It felt utterly peaceful here, and he took a moment to rest his head, to close his eyes and calm his thoughts. He hadn't acknowledged the tension in his chest until now, that awful pressure only apparent when it started to fade.

"It's just a case," he told himself. "It's not personal."

Except it *was* personal, the way everything felt personal now. Ever since he'd broken out of Hollenbeck's prison, out of their hellish maze, he hadn't been able to separate himself from everyone else. Because he'd been a victim, he'd been *their* victim, and part of him hadn't broken out, it hadn't escaped. It would be stuck inside Hell House forever, lost in the dark passageways, drowning in blood. He was a victim, just like Peter Carran, just like whoever those old bones had once belonged to. He couldn't find the place where he ended and they began any more. Their fear was his fear, their deaths were his death.

Their fury was his fury.

He felt it now as he climbed out of the car and gently closed the door behind him, an engine that beat alongside his heart, that drove him forwards.

He couldn't ignore the similarities between Foulger and Hollenbeck. He, like them, was wealthy, old, powerful, one of the elite. Kett had watched enough of the Hollenbeck interview tapes to see that same smugness, the same arrogance and entitlement that Foulger wore like a badge of honour. They'd been a few leagues above Foulger, of course, but he was a smaller fish swimming in the same stagnant pond, no doubt about it.

Kett crunched over the path and stumbled through the thick verge to the wall. It was a good two foot taller than him but the ancient bricks were full of grooves. He braced the toe of his boot in a gap and hauled himself up, peering over the top.

More trees lay ahead, the side of the rectory visible through them. It really was huge, as deep as it was wide and surrounded by a group of kowtowing outbuildings. There were people out the back, maybe four or five of them, one of whom was leading a black horse across a courtyard. The clop of its hooves was the loudest sound in the day. Three cars were parked in a low barn, too far back to make them out. He was pretty sure none of them were blue.

Kett dropped down, making his way further along the wall while he tried to figure out what to do. There were more people here than he'd expected, and suspicions weren't nearly enough to justify his presence. He climbed another section of wall, this one so worn by time that a brick came away in his hand as he tried to pull himself up. He threw it to the ground and looked through the gap, seeing more woodland thick with undergrowth. From this angle he couldn't see anyone, and the only sound was the quiet whisper of the trees and the gentle conversations of the birds.

He wrestled himself over the wall before he could talk himself out of it, missing his footing on the other side and dropping hard into a bush. He rolled out of its grip, staying low as he crept through the trees. The going was hard, this part of the estate neglected, the undergrowth reaching his knees. He caught glimpses of the main house through the spindly branches, broken voices caught on the wind.

The closest building was a brick and flint structure fifty yards away and he made his way to the back of it, grateful to finally be out of the thickets and the thorns. He took a moment to get some air, feeling the burn of the brambles on his legs. When he looked down at his suit, he saw the tears in it.

"For fuck's sake," he muttered, feeling angrier than ever at the arsehole who owned this place.

He crept to the corner of the outhouse and peeked around it. There was no door, and nothing inside, but there was another brick shed ahead, flirting with the woods on the far side of the estate. Every other building had its back to him so he skirted the gravel track, reaching the second shed. The door was open, this one full of coal, the earthy smell of it dredging up a powerful memory of childhood—his dad sending him out to fill the coal scuttle.

He pushed on, following the track as it curved around the motley crew of outbuildings. Despite the chill in the air he was sweating, his heart rattling in his chest. He really needed to improve his fitness.

"Don't want to end up like Pete," he said quietly, feeling guilty the moment he'd thought it.

He passed a third shed, this one with a locked door and no window, then crossed over the track to a bigger building. There he stopped, because he could hear voices from close by. He rested his shoulder against the wall, trying to listen over the roar of his pulse. It was a man talking—two, maybe—their feet crunching as they walked this way.

"... needs to be brought down here," said one. The accent was local, the voice rasping. Was it Foulger? He couldn't be sure. "Leave it outside, I'll get Rob to sort it. I don't want anyone in there who doesn't need to be."

The other man muttered a reply, the footsteps fading.

Kett pushed on, almost on tiptoes as he reached the end of the building. He edged around the corner, too late to see where the men had gone. Ahead was a smaller courtyard, the buildings opposite obviously stables. Kett couldn't see any other horses but he could smell them, the strangely comforting aroma of manure.

To his left was more woodland, to the right the track swept around towards the main house, whose top windows stared darkly at him from over the roofs of the stable and barn. He needed to get inside, but with so many people around there was no chance of it.

Kett spluttered out a sigh. He should probably turn around and head back. This place was so huge that even if there was something here that pointed to Foulger's guilt, the chances of finding it were remote.

He peeked around the corner again, drawing back immediately when he heard the grumble of an engine. A few seconds later the small, white van he'd seen earlier trundled down the path, an older man craned over the wheel. Kett pulled out his phone and made a note of its licence plate number, watching it disappear around the side of the stable.

Then, because he couldn't think of anything else to do, he followed it, keeping to the scrubby ground. He jogged from the shed to the next building over. From there, he had a much better view of the other side of the estate with its thicker, more established woodland. The van was following the track into the trees, its headlights crawling over a big, stone building that sat there in the relative dark.

A church.

There was a twenty-yard stretch of open space between the shed Kett was hiding behind and the treeline, but it wasn't like he had a choice. He could hear more voices behind him, and the bark of a dog. A *big* dog. He broke cover, sprinting to the trees, plunging into the shade. A stitch jabbed at his ribs, the pain radiating into his chest, and he put a hand to his heart.

"I am way too old for this shit," he said under his breath.

He made his way carefully forwards, the trees allowing him only the briefest glimpses of the stone building they were hiding. The church was old, its walls camouflaged with lichen, the glass in its windows black. It had been well looked after, though, because the slate tiles on the roof looked new. A squat, round tower jutted upwards like a finger, the point a sharpened nail scratching at the canopy above. A single crow sat there, watching Kett with black-eyed curiosity. It opened its mouth and loosed a hoarse caw, like it was sounding an alarm.

The white van had stopped on the other side of the church, and when its engine died Kett could hear a voice—the same one he'd heard before. It was obnoxiously loud, too abrasive surely to be anyone other than Derek Foulger, but he was still too far away to make any sense of it.

He glanced deeper into the woods, seeing the brick wall that marked the edge of the estate. If he needed to, he could always get out on this side and walk back around to his car.

Steeling himself, he proceeded towards the church, using the big, old trees to hide himself. It was impossible to be silent, too many brittle twigs underfoot, too many branches that tried to reach out and stop him. He broke left, circling the old building until the white van came into view, then the driver, who stood next to it, then another man with his back to Kett—skinny, with a mop of brown hair, dressed in blue overalls. They talked quietly, and the van driver laughed.

Kett moved along a little more until a wooden door

appeared in the side of the church, then he ducked down, keeping his breaths low and shallow in the hope of catching a word or two.

The men stopped talking, looking through the open door as that same braying voice rose up from inside. The driver nodded, walking to the back of the van and opening it up with a squeal that chased the crow from the turret. Both men looked up as it crashed into the branches overhead, the other guy starting to turn.

Kett ducked behind the tree, waiting for the man to shout out, for the cries of alarm. Nothing came. He counted to twenty before easing himself out again, just in time to see the driver carrying a large cardboard box into the church. The other man had gone but Kett thought he'd recognised him from somewhere—the glimpse he'd got had been too short to be sure.

The driver appeared again, closing the van doors.

"I'll go see if they're ready," he said, climbing back into the driver's seat and starting the engine. There was no place to turn around so he reversed up the track, his headlights like stage lights illuminating the exact spot where Kett was hiding. He hid himself until the engine had faded away, then peeked again.

The church was silent, no sign of life at all. There was a round window in the back wall, facing Kett, but it was blinded by leaded glass, the merest hint of saintly colour visible.

He puffed out an uncertain breath, looking back to make sure the wall was still there if he needed to get over it. He listened for voices and found nothing but that same barking dog—further away now.

The hell with it.

He crept out from behind the tree, his entire body rigid

with tension as he reached the church and pressed himself tight against the wall. The acidic smell of the old stone was overpowering, that and the mulch of the rotted ground. The building seemed to radiate something else, something more than a smell, more than an atmosphere, something that crinkled Kett's arms into goosebumps and made his scalp shrink swimming-cap tight.

It was freezing here, he realised, far colder than the day should have allowed. The chill crept up from below like it was growing on him, like it was *feeding*.

Enough, he told himself. *Focus*.

There was still no sound of life from inside the church, so he skirted around the corner and walked to the door. An old brass plaque had been screwed into the stone over it, the same emblem he'd seen inside the murder house—that circle of feet and a crowned eye. It was caked in dirt and crusted with lichen, as old as the wall it hung on.

The woodland was dark, but the interior of the church was like liquid night in comparison. Kett stared into it, seeing nothing, not knowing if somebody was looking right back at him.

Still no shouts, though, no cry of alarm.

He pushed his head through the door, his eyes adjusting. The stained-glass window—complete with an assortment of dead-eyed saints—let in a trickle of light, enough to make out three rows of wooden pews. There was no font, though, no altar that he could see. Instead, at the far end of the church, open like the mouth of some mythical beast, was a set of stairs leading below ground.

"For fuck's sake," he said.

That was where the cold was coming from, a whisper of lifeless air that leeched the warmth from his body. The longer he stared at the stairs, the more he could make of them—a flicker of firelight dancing on the stone as if something down there was burning.

Hell, he thought. *It's a gateway to hell.*

He almost laughed at how ridiculous he sounded.

He took in the rest of the church, seeing the cardboard box that the driver had brought in. It was sitting on the middle pew, halfway from the door to the stairs. There was no sign of the two other men.

Do it, he told himself, and he was through the door before he even knew he was moving, his boots sounding like tap shoes on the polished flagstones.

He reached the box and lifted the flap, seeing a bundle of dark cloth. The smell of fabric softener filled his nose, something coconutty. He grabbed a handful and lifted it, surprised at how heavy it was. It was a sheet of some kind, he thought, or maybe a bag. He couldn't make any sense of it until he'd draped it over the pew and switched on the torch on his phone.

"Oh."

It was a robe. He could see the empty curve of the hood, a brass chain that could be fastened around the neck. He delved back into the box, pushing deep, finding nothing but robes—six, seven, eight of them, he couldn't be sure.

"Frank?"

The voice barked up the stairs, so sudden and so unexpected that it felt like somebody had punched him in the gut. He stuffed the first robe back in the box, struggling with it, stopping when he heard footsteps. The light from below was rising, somebody coming this way.

He swore again, beneath his breath, and ran for the door, his steps too loud.

"Who's there?"

It was Foulger's voice, no doubt about it. Kett threw

himself out of the door, breaking for the trees and almost stumbling. The wall was too far away, Foulger would be outside in seconds and he'd spot him instantly if he tried to climb it. Kett passed one trunk, two, then flattened himself against a third that was almost big enough to hide him.

He waited, sucking every single part of himself in, the stitch once more tearing a hole in his side, his back aching from the angle he was holding himself. His pulse was so noisy there might have been a cement mixer inside his skull, but past it he could hear another shout.

"Frank?"

Silence, other than the chattering of a dozen crows.

"You see him?"

"Nope," said another voice.

"Someone's here," said Foulger. "Check that way."

Footsteps cracked through the undergrowth, getting closer. Kett held his breath, trying to be as still as the trunk he hid behind. Wind rattled through the branches, scattering sunlight, the whole forest seeming to sway.

The footsteps stopped, replaced by a haggard, wheezing breath, then they started again—right behind the tree.

The second man appeared, so close that Kett could have reached out and touched him. He took a couple of steps past the tree then stopped, the shoulders of his blue overalls rising and falling, rising and falling. In one hand he held a torch.

In the other was a twelve-inch knife—a *dagger*, really—the dark handle decorated with gold symbols, the blade long and thin and wickedly sharp.

Kett locked the air in his lungs, so desperate for breath that he could see fireworks sparking at the corners of his vision. He had seconds, he knew, before the man turned around and saw him.

Something moved deeper in the woods and the man's head jerked the other way. Kett looked past him, seeing a familiar pair of bright eyes. The deer looked back for a moment then bucked hard, almost bouncing between the trees as it bolted.

"Fucking things," said the man, his accent Northern.

He turned, still looking away from Kett—thank God—staring after the deer as he disappeared the way he'd come.

"Just a muntjac," he yelled.

Somebody grunted a reply in the distance, the footsteps fading.

For a moment, Kett didn't think he could move—as if he had willed himself so still that his body had paralysed itself. Then he forced his legs to work, his arms, creeping away from the tree towards the wall.

He didn't look back, he didn't *dare*, moving as slowly as he could until he reached the crumbling brick.

Only when he'd hauled himself over it—taking the top row of bricks with him—and collapsed on the other side, did he remember to breathe.

CHAPTER TWENTY-FIVE

KETT PUSHED THROUGH THE DOORS INTO THE MAJOR Investigation Team bullpen, looking past the handful of coppers to Clare's office. The door was closed, the blinds drawn. He spotted DS Alison Spalding sitting at Porter's desk, on the phone, and he walked over.

"The Super in?" he asked.

Spalding cupped the phone as she shook her head.

"Meeting with the Brass, sir, you need him?"

"No," said Kett. "Porter back?"

She nodded, pointing towards the back corridor and resuming her call. Kett headed for the Incident Room, finding Savage sitting at a desk almost hidden behind a pile of books. She was shivering in the chill, and she did a double take when she saw his suit.

"Another one, sir?" she asked. "What happened?"

"Had a fight with a brick wall," he told her. "And lost."

He pulled up a chair and sat opposite her. His body still felt weak from the adrenaline run-off, both hands trembling even though it was nearly an hour since he'd driven away from the Foulger place. That had been *too* close. He'd already been stabbed on this case—barely, but still—and he'd come pretty close to finding himself in another knife fight. If the man with the dagger had just turned the other way, Kett might have ended up in a shallow grave in the woods.

Worse still, he might have got another bollocking from Clare.

"You seen Porter?"

"He's around, sir," Savage said. She looked dreadful, although he'd never have said it. The exhaustion seemed to radiate from her. "You have any luck?"

"I don't know. I'll tell you in a minute, so I don't have to repeat myself."

He pulled out his phone and texted Porter.

"You're shaking, sir," said Savage, her brow furrowing.

"I'm okay, Kate. Just... just been a while since I've had a cuppa. I'll put the kettle on. You want one?"

"I'll do it, sir," she said, her chair scraping as she stood up. "Could do with stretching my legs. Have a look at this while I'm gone, see if it makes any sense."

She tapped the notebook on her desk then left the room. Kett swivelled the stack of books so that he could read their spines, seeing five titles on witchcraft and the occult and three on anatomy—all littered with neon post-its. He pulled the notepad to his side of the desk and put on his glasses, trying to make sense of Savage's scrawled handwriting. There were doodles too, including the eye with its crown.

"'*Bones, fangs, claws, feathers, hair all used in magick rituals*,'" he read. "'*Human bones considered most powerful*.'"

He turned back through five pages of notes, finding a photograph of the display of bones they'd uncovered in the cellar room. Next to it was a photocopy of an illustration which wasn't too dissimilar, an arrangement of three skulls surrounded by a triangle of bones. The caption read '*A selection of remains used in a ritual, as found in a grimoire of French Occultism.*' Savage had written a handful of notes next to it, including:

'*Each bone must come from a separate victim, it's the collection that holds the power.*'

The door opened and Kett looked back to see Duke walk into the room. He was holding two cups of tea, and he frowned when he saw Kett.

"Oh, sir," he said. "You're not Kate."

"I'm not. You'll have to make do with me, Duke."

Duke's frown deepened.

"To talk to, Aaron," Kett explained. "I'm not planning on kissing you."

"Uh..." Duke's mouth flopped open. He put the steaming cups down on Savage's desk, the air instantly filling with the sweet scent of tea.

"I probably *could* kiss you, though," Kett said as he shifted one of the mugs closer. "You do make a pretty perfect cuppa."

"Thank you, sir," said Duke. "But that's actually for Kate."

He looked for a moment like he was going to take it away, and Kett made a noise that was almost a growl. Duke stood back, hands up like he was face to face with a dragon.

"You can have it, sir, I'll go make another one."

There was no need, though, because Savage entered the room with three mugs, hop-skip and jumping to the desk and slamming them down.

"Ow, ow, ow, too hot."

She smiled at Duke.

"I didn't realise you were making tea, sorry."

"Wanted to surprise you," Duke said, smiling back. They giggled at each other, and Kett laughed.

"Somebody might need to fetch me a bucket," he said. Savage cleared her throat.

"Sorry, sir. Tea?"

He took a mug, putting it next to the first one.

"Two cups, I'm a happy man."

"Did you take a look at my notes?"

"I did, but I'm going to need you to tell me what I'm looking at. Where did you get all these books?"

"Well," she said, suddenly guilty. "There's a story there, and I'm not sure you'll like it. I paid a trip to Norman's house."

"Balls?" said Kett. "Why?"

"Because as annoying as he is, he actually does know everything there is to know about, you know."

"Weird shit," said Duke.

"Exactly. He wanted to come in to HQ. He demanded it, in fact, but I managed to barter him out of it."

"How?" asked Kett, getting a bad feeling.

"I agreed that you'd take him out for dinner, sir," she said with a sheepish look.

"A date?" said Kett, horrified.

"Not a date, sir, just food. He insisted on picking the place. It's the only way I could get him to hand over the books. Sorry."

Kett shook his head. All in all, it was a small price to pay if it gave them something they needed.

"So, talk me through it."

"Sure," said Savage, shooing Duke out of the way to get to her seat. "These—"

The Incident Room door opened again and Porter appeared. He'd obviously had the same idea because he was carrying two mugs, and he also had a bunch of flowers tucked under his arm.

"Oh," he said. "I can make more?"

"No," said everyone in the room.

"We're sorted," said Kett.

Porter placed his mugs on the desk. Kett didn't even have to look at them to know how awful they would be, he could feel it, the same way he'd felt the atmosphere back in the church. Some things were just *wrong*.

"I was just saying," Savage went on, "I told Balls about the bones, showed him a photo. I thought it was worth a shot because the way the bones were arranged, the pattern, it didn't seem random. Turns out it's pretty common."

"Common?" said Kett.

"Well, you know, not common, but it's a common sight when you're dealing with magick. *Magick* with a k on the end."

"What's the difference?" said Duke.

"Depends on who you believe. According to Balls, magick with a k is more linked to your occult stuff. Hermeticism, metaphysics, rituals, you know?"

Nobody answered.

"It's your typical Order of the Golden Dawn stuff."

Still nothing. Savage sighed.

"Am I the only one who reads books?" she said. "The Hermetic Order of the Golden Dawn was a group founded over 150 years ago by three men who wanted to study the arcane arts."

"Devil worship?" said Porter, taking a seat and putting his flowers on the desk.

"No. More complicated than that. It'll take too long to go into now, but the gist of it was communicating with the unknown, with the spirits. They had rituals and initiations, and the three guys who founded it were all freemasons."

"Like Foulger," said Kett, and Savage nodded.

"So there were a number of groups who believed in the same things as the Order of the Golden Age, splinter groups and copycats, there were dozens of them. From what I can see, Foulger's Harford Guild had its origins in one of these about 150 years ago. Balls couldn't find a direct link, but he had a file on these groups, and they shared a lot of the esoteric stuff."

"I don't even understand half these words," said Duke.

"One thing that cropped up in a couple of places was bone magick. It was thought the arrangement of bones could create, I don't know, powerful forces that could grant the practitioners strength or influence or money or whatever."

"The more bones you have, the more powerful you are?" said Kett, taking a sip of tea that was far too hot. He returned it to the huddle of mugs.

"Yes, sir. You know about this?" said Savage.

"I just read that bit in your notes," he confessed.

"Oh, right. Yeah, according to the books, you wanted each bone to come from an individual victim, because each one would grant additional strength to the next. Like batteries, I guess. They carry more power if they're fresh bones and..."

"And if you happen to have killed the victim yourself," Kett guessed.

"Yeah," said Savage. "Balls showed me a handful of examples where they've uncovered these things, but most are hidden in ossuaries, bone cemeteries, places like that, because nobody notices them, there are bones everywhere. Like not seeing the forest for the trees. But they always follow the same pattern, you have a skull in the middle, or two or three or whatever, and then you arrange smaller bones around the outside. Each bone represents something different."

She pulled the notepad closer and rifled through the pages until she found what she was looking for.

"So, a skull is for knowledge and vision, obviously. Ribs are for protection, because of the heart. Uh, the pelvis is, you know, sex stuff."

"What about the knuckle bones?" asked Kett. Savage shrugged.

"Honestly, I haven't seen them mentioned anywhere. They didn't seem to play a big role in the occult stuff."

"Okay," said Kett, picking up his tea again. "This points us harder towards Foulger, right? He's a freemason, or at least he was. He's a higher member of this Harford Guild, who have been known to engage in bone magick, or whatever you want to call it. The pieces all fit."

"There's more," said Savage. "When you read up on it, there are very strict rules for these arcane rituals. The bones only hold their power when they're in place, when they're undisturbed. Leave them be and they'll channel energy constantly, like an open tap. But as soon as you move them or disturb them or whatever, it shuts off."

"Which could explain our dead man," said Kett.

"Exactly," Savage went on. "The killer found out the bones had been moved, they panicked, murdered the first person they could find and tried to arrange his bones on the wall to recreate the pattern."

"But I thought you said the bones had to be from different victims," said Porter.

Savage shrugged.

"This is all pretty out there," she admitted.

"But it's good," said Kett. "It's taking us in the same direction."

He took a sip of tea and instantly recoiled, his head lashing back so hard he almost fell off his chair. Liquid exploded from his mouth alongside a cry that would have better suited an angry camel.

"Sir?" Savage cried out in alarm. "What's wrong?"

Kett slammed the mug back onto the desk and stared into its insipid, milky, almost-cold depths.

"I drank Porter's tea is what's wrong," he croaked. "It's inside me."

"No!" said Savage.

"Oh Christ, I can still taste it," he said, coughing. "It's like a donkey's pissed in my mouth."

"Here, sir, drink this one," said Duke, thrusting another mug in Kett's direction.

Kett took it, downing the contents in one go even though it scalded its way into his stomach. He wiped his watering eyes, licking his lips to make sure the taste had gone. It was still there, though. He felt a sudden terror that it would *always* be there.

"Are you okay, sir?" asked Savage with genuine alarm.

Kett thumped himself on the chest and nodded. Porter was staring into the mug like a little boy whose teacher had given him a D- for his macaroni artwork.

"Carry on, Kate," Kett croaked.

"That's the gist of it," she said. "But there's something even better. Balls and I found a newspaper article from the early 1900s. A man called Rupert Weston was accused of murdering a couple of kids from the poorer side of town. He got off because he was wealthy, a landowner from out Hethersett way. Want to know who he's related to?"

"Please tell me it's Foulger," said Kett, and she smiled.

"It's Derek's great-grandfather, on his mother's side. The house on Bracondale where we found the body yesterday belonged to him, he built it. There's records of Harford Guild meetings being held there. I haven't managed to check all the details yet, but he got rich at the end of the Nineteenth Century, something to do with the arms trade. He was knighted. But he was a smuggler, too; he had a dark side. He had a reputation for shifting things beneath the city."

"Shit," said Kett. "This is insane. So Foulger's grandfather was—"

"Great-grandfather, sir."

"Whatever, he was a wealthy smuggler with connections to the nobility, to government, and he was accused of murdering two kids but never found guilty. He was a member of the Harford Guild. Those things are hereditary, right?"

"They can be," said Savage. "Especially from father to son. They like to keep it in the family. But there's no proof that Foulger is involved in anything like that, it's all a massive leap."

"Except it isn't," said Kett. "Because I was at Foulger's house this afternoon, just an hour or two ago."

"What did he have to say for himself?" said Savage.

"Well... I didn't exactly talk to him."

"What did you do, sir?" asked Porter.

Kett sighed.

"I kind of jumped the wall and had a look around."

He tried to ignore Savage's look of disapproval.

"I had reasonable doubt. It's a massive place, people everywhere. There's a church in the woods beside the main house. Big old stone thing. It's got the Harford Guild symbol over the door, crowned eye and feet. I managed to get inside and I found a box of cloaks, just like the ones we saw at the Bracondale house."

"Shit," said Duke.

"There's a cellar beneath the church, and I heard Foulger saying that something was happening tonight."

"You saw Foulger?" said Savage.

"Not exactly, but I think it was his voice. I'm sure it was. There were two men with him, one called Frank, I think, who was driving a van. And another one, I didn't see his face. Northern accent, Yorkshire I think. But yeah, the one I thought might be Foulger definitely said that something was going to happen tonight."

"Could be anything, sir," said Savage. "And it's not exactly grounds to pursue him, especially given how you came across the information."

"I know that, Kate," Kett said. "It's not my first rodeo. Leave the explanations to me, we just need to figure out what he's planning."

"I might be able to help with that," said Porter. He lifted the bunch of flowers.

"You shouldn't have," said Duke.

"This is a bit out there as well," he said. "But bear with me. Yesterday, when I was looking around the woods next to County Hall, I met a young guy. A kid, he's seventeen. Daniel. He was walking his dog. He's ill, but I don't know with what, exactly. Lives just up the hill past the woods, council place."

"He bought you flowers?" said Duke, and Porter looked like he was ready to thump the big PC with them.

"No, he was leaving the flowers in the woods, by the big stone arch that used to be a part of Knucklebone Hall."

"Why, sir?" said Savage.

"I'm not entirely sure. I met him again a little while ago,

same place pretty much. Walked back down the hill with him. He..."

Porter swallowed, like he was wondering whether to carry on. After a moment he reached into his pocket and pulled out a Double Decker wrapper—identical to the one they'd found in the cellar.

"He gave me this before we parted," he said.

"He gave you a chocolate wrapper?" said Kett.

"Uh, no. He gave me a Double Decker. I just thought it was a weird coincidence, you know? Of all the chocolate bars he could have had."

"And you ate it?" said Kett.

Porter looked at the wrapper.

"I was hungry, sir."

"But it could be evidence, Pete."

"I was careful," he said. "I barely touched the wrapper."

"Jesus Christ," said Kett. "So, he gave you a Double Decker and then what?"

"You didn't eat *him*, did you, sir?" said Duke, and Kett fired him a warning look.

"No, I thought it was weird, that's all. So I followed him down the hill, saw him put the flowers by the arch. Waited until he'd gone and picked them up, read the note."

He fished an evidence bag from his pocket, placing it in front of Kett. Inside was a card, and written on it in small, shaky letters were four lines:

To all those who went before me,

I honour you.

And look forward to our reunion.

Do ut des.

"Do it, Des?" said Savage.

"No, *do ut des*. It's not English."

"What the hell does it mean?" asked Kett.

"No idea," Porter replied, pulling a second evidence bag from his pocket. "But I had a rummage through the flowers, dozens of bunches and half of them rotten, and found more of the same. One card in Daniel's handwriting, from yesterday, I think, and three more that look much older."

He placed the bag next to the other one and Kett saw a collection of florists' cards inside. The topmost one was yellow with age, the writing barely legible. But there was no denying it said the exact same thing.

"'*To all those who went before me*,'" he read. "Who are they talking about?"

"I thought it might be because he was ill," said Porter. "Makes sense, right? All the people who were ill before him. But that wouldn't explain why somebody else wrote the same thing God knows how many months or years ago."

"Anyone know what the last line means?"

Porter shook his head and so did Savage. To Kett's immense surprise, Duke put his hand up.

"I can take a crack at it, sir," he said. "I think it's Latin."

"What?" spat Porter. "You speak Latin?"

"Took it for A Levels, sir, quite enjoyed it. Was great being able to insult people who had no idea what I was talking about."

"Bullshit," said Porter.

"*Foetorem extremae latrinae*!" Duke said with a grin.

"What?" said Porter. "Take that back."

"Duke," said Kett. "The card."

"Oh, right." The PC bent over, his face grave. "*Do ut des*. Uh..."

"I knew he couldn't do it," said Porter.

"*Do* is give, I think," Duke said. "*Ut* is like so, and *Des* is give again."

"Give so give?" said Kett.

"No, it's about tenses and stuff. Verbs, you know? I think it says *I give so you can give.*"

"That doesn't help," said Kett, rubbing his temples. He could still taste Porter's godawful tea and it was giving him a headache.

"Still impressive though, right, sir?" said Duke.

"Here," said Savage, looking at her phone. "It's a Latin phrase, quite common. Aaron's right, it means almost exactly that. I give so that you *will* give."

Duke beamed, but Savage was frowning.

"Oh, but it's common for a reason," she said. "I give so that you will give. It means I give you something but in return, you have to give something back."

She swallowed hard.

"It's a message they wrote to the gods. It's what they used to say when they were offering a sacrifice."

CHAPTER TWENTY-SIX

"It's a gaping vacuum of nothingness, Kett!" roared Clare. "Duke's head is emptier than this. My *bollocks* are emptier, and I've had two vasectomies."

It was the response Kett had expected, even if the delivery was angrier than usual. He sat on the other side of the Superintendent's desk, the room as cold as a freezer. Clare was wrapped up tight in the monstrosity that was his Big Tossing Jacket, yelling so loudly that it was like sitting in a rainstorm. Kett wiped the spittle from his face, waiting for him to stop for breath.

"Sir, just hear me out."

"It's empty, Kett. There's nothing substantial in it. I can't let you go after Foulger with hearsay and history books. I asked you to bring me something concrete, not blow smoke up my tosshole."

"I was there, sir," he said, trying to reframe the truth. "I paid a visit to Foulger's house today and—"

"You did *what*?" Clare bellowed.

"He lied about his alibi," Kett went on, speaking fast.

"He left Yarmouth early yesterday, he could have easily made it back to Norwich to kill Carran."

"And you found this out how?"

"From his PA. Porter talked to her. Foulger lied, sir. I didn't speak to him today, but I saw... I saw deliveries being made to the house, and—"

"Well, maybe the Deliveroo driver did it, eh?" said Clare. "You think about that?"

"It was a box of robes," Kett said. "Just like the ones we found in the murder house. I saw an old church, a man with a dagger, looked like a ceremonial one. I heard them talking about something that was going to happen tonight."

"You heard this from all the way over the other side of the wall?" said Clare, his eyeballs like two enormous blisters. "Because I've been to Foulger's house, Kett. I have attended functions there, and I know how big that bastard's estate is. Unless you've turned into Dumbo with a pair of great big flapping ears, there's no way you overheard that from the street."

Kett puffed out a breath.

"I didn't sir," he confessed. "I may have... slipped over the wall... by accident."

Clare slammed himself back in his chair, his teeth gritted so tightly that they looked ready to shatter. He didn't say anything, but Kett thought he might have been vibrating with rage.

"If this *is* Foulger," Kett said. "If he's behind this and something's going to happen tonight, then we might have a shot at taking him down. This might be our only chance."

Clare shook his head.

"There's no way, Kett. No way in hell the Chief Constable is going to authorise this."

"I know, sir," said Kett. "And even if he did, he might give Foulger some warning."

"Be very careful what you say to me, Detective," Clare said, his voice low and dangerous. "Words like those have serious consequences, and never good ones."

Kett held up his hands defensively.

"I'm just saying, if we want to crash this party we have to keep it small. Just me and the Extreme Crime Task Force, you, and Gorski. We'll need a tactical team."

"Unbelievable," said Clare, rubbing his face so hard it was like he was trying to pull off a mask. "I just don't get how you could turn something as simple as a cellar full of forgotten bones into this, Kett. It was supposed to be a cold case, I just wanted to lure you back through the bloody door, and now you're asking for a firearms team to storm a church that belongs to the self-appointed Governor of Norfolk County Council and the godfather of the Chief Constable's kids? Is that right? Is that what you're asking me for?"

"Uh, yes, sir."

"You're a bucket of monkey toss, Kett. I hate you."

Kett didn't know what to say, so he kept his mouth shut. Clare stopped rubbing his face, glaring at Kett through splayed fingers.

"I want everything you have on my desk, and I want proof—*now*."

"Yes, sir," said Kett, getting up.

He opened the door, frowned, and looked back.

"You had *two* vasectomies, sir?"

A gargled roar and a lobbed stapler chased him from the room.

EVERYONE WAS WAITING for him when he walked back into the Incident Room, and he closed the door behind him before speaking.

"He's not happy about it, and he wants proof, but I think he might give us the green light."

"On Foulger, sir?" said Porter. "That's good, right?"

Kett hesitated, sitting on the end of a desk.

"Yeah," he said eventually. "It's good."

"I think it's him, sir," said Savage. "There's too much pointing his way. It was his house, it's his guild, he wasn't where he said he was yesterday—or where he said he'd be today, as a matter of fact. He had the means, he had the opportunity, and we know there's some kind of motive, the same justification his great-grandfather used for murder."

"Allegedly," said Kett. "His great-grandfather was never convicted."

"True," said Savage. "Different times."

"Only they're not, are they?" said Kett. "Nothing's changed. Doesn't matter what year it is, doesn't matter where you live. If you've got money you can do anything you want."

"No, you can't," said Porter. "Not today."

"It's why we have to catch him red-handed, sir," said Savage. "It has to be watertight."

Kett nodded, checking his watch to see that it was coming up for three.

"We don't have much time. Savage, Duke, can you head over to the Foulger place, watch from a distance. Do *not* let them see you. There's plenty of woods around there, you should be able to find a high point. Take some binoculars. Any sign of anything weird, call me."

"Yes, sir," they said together.

"I mean it, Kate, don't let them see you."

"I'm basically a ninja," said Duke.

"You're the opposite of a ninja," said Porter, looking at the giant copper. "You're a drunk Tyrannosaurus rex in a uniform."

"Porter," said Kett. "You really think this kid Daniel has something to do with it?"

"Can't say for definite, sir. But it kind of fits, doesn't it?"

"Kind of," said Kett. "Go talk to him, find out for sure. Bring him in if you have to."

"Yes, sir. What are you going to do?"

Kett looked at the images pinned to the wall, at the old bones and the new ones and the tissue-thin fabric of conspiracy that held them together.

"I'm going to keep convincing Superintendent Clare that we're not blowing smoke up his tosshole."

"YOU'RE SURE YOU'RE OKAY?" Porter said, speaking through the hands-free. "No aches or pains? You don't need anything?"

"I'm fine," Allie said for the third time. "And even if I did, you're at work, Pete."

"I can leave, anytime. Just say it and I'll come. You're sure you're okay?"

"I'm not okay right now, no," she said. "Because you won't stop asking if I'm okay. I'm bloody okay!"

She was laughing, and Porter did too.

"Okay, I believe you. But you call me as soon as you're not, you hear? And as soon as you feel anything, you know, weird."

"Pete, I've got an eight-pound lump of mini-you sitting on my bladder, nothing about this *doesn't* feel weird."

"Weirder, then," he said.

"We're like four weeks away," she said, and he could hear the strain in her voice as she moved, the way she tried to hide the pain from him. He hated it. He wished she could just be honest with him. "You can stand down for a month, soldier."

"Okay," he said. "As long as you're okay."

"Goodbye, Pete."

"Bye, Allie," he said, but she'd already hung up.

He got out of the car, the wind slipping up his sleeves and making him feel like he'd just jumped into a lake of ice water. There was no sign of Chainsaw the dog, so he let himself through the wire gate and walked to the door of Daniel's flat. Both sets of windows were blinded by curtains that looked like they hadn't been opened in decades, the fabric yellow with age.

He knocked on the flimsy uPVC door, hearing a shrill bark from inside, a snuffle of breath and a skittering of claws. When nothing else happened he knocked again, then bent down and opened the letterbox.

"Hello?" he called. "It's the police, can you open the door?"

Chainsaw barked again, although Porter couldn't see him from this angle.

"You alright, dog?" he said. "My shoes still smell like piss, thank you very much. Daniel home?"

Chainsaw snuffled a reply.

"Anyone else?"

The dog scampered off, stopping for a quick look back before vanishing into the dark.

"You've definitely lost it, Pete," Porter said as he straightened. "Talking to animals."

He made his way down the side of the building to a

flimsy wooden gate that almost came off its hinges when he pushed it open. Beyond was a garden whose size was obscured by the sheer volume of towering plants and bushes, an empty clothesline drooping almost to the ground and a metal bin that stank of weeks-old dog shit. He found a door at the back of the flat and knocked hard, cupping his hand to the window next to it to see a small kitchen. Somebody was doubled over the breakfast table, fast asleep.

Or worse.

Porter hammered on the glass but the person didn't stir. He walked to the door and tried the handle, shouldering it open. He was halfway across the kitchen in two steps, and by the time he'd taken a third, the figure at the table—a woman in her forties—had lifted her head and spotted him.

She screamed loud enough to make his ears ring, pushing herself away from the table with such force that her chair toppled over. Her legs pinged up, and she did an almost perfect backwards roll through the door into the hallway. Almost immediately Chainsaw reappeared, barking hoarsely and climbing onto her chest as she tried to roll over.

"Shit!" Porter yelled. "Shit, I'm sorry, I thought..."

He pulled out his warrant card, chasing the woman. She was crawling towards the front door, still screaming, Chainsaw running alongside her like it was a game.

"I'm police," he said. "I knocked, I knocked! I saw you through the window and just wanted to... I thought you'd had an accident or something. Look, I'm police!"

The woman had reached the front door and looked like she was trying to haul herself up it.

"Look!" Porter pleaded.

Chainsaw had finally noticed Porter, the old dog running over and bracing his paws on his shin. His tail was wagging so hard the little dog looked like he was about to take off. The woman turned back, her eyes wide, her dark skin covered in a sheen of sweat. Porter ducked, holding up the warrant card with a trembling hand and ruffling Chainsaw's head with the other.

"Can we start again?" he said, the dog licking his fingers. "I can go back outside, I can knock again. I swear, I thought you might be in trouble. I'm here to talk about Daniel, that's all."

"Heaven above," the woman said, turning around and sitting against the door. She wiped her arm over her sweaty forehead, then rested it on her chest. "I almost had a heart attack. Help me up?"

Porter put the warrant card away, offering the woman a hand. She was heavyset, and it took a surprising amount of effort to haul her to her feet. Even when she was up, she looked unsteady, her face creased with discomfort, her shoulder braced on the wall to stop herself from falling.

"I've got a stick," she said. "By the table."

Porter grabbed it for her and helped her back into the kitchen. He lifted the chair and she lowered herself into it with considerable effort.

"Are you okay?" said Porter. "I really am sorry. I was knocking, you weren't moving."

"I'm alright," she said. There was a hint of an accent in her voice, maybe Nigerian. She put a hand to her substantial chest, breathing hard. Her face was full of worry, the way only a mother's can be. "Is he okay? Daniel?"

"As far as I know he is," said Porter. "I was hoping to catch him, but I take it he's not here?"

She shook her head.

"He is out, I am sorry."

"I'm DI Peter Porter, by the way," he said. "You're Daniel's mother?"

"I am. Dola."

"Dola Porter," said Porter, musing quietly. He quite liked it.

"What? Not Porter, Dola Obasi."

"Got it. Can I make you a cuppa, Dola? Least I can do after waking you like that."

Dola shook her head, slowly recovering.

"You caught me at a quiet moment," she said. "I don't get too many of those. Life catches up pretty quickly these days." She gestured at the stick. "I am not very able, I'm afraid. My doctor, she calls it neurological. Functional, but I disagree. I cannot function, not the way I should."

"Functional Neurological Disorder," said Porter. "My mum has it, along with a heap of other things. Some good days, mainly bad. I get the feeling nobody really knows what's going on, not even the doctors. It's just a handy name to get you out of the office."

Dola laughed softly, wincing.

"I agree with you there, Mr Porter. It came on when Daniel got his diagnosis. The stress of it is... It has devastated me as much as it has him. It's such a worry, and when the house is quiet my body... As you can see, it switches itself off. My mind, too."

"I really am sorry," said Porter. "About everything. It must be incredibly hard. Can I ask what he has?"

"Hodgkin's," she said, and Porter struggled to remember exactly what it was. Nothing good, he knew that much.

"Do you have children?" she asked.

Chainsaw was sniffing at his feet and he ducked down again, as much to shoo the dog away if he looked like he was about to cock his leg. He ended up scratching his back, the dog's leg machine-gunning in ecstasy.

"First one on the way," he said. "Imminently."

"You may as well take out your heart and wear it on your sleeve," she said. "Because that's how it feels. You are utterly vulnerable. Can I ask, is Daniel in trouble? He is a good boy, he has the kindest soul."

"He's not in any trouble," said Porter. "I've met him a couple of times, in the woods by County Hall. We're investigating—"

"The bones," Dola finished for him, nodding. "I saw it on the news."

"Did Daniel ever mention them?"

"No," she said, frowning. "What would it have to do with him? The only time he ever leaves the house is to walk this thing or see his girlfriend. I wanted to rehome the dog when Daniel was diagnosed; the germs, you know? But he wouldn't let me. Only thing that brings him any happiness, other than his books and his games and his friend."

"Where is he now?" asked Porter, glancing at the dog, who was lying on his back with all four legs in the air waiting for his tummy to be scratched. "Out with his girlfriend?"

Dola opened her mouth to answer, but held back.

"I can promise you, he's not in any trouble," said Porter. "I just want to check that he's okay."

"He's okay," she said, her lips forming a tight line around whatever else she might have wanted to say.

"Dola, Daniel was leaving flowers in the woods. Do you know anything about that?"

She shook her head, her mouth a straight, grim line. Porter pulled his phone from his pocket, finding the photo he'd taken of the florist's card.

"'*To all those who went before me, I honour you. And look forward to our reunion.*' There's a line of Latin, too. '*Do ut des.*' It translates as something like 'I give so that you will give.' Does that mean anything to you? Do you know why he would be leaving flowers?"

This time, she didn't even shake her head. Porter sighed, returning his phone to his pocket. He looked around the kitchen, which was impeccably tidy. Five framed photos hung on the wall above the table, four of them showing Daniel and his mum, the fifth an older photo, creased and faded, of a big man with a bigger smile.

"Daniel's dad?" Porter asked, nodding to it.

"Yes. David." She heaved an almighty sigh. "He left us six years ago."

"Left you?"

"Left everything," she said. "Cancer. Like father like son in every way."

She made the sign of the cross over her chest, then kissed her finger.

"Look, Dola," said Porter. "Whatever's going on, whatever Daniel has told you, we can help. He hasn't done anything wrong, but we're concerned for his safety. I'm worried he's doing something dangerous."

"Because of the gifts?" Dola said, and there was a tear in her eye.

"What gifts?"

"The presents, the clothes. He told me he had found a girlfriend, that's why he took flowers with him. He told me they were for her."

"Have you met her?" said Porter, and she shook her head. "Did he tell you her name?"

"Of course not," she said. "He is a teenage boy and I am his mother. And I never saw her. I wonder if perhaps it is a *boy* he has met, and I don't mind. I couldn't care less, if that's what makes him happy. I wonder if that is why he never told me."

"Hang on," said Porter. "So Daniel's been hanging out with somebody, and this somebody has been buying him things? Gifts?"

Dola nodded.

"But the flowers weren't for this person, boy or girl. He's been leaving them in the woods, with that note. They're more like a tribute to something."

"I don't know anything about this," she said, genuinely confused. "I thought the flowers were for... You said there was something in the note, something about giving." Her expression changed, suddenly full of horror. "You don't think... He's not giving something in return for these gifts, is he? He's not *doing* things?"

"No," said Porter. "I don't want you to think that. There's no evidence at all that he's doing that."

Dola showed no sign of relaxing, gripping the table hard enough for her knuckles to go white. Her eyes scrolled back and forth like she was remembering something.

"Whatever it is, you can tell me," said Porter. "Is Daniel out with this person now?"

"Yes," she said, using the palm of her hand to scrub away the tears.

"Did he say where he was meeting them?"

"No, but I saw him leave," she said. "I watched him through the window. I saw him get into her car."

"You saw the driver?"

"No," Dola said, frowning. "Oh, my gosh, I shouldn't have let him go. It's so hard to think straight with all this, it's so hard to do anything. I just wanted him to be happy, to have something good. I shouldn't have let him go, should I?"

"Dola, think hard," said Porter. "This is really important. Can you remember anything at all about the car he got into? Any detail? Colour, type, big, small, clean, dirty, anything."

Dola nodded, letting go of the table and stretching her hand out to Porter as if meaning to check that he was real. He didn't know what else to do so he took it, holding tight, her palm soft and warm.

"I remember it was blue," she said. "Bright blue. I remember thinking the car looked too old for a young woman, too expensive."

Porter took out his phone with his free hand and found the photo he'd taken the day before.

"Is this the car? Or close, at least?"

"Yes," she said, holding him so tight that Porter felt his knuckle pop. "How did you know?"

"And what time did he leave?"

"About an hour ago," she said. "*Why*? Who is this person he's seeing?"

Porter pulled himself free as gently as he could.

"I have to go," he said.

"Is he going to be okay?" Dola said, picking up on his panic. She tried to get out of her chair but she couldn't manage it, her body trembling.

"He's going to be okay," Porter told her, pulling out a card and leaving it on the table. "You call me anytime if you're worried, or if you think of anything else. I'm going to go and get him, right now. I promise. I'll bring him home."

He ran for the door, gripping the phone hard, the photograph of Derek Foulger's Jaguar still on the screen.

CHAPTER TWENTY-SEVEN

"I THINK THAT'S A EUROPEAN GREEN WOODPECKER," said Duke.

He was kneeling in the thick undergrowth of the woods, Savage's binoculars up to his face. In the shifting shade of the woodland, and with his dark, bushy beard, he looked like a lumberjack. They were at the top of a small hillock—the tallest point in the flat land that had any view at all of Derek Foulger's sprawling estate. The perimeter wall was maybe fifty yards away, the side of the house fifty yards further than that. But Duke was looking in the opposite direction.

"Aaron," said Savage.

"I might be wrong," said Duke. "But that red-crested head is pretty distinctive."

"Aaron," she repeated.

"It could be a..." He stopped as a mechanical chattering noise filled the treetops. "Oh, ha! I was right, it's a woodpecker. I've not seen one this close before, did you know that they—"

"Duke!"

Her voice was too loud, filling the woods and chasing whatever bird it had been from the branches. Duke turned around, the binoculars still held up to his face.

"Huh?"

"We're on a stakeout," she told him, hooking a thumb over her shoulder. "The bad guys are that way."

"Oh, right, sorry."

He handed her the binoculars, adjusting his position so that he was lying on the ground like a Roman emperor at dinner, one knee pointing at the heavens. He had to shift his Taser out of the way so that it wasn't digging into his side. He picked up a twig, studying it like it was the most interesting thing he'd ever seen.

"It's a bit boring though, isn't it?" he said. "We've been out here for hours."

"It's been forty minutes," said Savage.

She lifted the binoculars and studied the house, adjusting the focus until the image grew sharp. The estate was obscured by a dozen trees, thankfully without their leaves, and the top of the wall, but she could still make out the long driveway that swept down from the gate, and she had a good view through five of the large windows. So far she'd seen four cars enter the estate, passing out of sight down the other side of the house, but even with the binoculars she was too far away to ID any of the drivers or passengers.

"Do you want a Starburst?" said Duke, holding out a handful of sweets.

"Where did you get them?"

"My pocket."

"Why have you got a pocketful of Starburst?"

Duke shrugged.

"Had to stop Pete getting hold of them," he said with a grin. Savage gave him a hard stare.

"That's DI Porter to you, mate," she said. "And give up, yeah? He's going through a hard time at the moment, he needs support."

"Like a motorised scooter?" said Duke. "They give great support."

Her hard stare grew harder.

"I'm sorry," he said. "I don't mean it. I only say it because..."

"Because what?" she asked when he petered out.

"Because I'm jealous of him. Porter. He's such a good copper, you don't meet many like him anymore. Like Kett, too, and you. I feel jealous of all of you, but especially him because he's... *him*. Great guy, great copper, fit as anything —or he used to be, anyway—and now he's going to be a great dad too, you just know it. I don't feel good enough to be here. I feel like you all think I'm some sort of walking gorilla."

"You realise gorillas *can* walk?" said Savage, and Duke's face fell.

"That's exactly what I mean!" he said. "That's why I do it, why I rib him so much, because he's so much cooler than me. I don't mean any of it. I wish I was more like him. Just not the expanding waistline bit."

He pushed the twig into the ground like he was planting it.

"I want to be part of your club too."

"Club? You mean the Task Force?"

"Yeah. At the moment it's like the Extreme Crime Task Force... and this other guy. I don't want to be the other guy."

"You're fine, Aaron," she said, lifting the binoculars again.

"*Fine?*" he said.

"You know what I mean."

Another car was coming through the gates, this one long and black—a few feet shy of being a fully-fledged limousine. It followed the path the others had taken, disappearing behind the bulk of the house. She wondered if they should move, try to find a vantage point to the west where all the action seemed to be happening.

"Maybe we should have kids?" said Duke, and she almost dropped the binoculars.

"*What?*"

"Not many," he went on with a goofy smile. "Five or six."

The laugh was out of her mouth before she could stop it.

"*Just* five or six?" she said.

"More, if you want?"

"Let's stick to meals out and cinema trips for now, yeah?" she said. "I've got too many kids to look after as it is."

What with you and the dog, she thought but didn't say.

"But maybe one day?" he persisted. "Like in a couple of years?"

She offered him a smile instead of an answer and he grinned back.

"You dope," she said.

"*Your* dope," he replied, prodding her shoulder with the twig.

Savage's phone started vibrating and she pulled it out, seeing Porter's name on the screen.

"Kate," he said when she'd answered. He sounded out of breath. "You at the Foulger place?"

"Yes, sir," she said.

"You've got eyes on?"

"Yeah."

"You seen Foulger's car, the blue Jag?"

"The XJS?" she said. "Yeah, it arrived about twenty minutes ago."

"Twenty-five," said Duke, consulting his pad.

"Twenty-five," she echoed. "Why?"

"Did you see a young man in it? Black, no hair?"

"We're not close enough," she said. "Couldn't really get a bead on any of the drivers. But I think there was somebody in the passenger seat of the Jag."

She closed her eyes, picturing it.

"Yeah, the passenger side was facing us and there was definitely somebody there. That your kid?"

"Yeah," said Porter. "Daniel Obasi. His mum says somebody's been buying him gifts, offering them in exchange for something. Grooming him, I'm guessing. Foulger—or somebody driving Foulger's car—picked him up just over an hour ago."

"And brought him here," said Savage. "Why, sir?"

"I don't know, but the robes, the church, the knife, the whole sacrifice thing, it's nothing good, Kate. Can you see what's going on?"

"Not much," she said, using her free hand to lift the binoculars. "But there's a lot of traffic. Five cars have entered the estate, none have left."

"Something's going to happen," said Porter. "I can feel it."

He hung up, and Savage turned to Duke. He'd obviously heard the call because his face was carved from stone, his eyes dark.

"What now?" he asked.

"We brace ourselves," said Savage, pushing herself up. "Because it's all about to kick off."

"IT'S RIGHT THERE, SIR," said Kett. "All you have to do is look."

Superintendent Clare stood with his eyes closed in front of the wall of evidence in the Incident Room, his fists clenched at his side. Kett was next to him, wondering if he was going to have to peel the Super's eyelids open to force him to confront the truth. After a handful of seconds, though, Clare spluttered out a sigh and stared at the wall.

"Savage has just confirmed it," Kett said. "Foulger's back at his estate, almost certainly with Daniel. We have multiple vehicles arriving, high-end cars. It's..."

He checked his watch.

"It's past five, sir, almost dark. I don't know for sure what's going to happen, but we've got one dead body connected to Foulger, sacrificed and displayed on the wall. This could end up being another. We're running out of time."

"I just don't believe it," said Clare. "Magick, rituals, it's just too..."

"Extreme, sir," Kett finished for him. "But that's what we do. It's who we are."

Clare shook his head.

"I think your judgement has been clouded by Hollenbeck, Kett," he said. "I think you're looking too hard. You're seeing things that aren't there. A group of wealthy psychopaths sacrificing innocent men, it doesn't feel right, it feels like something you've made up because it's exactly what happened to you. Your thought process has been polluted by what Hollenbeck put you through."

"You're wrong, sir," said Kett. "I'm seeing clearly, the pieces are right there."

And they were, clicking neatly into place inside his head.

"Something bad is going to happen to that kid tonight," he went on. "We're not going to get another chance."

Clare's red eyes trolled the board, settling on the butchered remains of Peter Carran.

"Gorski's waiting for you," he said. "She's the only one who knows. I need this to be clean. Do not Kett this up."

"Thank you, sir," Kett said, a cool explosion of adrenaline in his stomach. He ran for the door, stopping when Clare called his name.

"Kett, if you're wrong about this, we're all fucked. Foulger and the Chief Constable and all their golf buddies will rain fiery toss upon us until the end of days."

Kett offered him a grim smile.

"I'm not wrong, sir."

CHAPTER TWENTY-EIGHT

NIGHT DROPPED HARD AS KETT SET OUT TOWARDS THE Foulger estate, like he'd fallen into a trap. He floored the Volvo on the A47, the lights of Sergeant Julia Gorski's van filling his rearview mirror as the greying world flashed past.

As they approached Dereham, the traffic grew so thick that he pulled over and let her pass, motioning for her to put the blue lights on. Even then it was a struggle to get through the town, as if the whole world was trying to hold them back.

It was almost an hour after leaving the city that they hit the road that led to Foulger's house, and Kett flashed his lights in order to get the van to slow down. Gorski turned off her blues and wound the window down, leaning out.

"We can't afford to go in hard," Kett said through his own open window. "It's too big, too many places to hide. Savage is in the woods. She's found a place to breach the wall. We pull in, we watch, we wait. We don't let them see us."

"Watch and wait?" said Gorski, adjusting her helmet. "Who are you, and what have you done with DCI Kett?"

Kett breathed a laugh through his nose then pulled the car away, keeping his speed down as he negotiated the tight turns and high verges. It was almost pitch black out here, the woods a dark line to his right and sloping fields to the left. He couldn't quite remember where the house was, then he turned a corner and saw a dark shape in the road, flagging him down. It was DI Porter, and he moved over as Kett slowed to a halt, leaning on the roof.

"We're down there, sir," he said, pointing to an opening in the trees. "Path's a little rocky, so take it slow. House is about a hundred yards that way."

"Anything happening?" Kett asked.

"Plenty, sir," he said. "Like a fucking convention in there. You can give me a ride back."

Kett disengaged the central locking and Porter clambered in. Even with the headlights on it was almost impossible to see the break in the verge, the car almost losing its undercarriage as it bumped onto the track beyond. Instantly they were crowded by trees, branches battering at the windows and scraping the doors as they thumped their way forwards. Porter sat in the passenger seat and chewed his thumbnail, his expression full of worry.

"It's going to be okay, Pete," said Kett. "*He's* going to be okay."

"If that bastard touches him, I'll..." Porter started. "How many times have we seen it, Robbie? They think they can do whatever they want, they think they're untouchable."

"But they're wrong," said Kett.

"They're wrong," Porter echoed. "Over there."

The Volvo wound around the track and the headlights caused a sudden explosion of yellow ahead—PC Duke's jacket, brighter than the sun. Savage was standing on the colossal trunk of a felled tree next to him, binoculars up to her eyes.

There was no space to steer around Porter's Mondeo and the Audi that Savage had driven up in, so he parked behind them, cutting the engine. Gorski did the same, the sudden silence falling like a hammer, brutal enough to make Kett's ears ring. Even though he knew Foulger's house was just through the trees it felt like the middle of nowhere here, miles away from civilisation.

Miles away from help.

"I hate the countryside," said Porter as he got out. "Have I ever mentioned that?"

Kett followed him into the frozen dark, the cold making him double up for a moment.

"Jesus," he said through chattering teeth. "What's happening, Kate?"

"Come and have a look, sir," she called down from the horizontal trunk.

It was as tall as his chest, and it took him longer than he'd have liked to climb it—Porter taking pity on him after a minute or so and offering him a foot up. The dead tree was slippery, but there were plenty of branches to grab, and he wobbled unsteadily for a moment until he found his balance.

From here he could see over the wall into the western edge of the estate, those same woods he'd explored earlier. The church was a lump of shadow against the brighter lights of the house, the large, circular window in its back wall glowing faintly.

There was a grunt as Gorski climbed up beside him, so close that she almost knocked him off. Both she and Savage grabbed Kett's arms in order to stop him from falling.

"Thanks," he said.

"No worries, *Granddad*," said Gorski. She lifted a sleek, black monocular, studying the woods. "The church?"

"I've seen eleven people go inside in the last thirty minutes," said Savage. "Want to guess what they were wearing?"

"Robes," said Kett.

"Yeah, hoods up. Nobody has come out. There's another couple now, look."

Two shapes stalked through the trees, their long cloaks making them almost invisible. They approached the open door of the church and filed inside.

"That's thirteen," said Savage. "I haven't seen anyone who looks like Porter's lad, unless he's wearing a robe too. But we were on the other side of the house for a while, he might have been brought here earlier. We wouldn't have seen it."

"There's a basement," said Kett. "Steps are inside, at this end. I didn't see how deep it was, or how big. Going by what we've seen so far on this case, there may be tunnels too."

"How do you want to play this?" asked Gorski. "Full assault? I'm not going to lie, it'll be hard getting a team into a basement, narrow stairs, small spaces, lots of people. It'll be messy."

Kett chewed on it, watching another three hooded shapes make their way towards the building. Somebody was laughing, the sound of it echoing off the wall of the church. He waited until they'd entered the building before speaking again.

"We need a small group," he said. "Two or three. We take it slow. Kate, have you seen any security?"

"Nothing," she replied. "The front gates were shut but there's nobody guarding them. Some CCTV by the road but nothing back here. No guards, no guns."

"They think they're too clever for us," said Kett. "They're assuming nobody's going to find them."

"Or that there's nothing we can do about it if we do," said Savage.

He hopped down from the tree, wincing as the pain clawed up his knees. Gorski followed, Savage stayed put.

"You and me, Gorski," he said. "Pick another officer."

"And me," said Porter. "I want to make sure he's okay."

Kett nodded.

"Pochin," said Gorski, and one of the firearms team jogged over from where they'd all been huddled by the van. The man's face was inscrutable beneath a balaclava but he nodded at Kett and Porter, his rifle slung by his side, his pistol strapped to his leg, only the Taser showing any hint of colour.

"Four more on their way in," Savage called down. "Seventeen now, at least."

"Be very careful," Kett told Gorski. "There are some powerful people here, I'm sure of it. Foulger is connected, he has some wealthy mates."

"What is it with you and psychopathic rich folk?" said Gorski.

"One of his mates is the Chief Constable," Kett went on, and only now did Gorski start to look uncomfortable. "We think there's a young man in the church, Daniel Obasi. He's seventeen. His life might be in danger, this might be some kind of..."

Even thinking it now seemed utterly surreal, and Kett had a moment of doubt—only for a second, though, before he remembered the arrangement of bones in the cellar of the house, before he remembered the glistening mess of Carran's body strung up on the wall like a piece of modern art.

"Some kind of *ritual.* I saw somebody with a dagger when I was here earlier, looked like a ceremonial one. I don't know if there are any other weapons."

Gorski nodded to show that she'd understood.

"They're probably going to bolt when they see us," she said. "After they've shit their pants, that is. I'll secure the rest of the unit in the woods, round them up as soon as they run out the door."

"Sounds good," said Kett. "Thanks."

Gorski tutted.

"Rituals, magic, bloodshed, sacrifice. Only you, Kett."

"I didn't bloody organise it!" he said.

"Two more," said Savage. "Hang on... They've closed the door."

Silence fell. The quiet night held its breath.

"Let's go," said Kett.

He led the way down the length of the tree, passing Duke.

"You want me in there too?" said the PC.

"Not this time. But be ready in case anyone jumps the wall."

"Yes, sir," he said as he pulled out his Taser.

The tree's roots looked like a monstrous spider in the dark and Kett made his way around them, using the torch on his phone to navigate the uneven ground. Porter jogged alongside him, panting hard, while the tactical team followed as quietly as shadows, only the soft rattle of their rifles giving them away.

Kett could see the section of wall he'd climbed over earlier, the topmost row of bricks missing. He paused when he reached it, checking for silence on the other side before digging his boot into the crumbling mortar and hauling himself up.

The church sat twenty yards away in its cage of trees, muted candlelight flickering through the back window. Past it was the main house, every room lit up like it was Christmas. Other than the crack of branches in the wind it was completely still here, as if all those people in robes had simply dissolved into the night. Kett watched the window for a moment but there was no sign of life inside. They'd probably moved into the cellar.

"It's clear," he said when he dropped back down. "Nobody's watching the door."

He heard Gorski relaying quiet orders to her team, and one by one they ghosted over the wall. She was the last to go, vaulting the six-foot brick like a gymnast. Kett followed her, his boot slipping. He tried again, every muscle quivering as he pulled himself up.

"Sir, that's just embarrassing," said Porter, planting two hands on his backside and giving him a shove. Kett straddled the wall, offering Porter a hand and pulling him up. The pair of them were grunting like mules, earning a hiss from Gorski down below. She put her finger to her lips.

"If you can't move quietly, don't come," she said.

Porter rolled his eyes at Kett and then dropped down. Kett waited until he was clear before doing the same, the fall further than he'd expected it to be. He hobbled after the others, twigs cracking underfoot like an alarm as they drew closer to the church. Gorski reached the door first, her sharp eyes watching as her team dispersed into the trees. She checked her rifle and then lifted it to her shoulder, nodding to Pochin by her side, then to Kett as he caught up.

Kett turned the handle and gently pushed the heavy wooden door. It opened silently, as if the hinges had recently been oiled, revealing the same cramped interior that he'd seen earlier. At least a hundred candles burned on the floor between the pews and along the walls, producing a gentle, sputtering roar and a welcome warmth. He couldn't see anybody but the stairs were lit up once again by a brighter glow from below. He thought he could hear something from down there, a gentle, rhythmic song.

"They're chanting," whispered Porter, leaning in next to him.

"Looks clear," said Kett, standing aside to let Gorski in first.

She entered the church, her rifle sweeping left and right before centring on the stairs. Pochin followed, breaking to the side and traversing the narrow gap between the pews and the wall. Kett trod on Gorski's shadow, both of them moving swiftly down the middle of the room. The closer he got to the stone steps, the more he could see of where they led—straight down to a narrow, earthen corridor below. More candles burned there, and the rhythmic music was louder.

Porter was right, they were *definitely* chanting.

Gorski dropped onto the top step, then immediately pulled back. She fell to the side and Kett almost asked her what she was doing when he heard echoing footsteps below. He stepped away from the mouth of the stairs, colliding with Porter behind him, both of them hugging the wall as the steps grew closer.

A man's head rose into sight, staring intently at the phone he held in his hand. He looked like he was texting somebody, so engrossed in it that he reached the top of the stairs without seeing any of the four figures who flanked him.

"Fuck's sake," he whispered, poking the screen with a finger.

For a moment, nobody moved. Then Gorski punched

up from where she'd been crouching, moving fast. The man heard her, turned, then the barrel of Gorski's gun was in his face. He dropped onto his backside like a stack of bricks, drowning in his robe, the phone clattering away.

"Do not move," Gorski hissed. "And keep your mouth shut."

The wide-eyed man nodded, holding up his trembling hands. Pochin slapped on a pair of cuffs, grabbing the collar of the guy's robe and dragging him back up the central aisle towards the door.

Gorski was already moving again, stepping neatly down the stairs. Kett chased her, Porter right behind him. The chanting grew louder, resonating off the cold stone walls, the pitch of it vibrating inside his skull like a trapped fly. That same atmosphere he'd felt before seemed to crawl inside him, making his stomach churn, making his heart slam against his ribs like it was trying to break free.

They reached the bottom of the steps, staring along a short, narrow tunnel. At the end of it was another set of wooden doors and engraved in both was the same symbol they'd seen before—a gaping eye with its crown, that wheel of feet. One side was open a crack and through it Kett could see shifting, swaying shapes illuminated by firelight. The sound of their song was almost hypnotic, and there was a smell in the air here too, something pungent and floral. It made his eyes weep, made him feel like he was going to be sick.

Pochin was back, and he and Gorski approached the doors side by side. Kett squeezed between them, blinking through the gap and seeing something he couldn't quite believe.

Beyond the doors was a cellar room that looked almost identical to the one they'd found at County Hall—other than the fact that this one didn't have a central column. Crammed between the brick walls and beneath the low, vaulted ceiling, their backs thankfully to the doors, was a crowd of people in long, black robes, all chanting softly—so many of them that they almost blocked the view across the room.

Almost.

Because as they chanted they swayed, and every time they moved, Kett caught a glimpse of the far side of the room. There was a deep alcove in the wall there, just like in the cellar, and inside it was a bundle of cloth that twisted and writhed—a heavy chain stretching from the mouth of the sack to the wall.

Beside the sack was a monster of a man, his face hidden in the shadows of his hood, that ceremonial dagger clutched in his meaty fingers.

The man lifted his free hand and the chanting abruptly stopped, everyone in the room falling still and silent.

"And so it falls to us, once more," came a deep, resonant voice—instantly recognisable as Derek Foulger. "The honoured members of this guild. It is our duty, our honour, our *right*."

Kett glanced at Gorski, the expression on her face clear enough.

I'm ready.

"Our right," the big man said again. "*Do ut des!*"

Foulger grabbed the dagger with both hands and lifted it over his head, a series of small gasps filling the room from the eager crowd.

"Do it!" a woman called out, her words echoed by half a dozen others.

"Our right!" said another man.

Kett stood back, nodded at Gorski, then kicked the door wide open.

"Police!" he roared. "Everybody on the floor!"

The chaos was instant, the room full of screams, full of movement as everyone spun around. Gorski moved fast, Pochin beside her, both of them shouting.

"Armed police! On the ground!"

Two of the hooded figures bolted, their hoods flying back as they ran to reveal a man and a woman, both of them in their fifties, both of them perfectly manicured. The man made it three strides before Pochin cracked the butt of his rifle into his face, dropping him instantly. The woman ducked under Gorski and made it through the door but Porter tackled her, both of them crumpling into a heap.

"I mean it," Gorski shouted. "The next one to move won't get up."

The crowd was falling back towards the walls, trampling over each other as they parted. Somebody's robe had caught one of the candles, the fire climbing fast. Inside the alcove, the sack twisted even harder as whoever was inside it tried to get out. Foulger rose tall, the dagger still held over his head, his obese face visible through the folds of his hood.

"How dare you!" he roared. "How fucking dare you!"

"Drop it," Kett told him, breaking into a run.

He was fast, but Porter was faster, crossing the room like a locomotive. Foulger staggered back, then—just before the two men collided—he drove the dagger down towards Porter's chest.

"Move, Kett!" screamed Gorski. "I need a shot!"

Porter slammed into Foulger, driving him into the wall. The DI gasped wetly as both of them dropped to the floor.

"Jesus, Pete!" said Kett as he skidded down beside them.

Porter was on top, deadly still. Beneath him, Foulger

bucked and flopped like a landed whale, his eyes almost bursting from their sockets.

"Stay still," Kett told him. "Or I'll end you."

Foulger tried to get up but suddenly Gorski was there, the barrel of her rifle inches from his forehead. Porter was still groaning, doubled up, and Kett grabbed him, dragging him away from the other man.

"Shit, Pete," he said. "Talk to me."

"You idiot!" Foulger grunted, his fat face peeling open into a smile that was almost demonic. "You're finished!"

Kett ignored him, rolling the DI onto his back, expecting to see the hilt of the dagger protruding from his chest, expecting to find a river of blood. The weapon fell to the ground next to him, not with a clatter but with a thud. Porter's hands were on his crotch, not his chest, and after a second or two he opened his eyes. They were watering, and full of pain.

"You okay?" Kett asked him.

"No," wheezed Porter. "Bastard got me right in the balls."

"What's going on?" said Gorski, her rifle still aimed at Foulger.

Kett looked over his shoulder to see that the crowd had calmed. Pochin had managed to extinguish the burning cloak, and now everyone stood there with their hoods down, watching in horror and dismay. Even the sack had grown quiet, inflating and deflating as whoever was inside it took deep, gulping breaths. Gorski reached down and picked up the dagger.

"What is this, Kett?" she said, passing it to him.

He took it, flexing the blade. It was made of rubber, not even remotely convincing this close up.

He stood, the room reeling around him. Foulger had

erupted into wet, choking giggles. Porter struggled up and limped to the sack. He wrestled with the opening, tugging it down to reveal a teenage boy, his skin drenched in sweat, his eyes wide. There was a heavy manacle around his scrawny neck, connected to the chain.

"Daniel?" said Porter.

The kid broke into a bashful smile.

"Good to see you, PC McStalker," he said.

"What the hell is going on?" Kett demanded. The vertigo was so bad he had to rest a hand on the wall to stop himself falling.

"What's going on is that you just made your last mistake, Kett."

Foulger lay on the stone, speaking the words through more grunting laughter, his entire body rippling with it. Other people in the room were laughing too, the sound of it mixing with the adrenaline, with the acidic stench of whatever was burning, making Kett feel like he was trapped inside some sort of nightmare.

"Your last mistake," Foulger said again. "You're finished."

CHAPTER TWENTY-NINE

Superintendent Clare wasn't shouting, he wasn't swearing. He wasn't saying anything at all.

And that was infinitely worse.

He stood with his back to Kett, facing the old church, his shoulders slumped. He was lit by the flashing blue lights of the ambulance that waited by the main house. A uniformed officer was helping a man out of the church—the guy that Pochin had brained with his rifle. Even though his face was swollen, a tooth missing, Kett recognised him: Steven Fish, an anchor for the local East Anglia news. Fish turned his bloodshot eyes to Clare, then to Kett, firing them a murderous look before he walked away.

Daniel, the kid who'd been chained to the wall, was in the ambulance, even though he'd insisted he was okay and had shown absolutely no sign of injury. Porter was with him, as confused as Kett was.

Fish was the last of the guests to go. Everyone else had made their way towards the main house in the half-hour since they'd raided the church, since the dagger had been revealed to be fake. Kett could see them through the big windows, sipping champagne, talking animatedly, laughing. They'd shed their robes to reveal black ties and ballroom dresses, a small fortune of jewellery glittering like disco balls. There was music playing, something classical that wafted through the trees.

It was utterly surreal, and he was still convinced he was locked inside some kind of fever dream.

Only Foulger remained inside the church, and he was putting on quite a show. As soon as the entire display had been revealed to be a charade he'd begun screaming and howling, claiming that Porter had injured him during his attack. The paramedics had offered to check him out, of course, but he'd insisted that he was in too much pain. He'd ordered Kett out of the church and then made a dramatic display of calling his friend the Chief Constable.

Thankfully, Clare had shown up instead.

The Super rubbed his face, and looked back at Kett with eyes that might have belonged to a hundred-year-old man.

"Let's get this over with," he said, leading the way towards the church.

"I'm sorry, sir," Kett said as he followed. "I don't know—"

Clare held up his hand, shaking his head.

"I don't want a single thing to come out of that hole in your face, Detective, other than a series of grovelling apologies. I told you, didn't I? If you Kett this one up, we're all out of a job. I told you."

He walked through the low door, cracking his head on the lintel. A shudder of quiet fury passed through him, one that burned hotter than the candles. Kett turned to look at Savage, who stood with Gorski between the trees a short distance away. She offered him a sad smile, a wave, and he could read her mind even though she didn't speak.

Good luck.

He was going to need it.

He entered the church, following Clare down the stairs and along the short corridor to the chamber that lay at the end. The smell of smoke still hung heavy in the air, that and the pungent stench of whatever incense they'd been burning.

Somebody had brought one of the short pews down from upstairs and Derek Foulger sat on it, hunched over and wheezing theatrically. He had shrugged off his robe and untied his bowtie, his shirt missing a couple of buttons from the tussle and his pink flesh like gelatine underneath. He was sweating profusely in the heat from the candles, looking like a wax sculpture that was in the process of melting.

But the hatred in his eyes was as sharp as ever.

"About time," he said to Clare. "Where's Tim?"

"The Chief Constable is unavailable," said Clare. "He sends his apologies, but he's on his way back to the city. He will be in touch. Mr Foulger, on behalf of the entire Norfolk Constabulary, I'd—"

"I don't want to hear it from you," said Foulger, jabbing a fat finger in Kett's direction. "I want to hear it from him. Of all the... You realise people could have died? Mary was on fire, Steven's going to be off work for weeks, they think he might have a broken jaw. How dare you, Kett? How dare you attack me and my friends like that. I'll have your job, son, yours and *his*."

He glared at Clare for a moment before returning his attention to Kett.

"Now say it. Go on. I want to hear how sorry you are."

Kett felt like he had a brick in his throat. He coughed to clear it.

"You have my—"

"Louder."

"You have my apologies, Mr Foulger."

"He doesn't mean it," Foulger said, sitting back against the wall, folding his arms over his capacious chest. Behind him, in the alcove, sat the sack with its chains and its manacles.

"I can assure you, he does," said Clare, turning to Kett and speaking through gritted teeth. "Don't you?"

"I do," said Kett, hearing the insincerity there, trying again. "I am sorry. But you have to see it from our point of view, Foulger."

Clare hissed a warning but Kett ignored him.

"We had credible evidence that a child was in danger. We come down here to see him in chains and you with a dagger. In that split second we acted exactly how we should have done, how you'd have wanted us to act if that was *your* kid. We did our jobs."

Foulger smiled, and there was nothing kind about it. His eyes were dark.

"That's your apology, is it?" he said.

"Mr Foulger, as much as I hate to admit it, DCI Kett has a point," said Clare. "What were you doing down here?"

"Carry on down this path, Superintendent, and you won't have a job come the morning either," said Foulger.

"You've made that perfectly clear. So if I've lost my job I may as well ask again, what was going on?"

"A ceremony," Foulger said, sniffing. "A ritual that has its roots in the dawn of this great country, in the cradle of civilisation."

"A sacrifice," said Kett.

"Of sorts," Foulger replied, his face full of smug victory. "But a purely performative one. We sacrifice a victim, save him from poverty, and his bones shall grant us wealth and power forever more."

"So you kill the boy," said Kett. "You use his bones for... for ritual magick?"

Foulger huffed a laugh.

"Like I said. It's a performance. Do you know what that word means? Performance? It means it's not real."

"But it's based on something real," Kett pressed, earning another look from Clare. "It's what used to happen, right? The bones we found in the cellar by County Hall, linked by tunnels to your ancestral home. The Harford Guild crest on the walls, on the doors in this very room. Not so long ago, this thing wasn't a performance at all, was it? People died. It really happened."

"So what if it did?" Foulger said. "It was nothing to do with me. I can't be held responsible for the crimes of my ancestors."

Kett opened his mouth to argue, and realised he couldn't. Foulger's face split into a smile, sensing his hesitation.

"All we're doing here, Detective, is upholding a sacred tradition in a way that harms nobody. Daniel was well aware of what he was signing up for, he was perfectly happy to play our sacrificial lamb. And he will be well rewarded for it. We have no desire to kill an impoverished child. That practice—if indeed it ever truly existed—is vile, repugnant. No, we perform our sacrament, we go through the motions, we uphold the rites of the Harford Guild in a safe and welcoming environment. We keep history alive in a sacred way. We appease our gods and those who came before us, then Daniel gets paid and we get drunk."

He leaned forward again, hauling in an asthmatic breath.

"Only this time we were the victims of religious discrimination. We were persecuted for our beliefs. This isn't just an error of judgement, it's a heinous crime against a minority group."

The laugh exploded from Kett's mouth.

"A minority group?" he exclaimed.

"Yes, the wealthy. We're the one percent, are we not? It doesn't get much more of a minority than that."

"Unbelievable," said Kett, and Clare actually drove his elbow into Kett's arm.

"Like I said," the Super grovelled. "We are all deeply sorry for the inconvenience and the misunderstanding, Mr Foulger. It won't happen again, will it, Kett?"

Kett didn't reply immediately. He rubbed his hand over his watering eyes, feeling that same unpleasant smell scour the inside of his nostrils, fill his skull.

"While I'm here, Mr Foulger," he said. "I need to ask you some questions about the death of Peter Carran."

"Jesus Christ," muttered Clare.

"You told us you were in Yarmouth yesterday at the time of the murder, but a witness claims you left early. You could have been back in the city, inside your old house on Bracondale, at the time Carran was murdered."

Foulger simply stared at him with his bloated eyes.

"So where were you?"

"Fucking your mother," the big man said. "Got a problem with that?"

"Not if she can provide a witness statement," said Kett, trying to keep his cool. Foulger laughed again.

"I don't know if she was your mother or not. It was too

dark to see. I was at Goldie's, you can check with them. They have plenty of CCTV on the front door."

"Goldie's?" said Kett.

"Brothel," Clare told him. "In everything but name, that is. It's upmarket, way upmarket."

"And you know this how, sir?" said Kett.

"Because we've *raided* it, Kett," Clare spluttered back, outraged. "Several times. Not that we've had any luck shutting it down."

"Because it's not illegal to offer a lithe young kitten a gift," said Foulger, grinning smugly. "And it's not illegal for said kitten to return the gesture with a little affection. Just like it's not illegal to *pretend* to sacrifice a boy. You have to remember, gentlemen, that it's our God-given right as the protectors of this realm, as the cream of the crop, to do whatever the fuck we want. Now give me my apology and get out."

Clare sighed, nodding to Kett.

"Do it," he said.

Kett took a deep breath, closing his eyes for a moment, centring himself. Then he looked at Foulger.

"I genuinely am sorry," he said.

Foulger's grin grew wider, a fat cat who seemed to be lapping it up. It was too much to bear, and the next words were out of Kett's mouth before he could stop them.

"That you're such a fucking prick."

Clare grabbed Kett's jacket like he was manhandling a criminal, dragging him from the room and almost sending him flying up the stairs.

THE NIGHT WAS COLDER than ever, but Kett was grateful for it after the feverish heat of the church. There was no sign of Savage and Gorski when he walked outside, and from here he couldn't see through the open doors of the ambulance. Only Foulger's guests remained, cocooned inside the enormous rectory, oblivious as they danced.

"Kett," Clare called out behind him, and he almost ignored the Superintendent, pushing into the trees, just wanting to get away. He felt like he could keep walking forever and never look back. "*Kett*!"

He stopped, inhaling the crisp, clean air. Then he turned around to see the Super marching towards him.

"That was stupid," said Clare.

"Like you said, sir, if I've lost my job then it doesn't make any difference. And it sure made me feel better."

Incredibly, Clare laughed.

"Me too," he said. "You should have seen his face."

Their smiles fell away, scuttling into the dark.

"Have I lost my job, sir?" Kett asked.

"That's not up to me. Maybe. Maybe not. It wasn't like there wasn't evidence pointing to Foulger. But I was right, wasn't I? Hollenbeck has tossed all over your brain, Kett, they've made it so you can't see straight. Hell, they've done it to me, too. To all of us. I believed you. I believed Foulger was guilty because I was there when we rounded up those Hollenbeck tossbags, I saw who they were. The wealth, the arrogance, that sense of entitlement and immunity. I believed you and I shouldn't have."

"You're going to check Foulger's alibi?" Kett asked.

"Of course. But it'll be solid. This isn't him, it never was. He's a prick, just like you said, but that's all he is. He's not a killer. It wouldn't surprise me if he did all this just to trap you. Look at the timing, it's too neat."

Kett realised he was probably right, and the hatred he felt for Foulger burned even deeper.

"We'll find whoever killed Carran," he said. "Even if it wasn't Foulger, it's connected to his ritual, to the Guild, we'll..."

He tapered off when Clare raised his hand, holding it up like he was taking an oath.

"I can't say whether or not you've lost your job, Robbie," he said. "But I know one thing for sure, you're off this case."

"Sir—"

"Don't argue. There's nothing I can do." Clare walked past Kett, stopping for long enough to place a hand on his shoulder, squeezing hard. "Get some rest, take some time. Go home, and I'll tell you when it's safe to come back."

Then he was gone, leaving Kett alone in the woods.

CHAPTER THIRTY

"So," said Porter. "You want to tell me what on earth that was all about, mate?"

He was standing in the back of the ambulance that had shown up at Foulger's house. Inside the bed, covered with blankets, was Daniel. He looked like a wreck, like a hollowed out shell, his skin covered with a sheen of sweat and every limb trembling. But he was grinning, his eyes bright.

"That," he said, his voice hoarse, "was so much more fun than I thought it was going to be."

"You were about to be *sacrificed*," said Porter. "What's fun about that?"

Daniel laughed.

"It wasn't real, obviously. Didn't you get that, with the rubber dagger and the cheese-as-shit robes and everything? Who the hell does a real sacrifice or whatever? Only an idiot would think that."

Porter lifted his hands to admit to being an idiot.

"But how did you know?" he asked the boy. "How did

you know Foulger wasn't going to turn around and stab you?"

"He's alright," said Daniel. "We're never going to be best friends, like, but he's alright as far as old blokes go. Known him for ages."

Porter shook his head in disbelief, glancing through the open back doors to see a paramedic heading their way, helping a man through the trees. It was the guy who'd been laid out cold by Gorski's officer, his face such a ruin that Porter had no idea why he wasn't on a stretcher. He turned back to Daniel, noticing again how sweaty he looked. He examined his skin more closely, seeing that it looked almost greasy, as if he'd been slathered in oil. The smell of it, weirdly, was making him think of roast dinners.

"How did this all start?" he asked.

"Wouldn't you already know that?" the kid replied. "Seeing as how you've been following me everywhere."

"Fair point," said Porter. "But tell me anyway."

Daniel sighed. The smile was still on his face, but it seemed defensive now. He played with the sheet like it was a puzzle, twisting it between his fingers.

"It's nothing weird," he said. "He wasn't a paedo or anything."

"Good to know," said Porter.

"I used to bump into him all the time when I was walking the dog."

"You're talking about Derek Foulger?"

"Yeah, he always told me off for letting the dog shit everywhere, even though it was in the woods. So I used to make Chainsaw hold it in until we saw him coming and then do it right in front of him."

He laughed.

"Turned out Derek thought it was hilarious that I'd

trained him to shit on demand, like every time he saw his face. We got talking, he asked me stuff about my life, my house, my parents, about what's wrong with me. He wanted to know if I was, like..."

"Poor," said Porter, and he nodded.

"We're not *poor* poor. We can eat, we have a roof, I have a PS4."

"Call of Duty?" asked Porter, and Daniel pulled a face.

"Yeah, if I was born in 1962, maybe. We're not peasants or anything. But yeah, he asked if we were poor, and then he offered me a job. One night, a lot of money. So of course I thought he was a paedo, and I told him to fuck off, but it wasn't that at all. He said it was some play he was doing, a show. Theatre. This thing, that you guys majorly fucked up, by the way. He didn't tell me you lot were coming, obvs. Were they, like, real guns?"

Porter nodded, trying not to think about how much worse this would have been if Gorski and her team had started shooting. There was a knock on the ambulance door, the paramedic standing there with the injured man.

"Just gonna grab a couple of things if that's okay?" he said, and Porter gave him a hand up. The bloody-faced man started to follow, struggling with the step.

"Get that kid out of the bed," he said, sounding like he was speaking through a mouthful of toffee. "I'm hurt."

"He's not going anywhere," said Porter, blocking the way and forcing the man to drop back to the ground. "You can wait, mate."

"Do you know who I am?" the man said, holding his face.

Porter squinted, trying to ID him through the blood and the swollen tissue.

"Pretty hard to tell at the moment, sorry," he said. Then

he realised. "Oh, wait, don't you read the news? You're that guy... uh..."

"Fish," the man spat. "So move over, let me in."

"Nah," said Porter. "You look fine to me."

The paramedic grabbed what he needed and jumped out, steering his patient around the side of the ambulance.

"Hey, Fish, any chance of an autograph?" Porter called after them. "My wife watches your show all the time."

"Fuck off!" came the muffled reply.

"Worth a shot," said Porter. "So, you met Foulger, he asked you to be in this thing. Did he tell you what you had to do?"

"Sure," said Daniel. "Sit inside a sack with my hands chained for half an hour. He was going to pretend to stab me and I'd like, play dead or whatever while they all chanted. That was it, job done. Easy money."

"How much was he giving you?"

"Eight grand," said the kid, and Porter whistled. "He'd better still fork it over, too. I did my part. If you messed this up for me I'm going to send you, like, an invoice or whatever."

"He'll pay," said Porter, with no idea whether he was telling the truth or not. "You ever stop to think how nuts this was? How dangerous? Did Foulger ask you not to tell your mum? Because she has no idea about this."

"You spoke to her?" Daniel asked, a flash of guilt passing over his face. Porter nodded. "Derek *did* tell me to tell Mum. He insisted on it, but I lied. I said she was cool with it because I knew she'd never have let it happen. I faked her signature on his permission slip."

"He gave you a permission slip?"

"Yeah, a contract thing. I told you, it's all legit."

"And you didn't think to mention any of this to me when I spoke to you?"

Daniel shrugged his bony shoulders.

"Swore not to tell anyone. Part of the deal. How'd I know you were gonna chase me all the way out here, you weirdo?"

Porter blew out a breath, checking his phone.

"Did Foulger ever tell you what this was all about?" he asked after a moment.

"Yeah, he told me. Said it was something that used to happen in the olden days, that's *always* happened. You have a rich family, and they get worried they're going to lose their shit or whatever, so every year they kill some poor guy. Only it's not really bad because they think they're freeing the guy from being poor, if that makes sense. They're doing him a favour. He said in the olden days they used to think bones had power in them, that they could be used to make you richer, that sort of stuff. I don't know, I wasn't really listening, was just thinking about the money, you know?"

"Daniel, did Derek ever give the impression that he believed in all this?"

"Nah," he said, grinning harder than ever. "He told me it was a bunch of baloney but that they did it anyway, because of history or whatever."

"What about the other people who were there tonight? Did any of *them* seem to take this seriously?"

"You kidding? They were all pissing about in the house getting drunk off their arses, laughing and joking and shit. I didn't see them, wasn't allowed to talk to them, but I heard them. They were all giggling under those hoods, just a big game."

Porter swore beneath his breath.

"Why the flowers?"

"The flowers? Oh, yeah, I can't remember, just something Derek asked me to do. Tradition. In the olden days, the person who got, you know..." He drew a finger over his throat and pretended to die. "They had to be a volunteer, had to give permission or something. The flowers were part of that, I guess."

"And the grease? Whatever you're covered in?"

"Gross, right?" the kid said. "It's lamb fat, apparently."

That explained why he was thinking of roast dinners, at least.

"Why?"

The boy shrugged.

"Haven't a clue."

"Thanks, Daniel. And sorry again for crashing your party. I hope it hasn't cost you that money."

"Me too," he said, coughing. "Set Chainsaw on your arse if it has."

Porter dropped down from the ambulance.

"You call me if you think of anything else, yeah? Or if you need anything."

"All due respect, I've got Derek for that," said Daniel with a shrug. "Sorry."

Porter didn't fancy climbing the wall again so he made his way down the driveway, heading for the estate's open front gate. An IRV sat there, its lights rolling and a PC sitting in the driver's seat. He nodded to her before setting off down the road on foot, the cold air like a slap to the face, waking him up.

He spotted the lights in the wood, turning onto the track and stumbling down it until he saw cars ahead of him, and Duke's fluorescent jacket. Gorski's van had gone, and so had Kett's orange Volvo. Savage was leaning against the bonnet of her IRV, Duke standing beside her. Both of them looked miserable as sin.

"Well, that was a clusterfuck of epic proportions," said Porter as he closed in. "You seen Robbie?"

"Just left, sir," said Savage. "The Super tore him a new one, booted him off the case."

"He okay?"

Savage shrugged.

"You need us for anything else, sir?" she asked.

"We'll have to interview everyone here," Porter replied. "Figure out what they know, what they thought was going on. Even if Foulger's innocent, one of the others might have jumped Carran, they might believe in all this stuff."

Savage was shaking her head.

"We're not allowed anywhere near them, sir, Clare's orders. The Chief Constable's heading out this way tonight, he's going to take care of it."

"Take care of it?" said Porter.

"You know," she said with another shrug. "Honestly, I don't think there's much to uncover. Whoever killed Carran, I don't think they're here. This is something else."

He didn't disagree, but the thought of retracing their steps, of trying to open up a new lead, felt overwhelming.

"He's told us all to head home, sir," Savage said. "I was just waiting for you."

Porter dug his keys out of his pocket, unlocking the Mondeo. When he glanced back, Duke had his phone out, and he looked like he was about to take a photo.

"For the socials, sir?" said the PC, and Porter shook his head.

"Put it away, Aaron," he said, climbing into the car. "Nobody's ever going to want to remember this night."

PORTER CONSIDERED HEADING to HQ to get started on the paperwork, but halfway back into Norwich he changed his mind and headed home. He called Kett as he pulled onto the drive, but there was no answer.

"Don't let the bastards grind you down, sir," he told the voicemail. "It'll be okay."

He let himself into the house as quietly as he could, because it was coming up for ten and Allie was often asleep well before now. As it happened, though, when he looked into the living room he saw her lying on the sofa, a blanket over her enormous bump and the TV on. She gave him a lazy wave, her hand crashing back to the cushion.

"I would get up," she said. "But it'll take me all night."

"Hey," said Porter as he walked over. There was no room on the sofa so he slid onto the floor, running his fingers through her hair.

"Wash your hands, will you, Pete?" she said.

"Oh, right, sorry."

"In a minute, though," she told him when he started to get up. "Stay there, it's nice."

He rested his head against hers, staring at the TV without really focussing on what she was watching.

"Everything okay?" he said. "You're good? Baby's good?"

"We're fine. It's been going bonkers in there today, though. Think it's having a rave."

"He's ready to come out," Porter said.

"How many times have I got to say it, we don't know it's a he."

"He, she, whatever. It wants to break free."

"Not yet," said Allie. "It's too soon."

She groaned as she shifted her body.

"Although I don't know how I'm going to handle another month of this."

"You're doing amazingly," said Porter. "You *are* amazing."

She didn't reply, her face etched with worry.

"You are," he said.

"Don't know about that, Pete. I mean, a baby?"

She said it like she'd only just realised what it was that grew inside her. She put both hands on her stomach.

"Feel it."

Porter moved his hand to the bump, his pinky finger touching Allie's, and sure enough after just a second or two he felt a sturdy kick. His reaction was the same as it always was, nine parts boundless wonder and love, one part *oh shit oh shit this is so weird there's something inside there.*

"How're we going to manage?" Allie said when he'd pulled his hand away. "I mean me and you... It's not..."

"We're going to manage," Porter said before she could find the words she wanted, the words he didn't want to hear. "It's going to be amazing, I promise. Me and you, we've been waiting for this, all the... all the bad days, it's because we didn't have this little fella in our lives. And now we do, and it's going to be the missing piece that... that keeps everything else working perfectly. It's going to be perfect, Allie, every second of it."

"You promise?" she said.

"I do. I promise."

"But what if we can't cope?"

"We will," he said, remembering what Kett had told him. "You just *do*. Hardest thing in the world, but the easiest too. You just do."

She winced.

"What are you doing in there?"

"You need me to call anyone?" Porter asked, and she shook her head.

"I just need a cuppa, and a massage, with clean hands."

"I'm on it, boss," he said, pushing himself up. He made it to the door before looking back, seeing Allie wince again, her body arching. He thought of the child inside her, of that living, breathing, squirming baby that carried her genes and his, and the rush of excitement and terror hit him like a train. "You *sure* you're okay?"

"I'm fine, Pete," she said, obviously a lie. "Don't worry about me. I'm fine. We're both fine."

CHAPTER THIRTY-ONE

Saturday

"So..." SAID BILLIE ACROSS THE BREAKFAST TABLE.

"So..." echoed Kett.

It was the way it always was in the mornings, a few stops short of complete Bedlam. Alice was the only one of their children who was at the table, and she'd been talking almost continuously about getting a horse ever since she'd sat down. Evie and Moira were currently fighting about something in the living room, yelling at each other loud enough to bring the house down. Somebody had brought the chinchilla from its usual home in Evie's bedroom and it squeaked in its cage like it was trying to compete with the noise.

"So, here we are again," said Billie.

"I haven't been fired!" said Kett, helping himself to a slice of toast from the plate. "I'm just off the case. For now."

"Off this case, or off every case?" she asked, passing him the butter.

"And it's probably best we get a cob," said Alice, oblivious to the fact that nobody was listening to her. "Or a Welsh D, but something calm and not too spicy, otherwise I won't—"

"Just this case," said Kett, pausing. "I *think*. You'd have made the same call, Billie. The evidence was right there, it..."

He heard how hollow his words sounded, how far from the truth he'd been. Billie reached over and put her hand on his, squeezing for just a second.

"You don't have to explain anything to me," she said. "I'm on your side. Honestly, I don't know how you can even do it, going back. After what happened. Maybe this is..."

And she didn't have time to finish before Moira came running into the room, her blonde hair plastered to the tears on her cheeks. She ran straight to her mum, the way she always did, and Billie lifted her onto her lap.

"Evie took my iPad!" she said. "Hers is dead and she took mine."

"I'll sort it," said Kett, but Billie waved him down.

"Eat your breakfast, Moo-moo, then we'll figure it out. I don't want you sitting on your iPads all day."

"I'll take them out this morning," said Kett through a mouthful of toast. "How does that sound? A day out with your dad?"

Moira shrugged.

"I can't play with you, Dad," she said matter-of-factly. "Because your face isn't a screen."

He laughed.

"Right. What about soft play, though? How does that sound?"

Moira's face lit up.

"Yay! Soft play!"

She jumped off her mum's knee and bolted towards the living room, returning seconds later with Evie.

"Really?" said Evie, her eyes wide. "Can we go?"

"Sure," he said, taking a sip of his tea. "It's not like I've got anything better to do."

BY THE TIME they got into town it was heaving, and as Kett did his best to wrestle his kids out of the Volvo and stop them running off into the underground labyrinth of the Castle Mall car park, he couldn't help but question his decision to bring them here.

"Hold up!" he yelled at Alice, who was standing in the middle of the road looking at her phone while a Citroen waited patiently for her to move. "Alice, get over here, you're going to get squashed."

Alice shrugged, sidestepping out of the way. Kett offered the driver an apologetic wave as he lifted Moira into his arms, kicking her door closed before realising that Evie was still inside. He opened it again and she climbed out with a scowl.

"You forgot me!"

"I didn't forget you," he said. "I thought you were getting out your side. *Alice*, get out of the way!"

Alice was back in the road, standing in the path of two more cars, still staring at her phone. She trod heavily to the other side, looking like a Goth in her black jeans and oversized black hoodie, her hair over her face. She was getting so tall that she could have been thirteen, not ten.

"Right," said Kett. "Let's go."

They headed up in the lift, reaching the middle level where the soft play and bowling alley were. It seemed like half of Norwich had thought of the same plan for the weekend, because the mall was a sea of screaming children and foul-tempered parents, one that Kett felt like he was drowning in as soon as he stepped through the door.

"How about the beach instead?" he said without conviction. It was a battle he could never win, Moira squirming out of his arms and running into the melee, holding Evie's hand and dragging her big sister behind her. Kett sighed as he waited in the queue, shuffling forward like a zombie as the harassed teenage girl behind the counter fought to hear everyone over the music and the shouts.

"You playing or sitting?" Kett asked Alice.

She looked up from her phone, staring at the soft play cages and the teeming mass of children inside. He knew what she was going to say, because for a year or so now Alice had reached the age where she wasn't quite young enough to enjoy the fun things, but not quite old enough yet to want to sit them out. Her autism didn't help, because she'd also started to develop an innate terror of big crowds and an aversion to loud noise. She seemed to shrink into her hood, shaking her head.

"Can I sit with you and talk about horses, Dad?"

"Yeah," said Kett. "Course you can."

He paid for the two younger ones, even though they'd vanished into the climbing frames, then set about looking for a table. It was a lost cause, he realised as he crossed the room, because every single one was occupied. Some parents had resorted to standing around the edges of the space like wallflowers at the school dance, and he was on the way to joining them when he heard somebody call his name.

"Rob!"

He squinted through the crowd, seeing Ronald Lewington three tables over. He was sitting alone at a table that was covered in coats and bags, a paper cup in front of him and a weary look on his face that mirrored the one on Kett's. He waved again and Kett returned it, pushing through swarms of children until he reached the table.

"Ronald," he said. "Of all the places. How are you?"

"Ron," he said as he cleared the coats from the table, sliding them onto the floor by his feet. "Sit down, make yourself at home. And it's Robbie, isn't it? Not Rob. Sorry."

"You found me a chair, you can call me anything you like," said Kett, sitting down. "This place is..."

"Mental," said Ron. "I know. It's never this busy. I don't know what's going on."

"Your kids in there?" Kett said, nodding at the colossal play area.

"I bloody hope so," said Ron. "But in this place, who knows? Who's this?"

"Alice," said Kett as she took the seat next to his, studying Ron with the nervous expression she used for everybody new. "My oldest. Say hi."

She lifted her hand in an abrupt wave.

"Dad, can I get a Fanta?"

"Only if you go yourself," he told her, opening his wallet and pulling out a ten-pound note. "Can you get me a tea?"

"It's not tea," said Ron, looking mournfully at his cup. "It's like rainwater that's passed through a sewage system."

"A Diet Coke, then," he told Alice. "And some Fruit Shoots for the girls, if they have them. You need anything, Ron?"

He shook his head. Alice looked reluctant to go, but Kett waved her off and she scuttled through the crowd. With her hood up, she reminded Kett of the men and women from the previous night, the drunken worshippers and their sick performance. They hadn't been there to kill a boy, of course, but that didn't make it much better. Everything that ceremony represented was rancid.

He sighed. The trip out to Foulger's estate didn't feel real, but the rush of shame did.

"You okay?" asked Ron. "Hungover?"

"No," said Kett, sitting back in his chair. He caught sight of Evie and Moira behind the netting, already red-faced and sweaty. He waved to them, but if they saw him they didn't return it. "Just a bad night."

"I didn't sleep well either," said Ron, misunderstanding. "None of us did. That's why I'm here so early. Kids woke up at four so this feels like bloody lunchtime. I thought Mum might kill them if I didn't take them out for a bit."

He snapped his fingers.

"I knew you looked familiar when I met you. You've been here before, haven't you?"

Kett nodded, and realised that's where he'd known Ron from too—just a glance across a crowded room, that subtle nod of sympathy that fathers gave each other when they saw another man's children misbehaving.

"Was it one of your girls who threw a slushie off the top of the slide a while back?" Ron asked.

"Uh, no," lied Kett, trying not to remember it. "But yeah, I've seen you here before, now you mention it."

Ron laughed.

"My girl, Clara, was behind the counter once, she managed to get the till open and was helping herself to the money. I thought we were going to get banned, but she returned all the coins and they let us off. It's only when we got home I realised she had three twenties stuffed in her pocket."

Kett laughed with him.

"I had to bring them back the next day with a grovelling apology," Ron went on. A boy sped past, colliding with his chair hard enough to shunt him into the table, and he rubbed his elbow. "Why do we do it?"

"Because we love them," said Kett.

"Sometimes," added Ron, pulling a face. "Anyway, the lads from the group all thought you were a great guy, solid. Spencer was raving about you. You've passed your initiation, if you want to come next week. Although, be a little wary."

"Why?"

"I think Steve fancied you."

Kett laughed.

"Good to know. It was a nice evening. If I'm free, I'll come again."

"Great!" said Ron, genuinely delighted. "That's really great. So, how's work? Any luck with those old bones?"

"We hit a dead end," he said. "My fault. I went after the wrong person."

"You went after Derek Foulger, didn't you?" Ron said.

"I shouldn't say."

"He's just atrocious, that man. Full of..." He leaned in so that he wouldn't be overheard by the girls at the next table. "Shit. Utter shit. Dad hated him, even though they worked together. And as much as I didn't agree with Dad on a lot of things, I trusted his ability to judge a person's character."

"Yeah?"

"Yeah. And even Dad didn't hate him as much as Mum. She wouldn't hit the brakes if he was standing in the middle of the road. She'd speed up. She was dead chuffed, you know, that you came to see her for advice. Twice. She thinks she's quite the expert. I'll be surprised if she doesn't add police consultant to the list of accolades on her CV."

"Did she know that Foulger was conducting rituals?" Kett asked. "The same ones his ancestors did, but without the murder?"

"The Harford Guild stuff?" said Ron, blanching. "He's still doing them? Surely not. I don't think she's aware, no, but I couldn't be sure. She seems gregarious enough, but she keeps her cards close to her chest, does Mum."

He frowned at Kett.

"You're sure he's still doing the rituals? In this day and age?"

"Without the bloodshed, yes. It's more like a... a play, I guess. A recreation or whatever they're called. Pretend."

"Huh," said Ron. "Wait, this didn't have anything to do with what was on the news this morning? That TV guy who got his jaw broken. I swear I heard him say he'd been attacked by the police."

"Uh... I shouldn't really comment, sorry."

"World's a crazy place," commented Ron. "Ah, here she comes."

Kett looked over his shoulder to see Alice trying to make her way through the crowd, a gold standard scowl directed at anyone who got in her way. When she reached them she sank into her chair, her hood pulled so far over her face that Kett couldn't see her eyes. She handed the Fanta bottle to Kett to open and he twisted off the cap, passing it back.

"Alice, this is Ron, by the way. He's a..."

He wasn't quite sure what word to use, but Ron finished for him.

"Friend. Your father and I have war stories in common, that makes us friends."

"Speaking of which," said Kett, seeing Evie run out of

the play area with a face like thunder. She was followed by another young girl, and it took Kett a moment to recognise Ron's daughter, Clara.

"Moira isn't letting me go on the slide," said Evie when she reached the table. "She's not letting *anyone* go on it."

"Tell her she has to, or I'm putting her back in the bin where we found her," said Kett.

"You okay?" Ron asked Clara, and she nodded. The two girls ran back to the soft play hand in hand, and Ron laughed. "Usually takes her a long time to make friends. That's nice to see."

"Evie's great with people," said Kett. "Friendly as they come. Moira wants to punch everyone. And Alice..."

He looked at Alice and she grunted.

"She's just Alice."

For a minute or so there was silence—or as close to silence as you could get in a packed soft play. Kett was knackered, and so was Ron, the pair of them looking more like a couple of old men out with their grandkids than two dads in their forties. He checked his phone, wondering if he'd missed a call from Superintendent Clare or one of the team, but found nothing. He spluttered out a sigh that was louder than he'd intended, and Ron turned to him.

"Don't let Derek Foulger get you down, Robbie. He's a..." He glanced at Alice, biting his tongue. "He's a wind-up merchant, and he's good at it. I don't know what happened on your case, but if Foulger caught you out then I'm certain he did it deliberately. He comes across like a... well, a prat, I guess... but he's sharp as they come. Ask yourself, did he have anything to gain from what happened?"

Yeah, Kett replied, but he kept it inside his head. Foulger now had the Norfolk Constabulary well and truly in his pocket. He could do whatever the hell he wanted because there was no way anyone would come after him again unless they literally caught him in the act. If this was him, if he was the man behind the murder, then the raid last night had made it infinitely more difficult to go after him.

"Exactly," said Ron, reading his mind. "There you go. Foulger wins again."

There was a high-pitched scream from inside the soft play, but Kett couldn't tell if it was one of his or not.

"Can you go check on your sisters for me please, Alice?" he asked. "I'd go in, but I'd never get out again."

Alice grumbled a reply, slouching off.

"Your mum didn't fancy it today, Ron? Could have done with talking to her again, to be honest."

"Mum, in this place?" Ron laughed. "Not a chance."

"Didn't she say she was here with you the other day?"

Ron frowned, as if he couldn't remember, then he nodded uncertainly.

"She comes with us," he said, staring across the room. "But not inside. She wouldn't be caught dead in here. She always buggers off for afternoon tea with Muddle and leaves them to me. What did you need to talk to her about?"

"Just wanted to wrap my head around these rituals. I just want to try to figure it out."

"I can help a bit," he said. "I don't know much, but I've read some of Mum's papers. She used to take part with Dad and Derek, did she tell you that? I can't remember."

"No," Kett said. "She used to take part?"

"Sure."

"What the hell is going through their heads?" asked Kett. "Because they actually used to make a sacrifice, didn't they? Not your Mum, obviously, but if you go back far enough then somebody was actually murdered during the ritual."

"I'm not sure," said Ron. "Maybe. I wouldn't put it past them. People believed all kinds of crazy shit. Mum only ever spoke about the theoretical side of it, she never discussed what happened, she never wrote about it and she certainly never told me."

"Really?"

"Yeah," said Ron. "I guess it was more about the history for her. The ceremony was like a pact, I guess. Dark magic. You sacrificed a life, and in return the forces to whom you made the sacrifice would allow you to stay rich for another year. It's a pretty simple trade."

"But your Mum never told you what happened in the ritual itself?"

Ron shook his head.

"Don't you think that's a bit weird?" Kett asked.

"I guess," he said, looking uncomfortable.

"Ron, do you know where your mum was on Thursday, around lunchtime? She told me she was here with you, but you just said she wasn't."

"Afternoon tea," said Ron, his eyes growing dark. "Look, Robbie, I know you had a bad day yesterday, but this feels a little inappropriate. Mum didn't have anything to do with whatever you're investigating."

Kett held up his hands.

"I'm sorry. Really. It's the job, you can never shake it."

Ron watched him for a moment more before the smile landed back on his face.

"Honestly, she'd probably quite like the idea of being considered a criminal mastermind. But she's not. She can't even make a cup of tea without Muddle's help, as you saw."

Kett offered a smile back, nodding.

"Speaking of tea, let me get you one," said Ron, standing

up. "Not from here, there's a café across the way. Milk and sugar?"

"Just milk," said Kett. "Thanks, Ron."

Ron vanished into the crowd and Kett turned his attention back to the soft play. In the breaks between the equipment, through the netting, he could see all three of his girls playing with Ron's kids. Incredibly, they weren't trying to fight each other. They almost looked like they were having a good time.

He felt the vibration of his phone and pulled it out, seeing Savage's name on the screen.

"Hey, Kate. How's it going?"

"About as well as you'd expect, sir," she said. "The Superintendent is still fuming, and the Chief Constable was in this morning, an emergency meeting. He thinks Foulger's going to sue the department."

"Of course he is," said Kett, feeling that awful hot creep of shame again. "You've heard from him?"

"Foulger? No. Claims he's suffering from shock and whiplash, from when Porter took him down. And his alibi came through. He was on camera pretty much from the moment he got back into the city, at the brothel, other than the four minutes he spent inside one of the rooms."

"Four minutes?"

"Yeah, he's a real gentleman, obviously. He was in the bar for the rest of it. There's no way he could have killed Carran. The kid, Daniel, confirmed his side of the story. He had the down payment in his bank account. He'd signed a contract, too."

"Jesus," said Kett.

"Steven Fish has also lodged an official complaint. Andrew Pochin's been suspended for striking him with his weapon."

"What a mess," said Kett, rubbing his eyes until the room flashed.

"It is, sir, no doubt. But that's not why I'm calling. I watched the interview with Lord Montague when I got back to base last night. You remember he said something about Peter Carran having an argument with a site foreman a few years back?"

"Yeah."

"I looked into it. The foreman was Geoffrey Wileman."

"What?" Kett said, leaning forward.

"Yeah. Turns out Wileman actually lodged a complaint against Carran, for assault. Never made it as far as us but Carran got a warning, and apparently there's been bad blood between them ever since. Wileman left the job soon after, started with the company he's at now and moved pretty quickly onto the County Hall dig."

"So Wileman had a beef with Carran, and the day after Wileman found those bones, Carran ends up dead?"

"Yeah," said Savage.

"You going to talk to him?"

"I'm going now. Just wanted to loop you in."

"Thanks, Kate."

He bunched his fist and bounced it gently on the table, then looked across the room. There was no sign of Ron returning.

"Kate, can you do one more thing for me?"

"Sure, sir."

"Kitty Lewington's alibi for the day of the murder doesn't check out either. She told me she was helping her son look after the kids, but she wasn't. Can you see if you can pin down her whereabouts on Thursday? But quietly. I don't want her to know. Ron, her son, said she usually goes for afternoon tea with the maid, Muddle."

"Muddle?"

"It's a nickname."

"You think Mrs Lewington's involved, sir?"

"From what I hear, she was pretty keen to get down inside that cellar. And she was part of this whole thing, the rituals, once upon a time. She and her husband and Derek Foulger were tight."

"She's a bit old to be murdering people like Carran, isn't she, sir?"

"You said it yourself, Kate, a chainsaw is a good leveller. And I'm more concerned about Muddle. Did you see her when you were at the dig?"

"Was she the bigger lady?"

"That's a polite way of saying it. She could throw Miss Trunchbull over her shoulder. It might be nothing, but my gut's telling me to follow it."

"I'll look into it, sir," said Savage. He heard a car door slam, and when she spoke next her voice was muted. "And I'll let you know about Wileman."

"Thanks, Kate. And be careful, yeah?"

He heard a car engine start.

"Don't worry, sir," she said. "I'm taking the bear with me."

CHAPTER THIRTY-TWO

"Did you just call me a bear?" said Duke, grinning beneath his beard.

Savage put the IRV in gear and pulled out of the parking space, heading across the half-empty car park towards the main gates of HQ.

"Yeah," she said. "I meant teddy bear, though, obviously."

"Grizzly bear is better," said Duke, one hand holding the strap over the door as Savage accelerated. "Grrr."

"Because you never wash and you poop in the woods?" Savage asked. "Yeah, you might be onto something there."

"I do wash!" Duke protested, sniffing his armpit. "I have a routine. I'm very meticulous about my—"

"I'm kidding, Aaron," said Savage, reaching over and putting her hand on his. "I know you are. You use up the hot water every time you come over."

"A beard like this takes work," he said quietly, stroking it.

Savage squeezed his hand, then returned her attention to the road, rolling onto the A11. Fifteen minutes later, they were back in the city and heading south, County Hall appearing and then disappearing as they made their way up Bracondale and then off towards Riverside.

Savage had already called Wileman's employer, who'd told her the entire site was still shut down, the staff on standby until the investigation was over. The woman on the phone had given them the foreman's address, a temporary lodging on Yarmouth Road, and a phone number too, although nobody had answered.

"That way," said Duke, pointing over the wheel to the road that cut down the back of the football ground.

"Really?" said Savage with a little more sarcasm than she'd intended. "I've only lived here my whole life, mate."

"Savage," he said.

"What?"

"No, I meant *you're* savage."

She laughed as she turned right, and three minutes later she pulled up outside a row of terraced houses that sat on a small rise over the main road.

"That's the one," she said, nodding to the third from the right. At least seven wheelie bins of different colours crowded the gravelled front garden, two on their backs.

"Those bins must have been having some party," said Duke.

"Why does anyone need that many bins?" Savage said as they both got out.

She climbed the short set of crooked stone stairs, opening the lid of a black wheelie bin and seeing nothing inside. The blue one next to it was empty as well.

"Weird," she said, walking to the door and knocking hard enough for the echo of it to bounce back and forth across the street. "Mr Wileman? It's the police. Can you open the door?"

Nothing. Savage lifted the letterbox and peered inside, but it was too dark to see. She knocked again, standing back to take in the windows—all of which had their curtains drawn.

"See if you can get around the back," Savage told Duke. Then she tried the handle of the front door and it opened inwards. "Scratch that. You want to take the lead?"

"Because I'm a bear," said Duke, flicking out his baton. "A bear with a big stick."

"It's not that big," said Savage.

"Police," growled Duke. "We are inside the property. Please make yourself known."

The house creaked as they made their way down the corridor, sounding like a ship at sea. There was a smell in here, faint and familiar, something chemical. Duke used his baton to push open the living room door and Savage peeked past him to see that it was empty. A single chair sat in front of a small TV, a pyramid of beer cans stacked next to the window.

She took the lead, finding an empty dining room and past that a postage-stamp-sized kitchen. The garden visible through the grimy window wasn't much bigger, a concrete yard with a limp clothesline and a wooden fence that was green with age.

"I'll check upstairs," said Duke.

Savage opened the cupboards, finding little else other than Pot Noodles and chocolate digestives. The milk in the fridge was a week out of date. She tried the back door, finding it locked, then noticed a collection of folded paperwork by the kettle. They were payslips, she realised when she opened them, all with Wileman's name on them.

"Kate," Duke called. "You're going to want to see this."

She doubled back, grabbing the handrail to haul herself

up the stairs and almost pulling it out of the damp wall. The chemical smell was stronger up here, more familiar. There were three doors leading off the landing, a bathroom to the side that stank of rot, a room to the back, and then the front bedroom where Duke stood. He had his torch on, and he moved out of the way to let her through the door, shining it at the far wall.

It was covered in blood.

"What the hell?" said Savage.

She used her elbow to switch on the light, the dusty bulb taking a long time to find its courage. The room was bare, the wooden floor uncarpeted, the wallpaper almost completely stripped away. There was no furniture here at all, and no decoration whatsoever other than the streaks of dried blood that marked the opposite wall.

There was a pattern in the chaos, Savage realised: a circle marked with lumps, and inside it an eye wearing a crown.

Most of the design was crudely wrought, and almost lost inside a madness of drops and splashes, but whoever had done this had taken great care with the eye. It seemed to burn across the room.

"Don't touch anything," she told Duke, who still hadn't switched off his torch. "Can you call this in? Get Porter out here."

"Yeah," he said, leaving the room.

She heard him speaking into his radio, then he called her name again and she followed his voice to the back room. He'd turned on the light, revealing an unmade single bed and a pile of clothes in the corner. The only other items of furniture were a desk that looked too small to belong to an adult, and a kitchen chair that sat next to it.

"There," said Duke, pointing beneath the desk.

There was a can of paint, the lid resting lightly on the top. Runnels of dark red emulsion marked the sides, forming a puddle on the wooden boards of the floor.

"Same colour as the wall through there," Duke said.

"It's not blood," Savage finished, but she didn't feel much relief.

She found a set of latex gloves in her pocket and slipped them on, treading carefully across the room to the desk. There was nothing on top of it, and nothing else underneath, but when she opened the single drawer she saw a pile of papers. As carefully as she could, she pulled them free and spread them out over the surface of the desk.

"Oh my God," she said.

There had to be fifty sheets of A4, and half of them were photocopies from textbooks. She recognised some because they were the same books she'd been reading for the last couple of days, the ones she'd borrowed from Norman Balls—all about ancient rituals, bone magick and blood sacrifices. Somebody had outlined hundreds—maybe *thousands*—of lines in angry red pen, hard enough to go through the paper in places.

The rest of the documents included dozens of sketches, some of faces, some of emblems like the one that had been painted in the room next door, some of buildings. There was a lot of skill in them, the detail extraordinary.

"What is all that?" asked Duke, still standing in the door.

"He's obsessed," said Savage. "Look at these. They must have taken hours. *Days*. He's been doing this for a long time."

She slid a sheet of paper to one side and found another drawing beneath it, this one just as detailed but far worse. In front of her was an illustration of the bones they'd found on the cellar wall, every one of them brought to life with an almost photo-realistic skill. Savage could see every nail, every scratch, every fracture, every scuff on every brick, all brought to life with patient shading. It was astonishing.

She pushed this one to the side and the picture she saw beneath that one made her stomach churn. It wasn't as polished as the others, just an island of pencil strokes in a sea of white, but there was no mistaking the subject of the picture.

A head with no face, legs with no feet, an aberration of flesh.

"That's Peter Carran," she said, turning to Duke. "That's what he looked like when we found him."

"This is our killer," said Duke. "Wileman. This is him, right?"

He left the room, speaking into his radio. Savage continued to gently push the sheets of paper aside, and in the midst of them she found something else, something much smaller. It was a business card, a clip-art image of a lawnmower at the top and two lines of text underneath: *Pater Carran Yard Services and House Clearances, All Work Considered, Free Quotes, Just Call.* Beneath that was Carran's phone number, the same one she'd tried herself. The same one the killer had almost certainly called in order to lure him to his death.

"Yeah," Savage said quietly, even though she was now alone. "Wileman's our guy."

SAVAGE WAS on the phone when Porter arrived fifteen minutes later. She opened the door for him, spotting the forensic team gathering on the steps outside. When he started to speak she held up her hand, listening to the woman on the other end of the line—the HR manager from the construction company that employed Geoffrey Wileman.

"He was no trouble, as far as I know. The company rents out the accommodations. We've got three on that road alone, another seven in the city. Some of the men like to live together, it's like student life, really. Geoff always chose to stay on his own."

"He's got family back home?" Savage asked.

"Not as far as I know," the woman said. "Kept himself to himself a lot of the time. He seemed to be pretty devoted to the job, never showed much interest in anything else. Had a girlfriend for a bit, I know that much, she came to the Christmas party a couple of years back. Not sure what happened to her. Hard to keep a relationship going when you move around a lot."

"Where did you say his home was?"

"Derby, originally," said the woman. "Joined us five years ago, been working onsite in Norwich for the last three of them."

Porter jogged up the stairs, dust raining down from the ceiling as he went. The little house was struggling to hold them all.

"Can I ask, did Geoff ever have any complaints made against him? Was there ever any trouble? Bad blood?"

"Not as far as I know," said the woman. "There was an incident at the place he worked at before he came to us, a grudge. I can't remember the details, but he was honest about it."

"With a man called Peter Carran?"

"I couldn't tell you that, sorry. He fell out with a couple of our people over the years like everyone does, but never any violence and we never had to give him a warning, verbal or otherwise. By all accounts he was one of the good ones, lived for his work. But..."

She hesitated, and Savage heard Porter swear in the room over her head.

"Please, if there's anything at all, it could really help."

"And you can't tell me what this is all about?" the woman said for the fourth time since the call had started.

"I'm sorry."

"Well, I guess it could be important, but I hate to slander a man. I don't know all the facts, but according to his file, we've had to advance his salary a couple of times. More than a couple, actually, we're talking... eight times, and seven of those in the last couple of years."

"Why?" asked Savage.

"There's a note here that he was pulled up on his gambling habits. He skipped work early a couple of times to hit the betting shops. Nothing major. Doesn't say anything other than that, but I'm guessing he might have had a problem."

"Yeah," said Savage, taking in the state of the house around her. "You might be right. Are there any other addresses or phone numbers for him?"

"No," said the woman. "But I'll ask around. I work mainly with site recruitment, some of the management girls might have known him better. I'll call you back if I hear anything."

"Thanks," said Savage, hanging up.

"Bloody hell," Porter yelled from the landing overhead. "You have got to be shitting me, Kate."

Savage walked back into the kitchen, flicking through the paperwork that had been left there. It didn't take long to find a bank statement, and it took even less time to see that there was nothing in his account at all. She carried it back upstairs, scanning through it as she went and seeing the relentless debits to Betfred and Ladbrokes and Coral. Problem was an understatement, she realised. Wileman had a full-on gambling addiction.

"This is nuts," said Porter as she reached the landing. He was in the back room, squinting at the paperwork on the desk. "He has all this just stuffed in his desk drawer? I met Geoff Wileman, he seemed like the least murderous person in the world."

"And yet here we are," said Duke, who loitered on the other side of the room.

"Why was he so interested in the bones?" Porter asked. "The rituals? Why did he mark the Harford Guild emblem on his wall in blood-red paint? He was fixated on it, I've seen about twelve sketches of the same design in these papers."

"Maybe he found the bones before they were uncovered?" said Savage. "Wileman spent years surveying the County Hall site, he told us so himself. He spoke to all the history society people, Kitty Lewington included, he must have learned about the stuff that went on. Maybe he stumbled onto one of the tunnels and found the chamber, started doing some research. He never hid how much he hated Derek Foulger, right? Maybe it's because he knew about Foulger's family history, knew about the rituals? He started doing some research."

She petered out, because she couldn't work out what would come next.

"So he kills Carran?" Porter said, shaking his head. "Why wouldn't he just murder Foulger, if he hated him so much?"

"Because he had history with Carran," said Savage.

"They'd fallen out years ago. Maybe the more he looked into the bones, the rituals, the more he thought about the idea of revenge? Wileman was in serious financial trouble, I think he was a gambling addict, slung his entire monthly wage packet into the horses or dogs or whatever. Maybe the pressure of it was too much; he might have cracked."

"That's a lot of maybes, Savage," came another voice, booming up the stairs. A second later, Superintendent Clare appeared like some kind of bug-eyed spectre, his Big Tossing Jacket making him so wide he had to turn sideways to squeeze inside. "You know how much I hate maybes, so give me something concrete."

"Wileman lived here alone," Savage said. "Duke spoke to the neighbours while we were waiting for you lot. One of them talked to Wileman yesterday evening, but nobody has seen him since or heard anything weird. No door cams up the street, as far as I can see. Paint's still tacky, which means it's maybe..." She caught herself. "Which means it's *probably* a few hours old. No earlier than this morning. There are no clothes, no suitcase, no phone or wallet. Wileman's taken everything with him."

"Except these," said Porter, looking at the paperwork on the desk.

"Except all the evidence we'd need to charge him," said Clare, browsing through it. "Why leave that?"

"Yeah, it's not like he didn't have a bin to put it all in," said Porter. "There's about fifty of them in the front garden."

For a moment, nobody spoke. Savage could hear Cara Hay downstairs coordinating her team, her voice strangely muffled like the house was eating it.

"I spoke to Kett this morning, sir," Savage said after a moment. Clare grunted, but he didn't say anything. "He asked me to check Kitty Lewington's alibi because she'd lied about where she was yesterday. Kitty and Wileman were the two people who entered the cellar when it was discovered. They went down together. Maybe... I mean, what if it wasn't a coincidence?"

She shrugged, and said no more.

"What in the name of toss is going on here?" Clare said.

"If Wileman's our guy, then he's on the loose," said Savage. "It's pretty clear what he's obsessed with, and if he killed Carran, then he's going to kill again, I'm sure of it."

"And if he killed Carran because of a grudge, then the chances are he'll go after somebody else he doesn't like," Porter added. "My money's on Derek Foulger."

"I'm tempted to let him have Foulger," Clare said. "But I'll send somebody to watch him. Any other clues to where Wileman might be hiding?"

"He knows the tunnels beneath the city, sir," said Savage. "That's where I'd go, if I was him."

"Then thank God you're not," he replied.

The Superintendent checked his watch.

"If he's going to kill again then we don't have long," he said, retreating from the room. "Find him. And the hell with it all, my job's down the shitter anyway, somebody get Kett back in here."

CHAPTER THIRTY-THREE

"Are you sure I can't drop them home for you?" asked Ron.

Kett had finally managed to wrestle his girls from the soft play, although he'd had to climb to the topmost level to collect Moira, contorting his aching body around tight corners and through minuscule tubes before he managed to snatch her. He'd pretty much had to drag his youngest daughter to the bottom, his promises of endless tubes of Smarties and an afternoon on the iPad lost behind her ear-shredding screams. By the time he'd got her out, both of them were red-faced and sweaty, and he thought half the parents in the room had probably called the police on him.

She'd calmed down now, but only just. Kett did up the zip on her coat, swiping the hair from her sticky face. His heart was still going like the clappers, his head pounding.

"It's fine, honestly," he said, giving Ron an appreciative smile. "I know you'd get them home, but we've been through a lot, these kids and me. I don't like to let them out of my sight."

"Roger that," said Ron. "I totally get it. I'm the same.

You'd do anything for them, wouldn't you? Anything to keep them safe. Touch wood."

He rapped his knuckles on the table hard enough to knock over his empty paper cup.

"Yeah," said Kett. "You would."

He heard the crack of the hammer the way he always did, he felt the Pig Man's body go limp beneath him.

"Sorry to leave so abruptly."

"You've got a lead?" asked Ron.

"I think so. But let's do this again."

He pulled a Biro from his jacket pocket and scribbled his number on the back of a napkin.

"The kids seem to get on, we should arrange something. God knows it's nice to have a friend."

Ron looked genuinely chuffed, and he tore a piece of napkin away to write his own number on, handing it over.

"I'll hold you to that. I'll get the boys to come along too. We can be a proper gang."

"I'll get T-shirts made," said Kett, and they both laughed. "Come on, girls. Moira, no fingers in noses, please."

"It's not in my nose," she said. "It's in Evie's."

"Right. So it is. Let's go find those Smarties."

He ushered them out of the room, finding a vending machine on the way to the car park. There were no Smarties, but he bought two Twix bars and a Snickers, using them to lure the girls into the Volvo.

"I'm really sorry," he said to Billie when she opened the door to them all. "They want me back."

"It's fine," she said, giving him a kiss. "It's the job."

It was almost an hour after Savage's call that he bumped the Volvo onto the kerb at the city end of Yarmouth Road. There were half a dozen IRVs there now, plus Porter's

Mondeo and Clare's beastly Mercedes—all of which had reduced traffic to a one-way system. A crowd of onlookers had gathered on the opposite pavement, young men who jeered at him as he made his way through the open front door.

The house was full to bursting, Duke and another uniform dominating the hallway and Cara Hay and her team inside the microscopic kitchen. Duke pointed up the stairs and Kett took them two at a time to find Savage, Porter and Clare on the landing.

"Kett," Clare bellowed, cutting Savage off mid-sentence. "You're here, but you're also not here, is that clear?"

"Uh, not really, sir."

"You're invisible. You cannot be seen. If the Chief Constable finds out about this then he'll be using my balls for earmuffs."

"Nope," muttered Savage, covering her ears.

"So do what you have to do, Detective, but do it quietly."

"Yes, sir," said Kett.

Clare moved out of the way, letting him peek around the door of the front bedroom. Savage had sent him a photo so he knew what to expect, but seeing the crowned eye in its wheel of feet, scrawled there in red paint, still made his blood run cold.

"Wileman," he said. "I've got to admit, he didn't seem the type."

"It's always the quiet ones," said Clare.

"He's strong, though. I noticed that about him when I shook his hand, grip like a sailor."

"There's a whole raft of incriminating evidence in the back room," said Clare.

"Why would he leave it?" Kett asked. "He's cleared the

rest of the house out, why leave the stuff that would put him away?"

"We've all been wondering the same thing, sir," said Savage. "Wileman's an addict. We've spoken to a couple of betting shops and they've confirmed he was in there way too often. He's asked for help before to try to shake it. If he's addicted to gambling, he could be addicted to *this*. To killing. All addicts want to stop, right? So leaving all this could be a cry for help. He might want us to catch him."

"Have I ever told you you'd make an excellent profiler?" said Kett, and Savage smiled. "Any hint of where he might have gone? What might be going through his head?"

"I think it's pretty tossing clear what's going through his head," said Clare. "I think he's going to kill again."

"I think he's a creature of habit, sir," said Savage. "Ritual is important to him. Those bones had meaning. He killed Carran in a property that was connected to the same tunnels as the cellar room. It makes sense that he'd go back there."

"We found Carran's business card," said Porter. "But nothing else. No hint of who he might target next."

"He hated Derek Foulger," said Kett, and they all nodded.

"I've got a unit with Foulger," said Clare. "He's safe enough."

"It might not matter who the victim is, sir," Savage said. "I think the ritual is what's important. Carran might have been a happy coincidence, but judging by what we've found here, the urgency of it, Wileman just needs somebody to sacrifice."

"He'll find somebody in the tunnels," said Porter. "Those Montague twats weren't the only people living down there."

"Kett?" Clare asked, looking at him. "You agree?"

He didn't answer straight away. Wileman hadn't set off a single alarm bell, not one hint of suspicion, but Kett had been wrong before.

"Yeah," he said. "You're probably right. I can't think of anywhere else he'd go. Let's try the tunnels."

"Well toss me off," said Clare with mock appreciation. "How grateful I am to have you back, Kett, that big brain of yours. 'I can't think of anywhere else he'd go.' Get that man the Queen's Police Medal."

He pushed past Kett and clomped down the stairs, grumbling all the way to the bottom.

"Sir?" Savage asked Kett. "What's wrong?"

"I don't know," he told her. "This, I think. The house. Something's not clicking, the pieces aren't fitting together."

He scrubbed his hands in his hair like he was trying to physically arrange his thoughts, but his skull was full of muddy water.

"Now, you useless tossbags!" came Clare's roar.

They filed down the stairs, following the Super out into the freezing morning. He'd made it halfway to his Mercedes when there was a shout from up the street. A PC was walking out of the garden of a house in the same row, a binbag in her gloved hands. She jogged towards them with such enthusiasm that something fell out of the bag, landing on the ground with a slap. It looked like a wallet.

"Just put it down!" Clare yelled at her, and she did as she was told, standing back.

"I was checking the bins up the street," she said, breathless. "Just in case. Found this."

Savage was still wearing gloves, and she bent down and gently prised open the bag. Inside it was a mound of clothes, including what looked like a hi-vis jacket. She rummaged further, pulling out a lanyard. The writing was too small for Kett to make out without his glasses, but he recognised Geoffrey Wileman's face.

"That's his work pass," said Porter, leaning over.

"There was this, too," said the young constable, holding up the wallet that had fallen out of the bag. She opened it up, Wileman's driving licence peeking out of a transparent pocket.

"Some books in here," said Savage. "Couple of framed photos."

She held one up, a beautiful chocolate Labrador grinning at them.

"That's a good find," Clare told the PC. "Why would he dump his stuff?"

"Because he didn't want anyone to find it," said Duke. "I mean he had a good choice of bins here, he could have used any of these. Not the recycling one, though, obviously. You can't put binbags in—"

"Can it, Duke," barked Clare. "What else is in there?"

"Just clothes, I think," Savage said, rummaging inside the bag. "And this, hang on."

She pulled free a sheet of paper, unfolding it.

"It's a printout, from online," she said, holding it up. Kett slipped on his glasses, seeing a photograph of a church, and beneath that a second picture of a collection of bones. "That's St John and Mary's, over in Stiffkey. I think it's got some bones of its own."

"Stiffkey?" said Porter. "You think that's where he's gone?"

"Without his wallet and his clothes?" said Kett. "This doesn't make any sense."

"I'll get a unit over there," said Clare. "Tell them to keep an eye out, just in case."

He walked away, his phone to his ear.

"What now, sir?" asked Savage.

Kett glanced up at Wileman's house, the dark sky filling the windows.

"What if this *isn't* Wileman?" he said. "What if he's not our killer? What if somebody's framing him?"

"Sir?" said Porter.

"Who bundles up everything they own and throws it in a bin up the street? Nobody. Just like nobody leaves behind a desk full of evidence, it doesn't happen. Addict or not, Wileman isn't an idiot. Obsessives are exactly that, they obsess over every detail. Right? They're not careless. What if somebody else was in the house? They subdue Wileman, they paint the icon on the wall, they plant the paperwork. Then they take everything else and dump it."

"But not far enough away that we won't find it," said Savage, nodding. "Because they wanted us to see the printout of St John and Mary's."

"Because it will send us in the wrong direction," said Kett. "Exactly."

"But if it isn't Wileman, then who is it?" asked Duke. "And more importantly, where the hell is he?"

Nobody had an answer.

"Savage, did you check Kitty Lewington's alibi?" Kett asked after a moment. "Her and Muddle, the maid?"

"Oh, sorry sir, I farmed it out to Spalding because we were on the way out here. I can call her."

"Kitty Lewington?" said Porter. "Surely not."

"She had a beef with Wileman," said Kett. "They were arguing nonstop over the construction project."

He pulled out his phone and found Spalding's name. He counted the rings until he was sure it was going to go to voicemail. Eventually, though, she answered.

"I'm going to pretend this isn't you, sir," said Spalding. "Seeing as how you've been kicked off the job, again."

"Not the job, just the case," he said.

"So you're not working the case?"

"Uh... Savage says you were going to check Kitty Lewington's alibi for Thursday. Have you got to it yet?"

"I'm a busy woman, sir," she said. "Of course I have. We got a tonne of footage from the Castle Mall, she's right there with, I presume, the maid. Maid looks like she throws a mean shot-put."

"That's her."

"They got there late morning, left well after three. There's no chance they could have murdered Carran, sir."

Shit, thought Kett, saying, "Thanks, Alison."

"I'd love to say no problem, sir, but..."

She hung up.

"It wasn't Kitty, or Muddle," said Kett as he pocketed his phone.

"Got an IRV on the way out to Stiffkey," Clare boomed as he strolled back over.

"I don't think they're going that way," said Kett. "I think it's a diversion."

"Then—"

A call from Wileman's house cut the Superintendent off and Kett looked to see Cara Hay half in and half out of the front door.

"I've got everything I can," she said. "One set of prints, as far as I can see, almost certainly Wileman. I can only find hair belonging to him, too, although I will start a deep search in a moment. No sign of a break-in."

"Front door was unlocked when we got here," said Savage.

"I think the lock is broken," Hay said. "Wouldn't engage

when I tried. Back door is locked, no windows broken, no disturbance inside."

"So if somebody took Wileman, they did it quickly," said Porter.

"*Took* him?" said Clare. "What happened to it *being* him?"

"They might not have had to subdue him, sir," said Savage. "When I spoke to the company that employs him, they said they thought he only had one passion in life, other than the gambling."

"His job," said Kett.

"Right, sir. What if somebody called him, told him there was a problem on-site? That way, they get him out of the house without a struggle. That leaves the house empty for them to plant everything they need to plant."

"And they get him where they want him," said Kett. "They get him back to the tunnels. Good thinking, Kate."

"What somebody?" said Clare. "What the hell did I miss?"

"Maybe nothing, sir," said Kett. "Maybe everything."

"Don't you start on the bloody maybes."

"Hey, Robbie," Hay said. "Did Franklin get hold of you?"

Kett shook his head.

"She said it probably wasn't important, but she finally identified the bone she found inside the cellar, the little scrap that wasn't human. It belonged to a lamb."

"A lamb?"

Hay nodded.

"That's all she told me."

She vanished back into the dark house.

"A lamb?" said Savage.

"Wait a minute," said Porter. "When we found Daniel

at Foulger's place, in the sack, he'd been smothered in lamb fat."

"What?" said Kett.

"Yeah, they'd greased him up. He didn't know why, or couldn't remember."

"Why lamb?" asked Savage.

"The lambs can go toss themselves," said Clare. "What about Wileman?"

Kett looked at the house again, puffing out his cheeks before releasing a slow, deliberate breath.

"I don't think it matters whether Wileman's the killer or the victim," he said after a moment. "I think Kate's right, this thing's going full circle. We need to go back to where this all started. We need to go back underground."

CHAPTER THIRTY-FOUR

SAVAGE DROVE, EVEN THOUGH SHE WAS SO TIRED SHE was struggling to keep her eyes open. Porter had claimed the passenger seat, Kett and Duke clinging on for dear life in the back. The big PC had his phone in his hand, filming himself looking out of the window, the expression on his face the one the hero would wear in an action movie.

Kett would have asked him what he was doing, but his head was a box of jigsaw pieces, none of them connected. Every time Savage took a turn he could feel them sliding back and forth, any hope of a pattern scattering into chaos.

But he kept coming back to one thing: *lamb*.

A cellar full of bones, all of them human except for one —a fragment that belonged to a sheep. Why? The simplest explanation was that whoever had made the display had no idea where the bone had come from. If they'd simply been collecting relics from a graveyard, they could have added it to their collection without thinking.

But whoever was behind the ossuary they'd found at County Hall had been a perfectionist. Every bone in its place, carefully secured, every part of the pattern where it needed to be, and every bone from a separate victim. They'd known exactly what they were doing. They would have been able to tell the difference between the bone that came from a human and one that came from an animal, he was sure of it.

What, then?

If the bones were what Kett thought they were, if they had been part of the same sick ceremony that Foulger's ancestors had taken part in and that he still re-enacted, then perhaps at some point they'd started sacrificing lambs instead of people? But why just one? And why just a scrap? What had happened to the rest of the bone?

"County Hall?" Savage asked, taking a corner so fast that Kett could feel the tyres slip on the wet road. She corrected it with a flick of the wheel, gunning the engine.

"We can't get into the tunnels that way," Kett said. "They've been filled in. Head to the Foulger house on Bracondale, the place we found Carran."

"Yes, sir," Savage said, accelerating hard enough to make his stomach turn in loops.

"Lamb," he said quietly, trying to find his place.

The only other explanation he could think of was that the lamb bone had been switched for a human bone. Again, though, *why*? Had somebody stolen one of the human bones and left a lamb bone in its place? Had they taken it as a souvenir, or did they—like the original participants of the ritual—truly believe that the bones would give them power, keep them safe?

You'd do anything for them, wouldn't you? Anything to keep them safe.

Ron had said it himself, that very morning. Everyone had their rituals, didn't they? Ron touched wood for luck, Savage wore her grandfather's silver police whistle, and

Billie had her long list of obsessive rituals that she was convinced would keep danger away, including switching off the kettle before it boiled. Belief was a powerful thing, easily powerful enough to convince you to do something crazy, to take a life.

You'd do anything for them, wouldn't you?

Savage turned another corner and Kett's head cracked off the window. He grabbed the seat in front, bracing himself as the car braked hard. Savage steered them gently up the path, everyone joggling in their seats as she negotiated the potholes. Ahead, the trees peeled themselves reluctantly apart to reveal the enormous house on the hill, its big windows staring back like eyes, shocked to see them.

"This is as far as I can get," Savage said, cutting the engine. She looked back, frowning. "Where is everyone?"

"You drive too fast for them," said Duke. "They're probably still on Yarmouth Road, choking in your dust."

Kett's phone was ringing and he pulled it out to see Clare's name.

"Sir?"

"Somebody's called in a disturbance out in Stiffkey," the Superintendent said, his voice almost lost beneath the roar of his engine. "The Church of St John and St Mary. They say they saw two men fighting, one of them matches Wileman's description."

"What?" said Kett.

"Get out there, now."

Kett hung up, everyone looking at him.

"That was Clare. He thinks Wileman's out in Stiffkey, somebody said he saw him fighting another man."

"The church on the printout, sir?" said Savage, her hand on the key.

"Hang on," said Kett. "This all feels too easy, too neat."

"I was thinking the same thing," said Savage. "We find Wileman's bag with one convenient printout, then we get a call saying he's out there?"

"We're never that lucky," said Porter.

"So we're staying here?" asked Savage.

"I think it's worth a look," Kett said. "I think the killer's trying to play us, keep us out of the way. But I could be wrong."

He opened his door and climbed into the frozen February chill. His suit was already damp from the drizzle, his body feeling like it was entombed in ice. The house seemed somehow further away now that he was out of the car, as if it was retreating. He had the sudden notion that it might try to bolt, might lift itself up out of the ground and start running.

"The killer's trying to buy himself time," he went on. "I'm sure of it."

But who?

"You'd do anything to keep them safe," Kett said out loud.

"What's that, sir?" asked Savage.

"Hang on," he said, pulling out his phone again and calling Spalding. "Alison, you know when you checked the footage for Kitty Lewington's alibi, you saw her with the maid, right? And with the grandkids. And with her son?"

"I think so, sir," she said, and a shiver of relief had started to roll through Kett's body before she carried on. "Wait, her son?"

"Ron Lewington," said Kett. "He's a little older than me, tall, slim. Brown hair."

"I don't remember seeing him, sir," said Spalding. "Hang on."

He heard her typing something into her computer, the seconds ticking by, then the minutes.

"No, sir," she said. "No sign of him. It's just Kitty and Muggle—or whatever her name is—and the two kids. They're in the soft play from just after eleven until gone three. They leave together, head out the main doors."

"There's no man there at all?" said Kett, his skin puckering into goosebumps.

"Plenty of men, but none of them are him."

"Shit," said Kett. "Shit, shit, shit."

"What is it, sir?" asked Savage.

"Spalding, can you find out everything there is to know about Ron Lewington?" he said. "I need to know where he is."

He didn't wait for a reply, grabbing his face with his free hand as he tried to put the pieces together.

Feeling them click.

"Ron Lewington," he said. "He told me he was with the kids on Thursday and I believed him because his mum backed up his alibi, so did the maid."

"Kitty Lewington's son?" said Porter. "Didn't you go out for drinks with him?"

"Yeah," said Kett. "I've literally just left him, we bumped into him at soft play, he was there with his boy and girl."

He offered to drive my children home, he thought, that same icy chill sluicing through him. And it played out in his head: calling Billie, finding out they hadn't arrived, not knowing where they were. The memory of Bingo's house came back like a sledgehammer to his solar plexus, the horror of almost losing them.

"Not having an alibi doesn't mean this is him," said Savage. "There are a dozen reasons his mum could have been covering for him. Maybe he just wanted an afternoon off?"

"He knows about the rituals," said Kett. "He's grown up around them. His mum and dad used to take part in them. Maybe he did too?"

"That's a big leap," said Porter.

"He's an artist. The sketches we found at Wileman's place, they could be his."

Nobody looked convinced.

There was something else, though, something Kett couldn't put his finger on. He dug into his pocket, finding the scrap of napkin that Ron had given him and dialling the number into his phone. It went straight to his voicemail.

"Hi, you've reached Ron Lewington, I'm either at work or out with the kids, leave me a message and I'll try to call you back. Have a good one."

He hung up before the beep, suddenly full of doubt after hearing Ron's voice. He'd only known the man a couple of days, but in that short time he thought he'd found a genuine friend, somebody who understood the hardships of being a father, who struggled with his kids like Kett did, but who loved them just as hard and just as fiercely. It hadn't crossed his mind that he could be capable of killing a man, of cutting his body into pieces. Ron hadn't even been on his radar.

It can't be him, he thought.

He called the number again. No luck.

"His phone's off," he said.

"It's either off, or it's out of service," said Porter, pointing down. "Underground."

Kett's phone began to buzz and for a moment he thought it was Ron calling him back. When he answered, though, it was Spalding's voice he heard.

"You're sure he's Kitty Lewington's son?" she said. "Biological?"

"As far as I know," said Kett. "Why?"

"Because there's no record of her ever having a child. Her or her husband."

"What?" said Kett. "You're sure?"

"There's nothing on the registry, sir. Either they had a baby and never told anyone, never registered it—which would be almost impossible—or they somehow took him in without any official paperwork. I can't figure it out."

"Thanks, Alison," said Kett. "Can you keep looking for me?"

He hung up, everyone waiting.

"Ron isn't Kitty's child," he told them. "Or Keith's. Not biologically."

"Adopted?" asked Savage.

"It's more complicated than that," he said. "There's no official documentation, no record. It's more like—"

Lamb bones, he thought, and that piece of the puzzle suddenly connected to something else, something he and Billie had been joking about before this even began.

They can't be our children. We found them in a bin. And we just forgot about it, because there's no way they can be ours.

"Holy shit," said Kett. "Holy shit, what if..."

Another crippling wave of doubt ran through him, but he ignored it.

"Sir?" said Porter.

"What if Kitty and her husband took part in the Harford Guild ceremony for real? We know they were tight with Foulger, part of the same club. What if they were supposed to sacrifice a kid in a ritual but they got cold feet?"

"They didn't kill the boy," said Savage. "They killed a lamb instead."

"We saw it ourselves, the kid's bundled in a sack, chained to the wall. A lamb's about the same size, it would struggle, and if you gagged it you wouldn't know what it was, not from outside that little room where the sacrifice took place. They kill it, take off a limb or something, and by the time you've stripped off the flesh you wouldn't know the difference. Afterwards, you dump the body, or burn it. Nobody would ever know."

"That's insane," said Duke.

"Then what?" asked Porter. "They take the kid home?"

"And raise him," said Kett. "They bring him up as their own son. But you can't keep a secret like that, not forever."

"If that's true, though," said Savage, "why start killing now?"

"You said it yourself, Kate, the killer knew about the cellar, they knew about the ritual and they believed in the power of the bones. As soon as they were disturbed, as soon as we moved them, that power was stripped away."

"The ritual had to be performed again," said Savage, nodding.

"Exactly. Ron knows about the tunnels, he knows about this house because they used to hold the ritual here—we found the robes. He can't get to the cellar because there are too many people watching it, so he comes here. He sees Carran, maybe he calls him, and then he lures him into the basement and kills him. But it's not enough, because we moved Carran's body too."

"So he needs to kill somebody else," said Porter.

"I think he does," said Kett. "It was there, in what we spoke about. It's there in the way he talks about his kids. 'You'd do anything to keep them safe.' I can't be sure, but..."

"So he targets Wileman," said Savage. "He gets him out of the house, then plants enough evidence to frame Geoff and lure us away from the city."

"That's insane," Duke said again.

"It is," said Kett. "It's utterly insane."

But the pieces fit. The puzzle had come together inside his head.

You'd do anything for them, wouldn't you? Anything to keep them safe.

For Kett, it had been a hammer.

For Ron, it was a chainsaw and a pack of coach screws.

"Sir," said Savage. "Didn't you say you were just with him? How would he have got here so quickly? It's impossible, especially if he had to pick up Wileman."

"Unless he already had Wileman," said Kett. "He could have brought him underground earlier today, or yesterday."

And that, he thought, could only mean one thing. Porter said it for him.

"He's already dead."

"I'll call Clare, sir," said Savage.

"Do it," Kett said, checking his watch. "Let's find a way inside. If by some miracle Wileman hasn't been killed already, he's about to be."

CHAPTER THIRTY-FIVE

Kett ran up the hill towards the old house, his boots finding no purchase at all on the muddy track. Police tape barred the front door, snapping in the wind, and he ripped it away. The door was unlocked, but the swollen wood was as stubborn as a bouncer, even when he put his shoulder to it.

"Stand back, sir," said Duke. "Let me do it."

Kett moved out of the way and the big PC took a run up, only for Porter to step right into his path.

"I'll do it," he said.

"Together?" said Duke.

Porter thought about it for a moment before nodding. They charged the door side by side, kicking it with such force that the top hinge busted out of the damp frame. The door tilted like a punch-drunk boxer before collapsing completely, the house seeming to groan in horror.

"That's how you do it," said Duke with a grin. Porter smiled back, offering a nod as he walked inside.

"Police!" he shouted. "Make yourself known."

Kett hesitated, waiting for Savage to catch up to them. She had her phone to her ear, and she shook her head.

"Clare's not answering, sir."

"Leave a message," said Kett.

He ducked through the broken door into the dank interior. It seemed as though the building had deteriorated even further since he'd last been here. The roof had long since given up, rainwater dripping from a dozen different holes in the ceiling. The floor, too, looked like it was ready to give way, and he walked carefully down the hall.

"Ron?" he called out. "You here?"

Only the house replied, making a creaking noise that could have been sobs or could have been laughter. Duke was already at the top of the stairs, Porter clomping down into the cellar where they'd found Carran's body. There would be nobody in the house, Kett knew. It wouldn't be that easy. He opened the door that led to the main basement and stared into a pool of absolute darkness.

"Ron?" he shouted. "Geoff?"

Nothing, as if the world simply ended at the bottom of those stairs. Even his words were muted, swallowed alive.

"I left a message, sir," came Savage's voice, so close behind him that he flinched. "Called Gorski too, but she's *en route* to Stiffkey, she won't turn back without an order."

"With any luck, they're right and we're wrong," said Kett. "You got a torch?"

"Yes, sir," she said, pulling a slim one from her pocket and clicking it on. "You?"

He switched on the flashlight on his phone, aiming it down the stairs. It did nothing at all to part the shadows.

"You really need to buy a proper torch, sir."

"Tell me about it."

There was another click as Porter stepped into the

room, his Maglite cutting through the dark like a knife through warm butter. His phone was ringing and he took it out of his pocket, glanced at the screen, then slid it back.

"Just Allie," he said. "Wasn't supposed to be at work today and she's pissed."

Kett heard a noise that might have been Duke falling down the stairs. Seconds later he joined them, his own torch on. They crowded around the steps and finally the basement slunk into view.

"Duke can go first," said Porter.

"I really don't want—"

"Definitely Duke," said Savage.

"But I—"

"Duke, get down those steps," said Kett. "And get your Taser out."

"Sir," Duke grumbled, pulling out his weapon with his free hand. He descended slowly and Kett trod on his heels, feeling the temperature plummet as they sank beneath ground level. Shadows danced on the walls around him, surely too many to be cast by their torches. Porter's phone was going again, but he ignored it.

"Police!" roared Duke. "If anyone's down here, make your presence known!"

The PC vanished as he walked through the door. Kett followed him into the cellar, nothing there but a century's worth of junk that even the looters hadn't bothered with. The second set of stairs sat directly ahead of them, the opening far too much like a mouth for his liking.

"It's chuffing freezing down here," said Porter.

"Ron?" Kett called when he reached the stairs. "If you're down there, mate, we need to speak with you. We know what's going on."

That wasn't a hundred percent true, of course. They

didn't know for sure. But it felt right. As much as he hated it, the pieces had clicked together.

"Come out now and we'll see what we can do. It doesn't have to end like this."

A low moan answered him, followed by a gust of wind that felt far too much like a cold hand on his face. The sound came again, longer this time, lifted right from the soundtrack for a haunted house.

"Fuck this," said Porter. "I quit."

"It's just the wind," Kett said, but the terror was gnawing at his nerves too. The last thing he wanted to do in all the world was set foot on those steps, to go even deeper.

"Duke," he said.

"Yeah, yeah, I'm going, sir," muttered the PC.

He started downwards, his Taser rattling.

"I'm shivering because I'm cold," he said. "Not because I'm afraid."

"Yeah, me too," said Kett, his chattering teeth breaking the words into pieces.

The steps were steeper than he remembered and he lost his footing on the way down, almost tumbling into Duke. It seemed to take far longer to reach the bottom than it should have, the stairwell eventually opening out into the chalk-walled chamber below. They fanned out across the room, heading for the gate that still stood open. Beyond it, the tunnel waited for them, as cold and as silent as the grave.

"Police," Kett shouted, his voice reverberating. "Ron, can you hear me? Geoff? Anyone?"

"They could be anywhere," said Porter. "Even if you were right about Ron, there's no guarantee he entered the tunnels this way. They stretch beneath the whole city. We'll never find him."

A fist of wind punched down the passageway, kicking

up dust with a spectral howl. It was followed by another sound, one just as faint and just as ghostly.

But this one sounded almost like a word.

"You hear that?" said Duke, and Kett hushed him.

They all held their breath, waiting for the noise to come again. And when it did, there was no denying it.

It was a shout.

"Kate, get back to the surface will you?" said Kett. "Try Clare again, get backup down here."

"Yes, sir," she said. "Be careful. It's way too easy to get lost."

"Follow the paint," said Porter, shining his torch at the wall to the right. "We marked all the junctions when we were down here earlier. The arrows lead to the cavern we found before."

"Good work," said Kett, breaking into a jog. He took a breath and bellowed: "Police! Stay where you are. Geoff, if that's you, keep shouting."

If there was a reply, it was lost behind the echo of their feet. The tunnel curved to the left and in less than a minute they'd lost sight of the chamber that led back to the house. Ten seconds after that, they reached the first junction.

"Geoff?" Kett yelled, his pulse drumming in his skull.

Only the wind answered him, or so he thought until Duke angled his torch down the tunnel to the right.

"That way," he said, looking at the red arrow.

"You sure?" Kett replied. "I can't hear anything."

"Not a shout, a scuffle, I think."

"I can hear it," said Porter. "Somebody's fighting."

The two coppers were off before Kett could say anything, and he chased their swaying torches down the tunnel. The ceiling dropped as he ran, forcing him to duck down to avoid being scalped. The walls closed in, too, as if the tunnel was being squeezed. He felt like he was being suffocated, like there was no air down here, and he made himself take deep, lung-busting breaths.

"Another junction," said Porter. "Quiet."

Kett slowed to a crawl as he caught up, and this time he heard it, coming from the tunnel to the right—something clattering, followed by a muffled cry.

"It's them," said Porter, charging off with Duke right behind him.

"Pete, wait," said Kett, but his words fell on deaf ears.

The tunnel was opening up, the ceiling rising. The sound of a tussle was louder than ever, Porter's voice rising above it all.

"Oi! Put it down!"

Adrenaline kicked Kett's heart into overdrive as he followed Duke out of the end of the tunnel and skidded abruptly to a halt. He recognised where they were instantly, a wide chamber with seven tunnels leading out of it, lit by a portable hurricane lantern.

Two men fought in the middle of it, their enormous shadows splayed over the walls and the ceiling. Kett knew them both. Geoff Wileman lay on his back in a pool of blood, one arm hanging limply, the other grabbing the leg of the man above him. His ankles were bound with rope and he kicked at the air as he fought to get up.

Ron Lewington had a knee in Wileman's stomach, his left hand around the man's throat.

In his right hand he held an axe—the blade slick with blood.

"Oi!" Porter yelled again, and this time Ron heard him, twisting his head around. His face was so contorted by panic and terror that he was almost unrecognisable. It seemed utterly impossible that just over an hour ago Kett had been sitting with him, the pair of them laughing and joking while their children bounced around the soft play.

"Help!" croaked Wileman, the word exploding from his lips with a glut of blood.

Duke ran forward, the Taser raised, but Ron lifted the axe. There was nothing but madness in his eyes, and it was terrifying.

"Don't," he said, his voice high-pitched and full of urgency. "Don't take another step, or he loses his head."

Duke slowed, still too far away for a clean shot. He took another step and Ron, true to his word, chopped the axe down into Wileman's forehead. It wasn't hard, but the wet crack it made turned Kett's stomach. Blood began to leak out of the wound, Wileman's eyes rolling up in their sockets as if he was trying to see what had been done to him. He was making a noise that was half choke, half sob, his feet drumming the ground like he was having a fit.

"Not another step," said Ron, sounding out each word with great care. He was still panicking, his eyes darting from Duke to Porter, then landing on Kett. "What are you doing here, Robbie?"

"I was going to ask you the same question, Ron," he said. "Get up, let him go, and we can talk."

Ron shook his head. The collar of his shirt was open, revealing a necklace of yellow bones tied with string. They rattled every time he moved, and Kett didn't need Emily Franklin's help to know that they were knucklebones—human ones. Ron put his free hand to them as if checking they were still there.

"Can't do that, mate," he said. "I'm sorry. I have to finish this. You knew enough to find me down here, which means you know what'll happen if I stop now."

"Nothing will happen," said Kett. "This doesn't mean

anything, Ron. The ritual, the bones, it's not real. It doesn't give you power, it doesn't keep your children safe."

Ron laughed, but there was an immense sadness there, a terrible desperation. He kneaded the bones around his neck like they were a rosary.

"You say that, but how can you be sure?" he said. The axe must have been heavy because his arm was shaking. "How can you know, Robbie? Would you risk it, if it was your kids? You know the answer to that as well as I do. If you could keep your girls safe by killing a man, you would do it. You wouldn't even hesitate."

"Not like this," said Kett. "I promise you, you're wrong. Put it down, talk to me."

"It's too late," said Ron. "I didn't think I'd ever have to do it, but you made me. You didn't give me any choice. All those people over the years, they all died so that we could be safe. My mum and dad, the Foulgers, all those others. They killed because they had to, don't you see? That's why we live like we do. It's what keeps us rich, keeps us healthy, keeps us alive. It *works*, because of the bones, because of..."

He frowned, as if he'd lost his train of thought. Beneath him, Wileman's movements were growing slower, the puddle of blood spreading.

"You understand," Ron said again. "You have to understand. In the end, it's worth it. You have to see."

"I do," said Kett. "I think I do. You were supposed to die down here, weren't you? What, forty years ago? Longer? You were going to be sacrificed. But Kitty Lewington changed her mind, she sacrificed a lamb instead, and she took you home."

"It wasn't Mum," he said. "It was Dad. He chickened out, he couldn't do it. But it's okay, because the bones were still there, they still protected us, and none of the others ever knew what he'd done. It was you who moved the bones, you broke the spell, you *forced* me."

He lifted the axe and Kett took a step towards him.

"Don't," he said. "Please, Ron."

"Just promise me one thing," Ron said, tears rolling down his cheeks. "Please, because I think we're friends now, aren't we?"

Kett nodded.

"Just promise me you'll leave him the way I do. Don't move his body. If you just leave him, then it will still work, I know it will. It will keep my kids safe."

"Ron—"

"I'm sorry," the other man said.

He swung the axe down again.

Porter was already moving, hurling himself across the chamber. Ron saw him coming, panicking, and the blade of the axe missed its target, sinking instead into the meat of Wileman's shoulder. Then Porter slammed into him and the pair rolled over each other, hitting the back wall.

"Move!" Duke roared, rushing forward with the Taser.

Kett was running too, vaulting Wileman's thrashing body and ducking onto his knees next to Porter—only for one of Ron's shoes to crack him hard in the nose. He fell back, the world slipping off its axis for a moment, the chamber full of stars. He tried to push himself up but the floor was slick with Wileman's blood and he fell again, seeing Ron slip free, seeing him bolt into one of the tunnels.

Porter struggled up, moving to Kett.

"You okay?"

He nodded, then Porter was off again, vanishing from sight before Kett could find the words to stop him. Duke flew after them, their shouts echoing back, growing quieter.

"Wait!" Kett croaked. "Just—"

There was a blinding flash of light from inside the tunnel, followed almost instantly by a roar of thunder that punched Kett backwards once again. He landed hard, rolling, the chamber full of dust and smoke.

"Jesus Christ," he groaned, trying to push himself up. "Pete?"

He got to his feet, coughing hard, his skull ringing like there was a bell inside it. Somebody was staggering out of the carnage, and Kett limped towards him.

"Pete?" he said, then he realised it was Duke. "Aaron? What the hell happened?"

"Tunnel was rigged," said Duke, wiping a sleeve over the blood that drained from his nose. His face was covered in scratches, and he'd lost his hat. "I think it was a fucking bomb."

"Where's Pete?" said Kett, pushing past the PC.

The answer was clear enough. The roof of the tunnel had collapsed, giant boulders of chalky rock blocking the path ahead. Kett looked at Duke, the fear boiling inside him like water in a kettle, the pressure unbearable. He could hear the hysteria in his voice.

"Duke, where is he?"

"He's gone," Duke said, his voice hoarse. "He was under all that. I... I don't know..."

"Fuck!" Kett roared. "Pete?"

He dropped to his knees, digging at the rock with his bare hands.

"Pete, can you hear me?"

"Sir?"

Kett glanced back to see Savage enter the chamber, her hand over her mouth.

"Oh God," she said. "What happened?"

"It's Pete," Kett said. "We need help, Kate."

"They're coming," Savage told him, running to Wileman and dropping down beside him. "Tactical and ambulance are on their way, they'll be minutes."

It wasn't quick enough, Kett knew. They were going to be too late.

"Sir," said Savage. "There's something else."

"What?" he said, pulling out rocks and hurling them over his shoulder.

"Allie called me when I was up in the house," she said, her voice heavy with sadness. "She's been trying to get hold of Pete, sir. She's at the hospital. She's having the baby."

CHAPTER THIRTY-SIX

PORTER COULDN'T WORK OUT IF HE WAS ALIVE OR DEAD.

He lay in complete darkness, his head a cavern filled only with a roar of silence. His body was numb, as if it didn't exist anymore, and when he tried to move his hands to check himself he found that they didn't respond. Nothing responded, not even his eyes when he commanded them to open.

A blast of undiluted terror ripped through him.

Work, he told his body. *Fucking work!*

Something moved over his face, a cold hand, fingers pushing into his mouth and down his windpipe, choking him. He tried to spit them out and nothing happened. He tried to cough, but even that didn't work, his body made of stone.

No, please, anything but this.

Something hit his face, harder this time, like he was being punched. He screamed inside his head but all his body did was whimper.

Come on!

Whoever was touching him poked his eye, hard enough to make an explosion of light dance across the dark.

Stop it! he yelled. *Stop it, stop it.*

"Shtopt," he slurred, and the sound of his own voice was so good he almost burst into tears. He tried again, his lips freeing themselves from their paralysis, then the slab of his tongue. "Stop it, stop it."

One eye peeled open, then the other, but there was no light at all.

I can't see, he thought. *The explosion blinded me.*

Was that what had happened? An explosion? He couldn't remember. One second he'd been chasing the suspect, the next his world had ended. He tried to make a fist, feeling his fingers contract. He did the same with his other hand, the sensation returning with a cold fury of pins and needles.

As slowly as he could, he sat up. There was no sign of his torch but he dug his fingers into his pocket and worked his phone free, tapping the screen until it came to life. He saw Allie there—*thank God, I can see*—a photo he'd taken of her just a week ago when they'd spent the day at Pensthorpe, looking at the birds. She stood in a ray of rare sunshine, one hand on her bump, the other shielding her eyes. He almost started crying.

"Shit," he told her. "I'm sorry."

Somebody punched him on the back of the head and he turned on the phone's torch, aiming it upwards. Nobody stood there, but the ceiling was a web of cracks, pieces of stone dropping like fists, the dust caressing his skin like creeping fingers. He coughed, tasting blood alongside the chalk dust, then he manoeuvred his body so that he was on his hands and knees.

Only now did the pain seem to remember what it should be doing, filling him from head to toe. He couldn't do anything except put his forehead to the ground and open his mouth, spit hanging from his lips. At least it was confirmation that he was alive. *Dead men don't feel pain,* he thought. For a second, the darkness returned as he felt himself sliding out of consciousness.

"Don't you dare," he growled. "Don't you fucking dare."

He started to crawl, the phone gripped in his hand doing a poor job of lighting the way. Only when he was sure everything was working did he push himself to his feet, leaning on the wall of the tunnel to stop himself from keeling over. Ahead, the tunnel stretched into infinity, but behind him the ceiling had collapsed. If he'd been a few feet further back when the bomb had detonated, he realised, he'd have been crushed.

You'd never have met your kid, he told himself. *You dick.*

He cleared his throat and tried to shout, but all that came out was a dry wheeze. The air was still heavy with dust, making it difficult to breathe. He wasn't dead yet, but down here in the dark and the cold it wouldn't take long.

Stay where you are, he told himself. *They'll dig their way through.*

But what if they couldn't, and what if the entire tunnel had been damaged? If he waited here, the whole thing could come down on him any second. He wouldn't get lucky twice.

He started walking like he'd only just learned how, the pain receding a fraction more with every step, his strength returning. All the tunnels down here were connected, weren't they? If he kept going, he'd be sure to find his way back, or find a route to the surface.

But the further he went, the more the tunnel seemed to drop, the angle so steep that twice he lost his footing, his shoe slipping out from beneath him. He gripped the rough wall for support until, finally, it began to level out. He could see the end of the tunnel up ahead, and was that a streak of daylight across the floor there, golden and warm?

He doubled his pace, almost jogging as he left the tunnel and entered the wider space beyond. And only there did he realise it wasn't daylight at all.

Ron Lewington stood in a slim cavern in the rock, a torch gripped in one hand and the axe still held in the other. He wasn't wearing his shirt anymore, just that necklace of bone and a second skin of blood and chalk dust. He was almost completely still, only his mouth moving as he muttered beneath his breath. His eyes were open, but they weren't looking at Porter. They didn't seem to be looking at anything, locked on a vision that only he could see.

Porter lifted his phone to light him up, and Ron stopped muttering. He raised his head to reveal those lunatic eyes, two red blisters in his chalk-white face. Porter scanned the cavern. There was one more tunnel leading into darkness and Ron stood right at the entrance to it. There would be no way of getting past him, not without a fight.

"Put the axe down," Porter said, his voice a husk. He could barely hear himself over the ringing in his ears, and he struggled to understand the other man's reply.

"Why couldn't you just die?" Emotion flooded Ron's face, a genuine expression of grief. "Why? I wouldn't have had to do it, then, I wouldn't have had to kill you if you'd just died."

"You *don't* have to kill me, Ron," said Porter. "Put the axe down. We can both get out of here. Go on, mate."

"I *do* have to," Ron replied, tapping his axe gently against the bones that hung around his neck. "You must see it. Everything was going so well until you moved those bones, you broke the spell. All this..."

He stretched the axe out to the side, the walls so tight that the bloodied blade scraped against the chalk.

"All this is proof, don't you see it? Without the ritual, without the bones, everything falls apart."

"You've got it all wrong, Ron," said Porter. "It's bullshit, mate. Put the axe down."

"Robbie understands," said Ron, and he swivelled the axe so that it was pointing at Porter. "He gets it. He's been through it, he's been where I am now, and he knows all about the sacrifices you have to make to keep them safe."

"Then let's go and find him," said Porter. "Yeah? You can talk to him as much as you like. Put the axe down and we'll go together."

"He knows that nothing else matters when you've got kids. He knows you just do what you have to do to keep them safe, keep them alive."

His words were running together, making it hard to figure out what he was saying. Porter wondered if he'd been hurt by the explosion too.

"Ron, if you don't put that axe down and focus on getting out of here, then your kids are never going to see you again."

"It doesn't matter. That doesn't matter at all. I don't care if I'm here or not, I just have to know that they're going to be okay. I have to do this, I'm sorry."

He started to walk, his body so stiff he looked like a marionette.

"I really am sorry, I don't even know your name."

"Pete. Peter Porter."

Porter took a couple of steps back, loose scraps of rock doing their best to trip him up. There was nowhere to go, he knew, so he adjusted his stance instead, eyeing the razor-sharp blade of the axe. Once again he thought about Allie, he thought about the baby who grew inside her. The horror of knowing that he might die down here, that he might never see his wife and meet his child, made his head roar like a jet engine.

"Just stop," he said, pointing a finger at Ron. "I swear to God, mate, if you come at me, I'm going to fucking end you."

"You got children, Pete?" Ron asked, taking another step. He was definitely moving weirdly, pain flashing across his fear-maddened face with every step.

"Got my first on the way," Porter replied. "Nothing's going to stop me seeing him, you hear me? Nothing."

Ron's mouth split open into a joker's smile, a slash of red in his paper-white face.

"See," he said, stepping ever closer, his torch burning a hole in the back of Porter's eyes, blinding him. "You *do* get it. You do whatever it takes to keep them safe."

Ron lurched forwards, swinging the axe in a wide arc. Porter stepped away, his feet slipping again—fortunately, this time, because he tumbled out of the path of the blade. It struck the wall where his head had been, releasing a blinding spark of light.

Porter fell onto his backside, his phone hitting the ground, the torch shattering. He crawled backwards into the tunnel, Ron advancing, the axe raised for another strike. The ceiling was too low, the heavy blade knocking chunks of chalk free.

"I'll make it quick," Ron said. "I promise, I don't want to hurt you."

He swung the axe down again and slipped on the loose rubble, the blade scuffing the wall. He lost his balance, his torch clattering to the floor and rolling away. It didn't break, but the tunnel flooded with shadows, Ron a silhouette who picked himself up, who charged again.

"I won't hurt you. I won't hurt you."

"No!" Porter yelled. "Don't!"

The axe fell, the heavy blade cracking into his shin. Fireworks exploded, the pain just as bright and just as hot. Ron was already lifting his weapon again, throwing himself forward.

"I promise, I won't hurt you, just lie still."

Porter kicked out with his good leg, missed. He tried again and this time his shoe connected with Ron's knee. There was a pop as something tore, and Ron loosed a gargled scream. He fell onto Porter, a knee in his gut, the shaft of the axe cracking him in the nose.

Porter roared, the blood in his throat turning it into a gargle. Ron lay on top of him, thrashing and bucking, heavier than he had any right to be. The necklace of bones clacked against Porter's teeth, slipping between his lips. He tried to roll but there was no room in the tunnel, the walls pushing against him on either side, as tight as a coffin.

"No!" he said again, coughing blood.

He grabbed the sides of Ron's head, trying to shove him off. Then he felt the handle of the axe against his throat, pushing hard. He tried to snatch a breath and found he couldn't. Ron was on top of it, every ounce of his weight driving the axe down, crushing his windpipe. Over the howl in his ears, Porter could hear him muttering gentle words.

"Hush now, Pete, it won't take long, I swear, it'll be over soon. Shhhhh, it's just like going to sleep."

And then, incredibly, he started to sing—a nursery

rhyme so mangled by his heaving, grunting breaths that Porter couldn't make sense of it.

The horror of it, though, of this insane song, was worse than the injury in his leg, worse than the axe that pulverised his throat, worse than the blood that choked him.

Porter gripped Ron's head, his thumbs working their way over his cheeks and up to his eyes. He dug them in as hard as he could, hearing the other man shriek, feeling the pressure on his throat lessen.

"Get off!" Porter growled, the words barely there.

He drove his thumbs harder, deeper, feeling the weight of Ron's body pull away. Then he let go with his right hand, bunched his fist, and drove it into the other man's nose.

Ron groaned and Porter hit him again, then again, forcing him back until he could drag his body free of him. He lifted his leg, kicked out, striking something solid. The torch had rolled so far away now that it was impossible to make sense of anything, just a maddening kaleidoscope of light and shadow. But there was enough to see Ron standing there, enough to see him lift the axe again.

Porter struggled up, his left leg not working properly, the pain like a chainsaw was revving beneath the skin. Ron was staggering, unbalanced.

Porter seized his chance, tackling the other man like they were playing rugby. Ron hit the floor first, the axe skittering away. Porter dropped on top of him but the agony in his leg flared and he flopped onto his side, everything going dark.

Nononono.

He could feel Ron moving, he could hear the scrape of the axe blade on the stone.

Get up! he screamed at himself. *Get up!*

But he couldn't, his leg wasn't doing what it was

supposed to. Ron was on his feet, panting hard. The axe was back in his hand.

"You... could have made... this," the man said, struggling for breath. "So much... easier."

He lumbered forwards and Porter coiled his good leg, ready to strike.

He didn't have to.

A shape exploded from the mouth of the tunnel, bright yellow and the size of a truck. It flew into Ron hard enough to send the other man flying into the wall, the crack of a breaking bone like a gunshot.

"Duke?" croaked Porter.

Another figure appeared, both of them piling onto Ron. Kett kicked the axe away while Duke wrestled Ron onto his stomach, snapping a pair of handcuffs around his wrists. The man howled his misery into the air, the sound of it filling the narrow cavern until Duke sat heavily on his back, crushing the air from his lungs.

"Pete?" said Kett, running over. "Are you okay?"

I'm fine, he said, or at least thought he'd said. The words didn't have the power to reach his lips, getting caught in his throat. He swallowed them back down along with a mouthful of blood, and tried to sit up.

"Shit," he heard Duke say, but he couldn't see where the PC was looking. "Sir, that's a lot of blood."

Kett dropped down beside him.

"Pete? Can you hear me?"

Of course I can, Porter thought, and he would have laughed if his body had let him. Instead, he closed his eyes, because he couldn't think of a way to keep them open.

"Christ," he heard Kett say. "Aaron, get him up, get him up!"

He wasn't sure if Duke was listening, because once

again his body had gone almost completely numb. The sound of their voices tuned out, becoming the static hiss of a badly tuned radio, leaving him with nothing but his own voice.

I'm fine, I'm fine, I'm...

Then even that was gone.

CHAPTER THIRTY-SEVEN

Bleep-bleep, bleep-bleep, bleep-bleep, bleep—

Kett's own heart seemed to stop beating as the pulse monitor stuttered. He stood in the cramped room inside A&E, as close to the bed as the nurses would let him. Savage leaned against him, squeezing his hand so tightly he'd lost the sensation in his fingers. On his other side was Duke, and past him Superintendent Clare, all of them watching as the doctors tried their hardest to save a life.

It was a battle they couldn't win.

Bleep-bleep, bleep... bleeeeeeeeeeeeee.

"He's coding," said the surgeon, wiping the sweat from her brow. "Paddles!"

"Come on," said Kett. "Come on."

The defibrillator whined, and the entire bed seemed to jump as it discharged.

Nothing.

"Again!" cried the surgeon.

Eeeeeeeeeeeeeeeeeeee.

The defibrillator punched its charge into him. His body bucked.

But it was hopeless. He was gone.

"I'm calling it," said the surgeon, looking at the clock. "Time of death is 16:07."

"No," said Kett.

She turned to him, offering a sad nod.

"I'm sorry for your loss," she said. "The wound was just too severe, he lost too much blood. I don't know how he kept going for as long as he did."

Kett looked at the man on the bed, caked in so much blood and chalk dust that he was barely recognisable. It was impossible to believe that just hours ago this cooling body had been somebody he'd called a friend, somebody he'd laughed and joked with.

Somebody who'd turned out to be a monster.

"Can you give me his name again?" asked the surgeon. "It all happened so quickly."

"Ronald Lewington," said Kett. "Ron."

She wrote it down.

"Do you all need a moment with him?"

"No, we tossing don't," said Clare, walking out of the door. Duke followed, leaving a trail of dust behind him.

Kett gently pulled himself free of Savage's hand.

"Got a grip like an arm wrestler, Kate," he said, shaking the feeling back into his fingers.

"Oh, sorry sir," she said. "It's been an emotional day."

"You're not wrong."

For a moment, they studied the man in the bed. His eyes had been closed but there was nothing at peace about the way he lay there, his mouth twisted open and blood on the sheets.

"He didn't deserve it, did he?" Savage said. "I mean, nobody deserves this, right? Whatever they did."

Kett didn't know how to answer, so he said nothing. He

didn't think he'd ever truly understand what had happened to Ron, only that he had been broken beyond repair. He'd discovered the rituals his mum and dad had conducted, he'd grown up under that dark shadow, he'd learned the truth about who he was and where he had come from, and somewhere along the way he'd fallen into a madness that nothing could have saved him from.

"His kids are the ones who don't deserve it," Kett said. "He did all this for them, but now they have to grow up without their dad. I hope they never find out the truth of it."

"Me too," said Savage, blowing out a long sigh. "You want to go see how Pete and Allie are doing?"

He nodded, leading the way into the quiet corridor. It was a short journey to the maternity ward and Clare was already there, holding the door open for them. A midwife looked at them reproachfully from the other side of the desk.

"You realise you lot are bloody filthy," she said as they walked past.

"We won't stay long," said Kett. "Allie Porter?"

"Room three," she said. "She had it thirty minutes ago."

"They're okay?" Savage asked.

"Mother and baby are just fine," the midwife replied. "Dad's a big wet blanket."

Kett laughed, walking around the corner and knocking on the door.

"Come in," came a voice so croaky that Kett wasn't sure who had spoken.

As quietly as he could, he walked inside. Allie was propped up in a bed in the middle of the dimly lit room, her face still flushed and her tangled hair held back by a bright red hairband. She looked utterly exhausted, barely able to lift an arm to wave them in, but the smile on her face was huge and there was a happiness in her eyes that Kett had never seen before.

Cradled in her other arm, and so small that it didn't look real, was their baby, fast asleep. It was swaddled in blankets, just its round, wrinkled face and a single hand visible—its fingers impossibly tiny.

Sitting next to them in a hospital wheelchair, drowning beneath twice as many blankets as Allie and the baby, was Porter. The doctors had done their best to clean him up but there were still pockets of chalk everywhere, contrasting the dozen or so cuts and bruises on his face and neck. The worst of these covered his throat, which was so swollen and so purple that it looked like he was wearing a scarf. He didn't seem able to get his hands out of the blankets, so he nodded to them instead, offering a croak of greeting.

"Wow," Kett said softly. He waited for Savage, Clare and Duke to enter the room before closing the door. "Congratulations, both of you."

Porter croaked again.

"What's that, Pete?" said Kett.

"He's telling you it's a boy," said Allie, looking lovingly at the child. "Our beautiful baby boy."

Porter nodded, a lopsided smile appearing on his face. He finally managed to pull an arm free, reaching for Allie. She took his hand, holding tight, gazing at him with just as much joy and admiration.

"He's gorgeous," said Savage. "Looks like both of you."

"That's kind," said Allie. "But he looks just like Pete, don't you think?"

He did, boasting a mass of dark hair that was the same colour as Porter's.

"He's about the same shape as Porter," said Duke. "Round."

Porter shot him a dark look that didn't last, becoming a tired smile.

"You know I'm only kidding, sir," said Duke. "Happy you're okay."

"Baby's pretty early, so they're going to monitor him, make sure he's healthy," Allie said, so tired her words were a blur. "But they say he's doing well, thank God. Strong as an ox."

"Like you," said Kett. "Both of you. How're you doing, Pete?"

"Not good," he whispered.

"He's fine," said Allie. "The doctor's just been in. He's covered in cuts, but none of them are very deep."

"What about your leg?" asked Kett.

"It's fine," Allie said. "The axe split the skin but it didn't go any further than that. He got hit with the flat side of the blade."

"It was still a bloody axe," Porter snapped back.

"His throat's got contusions or something," said Allie, "but they said it'll heal. The thing that will take the longest is his sprained ankle."

"You sprained your ankle?" said Clare.

"It's really painful," said Porter.

"And, of course, his bruised ego," said Allie with a smile.

"That's never going to heal," said Duke. "How many times have I saved your life now, sir?"

Porter looked like he was about to throw himself at the PC, but after a second he relaxed, wincing.

"We'll get out of your hair," said Clare. "We just wanted to check you're okay."

"Did Ron make it?" Porter asked, and Kett shook his head. There was such a rush of emotion on the DI's face that Kett couldn't work out what he was thinking. Porter studied his blanket like there were answers written there.

"It wasn't you," said Kett. "It was the explosion. He had half a dozen scraps of rock embedded in his back, two had punctured his liver. If you hadn't gone after him, though, if you hadn't taken him down the way you did, he could have got away. And he would have killed again, you know that as well as I do."

"If it's any consolation, Geoff Wileman's out of surgery," added Savage. "He was cut up pretty bad but he's going to live."

"Hush," said Allie, letting go of Porter to cover the baby's ears. "No talk about the job, he's too little to hear it."

"Sorry," said Kett. "We'll go."

"Hang on," said Porter. "Before you do. Allie and I have spoken about it. It was one of the names we had on the list, but after today..."

He coughed hard, then smiled at Kett.

"After everything you've done for me, for us. We want to call him Robert."

For a moment, Kett was literally lost for words. A rush of warmth flowed through him, over him, like he'd just stepped into a hot bath.

"Only if it's okay with you," said Porter. "I mean, it's cool if it's not."

"It's not cool," said Allie. "Second choice was Warrior Porter, remember?"

"It's fine," said Kett. "It's more than fine, it's... I'm honoured, Pete, Allie. I truly am."

"Little Bobby Porter," said Allie. "It works."

"It does," said Savage.

"Doesn't," came a grumble from Duke, who was quietly fuming.

"What's that?" Kett asked him.

"Nothing, sir," Duke said. "But, I mean, I was the one who saved you, wasn't I? Ron was running right at you and—"

"Hold your horses, mate," said Porter. "I haven't forgotten. Bobby needs a middle name, doesn't he? We want it to be yours."

"Really?" said Duke, his eyes widening.

"Yeah," said Porter. "Robert Dickhead Porter."

"Pete!" yelled Allie, loud enough that the baby stirred.

"Sorry, I'm joking. Robert Aaron Porter. It feels right."

"I'm... That's..."

It looked like the big PC was going to cry.

"Colin would also make a good middle name," said Clare.

"No," said Allie, shaking her head.

"Robert Aaron Colin Porter," the Superintendent persisted.

"Sorry, sir," said Porter. "Never going to happen."

"It's a good name. An *appropriate* name, Porter. I urge you to think—"

"No!" said everyone together.

"Fine," Clare said through gritted teeth. "Well, congratu-*tossing*-lations."

He opened the door and stormed out. The baby was well and truly awake now, watching the world with dark eyes and a soft whimper.

"He's hungry," said Allie, trying to shuffle up the bed.

"We'll go," said Kett. "But you did good, both of you. He's perfect."

"He is," said Allie.

"Thanks," added Porter as Kett opened the door. "I mean it, thank you."

Kett nodded to him and walked out. Duke followed, Savage last.

"Love you guys," she said as she left the room, closing the door behind her. "Wow. What a beauty."

"Makes you broody, doesn't it?" said Duke. "Makes you want to have like fifty babies of your own."

The expression of horror on Savage's face made Kett laugh—too loud, because the midwife on duty pointed to the exit.

"Out, the lot of you!"

They apologised their way through the doors, finding Superintendent Clare waiting for them in the corridor beyond. He was leaning against the wall, rubbing his face with his big hands, and when he heard them coming he looked over with eyes that were red raw.

"What the toss is wrong with my name?" he said.

"Nothing," said Savage. "That's why we gave it to the dog."

Kett laughed again, and after a moment Clare's scowl turned to a grim smile.

"Fair enough," he said. "I can't quite believe this turned into such a mess. My own fault, I suppose, for giving you an innocent-looking cold case, Kett. I should have known."

"I keep telling everyone, none of this was my doing!" he protested. "We need to bring Kitty Lewington in, she's—"

"Already done," Clare replied. "She's going to be charged with aiding and abetting, and a lot more besides, if I have anything to do with it. But that's my job. You're all going home. You're all disgusting. Have a wash, get some rest, I'll see you in the morning for a debrief."

Nobody argued with him.

"You honestly think he believed all this?" Clare said before they could walk away. "Ron. You think he believed in bone magick and rituals? This wasn't just a grudge disguised as something else?"

"He believed it, sir," said Kett. "For everyone else these rituals were a joke, a piece of theatre. They were history. But not for Ron. For him, it was life and death. Everything that mattered to him hinged on those bones, on what he thought they represented, on what he thought they offered him. As soon as we moved them his world fell apart."

"Maybe there was something to it, then?" said Duke. "Maybe the bones were magic."

Everybody turned to him.

"Just saying," he muttered.

"It was a self-fulfilling prophecy," said Savage. "He believed it so much he made his own fears come true."

Clare nodded sadly.

"We do anything to make sure they're okay, don't we?" he said, an echo of Ron's own words. "Our kids, our family. It's hardwired into us."

"It is," said Kett.

And sometimes the wiring comes loose.

He heard the thud of the hammer, saw the Pig Man fall.

"Go on then," said Clare. "Before I change my mind. Oh, and Duke?"

Duke looked back.

"Once again, Constable, I'm impressed," said Clare. "Above and beyond. Your commitment to the job and to your fellow officers is something to be immensely proud of. Kett and Savage have recommended it, and so has Porter—passionately, I might add—and I'm going to make it official. You're on the Task Force permanently, if you want it."

"Yes, sir!" said Duke, grinning. "I want it, sir."

"Good lad," said Clare. "Now toss off."

"I am going to toss off like you wouldn't believe, sir!"

said Duke at the exact moment the same midwife walked through the doors of the maternity ward. She looked at Duke with profound horror.

"I'm not actually tossing off," he told her as she scurried past. "Sorry. It doesn't mean what you think it means."

They nodded their farewells to the Superintendent, piling into the elevator together and riding in silence down to the ground floor. It was still light outside, the air freezing and the rain harder than ever. They sheltered under the canopy for a moment, watching the people come and go with their injuries, watching an ambulance pulling away and painting the world blue. An IRV sat on the other side of the car park, empty.

"It never ends, does it?" said Savage. "We catch the bad guy, we close the case, we bring somebody home, we save a life, and the next day it happens all over again."

"It's the job," said Kett, and left it at that.

Duke was on his phone, staring intently at the screen.

"What are you doing, Aaron?" asked Savage.

"Just Facebook," he said, typing something and then turning the phone to face them. "He deserves it."

On the screen was a photograph of Porter, obviously taken before they'd entered the tunnels. He was standing outside the Bracondale house, his jaw set and his eyes serious as they prepared to go after Ron Lewington. It was a good photo of him. He looked younger, fitter, he looked like the Porter Kett had first met on the streets of London all those years ago, hungry for the job, always ready to do the right thing.

Underneath the photo, Duke had written a single word: *Hero*.

"You're a big softie," Savage said, giving Duke a gentle elbow.

"Yeah," he replied. "You were right, I'm a teddy bear."

"You want a lift?" she asked, but Kett shook his head.

"I'll get a taxi."

He left them to it, climbing into a black cab at the rank and settling into his seat. The driver was talking to him, making a comment about the state of his suit, but Kett didn't have the energy to reply, and after a while the man gave up. They rode in silence, the skies grey and heavy, the rain drumming the windscreen. The twenty-minute journey felt like it had taken seconds, and yet at the same time hours, and by the time the driver pulled up outside his house, Kett was ready to sleep for a century.

"Thanks," he said as he climbed out, leaving a chalky imprint on the seat behind him. "Sorry about that."

He crossed the road, stepping onto his drive. And there he stopped, because the house was lit up against the dull afternoon, the living room curtains wide open. He could see Evie and Moira bouncing on the sofa, Alice on the easy chair with her legs curled up beneath her, her face serious beneath the hood of her jumper as she studied her phone.

Watching them like this was like seeing them on a cinema screen, as if they somehow weren't real, and a jolt of adrenaline rocked through him. It seemed suddenly impossible that these three girls could be part of him, that they came from him, and the love he felt for them was physically painful.

He thought about Ron. He saw him the way he'd first met him, on the floor of Kitty's kitchen, his son and daughter jumping on him. He heard their laughter, and Ron's, and before he even knew it he was crying—trying to trap the sobs behind his hands so that his girls wouldn't hear him through the window.

You'd do anything to keep them safe, wouldn't you?

Ron had been no different to him, no different to any father, any mother. He'd done everything he could to keep them safe.

And he'd paid for it with his life.

The tears didn't last long, he just didn't have the strength for it. He scrubbed his eyes, he cleared his throat, and he forced a smile onto his numb face. Then he unlocked the door and stepped into the warmth.

"Hey, everyone. I'm home."

CHAPTER THIRTY-EIGHT

Sunday

"I WON'T BE LONG," SAID KETT, LEANING THROUGH THE window. "Promise."

"You'd better not be," Billie replied, raising her voice over the chorus of *Supercalifragilisticexpialidocious* that was threatening to take the roof off the car. The girls sat in the backseat, this current rendition—the seventh since they'd left the house—not so much singing as screaming. Billie's face was a portrait of quiet desperation.

"Promise," he said again. "Then I'll take them out."

He legged it across the rain-slick car park and through the doors of HQ. It was quiet today, and he gave Shelley a wave as he crossed the empty lobby. Somebody must have got the heating working, because by the time he'd reached the bullpen he was sweating.

He tugged off his overcoat as he pushed through the door, seeing Savage and Clare chatting quietly outside the

Superintendent's office. They turned their damp faces his way, giving him a nod of welcome.

"Hot enough for you, sir?" said Savage, tugging at her collar.

"Yeah, what's going on?"

"New boiler," said Clare, his face flushed. "Powered by the flaming arsehole of hell itself, apparently."

Kett slung his overcoat onto the nearest desk and pulled off his jacket too.

"Got to be forty degrees in here," he said.

"Better than the cold, though," Savage replied. "Anything is better than that. You okay, sir?"

"I'm okay," Kett said. "Couple of bruises and my ears are still ringing, but I got off lightly, all things considered. An explosion like that could have brought the entire tunnel system down. Do we know what caused it?"

"Fire Service says it was an IED, homemade," the Superintendent said. "Basic trigger and a couple of gas canisters. Ron had it ready to go. My guess is he didn't necessarily want to hurt anyone, he just needed a way to seal up the tunnel after he'd killed Wileman."

"To make sure nobody moved the body," said Savage. "It was almost certainly Ron who cemented the cellar door closed, to preserve the bones."

"Leaving his Double Decker wrapper in the process," added Clare.

"According to Franklin, the necklace Ron was wearing held three sets of knucklebones," Savage said. "Human ankle bones. She thinks two belonged to Peter Carran, but the others are older, we don't know where they came from. It was probably a twisted take on the whole bone magick thing, a totem he wore to keep himself safe."

"Another ritual," said Clare.

Kett shook his head.

"I still can't believe it. I just don't understand how... I mean, he seemed so normal. He was just like me."

"No, he wasn't," said Clare, giving Kett a warning look as if he knew exactly what was going through his mind. "He was nothing like you, Robbie. Nothing at all."

"Kitty Lewington's in holding," said Savage. "Did anyone tell you?"

"No. She said much?"

"Savage and I interviewed her this morning," said Clare. "She didn't deny anything we threw at her. She knew all about Ron, she knew what he'd done, and why. She was his alibi, but she was his enabler, too."

"She created him," said Kett. "She rescued him from a ritual forty years ago. She sacrificed a lamb instead of a child, but she never let him forget it. It warped him."

"She'll pay for it," said Clare. "Honestly, there's a sadness at his passing, of course. I mean, however you look at it, she was his mother. But there was relief too. I think she always knew it would happen one day."

"It's why she was the first person to go down into the cellar when it was uncovered, sir," said Savage. "It was no accident."

"I guessed that. She wanted to take back the lamb bone. She knew if it got out then people would realise she'd killed a sheep and kept the child. But she only managed to find part of it. Do we know who she was afraid of?"

Clare's mouth peeled open into a gargoyle's smile.

"That's the beautiful bit about all this, Robbie. Kitty confessed to taking part in the ritual, decades ago. She told us they used to use real victims."

"They, sir?" said Kett. "She's given us names?"

"She's given us one. Derek Foulger."

Kett laughed.

"That's amazing."

"It happened a long time ago," Clare went on. "We're talking back in the 1960s and 70s. It's going to be hard to prove, but not impossible. And there's no statute of limitations here, of course, so I have no doubt Foulger will go down for it along with Kitty Lewington and whoever else she fingers. Let's see who the limp-dicked weasel is after a couple of months in prison, eh?"

"I wouldn't be so sure, sir," said Kett. "Foulger has friends in high places, remember?"

"Not anymore. The Chief Constable has disowned him, told me so himself. And he's let you off the hook as well."

"Yeah?"

"Yeah, because they're going to spin it that we already had substantial intel on Foulger before we raided his house, that you weren't just scratching at a lead like a mad dog scratching his flea-bitten bollocks."

"I did have substantial—"

"You had itchy bollocks, Kett, and I won't hear anything else. But it's done, it's over."

Clare unfastened the top button of his shirt. Then the next one. Then two more. Kett gave Savage a look of concern.

"It's hot," Clare barked when he spotted it. "I'm not a stripper."

"Thank heavens," said Kett. "Not sure my heart could take it. How's Wileman?"

"Better," said Savage. "Well enough to try to sneak off the ward and place a bet on the horses, anyway. I don't think he remembers much about it all. He says he got a phone call from the site claiming to be from Foulger. This was on Friday night. Headed down there and somebody knocked him out. Turns out it was Ron, of course."

"Why the hell didn't Ron kill him there and then?" asked Kett.

"I don't know, but I spoke to County Hall security and they said they were called out to a disturbance near the pit where we found the cellar. They couldn't see anything, but I'm guessing Ron was spooked. He took Wileman through the woods to the Bracondale house and tied him up so he'd be ready when he came back. We know the ritual was important, he needed to do it properly, right? He couldn't just kill him, he needed to dismember the body, get to the bone, and display it in the right way. He needed more time."

"Right," said Kett. "But that's insane, because I was with him yesterday morning. He already had Wileman, he knew what he was going to do to him, but he didn't show any sign of it, of being a monster. He was just sitting there chatting, playing with his kids. But it was inside him, this... this evil."

"We can't see it, sir," said Savage. "It's like the tunnels, isn't it? Our minds. We see what's on the surface but you only have to dig down a bit and you find a warren of... I don't know, but there are hidden things there, dark passages that lead you to darker places. Sometimes you head down them and you don't come out."

"Alright, Charles Tossing Dickens, you're not writing a bloody book," said Clare.

"Sorry, sir," mumbled Savage.

"I think you're spot on, Kate," said Kett. "That's exactly it. Just some people never really see those tunnels, not even their own. And some of us are just good at pretending we've never been down there."

"Tossbollocks," said Clare.

"Any idea what will happen to Ron's kids?" asked Kett.

"We've spoken to their mother," Clare said. "Turns out there's a whole shedload of history there. She was terrified of him, feels he bullied her out of the family, exiled her from him and the children. I get the feeling it was as much Kitty as it was Ron. Paid her a lot of money to stay away and promised her a lot of pain if she came back. I couldn't tell if she was laughing or crying when I told her Ron was dead and Kitty had been arrested. But long story short, she's coming back to the city today. The kids are going to be just fine."

Kett breathed a sigh of relief.

"One bit of good news," he said. "And speaking of kids, have you talked to Porter this morning?"

"We have," said Clare. "All doing fine, and Robert Aaron Colin Porter is as healthy as can be."

"You can't just add your name to the—"

"It's a good bloody name!" Clare spat.

Kett laughed.

"I spoke to him too," he said. "Can't remember ever hearing him sound so happy. He's made to be a dad. A lifetime of joy ahead of him." He sighed. "Which reminds me, I'd better get back to mine. They're in the car, Billie too, and I'm not sure how long it'll be before she throws them all in the bin out back."

"Family day out, sir?" asked Savage.

"No, Billie's heading to the food bank, so I've got them. Not sure what we're doing yet."

"Something quiet and relaxing, I'm sure," said Clare, his voice heavy with sarcasm. "Well, I don't have to say it, Robbie, Kate, but thank you. Life keeps thrusting these sticky cases at us, but you yank at them with both hands and you keep squeezing them until the inevitable violent, cathartic climax."

"Sir, *no*..." Savage said with a grimace.

"You get the job done," he said, wiping his brow. "And I appreciate it."

The Superintendent gave them a nod of thanks as he retreated into his office. Kett watched him strip off his sweat-streaked shirt and start to unbutton his trousers.

"We should go," he said in horror.

"Oh God, yes," Savage said, and they both quick-marched out of the bullpen and into the corridor. "Literally can't think of anything more terrifying than the Super working in his underpants."

Neither could Kett, until they walked into the lobby to see an equally terrifying sight. Norman Balls, the conspiracy theorist, occasional police consultant and never-ending thorn in Kett's side, stood beside the reception desk. He was wearing an honest-to-God white tie tuxedo that seemed like it was designed for somebody twice as tall and half as round, with the pointiest pair of winkle-pickers Kett had ever seen. Balls turned when he heard the door, his eyes growing wide behind his wire-rimmed glasses.

"You *are* here!" he said. "I knew it!"

Sorry, mouthed Shelley behind the desk.

"Oh, Norman, how are you?" said Kett. "You look... smart. Is that your suit?"

"It's Mother's awful boyfriend's suit," said Balls. "He doesn't know I took it. But I wanted to wear something special."

"Something special for what?" said Kett, the panic rising inside him.

"For our date," said Balls.

"Our *what*?"

"Oh, sorry sir," said Savage. "I promised him. In return for the bone books, remember?"

"I'd been trying to forget," Kett said. "How did you even know I was here?"

"I keep track of your movements," Balls said proudly.

"Listen, Balls, this isn't a great time. And it's really not a date."

"Rubbish!" said Balls. "It's the greatest date of all, a friendship date, between two best friends, me and you. Norman and Robbie. Nobbie, as I have Christened us. I've got a list of places I think we can go. There's a new five-star restaurant in Swaffham that specialises in eels, and there's also a rare book exhibition on in the printworks by the river, some early edition Julians there that I can't wait to show you. But I'll let you pick."

"Jesus Christ," Kett said beneath his breath, offering Savage a glare. "Fine. A date it is. But just to warn you, I've got the kids in the car."

"Oh," said Balls, his face falling.

"You'll barely notice them," Kett said. "But I've got a great place we can all go together. Full of culture, good food, history—right near the castle."

Balls grinned.

"That sounds amazing!" he said. "Let us depart, best friend!"

Balls marched towards the doors.

"You're taking him to soft play, aren't you, sir?" Savage said quietly as they watched him go.

"Yes I am," said Kett, heading to the exit with a smile on his face. "Yes I am."

PAPER GIRLS
ALEX SMITH
BAD DOG
ALEX SMITH
THREE LITTLE PIGS
ALEX SMITH
WHIP CRACK
ALEX SMITH
RUN RABBIT RUN
ALEX SMITH
STONE COLD DEAD
ALEX SMITH
EVERY MOTHER'S SON
ALEX SMITH
SWEET BRIAR ROSE
ALEX SMITH
JAW BREAKER
ALEX SMITH
KNOCK KNOCK
ALEX SMITH
KING RAT
ALEX SMITH
KNUCKLE BONES
ALEX SMITH
LUCKY NUMBER SEVEN
ALEX SMITH
UNHOLY SAINTS
ALEX SMITH
READ THE FIRST FOURTEEN BOOKS NOW!

SOMETIMES YOU WIN
SOMETIMES YOU DIE
LUCKY
NUMBER
SEVEN
A DCI ROBERT KETT NOVEL
ALEX SMITH
THE INTERNATIONALLY BESTSELLING SERIES

LUCKY NUMBER SEVEN

THE THIRTEENTH DCI KETT CRIME THRILLER

Sometimes You Win. Sometimes You Die.

When seven packages are delivered to the staff of an insurance company in Norwich, the unthinkable happens: one of the packages explodes.

Six people survive, the seventh does not.
As the fire rages and the city reels, DCI Kett and the Extreme Crime Task Force are brought in to try to figure out why anybody would murder an innocent woman in such a violent manner.

But the killer has only just started. Seven more people are targeted, seemingly at random, and it soon becomes clear that somebody is playing a deadly game of chance—if you lose, you lose everything.

The hunt is on for one of the most sadistic criminals the team has ever faced.

Sometimes you beat the odds. Sometimes you don't.

And Kett knows that sooner or later, everybody's luck runs out...

Lucky Number Seven is the thirteenth book in the million-selling DCI Robert Kett series. Relentless action, compulsive mystery and dark humour abound in the series that Thrilling Fiction calls "Heart-stoppingly gripping!" from the author that James Patterson describes as "fresh and ferocious!"

ABOUT THE AUTHOR

Alex Smith wrote his first book when he was six. It wasn't particularly good, but it did have some supernatural monsters in it. His latest books, the DCI Robert Kett thrillers, have monsters in them too, although these monsters are very human, and all the more terrifying for it. In between, he has published fourteen novels for children and teenagers under his full name, Alexander Gordon Smith—including the number one bestselling series Escape From Furnace, which is loved by millions of readers worldwide and which is soon to become a motion picture. He lives in Norwich with his wife and three young daughters.

Find out more at alexsmithbooks.com

Printed in Dunstable, United Kingdom

80754099R00275